WREN JANE BEACON GOES TO WAR

VOLUME ONE
IN THE BEGINNING

A NOVEL BY

DJ Lindsay

Book cover design: Jem Butcher. Picture © Imperial War Museum

© D J Lindsay December 2015

All rights reserved. No part of this book may be reproduced or transmitted in any form or by any means without written permission from the publisher, except by a reviewer who wishes to quote brief passages in connection with a review written for insertion in a newspaper, magazine or broadcast.

A CIP catalogue record for this book is available from the British Library.

About this book

The story of a brave, independent-spirited and outstanding seaman who stands tall against the enemy, the sea and the Royal Navy during World War Two.

The author acknowledges that *t*here are many published autobiographies written by ex-wrens, including at least five by former boat crew wrens. Many are excellent well-written books, but they were written long after the war and all have a sense of setting the record straight as an underlying and unspoken moral theme. These books provide excellent context and background and naval operational information, but they are less candid about personal lives.

In this book, the author has set out to pierce that veil, which of course, is very difficult because of the drastically different moral climate of that time. In writing *Wren Jane Beacon Goes to War*, the author has delved deeper into the Wren's personal lives, which the bulk of existing literature does not.

What Other People Are Saying About This Book

'I have just finished reading **Wren Jane Beacon Goes to War** *and think it is a splendid and unusual book. A very good read.* Your command of naval slang is amazing and there is a lot of fascinating description. I am filled with admiration that you have taken to writing after being so deeply involved in naval matters and that you are able to write in such a fantastic detailed way. Congratulations Douglas!'

Chris Moore

'Wren Jane Beacon Goes to War, *is such an original idea, which so brilliantly describes the hardships and humour, they experienced, especially in the war years.'*

Lotte Moore

'D J Lindsay gets this just right - enough background on WW2, naval jargon and things nautical to carry you along without getting too deep and the story line is certainly unusual - even socially significant! The role of women in the services these days is widely accepted, but back then it was an uphill struggle to get accepted and the account of Wren Jane, while fictitious, has an authentic feel. The attitudes and language of nearly 80 years ago take a bit of getting used to but it all helps to re-create a period now increasingly unfamiliar and makes a fictitious story credible. This is, however, told warts and all and gives an insight into life in the midst of war. It has its humorous and its romantic moments, but the horror of war is not left out. At bottom though, Wren Jane is a ripping good yarn - and you are left wondering what Jane will get up to next - and when the next book will come out!'

Peter Leppard

'This novel was especially fascinating for me because my own mother served in the ATS during WW2 and - like Wren Jane Beacon - played her part in the ultimate allied victory. I already knew a lot about life in the women's army but very little about the women's navy. Jane's experiences were hugely interesting and the attitude of men towards women in the armed forces rang completely true for me. This is a rattling good read that tells a great story and would also be invaluable to anyone researching women's roles at the time.'

Polly Floss

'I have vivid memories of tales told to me as a youngster by my mother about her life as a Wren during WWII. My mother's experiences were as a Radio Operator while Wren Jane Beacon is 'Boat Crew'. Nevertheless, the background and detail are as I recall being told. The world the book recreates is one where the normal social order was overturned, people's expectations were challenged and individuals found themselves learning new skills, finding new responsibilities and making new friends from places beyond their pre war ken. This accuracy and detail, together with D J Lindsay's vivid writing and a believable story make this book well worth reading. As has been said – this is a 'ripping yarn' and recommended.'

Ian Whitehouse, Publisher, 'Navy Books'.

Dedication

'Bless 'em all'

Acknowledgements

During the six years writing this first book, a wide range of people provided support and contributions, which have inspired the book series and I thank them most sincerely.

These include: Peter Leppard, the book's best friend; Glenda Whitley, ex-Wren, Sea Cadet officer and keen sailor and boat person, who informed the books on all matters Wren and ceremonial; Caroline Anns Baldock who advised on literary aspects; at some times Jennifer Russell, Jessica Smith and in the early stages Dr Jo Stanley.

Three established authors, Richard Woodman, Sam Llewellyn and Frank Welsh were supportive with their comments as was the tough professional approach provided by the Hillary Johnson Authors' Advisory Service, which helped the story to be completed.

Alan Cooper and JJ Jenkins nursed the book into life in its first published form.

I also thank Yvonne Downer, a delightful 94-yer-old lady who I had the privilege to meet. She had been a boat crew Wren in World War Two in *HMS Tormentor*, on the River Hamble.

Thanks also to Book Coach and Editor, Wendy Yorke, who has also helped me to reset my sails; republishing this first book and inspiring me to continue writing the rest of the series.

Contents

VOLUME ONE: IN THE BEGINNING 11
PROLOGUE 13

PART ONE: THE BEACHES OF DUNKIRK 17
    CHAPTER 1: The Good Theft 19
    CHAPTER 2: The Good Collection 27
    CHAPTER 3: The Good Support 32
    CHAPTER 4: The Good Rescue 45
    CHAPTER 5: The Good Return 55

PART TWO: BOAT GIRL 63
    CHAPTER 6: On Being a Sailor 65
    CHAPTER 7: On Laying Up 72
    CHAPTER 8: On Being a Girl 80

PART THREE: INITIATION 87
    CHAPTER 9: Back to the Surface 89
    CHAPTER 10: It's not the Body, it's the Mind 94
    CHAPTER 11: Day One 98
    CHAPTER 12: Moving Up 114
    CHAPTER 13: Losing It 122
    CHAPTER 14: On Relative Morality 129
    CHAPTER 15: The Water Takes and Gives 138
    CHAPTER 16: The Highs and Lows 145

PART FOUR: PROBATIONER BEACON 153
    CHAPTER 17: Back Among the Girls 155
    CHAPTER 18: Mixing in 165
    CHAPTER 19: Solidarity in the Abyss 176
    CHAPTER 20: Not Defeated 188

PART FIVE: VOYAGER 203
    CHAPTER 21: Back Home 204
    CHAPTER 22: Up The River 211
    CHAPTER 23: Weathering the Storm 217
    CHAPTER 24: Planes and Prejudice 224
    CHAPTER 25: Sailing to the Future 231

BIBLIOGRAPHY 238
About the Author 242
Tailpiece by D J Lindsay 244

VOLUME ONE:
IN THE BEGINNING

Prologue

There was something special about her: a strikingly handsome woman, tall, lean and poised, but there was so much more. She came in at the rear of a group of chattering, laughing Wren officer cadets and although she also had Wren cadet flashes on her uniform and could not have been much older than them, she was quite different to the fresh faces ahead of her. The gulf in experience was huge. Her uniform was well worn, with chief petty officer's buttons on her sleeve, a boat crew Wren's white lanyard at her neck and more medal ribbons than the average admiral. She exuded a calm battle-hardened authority from hawk-like features but there was a sensuous air to her too. She caught me staring at her from the entrance where I was standing with Miss French, her course superintendent. Her face tightened, displeasure plain to see. As she sat down the Wren stewards hurried to serve her, almost obsequiously.

I made a vow to find out about her. I was in the painted hall at Greenwich for stories; it was a privilege to be in that most wonderful of dining halls and to be mixing with the trainee officers, so I had to make maximum use of it. After five years of war I had heard fascinating tales from men who had seen much of it from the lower deck before being offered a commission; a similar Wren would be a new challenge. Later that day, talking again to Miss French, I asked about this more senior cadet.

"You mean Chief Jane Beacon? Our Stormy Petrel? Yes, there's a story there to curl your hair but I doubt if you'll get much out of her. I know you're brilliant at getting people to talk about themselves but others have tried and got nowhere. She's famous as the Dunkirk Wren among a host of exploits, but also has the most lurid disciplinary record in the service. Like a lot of exceptional people she's entirely her own person and tends to live on the edge. When it's what the Navy wants the results have been phenomenal. But she doesn't give a damn about authority and that has caused problems. I've seen her give an admiral a dressing-down. We had a devil of a job getting her onto this course – after five years as a rating she wasn't in the least bothered about being here and it took an 'officer or out' ultimatum from the Director herself to get Beacon to come. I just let her get on with it – the guidance I usually give cadets is meaningless to Beacon."

Getting a word in edgeways with Miss French in full Irish flow was impossible but she paused and I jumped in. "The Dunkirk Wren, eh? I've heard the tales but never imagined I'd meet her. Do you think I could get some time with her?"

"Well, I can arrange that but don't expect results. I doubt if even your honeyed tongue will get much from her." Although I relished the thought of the challenge, I knew it might not be easy. Boat crew Wrens, operating Naval small craft in all weathers round the clock, were about the wildest and toughest females I had come across in the Services and an experienced senior one might be doubly so. Despite – or perhaps because of – the demands of the job, boat crew Wrens tended to be a pretty top drawer lot; being sworn at ferociously in a cut-glass accent was a disconcerting mix.

Miss French called her in. "Beacon, I have a proposition for you". She started and stared incredulously at Miss French. "No, you silly woman, not that kind of proposition. This gentleman is a journalist who has been commissioned to collect stories from the lower deck for an official record of the war. He has full authority from WRNS headquarters and from their Lordships to interview people here and I'd like you to co-operate with him. Don't look mulish – those are orders."

She smiled, a lop-sided and slightly bitter smile born of many previous clashes with Authority. "All right ma'am, you know I hate talking about myself but I'll try." And with that she was dismissed.

But Miss French's – and my - doubts were right. Mature way beyond her twenty-four years, Chief Beacon proved a tough nut in every way. It wasn't reticence so much as a hardened war-weary cynicism and a sense that it was history she didn't want to delve into too deeply. On our next meeting she came in, her height and aura commanding the room even when she sat down. Normally when I interview, a little warm eye contact breaks the ice nicely; there was none of that with Chief Beacon. A calculating look and a raised eyebrow put me in my place. "I understand you want to interview me about my Wrens career? Who are you and what do you intend to do with any results?"

This set me back a bit, and the rest of the first session was spent sparring about what I was doing there. Her story never got touched. Another dry session passed by, but I was determined not let this one go. So, on the third encounter I deliberately led off with questions about relations between the Wrens and the Navy. For the first time I got sparks. "Very largely the Navy has accepted us and they know that we Wrens have done a huge amount of good work. But there is always a limit to male tolerance and if you cross it, as I have done frequently, the barriers can suddenly be very high."

"Give me examples?" I encouraged.

"You know I was at Dunkirk don't you? There were very senior officers who tried hard to have me chucked out for disobeying orders and daring to go into what they thought was a man's world. Some of those people would still have me slung out if they got half a chance. But I'm still knocking about and still just a Wren which infuriates them."

Sessions four and five were more relaxed. She had started to talk and by getting her to move from the general to giving me examples, I was getting just a hint of her story. By session five I felt the atmosphere was easy enough to mention her scarred face and missing fingers, which somehow enhanced her attractiveness. "At the last count I have fifteen scars – not that I'm going to show you them all." She pointed to the three vertical gold *braid stripes on her left cuff.* "See these? Wound stripes earned the hard way. It's the price you pay for being on the front line." *I waited for her to enlarge on this but she fell silent again. So many of our early exchanges were like this – tantalising glimpses of a bigger story. Why had she been wounded, and where? Fifteen scars were a lot even in wartime and I wanted to know more. But she had a capacity for suddenly clamming up and when she did I knew that asking her to carry on with the story would be futile.* "Do you know what a bullet sounds like when it passes so close to your head that you can hear it?"

I shook my head, waiting. But again I was left in suspense. Chief Beacon negotiated as an equal with nothing to prove and often I found myself pushed onto the back foot while trying to get her to open up. I never did find out whether this was just her avoiding painful topics or if it was deliberate intellectual jousting to entertain herself. After half a dozen sessions I wasn't much further forward and all I knew from the hints was that hers was the story of stories; the whole war was to be found in her tale and it deserved to be a central theme of the record I was making. But she seemed indifferent to that. By now we were on easy terms with some meeting of minds; she was friendly enough but there was a deeper reserve I just wasn't getting through. With her course nearing its end I felt the opportunity slipping away and asked her what she was doing once the course finished.

"I'm not allowed to mention my next draft but I've got some leave due first. I might visit my family down in Devon or I might just go into Town for a few days."

"You don't have a boyfriend?"

"Not now."

And again I was left dangling; gentle encouragement was ignored. Yet another glimpse, which could have led so much further, was left unopened.

"Well, you know I have been authorised to collect the stories of people like you. I really do need a bit more than the snippets you have given me so far. Can we try a bit harder once this course is over?"

"You're wasting your time threatening me with their Lordships. I've crossed swords with them often enough to know that they are very cagey about getting heavy with difficult Wrens."

I must have looked particularly crushed – not my usual condition and she recognised it. But then something let go in her mind, we grinned at each other and, with the fencing over, she suddenly lit up. She barked a short but sympathetic laugh and the tiniest corner of the veil started to lift.

"You certainly are persistent. All right, do you know anything about yachts and can you cook?"

Startled, I replied "Oh yes, I was a keen yachtsman before the war and my cooking is plain but nourishing."

"Right, that decides it. I have to do some maintenance work on my boat. If you're *willing to work on her and do the cooking I'll tell you a bit of my story in the evenings. But don't be misled – I will sleep in the foc'sle and you in the saloon."*

I took a deep breath and decided to chance my reply. "That won't actually be a problem. I swing from the other tree, if you get what I mean."

This drew one of her wry lopsided smiles. She clearly understood what I meant. "Well that removes one little pressure point and might actually make it all a bit easier. Let's do it."

That was how I found myself down in the West Country scraping and painting between cooking duties. And, by lamplight in the cabin in the evenings, I finally began to get the story I had been looking for. Yet even my hunch was only a fraction of this young veteran's remarkable war.

"Tell me about your going to Dunkirk. That was a strange thing to do, wasn't it?"

She stared deep into the lamp. "It seemed quite logical at the time but I was still very young - I'd just turned twenty - and inclined to do things without thinking them through. I was based at Dover anyway and had heard of the desperate need for boats to work off the beaches. The naval cutter I was in seemed ideal. It was a thirty-six foot open boat with a diesel engine and Kitchen gear steering so I could handle it myself. No-one else seemed inclined to take it so I did without giving much thought to what conditions would be like when I got there. Having got there I just had to get on with it. "

PART ONE:

THE BEACHES OF DUNKIRK

CHAPTER 1:
The Good Theft

THURSDAY 30 MAY 1940

Living in the killick's cabin at the Dover Wrennery had its advantages. With just two cabin mates, both sound asleep, Jane was able to get her head down for a few hours in the evening and woke up again at midnight by sheer willpower. Moving silently – by now a well practised routine – she dressed in a boiler suit overall, added her uniform hat, and sneaked out of the cabin leaving her pillows and Rufus the big teddy bear along her bunk to look as though she was still in it. She raided the galley and as well as her own lunch took all the leftovers and food she could find, stuffed into a canvas bag. With her oilskins under her arm, she walked quietly down to the boat moorings. She picked up the cache of fuel cans, fresh water and supplies she had hidden earlier, along with the boat's compass. She had made sure the boat was fuelled in the afternoon, and its tank was almost full, which meant three days of continuous running. Mercifully the engine was still warm and fired at the first asking – lift the decompression levers, give it a good spin and drop one of them. As soon as it fired, drop the other. Blessing the air-cooled Dorman for its simple reliability she threw off the mooring lines, gently moved the gear ahead slightly, and heart in mouth eased out of the boats' trot as quietly as she could. The harbour was still busy, with ships coming and going so a boat on the move attracted no attention. Outside the entrance she found just a gentle westerly swell, which was fine for getting over there. She swung to port outside the entrance to keep clear of the inspection vessel, and once sure she'd avoided it, set a course of east by south. It is just over forty nautical miles from Dover to Dunkirk in a straight line and as P36, her cutter, had only eighteen inches draft Jane saw no reason why she shouldn't go straight over the banks.

It was a dull, overcast night and Jane pulled on her oilskins to keep out the drizzle. Visibility at sea level was good, which was just as well as darkened ships of various sorts charged past her and picking up their dark bulk to avoid them was tricky. The cloud cover was thick. But as she chugged along the visibility reduced; a fine mist thickening then suddenly she ran into dense fog. This was bad news. Jane had not bothered with a chart, assuming she would just follow the other vessels going to and fro. For a little she dithered over whether to turn back, but logically she would be as likely to find Dunkirk as Dover so she might as well keep going. She had estimated six hours for the passage over, so at 0630 she stopped and listened; apart from a distant rumble to the south there was nothing. What to do now? By convenient chance Jane had left Dover at high water and so had had the tide behind her the whole way, although it would be turning soon. This meant that if anything she would be too far north, and further ahead than her rough dead reckoning suggested. To port was the North Sea – next stop the Arctic. To starboard lay France, so the only sensible thing to do was to turn towards the land mass and keep a sharp lookout. She headed South on the compass and pushed on.

Within forty minutes this was rewarded as a grey warship lying at anchor, loomed out of the blankness. And the rumble was a lot louder. Again, she paused, ate a sandwich and took a drink from her water breaker while taking in the sounds round her. She listened carefully: to landward she could hear people, distorted and distant in the fog but a continuous dull roar from a multitude of voices. To seaward she could hear engines, the rattle of anchor chains, the rattle and squeak of blocks and pulleys, and the odd shouted order. Well, she'd come to pick up soldiers so she might as well get on with it although it was going to be tricky in poor visibility. She eased the gear ahead and nosed in.

Soon the beach loomed up in front of her, less than a hundred yards away. With the tide rising she approached the shoreline cautiously, putting the boat's forefoot onto the sand. She called "Anyone there?" and immediately out of the fog came a group of dishevelled soldiers. All sorts, with no-one in charge. They piled on board, nearly tipping the cutter over. Some were in full uniform and with their kit, others half-dressed. Several Frenchmen were among them. Quickly too full for comfort she put the boat astern, backing off leaving men floundering and trailing in its wake. She called, "What regiment are you from?" The soldiers look at each other.

"Lots of different ones. What does it matter to you? Get us out of here." There was a threatening edge to the reply so she didn't argue, swung the cutter's nose to seaward and headed towards one of the noise sources she could hear. Coming alongside a fleet minesweeper the mixed bunch leapt off without a backward glance. 'Well, that was an appreciative start,' she thought.

Worried, she turned to the shore again, aiming slightly higher up the beach. But no luck – as soon as she came visible to the shore the boat was rushed by another mixed group of uncontrolled men who piled aboard and would have sunk the boat had she not slapped it into reverse and backed off quickly to howls and curses from those left behind.

"Sit down, you lot", she shouted at them as she swung the boat to seaward.

"Hey lads, it's a woman" the cry went up and instead of sitting down they crowded round her. "Give us a kiss, love" and "A woman! Haven't seen one of those for months," were the least of the shouts as they closed in on her hungrily. Suddenly Jane felt vulnerable and very alone. "Keep back" she shouted but they just squeezed closer. Her spare tiller bar was going to be useless against this mob. Suddenly there were hands on her legs, on her bottom and breasts. Hands were pushing down inside her clothing and her head was pulled back for a ravening kiss. She struggled but it was pointless, there were far too many of them, all unshaven filthy and stinking. For a moment blind panic seized her as a hand pushed inside her knickers then clarity shot through – the only way out was to get to a ship as quickly as possible and get rid of this lot. So she steeled herself to ignore the hands all over her body and aimed at the nearest ship she could hear. It only took a few minutes to get there but it seemed like an eternity. As the boat came alongside she screamed "Get off, you bunch of filthy shits" at the top of her voice and slowly, unwillingly, the troops pulled away, piling on board the ship without a backward glance. A leering face appeared over the ship's rails "Thanks for the grope, love" it called. She swore at him but he just laughed.

Shaken to the core, she pulled away from the ship's side and did up her clothing, a couple of buttons missing from her boiler suit. She was disgusted to see several white stains on it. Trembling all over she sat down and sobbed, wailing tears of despair and misery. She had come here to help the soldiers and what had she got? Assaulted. Her whole body crawled at the still vivid feeling. For a moment the urge to run away was overwhelming and she started turning to the west but then a voice in her head murmured 'What else did you expect? These are desperate men'. Traumatised though she was, she knew deep inside herself that her boat was equally desperately needed. Running away was not an option.

Through the fog she heard a constant buzz of voices, shouts and low hum intermingled. The thought of going back to the beaches terrified her but to do the job she'd come for she knew she would have to return and hope she could avoid any more assaults. It might have been all right if she could see where she was going but in fog it was chance where and who she ended up with. She took a deep if shaky breath and headed the boat inwards. Then anger kicked in and she charged at the beach "I will not be defeated," She shouted at the wall of fog; but a detached bit of her mind knew it was bravado.

Nervously running the boat's nose through the fog onto the beach she startled a padre squatting with his trousers down at the water's edge. "Excuse me, my child, oh please excuse me" He wailed, hastily restoring his dignity.

"Oh, no problem father" she called laughingly, "Being of the cloth doesn't exempt you from human basics."

The effect was electric. "My dear God," he exclaimed. "Are you a girl?"

"Yes, I think so. Do you want taken off?"

"No my child, I must stay here. But why are you here?"

"I'm here to take soldiers off to the ships".

"But a girl? You should be home tending the sick and lame, not running a boat in this dreadful vision of Hell. The Blessed Virgin did no such thing."

"Well that may be true but the Blessed Virgin wasn't an expert boat handler and I am so here I am."

By now the padre had come to the boat's gunwale and looked at Jane more closely. "Are you a Wren?"

"Yes, that's right, the Navy's first boat crew Wren since 1918."

"Well I never. Can you take some men off?"

"Yes of course, that's why I'm here. Do you really think the Blessed Virgin would never have been a boat handler?"

"The Bible does not say so, my dear. Our Lord was a fisherman but I don't think his mother ever went afloat."

"Seems a shame really – we can be ever so good at it."

The padre had to laugh "Perhaps she is watching over you. Now did you say you would take men off?"

Jane nodded.

"I will bring my flock to you, leading them out of the wilderness in a way I suppose." He laughed more loudly.

Soon the padre was back with a mixed group of French and British soldiers including a group of highlanders in their kilts. "One each side, come in over the fore end" she called. At the water's edge each knelt and kissed the priest's ring prior to clambering on board. Through the morning Jane did six runs like this of shattered but quiet well-behaved and clearly devout young men, many saying their rosaries as they sat in the boat trembling. By midday the last group had been taken off, and when Jane came back to the beach she found only the padre. "Come on Father, your turn now."

He called back "But my ministry is with the men still here. I must tend to them too."

Clearly he was not going to come. Jane had never been particularly religious but on an impulse she went forward to where he was hanging over the bow and asked "Bless me, father."

"I am sure the Lord is already watching over you, my child." He laid his hand on her head. "Heavenly Father, we ask that you watch over this brave soul. Bless and protect her from the slings and arrows and bring her safe home. Almighty God,

CHAPTER 1: The Good Theft

this we ask of you. Amen." And he was gone into the fog.

Jane felt strengthened, purified in a way and at peace after the turbulent horror of earlier on. A sense of being a decent person again swept over her and she had to control an impulse to shout defiance at the world as she sat down and took a long drink from her breaker. Her brief sense of omnipotence was broken by a very large Sergeant Major looming out of the now thinning mist. "You takin' people off?" He asked, chin and huge florid moustache to the fore. Jane just gave a beckoning wave, not feeling like yet another debate about her apparently dubious gender.

"Right stay there. I've got 'em in spades."

So she waited and within five minute the moustache was back with a ragged bunch of infantrymen, still clutching their rifles.

"Take it easy" she called "One over each side forward." Once again her voice betrayed her.

"Blooming heck, it's a girl."

The Sergeant Major waded aft to look at her closely. "What the Hell are you doing here my lovely?"

"What does it look like? I'm driving a boat taking you lot off to the ships."

The RSM shook his head in bemusement. "Yes, but a girl? You shouldn't be here my lovely."

"Why not? There's a job to do and I'm doing it.

"Yes but not a girl....." And his voice trailed off, suddenly the parade ground bellow and bluster punctured.

"Oh come on, There isn't time for debates about my gender. Get 'em on."

Still shaking his head he waded ashore and supervised a load onto the cutter. Another eight trips followed with the RSM keeping control. By six o'clock they were down to the last load and she called to the moustache "If that's your lot you come too."

He looked around guiltily at the masses of men still on the beach.

Jane sensed his doubt. "Come on, you're more use to us back in Blighty rebuilding the army than you are hanging about here and getting killed. Now get in, you great dumb hero."

Still looking shifty he climbed in and came aft to her controls. As they chugged off to the waiting destroyer he looked at her, about to say something. But suddenly the engine growled, coughed and died. "Oh dear, now what?"

"Your engine's stopped."

"I know that, but why. Who's the strongest person here."

The Sergeant Major grinned, cold and grim. "Probably me. I used to be the army heavyweight boxing champion."

"Right that's just what we need. Get on that handle and swing it hard." Jane lifted the decompression levers.

But the engine was solid; even brute strength could not spin it. "I hope it's not seized up" ventured Jane.

"More likely something round the propeller" grunted the Sergeant Major.

"You could be right there. I'd better take a look." And Jane lowered herself over the side of the boat. "God it's cold". She dived under and although she could see almost nothing in the cloudy water, she could feel that the Sergeant Major had been right "There's an army greatcoat wrapped around the gear with its arms tangled in the propeller. I'll try to cut it away." She opened her pusser's clasp knife, which she always kept razor sharp, looped the lanyard round her neck and went to work, finding that she could actually stand on the sand beneath the boat for more purchase. She was sawing away at the greatcoat arm when she felt something more solid, like a hand. Puzzled, she followed the arm along and suddenly there was a face inches from her own, its mouth gaping open. She panicked and shot to the surface. "There's a bloke down there" she screamed. The Sergeant Major looked over the side, pulled the corners of his mouth down and said "Must be dead. Just push him out of the way."

Jane looked desperate. "I can't, I just can't," she wailed.

"Yes, you can. He won't harm you."

She shook her head in desperation, took a deep breath and dived again. This time encountering the body was horrible enough but not so spooky. Feeling round, she found he was attached to the greatcoat by his belt so she cut that and pushed him out of the way.

It took nine dives to cut the first arm; the second was now more accessible so only needed four dives. With its arms cut off the rest of the coat pulled off fairly readily, much to Jane's relief, and she passed it up into the boat. The body had drifted away on the tide. She checked the gear as best she could by feel, and it seemed undamaged. "Right, pull me out, please" Back on board she commented "I think it should be all right now. Let's try the engine" The moustached one seized the starting handle, and found the engine rotated freely. "Looks like it's fine at this end."

"Good. Give it a real cranking." He made it look effortless and once up to speed Jane dropped a compression lever. The still hot engine fired immediately; a cheer went up from the squaddies on board, and they were back in business. Jane tried the gear ahead and astern; it seemed to be functioning normally so she pointed the boat outwards and headed for the last ship lying off. The Sergeant Major came aft and stood beside the shivering teeth-chattering girl. Whether that was cold or fright she couldn't tell, the image of the face in the water still haunting her. The pool of water round her feet spread slowly.

"You're some girl you are. Who on earth are you?"

"Leading Wren Jane Beacon at your service, sar'nt major. The Navy's only boat crew Wren."

"The Navy sent you here on your own? That's unbelievable."

"You're right it is. They don't know I'm here but I felt I had to do my bit. Hope they don't mind."

"You're something different you are. Good luck Jenny. Here, you'll need something to keep you warm." And he peeled off his greatcoat and put it round her shoulders.

They swung in alongside the destroyer and the RSM supervised his men on board. He then turned to her and snapped off his smartest parade ground salute, arm quivering – a gesture so unexpected that Jane was taken flat aback but just managed to come to attention and return the salute. "Thank you, kind sir. Good luck to you too."

As she moved away she tucked her clasp knife's lanyard under the overall's collar and pulled it tight across her chest. She found it so convenient this way that she took to wearing it there all the time.

Through the afternoon the weather had eased, the fog gone from the water but only lifted to a low and heavy cloud base. This had been an enormous blessing as the visibility had been too poor for flying and the evacuation had been able to go ahead without destruction raining down on it from the *Luftwaffe*. But at dusk a flight of ME 109 fighters swept in low, just under the cloud canopy, and shot up beaches and ships. Jane was lying off, debating where to go next as the flight swept in. There was a sudden bang on her shoulder and everything went black. Coming to, she looked around from lying on the bottom boards. The pain in her left shoulder was acute, lancing through her. Gingerly she felt the shoulder: There was a lump of wood sticking out behind. Getting hold of it hurt but she took a firm hold and yanked. Mercifully it came out – looking around she could see it was a chunk of the boat's counter, which had been blasted by canon shell. Although there was a good deal of blood about, she did not appear to be bleeding now. Carefully she got to her feet and tried the left arm, which seemed to function reasonably through the pain. She looked at the boat – water was over the bottom boards and rising, so she worked her way round the boat, finding three bullet holes through which water was spouting. Among the stores she had smuggled on board was a string of corks. They fitted smaller boreholes neatly, so she banged one into each hole wincing with each movement of her left arm. Then she got onto the hand pump and spent half an hour pumping the boat dry again. The good old Dorman gently chugged away throughout. This done, she look around. In the darkness she could not see any ships lying off. 'Oh well, time for some kip' she thought. Checking she was safely away from the tideline she chucked her grapnel anchor out, made sure it had a grip in the sand, and with a silent prayer that it would start again, stopped the engine. A drink from her breaker and some sandwiches made up supper. She peeled off her wet boiler suit and spread it over the warm engine to dry, then snuggled down on the bottom boards under the Sergeant Major's greatcoat.

CHAPTER 2:
The Good Collection

FRIDAY 31 MAY

Creeping daylight woke her early. Scratching her salt-encrusted mane and rubbing the sleep out of her eyes, Jane took in that the boat was rolling and yawing about. What to do? She pulled on her damp boiler suit while debating and breakfasting on the remains of her sandwiches and some more water. Starting the engine was a challenge with only one good arm: Prime the fuel system, lift the compression levers and give the engine a swing. Nothing. Annoyed, she primed it again and using all the lean strength she had acquired, gave it a fierce turning, dropped one lever and – mercifully – it fired. Allowing it a few minutes to settle to a steady rhythm she looked around. The day was clear but with a low cloud cover. The wind had freshened overnight from the North East and although not strong was sufficient to be sending a lumpy lop onto the shore where the waves were breaking. High water was not due for a couple of hours so Jane decided the Kitchen gear would be an advantage in holding the boat's stern to the swell while loading up. Looking further off she saw Dunkirk itself for the first time, with the towering columns of black smoke from its bombed oil tanks and sunken ships lying offshore. It was a scene from the second circle of Hell.

But where should she go? She had evidently arrived at the eastern end of the beaches with the mass of soldiers extending to the west towards Dunkirk itself. She surveyed the soldiers on the beach, mostly without visible organisation but there were also neat columns snaking down to the water and in some cases into the water where the breaking waves were making life difficult for them. Although there were other boats about, few seemed to be trying to work through the surf. One of those columns looked like a good bet to Jane. Offshore, destroyers, small passenger vessels and trawlers all lay, but there was little traffic going to them because of the surf. Selecting one of the more orderly-looking columns she headed in. At its head was a young lieutenant. "Two at a time please" she called, "One over each bow." The boat was ranging and twisting about and holding it close to the column was difficult.

"Good God," the lieutenant said. "Are you a woman?"

Jane decided that sarcasm would be wasted at this point so just said "A Wren" and waved them in. But in the surf, often up to their necks, the soldiers found getting over the bow impossible. "What we need are some boarding ladders" called the lieutenant.

"Hang on, I've got an idea" She backed the boat off clear of the column then went forward. Blessing her ability to tie bowlines-on-the-bight, she put a series of loops into her two forward ropes and hung them over the bows. The soldiers found this enough to climb on board and it meant that once they had a grip of the ropes it didn't matter if the boat was ranging about a bit. One by one they scrambled over the cutter's bows and settled down. Once full Jane said "That's enough. I'll be back," and gave the lieutenant a grin. Chugging back out she passed a rowing whaler, which made the age-old signal for requesting a tow by holding up a rope's end. She slowed, tossed them her after mooring line and caught the end on her quarter towing horn. The effect was dramatic. The cutter's speed was cut by three-quarters but the whaler's increased many times and five minutes later they were alongside an old 'V' class destroyer. Her soldiers were all tall strong men, properly dressed and with their full kit. There was sense of undefeated militariness about them and they were still fresh enough to go up the scrambling nets easily. "Can I have my line back?" She called to the whaler, now tied up behind her. There were some signs of disappointment at this – the whaler's crew had evidently been hoping to escape the endless rowing – but Jane doubted if they would achieve much in the surf anyway and also felt she had to get back to the young lieutenant and his orderly queue. Coming back he greeted her with a grin and a wave. "What regiment are you?" she asked.

"Welsh Guards. Couldn't you tell?"

"Well you're certainly tall and well ordered."

"If the cream of the army can't be, there's not much hope."

She smiled in reply and watched as the next group came on board and sat down in strict order. The whole morning passed this way, Jane keeping up a running battle to hold the boat against the surf while picking up groups from the column which seemed to have no end, and getting a rapport going with the destroyer's crew. She kept a tally of the number on each time, and with yesterday's loads as well, by midday had moved seven hundred and five soldiers off. The destroyer picked up and left then, leaving Jane without a convenient vessel to deliver to. But soon some skoots, the little Dutch motor cargo ships (they call them Schuyts) commandeered by the Navy, dropped anchor close by and she was soon running to them instead. Despite the conditions the men's discipline allowed the process to carry on effectively.

During the morning big splashes were becoming more common, sometimes close enough to send spray over the boat. "What are these splashes?" she asked the lieutenant. He looked at her in wide-eyed amazement. "You mean you don't know?

That's gunfire. Jerry has got his artillery close enough now to be shelling us"

Jane looked suitably startled. "Oh dear. No I didn't know. I suppose that makes it more dangerous here?"

"A hundred times more dangerous Jenny. I thought you were being awfully cool about it. Are you going to keep running?"

"I suppose so. I've just got to get on with, really."

So far it had been easy despite the swell and the increasing shelling, and she was wondering what all the fuss was about. But overhead the cloud was breaking up and by mid afternoon the sky was clear. This abruptly led to a quite different situation – the Stukas came back. From peacefully shifting people from the beach Jane suddenly found the world full of crashes, bangs, and screaming sirens. Around her ships were exploding, guns barking, and the atmosphere filled with fury. The noise was appalling, compressing her head and hurting her ears. Yet with the swell dying away the shifting went on; her lieutenant and his column continued to wait patiently and thirty-odd at a time she took them off to the skoots until they were full and in their turn upped anchor. After that delivery, it was to whichever ship was closest. At nightfall, with fires and explosions and the clatter of gunfire all around her, she paused alongside a big minesweeper to check her boat. A bit more lub oil, top up the fuel tank, a quick nip to the upper deck heads. Suitably replenished, she cast off and headed back to the beach, picked up the lieutenant and the last of his column, and ran them off to the waiting minesweeper. Having been in the water for much of the day the lieutenant was frozen and stood by Jane shivering violently. With his men offloaded, he came aft to Jane and without warning seized her, gave her a big kiss, said "Thanks Jenny. See you in London." And was gone. Startled, damp and chilled down the front she nevertheless felt warmed inside. Coming to the beaches was feeling like the right thing; P36 was making a useful contribution. She waved to his retreating form and looked around for what to do next.

Although she was unaware of it, her disappearance with P36 had caused a major flap back in Dover. First, her cabin mates had been startled to find the teddy bear in her bunk and No Jane. They had reported her disappearance to the Quarters Officer who, knowing of her recent fling with the PTI, assumed the worst. At the same time the boats chief petty officer was raising a panic because P36 was missing. And the fuel supplies depot reported some fuel cans missing. The cooks at the Wrennery reported that their food stocks had been raided, and a guard on the pier end remembered seeing a cutter go out late in the evening. Before long they were starting to knit the elements together, the boats officer recalling his conversation with Jane to make the missing link. A message was flashed over to the shore party at Dunkirk – "Was there a Wren in a cutter around the beaches?" But the young communications petty officer who received it presumed it was a spoof and did not pass it on. So reply came there none and for the first two days no-one was on the look-out for her.

By now there were other boats around her, some running men off to the waiting ships and some collecting a group then disappearing into the gathering gloom. Clearly evacuation was still going on. Jane had seen that soldiers had built a pier of sorts consisting of lorries with boards on top jutting out into the sea. This looked like a good place to be loading from as it looked as though there was a good deal of order and control – Jane was scared stiff of more threatening and uncontrolled lots on board like the first couple she'd picked up. So despite the ever-increasing shelling she eased in to the lee side of this rough and ready boarding point and found army officers and senior NCOs in charge, supervising an orderly loading process. The tide was now about half flood, so there was water around the end of the lorries and she was able to put P36 alongside, taking advantage of its light draft to get close in. The pongoes she found here were base staff, still strictly disciplined but not front-line fighters, plus other support elements. The shelling was getting intense and the sergeant at the end of the quay warned her they'd be pulling out later that night. "Where are you going?" She queried.
"Farther west, probably Braye beach" he replied.
"Where's that?"
"About four miles along the coast."
"Oh, right, I suppose I'll have to go there too."
"It's getting pretty hot here, that's for sure."

High water at eight o'clock allowed a swarm of boats to get alongside in turn, and evacuation was going well. Jane did a series of runs with remarkably calm and clean staff officers along with their support staff, and after some of her earlier traumas found this much more pleasant despite the constant shellfire splashing around her. A feature of ebb tide on flat sands, however, is the way the water suddenly disappears and twice she had to pull off in a hurry to avoid being left stranded. By midnight the tide had dropped so that there was only just enough water to put her bow onto the bonnet of the outermost lorry when there was a commotion on the quay. A group of officers had come down to the end, wanting to be taken off. Jane's boat was the only one left on the lorry jetty so the group got in, scrambling over the lorry bonnet and P36's bow. Jane gulped as she recognised the insignia of a full general. What she didn't know was that the army headquarters at La Panne, just behind the jetty, were being evacuated and this was the last party from it. Taking a deep breath, Jane came to attention and saluted the general. "At ease, sailor. Carry on with your duties."

"Aye aye, sir," she quavered in reply. She'd been keeping her voice as low-pitched as possible when she had to speak and mostly had avoided drawing attention to her gender. But now her suddenly surprised squeak gave her away. As the cutter pulled away the general came aft and looked at her closely. "Are you a woman?" he demanded gruffly.

"Yes sir, Leading Wren Jane Beacon sir."

"Good God, is the Navy so desperate that it's sending Wrens over?"

"Not really sir. I came on my own initiative as I felt I could do more good with this boat than simply running round Dover harbour. I've now moved about fifteen hundred soldiers off."

"By Jove, that's going some. How long have you been here?"

"Two days so far sir."

"And you've survived unscathed?"

"Well, I've got a wound in my shoulder but I don't think it's serious. Apart from that and being a bit tired I'm fine."

"Well I'll be damned. You deserve a medal. I'll see to it when I get back."

"Well thank you sir but that's not really why I'm here."

"I don't suppose it is. I'm General Brownlow. Get in touch with me when you get back."

"That's very kind sir."

They all instinctively ducked as a shell splashed in close enough to shower them with solid water – all that, is, except an unflustered Jane who had got used to this and just spat out the salt water as she kept the boat heading out. Getting to his feet the general gave Jane a long look and muttered "Well well" under his breath. "Doesn't that bother you?"

Jane shrugged. "Not really sir. The way I see it, if a shell hits the boat it's curtains anyway and I'll probably know nothing about it. Shells that miss don't do us any harm."

The general laughed, a short bark, and shook his head in disbelief.

The cutter was coming alongside one of the big modern destroyers and as she did so she automatically called out "Flag" which caused some scurrying aboard the destroyer. But at least one Bosun's mate piped the general on board. "Good luck young lady" He called from the deck.

"Thank you sir" and she gave him her best naval salute at which he smiled and returned her an army salute to rival the Sergeant Major's.

CHAPTER 3:
The Good Support

SATURDAY 1 JUNE

With the tide gone from the lorry jetty and the soldiers heading west, Jane too tried her luck further along. She motored along slowly, as close to the shore as she dared, looking for a reasonably organised column of men to carry. Spotting one, she stopped with a little water still under the boat and beckoned to the column to come forward. The soldiers at its head were just starting to come in over the bow when a young army officer charged past them, bellowing incoherently as he came. He hurdled into the boat amidships, fired a shot from his pistol over the heads of the soldiers at the bow and screamed

"Get back. This is an officers' boat." Startled, the soldiers stopped coming.

Jane, thoroughly cross about this, shouted "Oh no it isn't. This boat is for all ranks."

The officer - a captain – came aft and screamed at Jane

"This is my boat. Get me out of here." He was waving his pistol around dangerously, manic of eye and shaking violently.

Jane was having none of it. "Listen, chum I go when the boat is full"

The officer fired a shot into the bottom of the boat through which water immediately spurted. "Don't shoot holes in my boat, you bloody idiot, you'll make it sink."

"As long as it takes me off I don't care what happens to it. Now get me out of here."

Jane waved angrily at him then at the long column of soldiers at the boat's bow.

He came charging aft, shoved the muzzle of his pistol against her throat and yelled. "Get me out now. Never mind these oiks. That's an order."

Terrified but angry Jane shouted back "Listen, you nutter, I can't handle the boat with a pistol held against me. Now back off."

Grudgingly he took a couple of steps back but kept the pistol levelled at her head.

Fear just overcame rage and Jane backed off the beach, spun the boat round and headed out to an elderly destroyer conveniently close. Coming alongside it the young officer sprang for the scrambling nets, leapt on board and fired another shot from his pistol screaming "Get going now. I order you to take me away now." The deck party had ducked, but a large marine loomed up behind the young captain and karate-chopped him in the neck with practised expertise. He went down in a heap and a sigh of relief went round the deck. Jane called up to the quartermaster on deck "You've got a real head case there."

"Don't we know it Jane."

This use of her name startled Jane who had been focused on getting to the ship and getting rid of the deranged young captain. Suddenly it dawned on her – she was alongside *Venomous* and talking to her cabin-mate Jo's boyfriend.

"Hello Joey," she called back "how nice to meet you again."

"Hey listen Jane, we heard you were here. Would you like to come back with us? Pusser's on the warpath for you and you'd better watch out. If you go near any brass at all they'll collar you."

"Thanks Joey but I've still got plenty to do here so I'll stay. Why are they after me?"

"The word is out that they don't like a girl on the beaches here and what's more you defied orders to come. Do take care."

"Well thanks but really they're being a bit silly. I'm doing a useful job here. What's wrong with that?"

"I'm not sure that's the point Jane."

She laughed, got out her string of corks and banged one into the bullet hole. This done and the boat watertight again, she nipped aboard *Venomous* to its upper deck heads, scrounged a large bowl of burgoo from the galley then returned to her boat blessing the friendly contacts she had made. Back in her boat she motored away from the ship's side; turning sharp round, she waved to Joey and headed for the beach, pumping vigorously as she went.

Boat dried out once more she returned to the orderly column she had been about to start embarking. She went forward to where they were still hesitating and called "Sorry about the delay gents. Come on board, one at a time over each bow." Boat filled, she headed back to *Venomous*. Now she was back in what had become a well-practised routine, shuttling from the column to first *Venomous* then to a series of trawlers that kept coming out of the darkness. By dawn her tally of soldiers carried had passed two thousand and, apart from the constant shelling it seemed a little routine. These were front line fighters, exhausted, ragged and unshaven but unbowed and with their discipline intact; it allowed movements to go much faster. One of them was wearing a blue helmet with RN stencilled on it in large letters. "Ooh, can I have that?" She asked. It was presented to her with a laugh, although the squaddie insisted on fitting it himself which allowed for somewhat closer contact. Jane shrugged – this was harmless.

This loading went on all night; she managed to keep her mouth shut and with her RN helmet on no-one queried her status. On each trip she pencilled carefully on her thwart the number in each boatload and by dawn had moved two thousand three hundred and forty-two men. Pausing at dawn for the last of her food and water, she noticed another rough lorry jetty to the west but she also saw naval officers on it. Instinct suggested to her that perhaps she ought to keep clear of them.

June the first dawned clear blue skies and virtually no wind, which made it a lovely day for boating. Unfortunately it was also a perfect day for the Stukas and they were back with a vengeance just half an hour after full daylight. Once again the noise was appalling, with bombs and guns adding to the relentless shelling. Through this Jane just kept plodding on. Ships seemed to be getting blasted and sunk all around her. Approaching nine in the morning she was passing the fleet minesweeper *HMS Skipjack* when it was pounced on by ten Stukas and blew up. There was an almighty explosion, which knocked Jane off her feet and almost capsized P36. Struggling up with an intense pain in her ears Jane saw the unfortunate ship roll over, hesitate for a couple of minutes bottom up, and sink. Although she did not know it, her ears were bleeding from the blast. For no obvious reason she also had a sharp pain in her lower tummy, but this passed after ten minutes. Seeing people struggling in the water she got among them and managed to pull around a dozen inboard. But it seemed very few. Most of those on board were injured to some extent so she headed for a big modern destroyer. It proved to have a doctor on board and she passed her little handful of survivors to it. She cleared off and a recurrence of her tummy pain made her explore between her legs – her hand came away bloody.

"Gah, who'd be female" she grumbled to herself but as the pain passed she forgot about it.

Then it was back to the beach. There was no lack of places to load men, with columns snaking down the beaches to the waters' edge all along the sands. Once her present column was completed she selected one at random and ran in to its head. Here were wilder men: hungry, thirsty, and driven by desperation. She had to shout at them good and loud to stop hundreds piling in and overturning her boat, but with the spare tiller bar as a weapon and fear driving her on she kept control. Nearby she saw a rowing whaler overwhelmed, turned over and its crew thrown into the water by a wave of khaki desperation that poured over it. Vowing not to be caught this way she made sure of being handy with her bar whenever she came in. On her next trip she came alongside the upturned whaler with its crew up to their watery armpits standing on the sand. "Can I help? Use the cutter as a base." So they climbed in, and lifting its gunwale turned the whaler over. "Thanks hookie" said the leading hand in charge. This pleased Jane as he didn't seem to notice or care about her gender. The tin helmet helped a lot, she decided. "What ship are you from?" she enquired.

"We're from *Venomous* but she went leaving us behind so now we'll have to look for another ship."

"Oh, I know *Venomous* – been to a party in your chief's mess. One of my cabin-mates is sweet on your jaunty."

"Oh yeah, we know her – nice girl. Jo, isn't she?"

"That's right." This social chit-chat had been going on while soldiers climbed onto the cutter and Jane eyed up the whaler, still awash with all the water inside it.

"Want a tow?"

"Oh yes please. We'll bale her out and you can pick us up next trip."

"Fine – see you soon." And Jane pushed off with her load of pongoes. By the time she got back the whaler was dry and full of soldiers so Jane took a load, swung her stern to the whaler and caught their line. This proved to be a good way of doubling up the numbers her engine was moving, and for the rest of the morning they ran together. Two of the whaler's crew transferred to the cutter and helped Jane with crowd control and operating the boat. A certain good-natured banter got up between the boats, 'Hookie Tommy' on the whaler giving 'Hookie Jane' a hard time whenever her inexperience with towing showed. "Are you driving a boat or a snake?" he called at one stage when the combination of swell and the deadweight of the whaler caused her to sheer off wildly to port. Her reply was not ladylike. By midday the sweeper they had been ferrying men to was full, and abruptly Hookie Tommy announced that they were going to get a lift back on it, taking their whaler with them. "All right, give my love to Dover. See you around some time. You owe me a drink."

"Be our pleasure Jane. Take care." She cast them off and headed back to the beach.

A long swell set in during the morning, and by early afternoon was making operations straight from the beach difficult. This was a problem for Jane – she could go to the lorry jetty to the west and see if she could load from its lee side, but there were a few naval types about who might order her home. So she persevered with working from the beach despite the difficulties. Several boats full of soldiers had broached to and were pounding helplessly side on to the sand, so Jane decided to see if she could sort them out. One great advantage of Kitchen gear is that it gives full power astern so towing was easier than for most boats. In the course of a couple of hours she took off the loads of soldiers, put a line from her bow onto each stranded craft and pulled hard.

The first to come was an open trip-round-the-bay launch with a couple of matelots in it. She went to pull it off bows first but they called to her "Can you pull us off stern first, please? Our props stick out below the boat and we need to get them into deeper water." So she got a line onto its stern, and with the swell helping to lift it, tugged the stern round. They needed help to back out as the swell smacking the broad transom stern kept knocking the launch about but eventually they got it into deep enough water to turn and motor away. Casting them off Jane called "You'd be better off working from the lorry pier there. From half tide rising there's enough depth of water for you at the end." They waved acknowledgement, blew her a kiss and pushed out to seaward.

Next was a good-sized motor yacht with a long cabin and small cockpit aft. This was more of a problem, deeper-drafted and with a civilian crew who didn't know much about handling the boat. In manoeuvring to put a line on it P36 also fell across the swell and grounded athwart the tideline. Cursing, Jane put her gear hard over and using the forefoot on the sand as a fulcrum drove the stern out, the breaking swell splashing her a good deal in the process. Then straight back to the job; with some yelled instructions the yacht's crew got a line onto the windlass and giving her engine full astern she inched them off. Once off, the yacht came alongside to thank Jane for her help. Her crew, military-looking old gentlemen with big moustaches and gin-soaked accents, were appreciative.

"You must be that Wren we've been hearing about. We never expected to meet you but thanks for your help – real seamanship. We'll tell them about that." And the yacht with its thirty-two soldiers set off with its bows firmly pointed back to England.

Number three was an old fishing boat, rough and battered but strongly-built. Again, it was deep-drafted and it took some dragging to get it unstuck from the sand but with the towline tight each rise of the swell saw its bow bump a little further round and after twenty minutes of tugging the boat came free. Her fishermen crew waved thanks to Jane in passing, and again she suggested they'd be better off working from the lorries. "Sod that," called the fishing skipper. "We've got twenty-five men on board and we're off back home. We've had enough of this nonsense. See you sometime." And like the yacht they turned their bows to the North West and set off.

That left one stranded boat in this collection. She was a beautiful Thames cruiser, all polished brass and shiny brightwork, obviously a well-loved craft. Her owner was on board with a couple of matelots for crew, and between them they didn't seem to have much idea. To complicate it all, as Jane approached it shells suddenly got closer – the *Wehrmacht* artillery had got their range. With splashes and crashes around her, Jane put her bow onto the elegant old yacht, passed them a line and using the time-honoured sailors' phrase for a tow, asked "Would you like a pluck?" This startled the matelots a little and with sly grins they chorused. "Ooh yes please" but the old owner had understood her. With a line made fast round the bow fairlead she backed off and pulled hard. Nothing happened. Despite the swell the boat did not seem to be lifting. Between the rising swell and falling shells it was getting uncomfortable on the beach. Jane took the soldiers from the yacht, but still no luck with it coming off. After half an hour of pulling and twisting and getting nowhere, Jane called to the crew "I'm sorry, we're going to have to give up. I can give you a lift out to one of the ships if you want." The two matelots didn't need a second invitation but the old owner refused, tears in his eyes. "I can't leave her like this, she's too precious. Perhaps she'll come off at high water." Well, it was only an hour after low water so perhaps, but Jane doubted it – the boat was well settled into the sand. So she just said "All right, up to you. Good luck." And she set off out to the waiting ships, dodging shellfire as she went –this was scary stuff. She never did find out what happened to the old owner, but next day his beautiful boat was a charred ruin, burnt to the waterline with polished brass debris around it.

Jane looked around. Now what - salvage or moving men? She was debating this but there wasn't much to salvage where she was. Abandoned rowing whalers were being pounded in the surf but their usefulness was limited so she didn't bother. Looking further along the beach she saw a Thames sailing barge sitting forlornly on the tideline, looking abandoned. Curious, she motored over to it and saw a lot of soldiers on its deck, not doing very much so she laid alongside and called up "Hello, are you trying to sail this boat?"

A sergeant looked over the side "Well we would if we could but we don't know how."

"Shall I show you?" queried Jane.

"Yes please. Do you know what to do with one of these?"

'If only Punch was here,' thought Jane 'she'd show them." So she shinned up a rope ladder and looked around the deck. The barge seemed to be in good order and she could feel it lifting to the swell, so it was almost afloat. Jane checked her watch – now two hours after low water, so there was time enough to do something. There was an anchor out forward; she detailed some of the troops to get it in smartish, looked aft and found the barge had no engine so she dropped down into P36, lashed it securely alongside the barge and as soon as the anchor was up she put the boat full astern. Slowly, slowly, with each lift of a swell, the barge dropped a little further astern until suddenly it was afloat all the time. It started yawing about badly with the swell on its square stern, so she turned it round as tightly as she could to avoid going aground again, and headed out into deeper water. The Squaddies on board cheered as the barge turned to seaward. Safely out of the shallows Jane stopped and climbed aboard the barge again. "Who' in charge here?" she queried.

"I suppose I am" said the sergeant "but I don't know anything about boats." There was a gentle breeze blowing from North-East so Jane figured even the totally ignorant could get the barge going in the right direction. "All right sergeant, pick half a dozen men and come for a quick lesson." She explained how the sails caught the wind and made the barge go, very roughly how to set the sails, and checked their condition. The mainsail had been set anyway and was a bit ragged with holes in it, but its tan form was still good enough to work. She got the Squaddies to set the jibs and the mizzen, which seemed to be untouched, and decided against trying to set the tops'l. With this done she explained the compass - at least they understood that from their land navigation. A quick run-through steering – "Remember it's the ship you are steering, not the compass. It stays still and the boat moves round it. Move the steering wheel the same way as the compass card seems to be going." They appeared to grasp that fairly readily. Finally, she explained that if a tug or similar passed them going west, the universal signal for a tow was to hold up a rope's end. A tow would make their lives much easier. "Aren't you coming with us?" Asked the sergeant.

"No, I'm afraid not. I've lots more work to do here. But I'll get you going in the right direction." And with sails trimmed the bow pointed to the West North West. Being light it only drew a few feet and could go over the banks but she dropped the leeboards for extra security. It was some time later that an ecstatic letter from Punch thanked her for rescuing her father's barge. The squaddies did very well overnight, making steady westward progress and at dawn got the tow Jane hoped for them. Tug and barge arrived in Dover in some triumph. Throughout her gender had not been mentioned but the sergeant's report paid full tribute to the helpful Wren.

During this time the bombs went on falling and guns shelling. It was noisy but so far Jane had only her shoulder wound and damaged ears. 'How long can my luck last?' she wondered, looking at the mess of sunken ships, bits of boats and bodies floating in the water. That damn face kept coming back in her mind's eye, its mouth hanging open like a hungry fish. Getting the barge going had taken her away from the beaches and it took her a while to get close again. Ever mindful of a Navy looking for her she had been gently chugging east again, to where the shells were heavier but the mass of soldiers much thinner. Despite her injuries there was no point, she reflected, in hanging about – either go and pick people up or clear off. And there were lots of people still to be collected so really it was no choice.

Running P36 in to the beach again, debating who to work with next, she was startled to hear a female voice calling to her. "Hello, can you help?" Looking to port Jane saw a figure with a Red Cross armband. She waved to it to come over. "Hello, We're QA sisters. We've got six ambulances of stretcher cases in the dunes. Can you take us off to a ship?" Round this lone figure a clump of soldiers had gathered, eyeing the nurse and the boat equally hungrily. Jane weighed up the situation. "Yes I should think so. Have you anyone to carry them down to here?"

The QA sister shook her head wearily. "Afraid not, just us."

"Right" said Jane decisively. She stood on a thwart. "Listen, you men. There are ambulances with stretcher cases in the dunes there. Any of you who carries one down can come with it to a ship. Now get busy." On occasion Jane could still sound very head girl.

Her instruction caused a stampede. The QA smiled at Jane. "Thanks for that. I'd got nowhere."

In no time the first stretchers arrived, were passed over the bulwark closely followed by their bearers. With six stretchers and two nurses to each ambulance plus their four carriers, it was a case of one ambulance load at a time. Jane pulled off and looked around for a suitable ship. There, just arrived, was her old friend the *Medway Queen*. That would be a good place for them. As she came alongside she called up to the car salesman who seemed to be in charge on the upper deck "Hello Dylan, got some specials for you. Can you take thirty-six stretcher cases?"

"Don't see why not, Jane. Pass 'em up."

By the time she got back to the beach most of the stretchers were assembled at the water's edge and the QA sister was having difficulty keeping order. Before they rushed the cutter Jane stood up and shouted at them "Take it steady. You'll all get off. Now, in an orderly fashion bring them aboard one at a time." Discipline is a remarkable thing, and despite their exhaustion and desperation the soldiers did as they were told. With the last load the QA sister also came aboard, and came aft to Jane as she turned the boat seaward. "You're a girl, aren't you?"

"With your knowledge of anatomy you ought to be able to tell that."

"Yes, but what on earth are you doing here?"

"Oh, I'm a boat crew Wren and just using my skills to rescue lots of pongoes. Before you ask, no the Navy doesn't know I'm here."

"Well I'll be damned. I've never seen anything like it. I thought I was tough but you......." And her voice trailed off, looking at Jane's shoulder. "That's a nasty looking wound. What happened?

"Oh, a splinter from my boat caused by a bullet from a passing Messerschmitt."

"Let me look at it." So Jane slipped the shoulder of her boiler suit off. "Hmm. Nice and clean and it looks like it missed everything vital. You should get it seen to, though. It's clean now but won't stay that way."

"Thanks, I'll do that as soon as I get back."

The QA looked at her quizzically. "I'm Louise Joycey, senior sister with QAIMNS. We only just got out with Jerries chasing us down the road. Talk about chaos. I'm not sorry to be away. But who on earth are you?"

"Leading Wren Jane Beacon at you service Ma'am. I've been here for a couple of days now. With you lot I've moved a bit over two thousand people off to the ships."

They were now coming alongside the *Medway Queen* and Jane berthed with casual skill. The offloading went well until there were just the two women in the cutter. They looked at each other, a spark of mutual respect and recognition flashing between them. "Can I write to you? I wouldn't mind staying in touch."

"Yes sure. I'm at *HMS Lynx*, Dover. 1095 Leading Wren Beacon. Maybe we could meet in London sometime."

"Duty permitting that would be nice."

Jane waved to her as she climbed the scrambling net, watched by the car salesman.

"Dylan, any chance of a meal and a cup of tea? I'm famished."

"For you Jane, anything. Come on board." Climbing the net with her damaged shoulder proved difficult but the thought of a square meal spurred her on. Coming on deck she asked "any chance of a tiffy checking my engine? I think it's fine but it wouldn't hurt to have it checked over."

"I'll fix it Jane. Go to the wardroom.

"But I'm a rating on duty. I can't go into the wardroom"

"Oh don't be silly. The mess decks are heaving." So she was well fed in the cosy womb of the wardroom. Feeling warm and comfortable she went round to the galley "Thanks for that Tommy. It was great. Any chance of some sandwiches to keep me going?"

"Be my pleasure Jane. Wait one." Five minutes later a whole loaf had been sliced and wrapped round corned beef, and cheese, and jam so she had a nice assortment all stuffed into a muslin bag. "Here Jane, got something special for you. " And with a broad wink he produced a bottle, which proved to be well filled with Pusser's rum. A generous tot rounded off her visit nicely. She was so pleased with it all that she gave him a hug and kiss then wandered off wondering why these middle-aged men went pink when she did it. Coming on deck again she found the same old engineer who had bored her with his boiler problems, coming up from her cutter.

CHAPTER 3: The Good Support

"It's all fine. I've greased the gear and shaft bearing, given the engine some lub oil and checked the cooling system and it looks good to me."

She smiled her thanks and eased back into the cutter. As she cast off Dylan appeared again. "Good luck Jane. We're weighing now. Maybe see you in a day or two back in Dover." A wave and she was gone. Night was falling as she headed back to the beach, debating where to go next. Approaching the beach in the gathering gloom she heard weird honks and screeches. This was something strange that merited investigation. As she ran the bow onto the beach she found a tall strikingly handsome Indian major waiting. "Good heavens, was that you making those funny noises?"

The major laughed. "No memsahib, not me but my most precious friend. Can you help me? We are a troop of muleteers and I want to get my men away."

"Yes of course, get them on board"

"Well thank you, but I have another request. We have killed or abandoned our animals except for The Emperor and we desperately want to take him with us. Can you do that?"

"Who's The Emperor?"

The major smiled, that sweet gentle smile so characteristic of India. "He is my prize stallion donkey."

"Good Lord, you're mad. How on earth are we going to get a donkey off? We'd never get him into the boat." She thought about it for a moment. "Tell you what, if you can get him in, I'll take him off but then we'd have to get him onto a ship. It'd be awfully difficult."

"I have some planks so maybe we can walk him on board."

Jane laughed and shook her head in disbelief. "I'll give it a go if you will but you'll have to do the work. I'm injured you see."

"No problem Mem" and he called out loudly in a language Jane didn't recognise. Twenty-three men came out of the dunes leading the donkey, which brayed loudly whenever a loud noise went off nearby. It was plainly terrified. They brought planks with them and there was a lot of shouting and waving hands in the air as they went to work. A couple of the team stayed close to the donkey's head, whispering into its huge ears and gently stroking it. This seemed to keep it calm enough to be coaxed up the planks, over the bulwark and into the bow of the boat. Even Jane, whose knowledge of donkeys was effectively zero, could see that this was an exceptional animal. The major looked pleased. "Acha, bot tighai. Thank you Mem, can we go?"

Jane did not need a second invitation.

But now, with the poor beast in the boat, what on earth was she going to do with him? She pulled off the beach and went out into the darkness to find a ship that would take him. As they went she asked the major "What on earth are you doing here with a prize donkey? It's totally crackers."

In the darkness s the major laughed gently. "The British Raj extends a long way, you know. I am being sent from India with my donkeys and mules to help your army move things around where there are no roads. My animals do it very well. We are all sad to leave them behind but The Emperor we could not give up – we would as soon lose our own lives. Y'know, he came to us as just another working donkey in the last draft but he has been so brave and is such a noble specimen that we decided we wanted to save him for breeding. He kept on working hard when the other animals were paralysed by fear and nothing daunted him. But I am thinking your army has been given a big defeat and we are very lucky to get out. Maybe we have to go further than England to escape the enemy but that is far enough for now."

The first two ships she tried laughed derisively and told her in no uncertain terms what she could do with a donkey. The major stood impassively beside her while the negotiations went on. Jane was starting to feel a little desperate – to be stuck with a donkey in the boat seemed the height of craziness. Then she spotted a Naval tug, with low freeboard and a useful-looking derrick. "Hello, can you deal with a strange request? I've got a prize donkey and its handlers here. Could you take them to England?

"You what?" The incredulity was plain. But the British seaman is famous for his adaptability; the first lieutenant on the deck snorted a laugh and said "Anything for a challenge. How do propose to get him on?"

"Well we've got planks – perhaps we could walk him on."

"All right, give it a try." So they rigged the planks and started to coax The Emperor up them. As he started Jane went forward and patted his nose. He was trembling with fear but nuzzled up, seeming to want to be friendly – perhaps responding to her femininity - so she gave him a hug and his warm woolly coat was oddly comforting. His handlers clearly knew just how to deal with him but the poor animal was terrified and honked continuously as he was coaxed and pushed onto the planks. Half way up disaster happened. The tug swung a bit to put the rising swell beam on, the cutter took a roll one way while the tug rolled the other. The planks slipped off the bulwark and with a splash The Emperor fell in. There was a shout of "Kabada nichi" as he went in; his handlers roaring with laughter at this and seeming to find it all very funny. The Emperor proved to be a powerful swimmer but was panic-stricken; his two handlers immediately dived in and got hold of his halter, again making soothing noises in his ears. The first lieutenant looked pained.

CHAPTER 3: The Good Support

"Now what are we going to do? We can't mess around here with a donkey all night."

The major who had stood silently watching the drama, now took charge. "Do you have some canvas?" He called.

"Yes"

"We'll make a belly-band sling and lift him on your derrick. He's not very heavy." So they rapidly improvised a belly-band, attached it to the derrick's hook and swung it over. The two handlers in the water fed the band round the squealing animal and back onto the hook, waved to the sailors on the tug's deck "Ast Asti Tano" and slowly the dripping animal was hauled out. Hanging in the belly-band the fight seemed to go out of The Emperor who hung limply as he was swung over. "Aria, aria, ast asti" they called as he was lowered. Limp he might have been in the air but landed on the deck, he tried to charge the tug's deck party; fortunately some of his handlers were there waiting for him and managed to restrain him. The mule troop took all this in high spirits, laughing and joking to each other in their own language as they settled the Emperor down, tethering him to the towing hook. "Now we can see who is the stronger" joked the major.

The tug captain came down from his bridge. "I don't know, I've done some strange things in my time but rescuing a donkey from these beaches has to be the daftest yet. What do I do with him now?"

The major appeared out of the dark, shook the captain's hand and said. "Please sir, you take him and my troop over to England. The future quality of donkeys and mules has just been saved." He turned to Jane. "Ekdum Kolass. I thank you, mem. I will tell them how helpful you were." Jane gave him an ironic grin then saluted, acknowledging his officer status. "Good luck. I'll have one of his offspring one of these days." And that was how, sometime later, a useful young donkey, looking remarkably like his father, came to take up residence in the Grange's garden.

As Jane cast off, the tug was already weighing its anchor, England's green fields suddenly its priority. Jane was left with a cleaning job before the cutter was fit for use again. The swell had mercifully fallen light while she took off the stretcher cases and The Emperor, but was rising again. In the dark running onto the beach with a swell high enough to throw the cutter about did not seem to be a very good option. So she took her chances on the western lorry-built jetty, and headed that way. There were still Naval officers about but on the quay end it seemed to be mainly army people. By saying as little as possible and keeping her helmet on she hoped nobody would notice her – she would pass as just one more matelot running a boat. But there were a couple of naval personnel on the quay end, directing the boat traffic. As she came alongside a chief petty officer looked at her closely "Ere, you're not that daft Wren are you? We've been looking for you."

"What's it to you?" She demanded crossly.

"There are orders out for you to go back to Dover immediately. This is no place for a woman."

"This is my fourth day here so it's a bit late. And anyway, there are still lots of soldiers to lift. So you know what you can do with your orders." The cutter had been loading during this exchange and as soon as it was full, she backed out before the Chief could say any more. He reported back to the beach officer that he'd found the Wren, but that she'd refused to go. "What did she say?" queried the officer.

"Well, actually sir, she told me to go and fuck myself and then pushed off. But at least we've found her."

"Yes, we'll keep an eye open. She seems to be a fairly determined young lady."

A message was flashed back to Dover that the errant Wren had been found but was resisting orders to return. This got a terse response from Dover Command.

Jane was now in a quandary. Working from the jetty would mean falling into the hands of Naval authority. After two days and nights without sleep she was beginning to understand the absolute exhaustion shown by the soldiers, and the temptation to pack it in was strong. But, on the beaches masses of men remained and it seemed wrong to give up when there was still work to be done. So once she had delivered her load she took a long drink of water, demolished some of her sandwich stock, and headed in again. There were plenty of soldiers who had waded out, some up to their necks in water, and they seemed like a good bet for rescue while keeping out of the Navy's clutches. This worked fairly well but slowly, the men taking time to scramble in using the loops in the bow ropes. With three boatloads delivered to a trawler, which had come quite close in she turned to the shore again, passing close under the stern of her trawler's neighbour. This boat shone a light to see what was happening; this was a big mistake. The *Luftwaffe* was still prowling overhead and immediately pounced on the light source, bomb after bomb raining down. For Jane there was a dazzling flash then blackness.

CHAPTER 4:
The Good Rescue

SUNDAY 2 JUNE

The creeping light of dawn brought consciousness again, slowly. First there was a sense of light, then a savage pain lanced through her chest, then an awareness of lying on the cutter's bottom boards. When she tried to move it was agony. Cautiously she felt her left side and felt metal embedded in her ribs – shrapnel presumably. Then she tasted blood in her mouth and found her left eye wouldn't open. Gently, she felt her face and felt a raw pain from a bloody mess up her left cheek and into her scalp. She tried to look at her watch to see how long she had been unconscious but for the first time since being given it, it had stopped, looking battered. Dawn would be about four in the morning, she thought. Breathing was not easy – it hurt. Slowly she sat up and found the pain eased a bit so kept going, prising herself onto her feet. She found the cutter bumping gently against the tripod mast of a sunken French destroyer; the dear old Dorman was still chugging away on tickover. A fierce thirst drove her to overcome the pain and lift her water breaker. With handfuls of water she washed the dried blood off her left eyelid and managed to open the eye again. Mercifully, it seemed to work. Checking carefully round the cutter she found its port side peppered with shrapnel and the paint burnt and peeling. 'They'll kill me for this back at base' she thought in an idle, detached way. But everything still seemed to work and the boat was watertight, which was a useful start. As she moved around the pain in her side eased to a steady ache, which no longer made her wince and catch her breath with each movement, so perhaps she could still do something.

In one small way her going missing from the beaches had been useful – the Navy had been searching for her during the night. Having once located her they were determined to send her back to Dover, but found nothing. There were many small boats drifting unmanned, others attached to sunken ships or upturned on the beach, so a cutter lying in the masts of a sunken destroyer had not caught their attention. By the time Jane surfaced they had given up, presumed her dead or gone, and turned to more important matters.

With dear old P36 still in working order, if a bit battered, Jane looked around to see what was happening. Although there were still troops to be seen on the beaches there were no ships loading. This seemed strange to Jane. One elderly destroyer, close inshore, was still ablaze after being bombed and sunk, but had settled in shallow water with its upper works and forecastle still showing. Curious, Jane motored over to it and saw a group of men on its foc'sle frantically waving for help. With the ship surrounded by flames ten feet high, that would be difficult but circling the blazing wreck she noticed that the flames were smaller and almost separate right ahead of the ship, and there might be a way in there. She approached it cautiously, then gave a burst of power, blessing the Kitchen gear that allowed her to put power on then stop the boat quickly under the destroyer's bow. "Come on, quick as you like" she called to the dozen men. Although not actually in the flames under the bow, the heat was intense.

"We've got a couple of injured ones here, can you take them?"

"Yes of course, but hurry." Two helpless bodies were lowered down, the first strapped to a stretcher and the second hastily stuffed into a bosun's chair. Jane received them as best she could, laying them groaning on the bottom boards. Then the fit ones came sliding down a rope, with a Lieutenant Commander bringing up the rear. They were all black-faced and bloody, wounded to some extent with their uniforms ragged and scorched. "Get down low in the boat" she ordered, giving the cutter full power astern and charging the flame wall, closing in on them even as she did so. There was a moment of searing heat – and a smell of singed hair – then they were out. "All right gents, where to?"

The two and a half made his way aft, favouring his damaged left leg. "Thank you so much for coming to our rescue. We thought we'd had it. Are you the Wren we've been hearing about? After that rescue it looks like you deserve your reputation but my God, you are in a mess. Can you take us to the pier ends?"

She winced at the pain in her ribs and replied. "Yes, I'm your Wren. Why?"

"Because there are all sorts of stories going round about you." Even by Naval standards this officer was well spoken in an upper-class English way. "I must say it's jolly interesting to meet you but you really should get those wounds seen to. You're covered in blood."

"Is that right? Not much I can do about it just now. I didn't bring a mirror with me. D'you know how much longer this is going to go on for?"

"I think this will be the last night tonight although there was some talk of continuing tomorrow night as well to get as many French off as possible. They've given up on loading during the day."

"Oh, is that why there are no ships around?"

"I'm afraid so. We lost so many yesterday that we can't go on like that. There's to be a big mass rush of ships tonight to pick up the rearguard and as many Frogs

CHAPTER 4: The Good Rescue

as we can manage."

For the first time since arriving Jane passed through the Dunkirk pier ends. Here was more devastation: sunken ships, smashed piers and buildings, and over it all the constant black pall of smoke from the burning oil tanks. At the base of the East Mole a white ensign was flying. "That looks like a good place to land us."

So she put the boat alongside the steps and watched as the officer turned to supervise his wounded off the cutter. With his men ashore the officer very formally shook her hand, wished her 'Good luck' and went up the steps himself with some difficulty, dragging his left leg. From the top he turned and with a wave to her was gone. 'Now what?' Wondered Jane. There were still men on the beach so presumably they would need her tonight, but in the meantime there seemed little to do.

She was still sitting there debating when the next Stuka attack came raining down on the harbour. 'Bloody Hell,' she thought ' I was lot safer outside.' In the midst of this one of the Navy's younger and more dynamic commanders came down the steps to her boat. "Are you Wren Jane Beacon?" the three stripes asked.

"Leading Wren Jane Beacon actually" she corrected him.

"Yes, yes, we'll not quibble about that. Are you aware that there's a general order out for you to be sent back to Dover forthwith?"

"No sir, I'm not. This is the first time I've been inside the harbour and no-one mentioned any order to me out on the beaches."

"We thought you were a-gonner then saw you rescue those people from *Voracious*. That was a brave thing to do and we'll say so, but even then you shouldn't be here."

"I don't see why not sir. I've now picked up around three thousand pongoes from the beach which I'd have thought more than justified my being here."

The commander looked closely at Jane's face. "You're in a bit of a mess. How did that happen?"

"Bomb blast sir."

"Indeed. Another reason for sending you back. We're nearly finished anyway. Just the rearguard to get off tonight and we should be done."

"But my cutter is ideal for that sir. Its Kitchen gear makes it handy about the beaches."

"It's got Kitchener gear, has it? You might be right. We'll get a crew for it."

"It's got a crew already sir – I'll do it. I know it far better than any stray matelots and by now I know just how to pick men up from the beach."

"Young lady your determination is admirable but I really think from the state of you that you should be going home." He tried to look stern while saying this but ended up smiling at her woebegone expression.

"You can't go just now anyway – the Stukas would get you. Watch out for the ships arriving around dusk this evening. You can help get the rearguard off then you must go back to Blighty."

"Aye aye, sir." This sounded like the end of the job anyway so Jane was less bothered. She saluted him as he left the cutter. The Stukas seemed to have gone so she decided to go outside, and moored up to the tripod mast of the sunken French destroyer. Here, she thought, she should be inconspicuous and able to rest in peace.

She was waiting for them when the first of the night's ships arrived. The good old Dorman, left on tickover during the day, revved up as though it knew the end was near. She topped up the fuel, checked oil and stern gland grease, and give or take the intense spasms of pain from her ribs and face, was ready to go. From the start the troops on the beach were a mixture of guardsmen from the rearguard and French troops of all sorts, many non-combatants who had suddenly emerged from hiding places. She had carried two boatloads of mixed rearguard and French from Bray Beach when a young lieutenant came to her boat as it arrived at the shore. "Beacon, we've had word of part of the rearguard trapped in a pocket at the base of the lorry pier at La Panne. They're right under the nose of the enemy but we'd like to try to rescue them. Do you think you could do it? Your boat's ideal for the job."

"Well I'll give it a go. Where are the nearest ships?"

"Off Braye Beach I'm afraid."

"That's four miles each way so it's not going to be easy. But I suppose we've got to try. I'll get going now."

"Good girl." Whatever orders might be coming from high command about her, the more junior ranks on the spot seemed happy to include her as part of the effort and to be on her side.

Jane arrived about 2130, just after high water, and in the dusk nosed in cautiously close on the east side of the lorry jetty. There she found a small group on the beach looking a bit lost. Smaller, deeper explosions seemed to be falling about them and a great deal of small arms firing was going on. By now a slightly delirious light-headedness was gripping her. "Evening Gents. Leading Wren Jane Beacon at your service. Where are the men for Piccadilly?"

In the semi-darkness they looked at her in disbelief. "You're driving this boat? That's incredible. My men are in the dunes just behind me in close contact with the enemy. What do you suggest?"

"Get a boatload of about forty down now. I'll take 'em off to the ships but those are a few miles away so it'll be a slow process. I suggest you post someone on the jetty here, and next time I come back get another boatload to come down to the end of the jetty and I'll take them off from the west side."

"Those are your orders?"

"Well sir I'm only a Wren rating so I can hardly give you orders but yes, that's what makes sense."

"Right we'll do it. Messenger, get forty men down here now."

"Who are you sir?"

"Colonel Jerome of the Guards."

'I'm giving orders to a colonel?' thought Jane. 'Crikey.' And she ducked as machine gun bullets went screaming by close overhead. This was a very active war zone. With forty rapidly embarked troops she set off to the West, found a paddle minesweeper, and was back at the jetty in just over an hour. "How many men have you still got here, colonel?" She asked.

"About a hundred and fifty left"

With a falling tide she knew her time was limited. "Ye Gods. We've only got three hours left. We'll have to move you in three lots and I'll have to overload to get you all on, but that's a chance we've no choice but take. Hope you can swim."

The Colonel barked a grim laugh. We'll take our chances." Just then one of the smaller deeper explosions erupted close by them. "What are those?" she queried.

"Mortar shells. Don't you recognise them?"

"Afraid not colonel. We don't get them at sea."

He laughed and shook his head in slow irony. With fifty men squeezed in, all having to stand and warned not move, the boat had only inches of freeboard and although unstable stayed afloat. With this load on, P36's speed was maddeningly slow but she got to the paddler and offloaded again. Another load then she was down to the last of them, being close pressed by the surrounding Germans. The last fifty-five came backing down the lorries firing as they came and Jane could see answering fire coming from the top of the dunes. Loaded, but with only inches of tide left under her keel, she reversed out cautiously with men in the bows firing landwards, keeping the enemy at bay. Fifty-five in the boat would put it in serious danger of swamping but she was damned if she would leave any behind. Even the splash from a mortar round could have sunk them but her priest's benediction held good and they got going with water gently slopping over the bow. Safely away from the immediate firing zone and on the move, the colonel squeezed in beside Jane with an arm round her waist. 'Bloody Hell, rank doesn't stop them, does it?' she thought. The colonel squeezed a little harder and asked "You say you're a Wren? I didn't know the navy sent its women to sea."

"Well, not in general but I rather came here on my own initiative, colonel. With you lot I'm up to three thousand three hundred and fifty-odd pongoes rescued."

"Really? That's remarkable. I have to say we were looking pretty hopeless before you loomed unexpectedly out of the darkness so we're almightily grateful to you, official or not. Did you know the Jerries were less than half a mile away?"

"Well, I could see movement in the dunes – I presume that was them?"

He nodded.

"But that wouldn't have made any difference. If I could get you off I'd give it a go – as I did."

"Good girl, that deserves some sort of recognition. That was real courage."

" Oh, I doubt if it will be acknowledged. The Navy's not very pleased with me for disobeying orders to come here in the first place. When I picked up General Brownlow he said that he'd see me right but it will take more than the Army to keep the Navy's wrath off my back."

"Oh, that's ridiculous. Grabbing us from under the Huns' nose was a remarkable thing to do and I'll say so."

"Well thank you sir. Let's see what happens."

They were now coming alongside a minesweeper. The colonel just happened to lift his hand to Jane's right breast, which he squeezed gently and encouragingly. "Thanks for that. Jane Beacon did you say your name was? It's a first for me, being rescued in combat by a girl. But we owe our freedom to you so you can be sure we've no prejudice against you. Good luck." He then followed his men up the scrambling net. 'Typical' thought Jane, but somehow couldn't care any more about the casual grope. As she motored away she puzzled over his prejudice comment. Why should there be any prejudice if she was being useful? Men could be very strange sometimes.

Her pongoes offloaded, she found six inches of water in the bottom of the boat and realised they must have been within fractions of gently sinking. But the trapped troops had been rescued and feeling good with life she headed back into the harbour just after midnight pumping vigorously as she went. Dunkirk Harbour was swarming with traffic. Destroyers and minesweepers and ferry boats were all moving about, loading then going in rapid succession from the Eastern Mole at the entrance to the harbour. Smaller stuff, trawlers and drifters and the odd tug, pushed into the spaces left between the bigger ships and fast motor gunboats were charging about. P36 seemed very small and inconspicuous. In the intense darkness of the blackout Jane had to keep her eyes wide open for sudden ships looming up out of the darkness, and narrowly avoided colliding with a couple of wrecks lying semi-submerged in the fairway, but she threaded her way through to the base steps. A petty officer was waiting for her. "Go and report to Commander Leslie right away."

By now pain seemed to have left her and everything just flowed, a lightness of sense and touch coursing through her. Commander Leslie was intensely harassed but brightened up when he saw Jane. "Right Beacon, you got those trapped soldiers off the beach?"

Jane nodded. "It was pretty close stuff - lots of mortar shells and bullets flying around but I did it. We had to leave a few injured behind but the rest all got off."

"Hmm. We didn't intend you to go into an actual firefight area – girls aren't supposed to do that."

"But I did sir so at least it shows girls can do it."

Commander Leslie glared at her then laughed. "You don't say."

In the darkness, lit up mainly by the fires raging in the port, Jane grinned. "Too late to worry now, sir. It's done."

"Good girl. Now, we've got a special job for your boat. This is Lieutenant de Vaiseau LeMaitre. He tells me there are English and French troops trapped further up the docks and in the town and we want you to go up through the canals to rescue them."

"You're keeping us busy tonight sir."

"Yes, well P36 is the best boat we've got now for this sort of job"

Jane smiled at the French Lieutenant. "*Bonjour, m'sieur*" He brightened up immediately. "*Parlez vous Francaise?*" He queried.

"*Oui bien sur*" She replied.

Commander Leslie cut in, "I didn't know you spoke French?"

"Well, you didn't ask and it didn't seem like the most important thing to mention. How do I find these troops?"

"Take your boat up through the docks and into the canal. There's a big crossroads of canals further up and we understand the people are trapped there. Lieutenant LeMaitre will go with you as pilot. We've arranged for you to take some French sailors to operate the locks into the canal. One other thing: We'll be blowing the last of the main dock locks at 0230 and that's only survived because the charges failed last night but it gives us a final chance to look for these trapped pongoes. The last ship leaves at 0330. Don't be late or you will be left behind."

"Crikey, we're going to have to hurry to be back by then. Are we ready to go?" The French Lieutenant waved his readiness, shouted at a couple of sailors sitting in a corner, and they were off.

Going further into the docks was like entering a mediaeval image of Hades. The whole place seemed to be in flames, roaring forty and fifty feet high, and with continuous shelling buildings were collapsing on the docksides with great crashes of falling masonry. Reflections of fire glinted on the dockwater and roiling clouds of smoke eddied about glowing red from the fires. The heat was intense. It was impossible to imagine that anyone could be alive in this inferno. The docksides were littered with wrecked ships, some still in flames, others just masts and funnels poking above the water. From a quayside a dog howled at them in despair and misery. Jane looked at it and said "Let's go and rescue it"

LeMaitre demurred. "No time. No time."

Jane just waved him aside and altered in to the quayside. The heat was intense but as the boat's bow touched the quay wall the dog launched itself and landed in the bow in a heap. Backing off rapidly Jane called to the dog, which came aft wagging its tail and cuddled up to her.

"You English are crazy. Come on, let's get on with it."

Jane pushed the throttle wide open and they went roaring up to the canal lock gates.

The sailors jumped ashore and hustled the lock keeper out of the cellar he was hiding in. When the gates closed behind them Jane was seized of a panicky feeling of being trapped. After four days out in the open of the roads, despite the bombing and shelling, she had felt free and in her element. Now, she was behind gates and it felt claustrophobic. But there was a job to be done so as the inner gates swung open she moved the gear ahead and chugged gently out of the lock. As they went the Lieutenant bellowed at the lockkeeper, "We'll be back. Keep everything ready for us." The lockkeeper crossed himself but nodded.

It was only quarter of a mile to the junction they had been told to go to, and as they approached they yelled "anyone there?" but no-one showed themself. The buildings here were less damaged but the backdrop of fire and explosions was close enough to dominate. They scouted round for five minutes but the area seemed deserted. "There's another junction half a kilometre away" he shouted, waving the direction. Arriving, they found more devastation with buildings flattened and fire flickering in the piles of rubble. The occasional shell landed with a roar. Yelling as they ran close to the bank, they spotted movement from a cellar doorway. Suddenly half a dozen khaki-clad men sprinted over and Jane put P36's nose to the bank. On board, they came aft "Thank goodness you've come. We're NAAFI staff and have been holed up in that cellar for the past week. We'd no idea how to get further. Can you rescue us?"

"That's the plan although it's going to be tricky. Do you know of anyone else round here?"

"There are half a dozen roaring drunk soldiers in the next cellar. I don't think

CHAPTER 4: The Good Rescue

they care about rescue. And in one of the houses nearby are two shot-down airmen being hidden by a local family."

"Right – one of you go and call the soldiers. If they don't come immediately they'll be abandoned. Another go find the airmen and tell them they've got five minutes to be aboard the boat. With any luck I'll get you all out."

The soldiers came reeling and singing down the bank, oblivious to any danger. "Cheers, mate. Shame we had to go"

Then the two airmen arrived bleary-eyed, having been woken up. Still in their flying kit, and bandaged round the head, they looked thoroughly incongruous. With this motley collection on board Jane was about to turn back when there was a shout from the far bank. French soldiers waved to them. They were equally drunk and Jane would have left them but Lieutenant LeMaitre was insistent and the boat rapidly filled up with happy Poilus. Again, she was about to leave when a family with two little children arrived. "*S'il vous plait,* can you take us too. We're Jewish and we've heard what is happening to Jewish people. Please please, you must take us." Jane and the lieutenant looked at each other with shrugs of the shoulders. Without her watch Jane had lost the time but a quick check with LeMaitre told her 0145. Getting very tight for escaping from the locks. "All right, I can take you to the docks. Whether they'll let you on a ship is another matter. But hurry." And, dangerously overloaded again, she turned back. The canal lock was as they had left it but there was no sign of the lock keeper. Lieutenant LeMaitre took charge with his men, closing the gates and opening the paddles. The water drained from the lock but they could not get the lower gates to open. 'So near, yet so far', thought Jane in rising panic. But the matelots had been scouting round and worked out that the locks could be opened by pulling on the safety chains. This seemed to take an age but eventually the gates opened just enough for P36 to slip through. Pausing to collect LeMaitre and his men at 0225, Jane rushed through the twists of the dock system accompanied by heat and fire and explosions. She could see the main sea lock in the distance with men moving about on it. Frantically she shouted, then got everyone to yell together. The demolition party heard them and waved to hurry up but as they came down the dock Jane saw movement on a scruffy cargo ship tied up on the quayside. She dived over to it and shouted against the roar of the flames "Who's there?"

"We Norwegian crew of this ship. We didn't want to leave her but now we must. Please can you take us off?"

"Yes, but right now. Come on, jump in."

Eight of them came flying into the mass of bodies already in P36. "We so glad to see you. We only the crew of a coal coaster but we thought we was finished."

"My pleasure. Stay still will you. This thing's seriously overloaded."

P36 was going flat out. Charging through the half-wrecked locks on a level, Jane gave the demolition team a wave, her sense of relief overwhelming. Moments later there was an almighty explosion behind her close enough for the blast to singe the back of her head, and the last of the locks was demolished. She went alongside a destroyer lying on the East Mole and thankfully watched her passengers scramble on board. The Jewish family quietly melted into the people on board, mainly French soldiers who hid them. The drunks seemed singularly unimpressed about being rescued, but had taken to the dog and lifted it onto the ship. "Don't worry, miss, we'll look after it."

Job done, Jane went back to the steps and saw her French boat team disembarked. She was about to return to the tripod masts outside when Commander Leslie came down the steps. "Well done, young lady. That has been impressive work. We'll not forget it. I want you to stay handy here in case there's any other launch work."

Jane just shrugged. "Aye aye, sir." She lay down on her good side on the bottom boards and went to sleep as the shells rained down but really she was too tired to care. Even the pains from her wounds, which she had barely noticed, were not enough to delay the urge to sleep. But as the adrenalin drained away and she came down from the high, which had been pushing her on, the pains came back with a vengeance so the sleep was fitful and disturbed.

CHAPTER 5:
The Good Return

MONDAY 3 JUNE

She woke late in the morning, disturbed by a petty officer prodding her with his boot. "Come on you, wake up. The commander wants to take a trip."

"Well thanks. Any chance of a cup of tea?"

"You'll be lucky. I'll send a bottle of water down."

Five minutes later Commander Leslie arrived, a signals chief with him who handed Jane a bottle of water.

Jane looked at the chief. "Can you spin my engine for me? I'm injured."

With ill grace the chief wound the engine up to firing speed, Jane dropped a compression lever and it fired. Blessing the Dorman's reliability they set off, first to the Eastern Mole to see what was happening there. Large concentrations of French troops still milled around, and after watching the commander and a French Brigadier struggle to communicate Jane translated, warning the French that they would only have the coming night to complete their evacuation. That done, they toured the rest of the moles and outer harbour. "Have you noticed something, sir? No Stukas."

"Yes, peaceful isn't it?" This despite the sporadic shelling that was still going on. "I wonder where they've gone to?"

"I suppose there's not much left for them to bomb round here. Perhaps they've gone looking for better targets".

Inspection completed Jane returned to the steps and settled down to wait, the fierce pain in her side making any relaxation very difficult. The wounds kept opening and bleeding again, so her left side was soaked in blood. Around 1800 she was summoned to the commander. "Right, Beacon, this is the last night and we've got a special job for you. The main French headquarters are at Bastion 32, in the ramparts on the east side of the city. There's a moat lies alongside it. Normally we wouldn't be able to get there by boat but Lieutenant LeMaitre tells me that the barrage between the moat and the docks has been shelled and is lying open so that a boat can get through and yours should be ideal. We want you to go to Bastion 32 around midnight to pick up a group of French senior officers. Lieutenant LeMaitre will go with you as pilot. Bring 'em down here to board a destroyer to England. Then you can go home yourself. It's high time you went."

"Aye aye sir. Anything before then?"

"No, I don't think so. You can try squeezing up there before dark if you like. I don't think Jerry will be close enough to trouble you."

A couple of hours later the Lieutenant arrived with the same group of matelots, and they nosed up to the barrage. This consisted of a series of gates; the central sections had been blasted by shellfire and hung open, leaving the moat at the mercy of the tide. P36 squeezed through without difficulty and slowly eased along the moat on the rising tide, going softly aground a couple of times. Once moored up at Bastion 32, the Lieutenant disappeared into the headquarters, returning to tell Jane that it would be at least midnight before the group of very senior officers were free to come. "Well, the last ships go at 0300 so they'd better not be too late." And with that Jane settled down as best she could to wait. Occasional mortar shells landed nearby but the main fighting seemed to be further to the east and south.

Midnight came and went without any sign of her passengers.

TUESDAY 4 JUNE

0100 passed, then 0200 and Jane was getting worried. She had clear orders to pick these people up but if they didn't come what was she to do? Finally, shortly after 0300, a group emerged led by Lieutenant Lemaitre. The small arms fire, which had been distant, was getting ever louder. Perhaps they had been under enemy observation or perhaps it was just a chance thing, but as these senior officers emerged a mortar shell landed on the quayside, blasting people and masonry. Jane was knocked over and took several minutes to come to her senses again. As she opened her eyes lying on the boat's bottom boards, she found she was looking into Lieutenant LeMaitre's eyes, several inches from her face. Unfortunately, his head was not attached to his body. Recoiling from this horror, Jane jumped up and looked around. Bits of bodies lay around; other people lay groaning. But by chance, the main senior officer group had still been in the Bastion's doorway and had survived unharmed. They rushed over to the boat, threw heavy briefcases in, and shouted at Jane to get going immediately. Jane, reaching into the depths of her French, shouted back, "What about the injured people?"

"Too bad. Get going now."

Several of Lieutenant LeMaitre's matelots reappeared and jumped aboard. One saw the severed head, picked it up and threw it overboard. At least it wasn't staring at Jane any more. Trying hard not to retch, Jane waved at the sailors to let go, and cautiously backed out. Without the lieutenant's pilotage and on a falling tide Jane had to guess where the deeper water might be in the moat, not intended for navigation and now tidal where it had never been before. As a result she went aground several times and had to struggle to get the boat off. This lost time and it was almost 0400 with dawn breaking before she got to the barrage. It was now nearly low tide and the inevitable happened – the boat grounded on the debris from the broken barrage gates. Jane tried to back off but the boat was stuck fast. "Sorry, gentlemen, because you were so late coming we've missed the tide. We will have to wait until it makes and hope that it will float us off." This produced a lot of shouting among the senior officers – admirals and generals - who appeared to be blaming each other for the delay but it made little difference. With full daylight their precarious position became obvious. Jane could see grey uniforms moving around over on the west side of the harbour, and if they were there presumably they couldn't be far away on the east side. Jane had the same 'so near yet so far' trapped feeling as she had had in the canal locks. It was nearly 0800 before the boat lifted clear. Finally Jane could feel it disengaging, but gave it another ten minutes before she very cautiously put the gear ahead and slipped slowly over the obstacles. Her spirits briefly soared as she saw the harbour mouth over the bow then a rattle of machine gun fire punctured the optimism. There were grey uniforms on both sides of the harbour mouth. P36 still showed its tattered white ensign so inevitably attracted a lot of hostile attention. She gave the engine maximum throttle and weaving in and out of the wrecks got to the harbour mouth unscathed. Only Jane stayed standing; the senior French officers had all flattened themselves in the bottom of the boat and only slowly came upright again as the last of the shooting died away. Her ensign, Jane noted, had several new holes in it. Outside, she headed straight out to sea for a bit then swung the boat to the west and headed for home. A wonderful sense of freedom swept over her.

Approaching a large navigation buoy a couple of miles further on, there was a strange sight. Three men, naked but for their underpants, were clinging to it and frantically waving to her. So she altered, went over to them and asked. "Are you English?"

"Too right we are – British soldiers."

"What happened to you?"

"We got separated from our regiment, tried to make a raft and sail back to England but it sank and we've been hanging on to this buoy for hours. Please take us back home."

Jane turned to her collection of important Frenchmen and shrugged in an apologetic way before putting the cutter's bow onto the buoy. With the three stray soldiers on board she turned and set a course West by North on her boat compass, which had survived unscathed. It was a fine sunny morning and mercifully the cutter was too small to attract the attention of the German artillery – or so they thought – and a general mood of relaxation spread through the boat.

That was premature. As they approached the West Dijk buoy a couple of enormous splashes in the water close to them announced that the German artillery had opened up on them. Instantly Jane swung the cutter to starboard, turning her stern to the threat and zigzagging furiously to try to throw them off. More splashes so close that spray showered into the boat told her she was not succeeding. She turned and watched: the flash from the guns was clear and about ten seconds later the shells arrived. This was just long enough to dodge out of the way and by watching aft she was able to swing the boat away each time the guns were fired, putting a few boat's lengths between it and the target point. After about twenty salvoes the shore batteries gave up - presumably the little cutter didn't justify the expenditure of much large weaponry.

While this was going on the high-ranking group had huddled in the middle of the boat but with peace restored and the boat back on course, a general and an admiral came aft to speak to Jane. Since coming on board they had largely kept to themselves in their conclave amidships, but the sudden shelling seemed to bring them out of their own shells. The general spoke *"Mam'selle,* we must congratulate you on your brave and brilliant boat handling. We are sure we would never have got away nor avoided being hit just now had you not dealt with the situations so well. You were at the beaches for long?"

"Six days, sir"

"Mon dieu, that is a long time. How did you get injured?"

"Messerschmitt bullet and Stuka bombs."

"Incroyable. We are in your debt and will remember that. What is your name?"

"Leading Wren Jane Beacon, sir"

"Your Navy sent you over there?" He asked, clearly puzzled.

"No, sir, I'm afraid I disobeyed orders to come but felt I had to do something. I work on the boats all the time, you see."

They clearly didn't see but nodded in acceptance, going back to their huddle to explain. Settled on course again she handed the tiller to one of the French matelots and sat totting up the numbers pencilled on the thwart. With the groups now in the boat it came to three thousand, four hundred and twenty-seven.

As they approached Dover a major dogfight was going on overhead, Messerschmitts and Hurricanes weaving over the sky. From the midst of it a parachute was seen descending, clearly going to land close to the cutter. Jane eased back on the throttle and waited till the pilot landed in the water close by, swung round to

CHAPTER 5: The Good Return

him, and the French crewmen pulled him inboard. Perhaps this was a mistake – he was a German pilot. For a minute or so he sat there, clearly getting his breath back, then suddenly jumped to his feet, waving a pistol around. "You go France, not England" he shouted. He made the mistake of facing the main group in the boat, which meant turning his back on Jane. Unhesitatingly she grabbed the spare tiller bar, and despite wound pain swung it with great ferocity, cracking him over the head. His leather flying helmet was no protection and he went down in a heap, out cold. The startled eyes of the senior officers told their own story as they let out great sighs of relief. Jane called to the French crew members. "Tie him up, lash him to a thwart and see you make a good job of it." She picked up the pistol from the bottom boards and stuffed it in her boiler suit pocket. All this time the boat was chugging along, off course a bit but still heading Westerly. A surge of affection for the misused craft passed through Jane.

A strong West flowing ebb tide was running across Dover harbour entrance so Jane swung to stem it, eased across the current then turned into the harbour mouth. Inside was eerily calm; after the frenetic activities of the last days the non-stop flow of ships and men had slowed to a trickle with only a handful of damaged ships lying on the berths. She headed in along the side of Admiralty Pier, through the inner entrance and swung to come alongside the boat moorings. Like her return from sailing in the Mediterranean she got that odd feeling of coming home, yet arriving in a strange place. The French matelots tied the cutter up with practised ease, Jane pulled the decompression lever on the engine and it expired with a sigh. She couldn't resist giving it an affectionate pat and murmuring, "well done" as it stopped. Everything came to a suspended halt for a moment or two. They all sat there looking at each other, still stunned by their experiences, until there was a hail from quayside. "Boat ahoy. Which boat?"

"Cutter P36" Jane called back.

"Good God, we thought you were a-gonner. Wait one."

Within moments a crowd had gathered on the quay edge. Jane called again. "I've got a Hun pilot here." And she indicated the tied-up figure, by now wide awake and jerking furiously at his lashings. "Can you get the crushers to come and take him away?"

She then turned to the French group. "That big hotel building is *H M S Wasp*. It's now the wardroom and headquarters for the docks. I'd suggest you make your number there first and I'm sure they will sort you out."

One by one they climbed the quayside ladder, getting a salute from Jane as they passed over the bulwark. The senior admiral was last off and to her surprise he seized Jane's shoulders and kissed her good cheek. "*Au revoir mam'selle.* We will not forget you." He promised. She noticed that the three semi-naked soldiers had quietly vanished without saying a word. 'Odd' she thought then dismissed them from her mind.

A couple of minutes later an armed detachment arrived. "You got a Hun there?"

"That's right. Him on the thwart. He's a downed pilot we picked up. Will you come and get him?"

A few minutes of gun waving and untying followed but the pilot seemed to accept that he was now a prisoner and went ashore meekly, giving Jane a glare in passing. Now she was alone on the boat; the crowd on the quayside had dispersed, and she sat down rather blankly. This reverie was disturbed by another hail from the shore. HMS Lynx's jaunty with four of the largest Masters-at-Arms she'd ever seen stood there. "Are you Leading Wren Jane Beacon?"

Jane nodded in return. "All right, get yourself ashore at the double young lady. You're under arrest."

"You what? I've just got back from Dunkirk."

"I rather think that's why you're under arrest. Come on, lively now."

Jane felt anything but lively and her left arm was more or less completely seized up. She had been idly debating how she was going to get up the ladder. But she clapped her rather battered hat on and scrambled to the ladder; by holding on with her left hand and using her right to pull herself up, she got to the quay edge where an impatient Jossman grabbed and yanked her onto the quay. She squealed with pain. "Careful now, I've got broken ribs I think."

"You'll have more than broken ribs by the time pusser's finished with you" growled the jaunty, and they marched her off to the wardroom. Inside, she was told to sit and wait. Thanks to the ministrations of the jossman her ribs were hurting fiercely, the wounds were bleeding freely, and she was struggling to breath. Filthy, her hair a blood-soaked mat and black of face, ragged and covered in blood, she looked more like a feral animal and was getting strange looks from passers-by. Her smell didn't help – a rank mixture of body odours, cordite and dried blood meant she stank fiercely although she was sublimely unaware of it. The jaunty came back. "Right, follow me" and she was led into an office. Here she was a bit nonplussed to find her own chief officer, a commander and the boats officer sitting behind a table. None of them were looking friendly. When they saw the state Jane was in, they all looked startled and her chief officer went pale. Jane came to attention and shakily she saluted the assembly. The salute was not returned, and she was left standing to attention.

"Just what do you think you've been doing, young lady?"

"Rescuing soldiers, sir."

"Quite, but what on earth possessed you to disobey orders, take a badly needed boat, and go gallivanting off?"

"Well, I felt it was the right thing to do."

"Your duty is to do what you're told. You had clear orders to stay in Dover and work on the boats. Do you realise the chaos you've caused while you've been away?"

This puzzled Jane. "Why should I have caused chaos? I don't understand."

Her chief officer replied "We've been going frantic with worry about you, not knowing where you were until reports started to come back from the beaches about a Wren running a boat there. Then we put two and two together and knew what you were up to."

The commander cut in. "The Navy cannot be doing with disobedience like this. If every rating started to act like you the service would disintegrate very rapidly and we just can't have that. And even more so a female should not be going into a battle zone like that. It can't be done."

"But I did it sir, so females can do it."

Jane found the group behind the table were coming and going, fading into the distance then spinning back into her face again. There was a roaring and a buzzing in her head and waves seemed to be thundering over her. Then everything went black.

PART TWO:

BOAT GIRL

CHAPTER 6:
On Being a Sailor

Out of the blackness her world was a whirling kaleidoscope of mists and rainbows and confusion. Voices were calling and singing, drawing her on to an ethereal void. Out in the darkness somewhere a dimly perceived voice was calling, getting stronger through the other whirling senses.

The voice was coming to her, calling "Jane, Jane, where did you learn to sail like that, how did it come to this?" And from the fuzzy fog another voice was singing in response. It spun out of August 1939: and It was her younger self. In the dark of the midnight watch she was singing to herself "Jane Beacon, sailor: That's what I'm made for" and this voice now rang clearly, overriding the kaleidoscopic whirl in her head. The voices were taking her back to the yacht *Osprey* as it rushed its young crew northwards towards an England just over the horizon. She shivered a bit, the sharp sting of the North West wind biting into her cheekbones as she snuggled deeper into her oilskin and neck towel. Despite the cold, her senses soared as she looked around from the yacht's deck; the sky a black bowl pierced by a million shards of starlight, the sea white-flecked. The vessel itself a mere speck on the face of dark, the infinitely small passing beneath the infinitely huge to a new world which would be heralded by the dawn. Jane felt as one with the vessel and its surrounds – the faint taste of salt on her skin, the sound of the waves and the easy motion of the boat to which she swayed as it bowled along heeling to the fresh breeze.

Yet sadness mixed with the joy in her heart. So soon it would all be over, and she would have to leave behind not just the simpler pleasures of childhood, but also the good companions who had been her shipmates in the sensuous warmth of the Mediterranean these past six months. It was all right for them: They knew what duty they were hurrying back to serve, answering the urgent call of impending war. For a nineteen-year old girl it was less clear and she shook her head, groping for a sense of purpose. The uncertainty ahead worried her; so many choices and so little idea what to do.

A trembling of the flying jib sent her eye to the compass. Right on course, so the wind must be veering and heading them a little. Gently she leant her left hip against the tiller, eased its securing beckets and let the yacht fall off until the flying jib drew comfortably again. Old sailing pilot cutters were designed for balance, to be able to sail untouched for long periods, which meant that one person on the watch was sufficient. But the only girl, and youngest crew member? That was something else and the trust being shown in her was deeply gratifying. She checked the course – a point further to the East, which meant they were no longer laying the Yealm. 'Still', she thought, 'we've got the ebb tide on the lee bow so shouldn't lose too much ground.' An odd tack on starboard would be nothing to a crew, which had sailed every point of the compass together. Jane loved being on her own like this. It wasn't just the sense of being trusted, it was being in charge and knowing that it was up to her to do it and to do it right, whatever 'it' might be. The solitude spoke to her as part of this complex sense of wellbeing. Being on her own had never bothered Jane: 'I'd be happy marooned on a tropical island,' she half muttered to herself. 'I've got two feet and I can stand on them'.

With the boat settled again, Jane looked to the skies, the sense of infinity arching overhead uplifting and oppressing her spirit in equal measure. Under a sky like this, human insignificance would make it so easy to feel helpless in the face of the unfolding drama ashore. But that needn't be so, she thought, as her positive nature rebelled. Looking to the stars she smiled, her strong emotions tugging this way and that. Perhaps dawn would bring better vision. Which was all very well, but what was she going to do? These past six months had been a wonderful time of transition, from head girl to competent adult seaman in the encircling safety of trusted shipmates and a well-found yacht. But that suspension of reality couldn't go on. With this wretched war threatening she supposed she would have to get involved, to do something useful that helped her country.

Finishing schooling had seemed to open up an exciting new world. The interview at Oxford had been tough, but she had refused to be browbeaten by the grumpy old professor and the reward had been the prospect of Somerville and studying the French literature and philosophy that she loved. Sitting around in studies drinking sherry and debating Rousseau had seemed like an exciting prospect. But that university place seemed irrelevant now. With the Germans getting ever more threatening, that sort of life seemed shallow and her family's commitment to duty was coming to the fore in her mind.

In the crystal sharp darkness the loom of the Eddystone lighthouse rotated ever more strongly out on the port bow, the first harbinger of England and home. Soon it would rise over the horizon to be a clear light giving two flashes every ten seconds. Time to get organised for a rising bearing, she thought, and a firm fix of the yacht's position. Height of eye? Two feet of compass binnacle set on five feet of hull – allow eight feet altogether. The Eddystone light is 133 ft high, so the navigation tables told her she would see it rise over the horizon and flash as a light when 17.2 nautical miles away. Calmly she removed the binnacle top and adjusted the azimuth prism, watching and waiting. Within five minutes it showed, bearing NE by N a half N. Deviation a quarter point E, variation one and a quarter points W, true bearing NE a half N. Bearing and range she laid off on the chart, and with some satisfaction drew the circle of confidence round the position, noting the time – 0327. Nearly the end of her watch, she realised with a start. She looked out on deck, saw all well, and went below to shake up the coals in the bogey stove to boil the kettle for the next watch. Briefly, she warmed her hands at the stove, then called the watch and returned to the peace of the deck.

The voice echoed in her head "And that's where it all came from?"

'Well yes', her echo replied, 'it is'.

Jane's mind drifted over her life on the water, from her father's motor cruiser to the dinghies she had raced and had adventures with from early childhood. Then on to sailing with the Pechot family around the Isle du Re, and to the Sea Rangers group she had helped start at school. These strands, along with the work of the past six months, had led to this moment. Experience and teaching had built into the confidence to be left in charge alone on the deck of a large yacht being sailed hard. She wished she felt so confident about the rest of her life.

She smiled as she greeted her relief, "Morning, Billy. That's Eddystone flashing on port, we're laying about NE by E, as close-hauled as I can manage. Tide turns at six, so we should pick up a bit then – we're making about five knots just now. There's a position on the chart. No ships to bother you. Don't sink her, will you?" Billy took a long swig of tea, looked around and grunted morose acceptance. Jane smiled sweetly and was gone; ten minutes later she was sound asleep, burrowed deep beneath the blankets in her foc's'le bunk.

Past the Great Mewstone, over the bar, the flooding tide swept *Osprey* into the Pool where she was all fast on a mooring at 1020 that morning. The River Yealm in its summer glory had never looked more beautiful. Pratique granted and yellow flag hauled down, visitors came pouring aboard from the surrounding dinghies until the deck was thick with people, each group seeking out its own among the crew. Many of them had been away for the best part of a year. Among this throng came Jane's mother and brother David, keen to carry her off to the Old Grange and into family life again. She hesitated. Her mother looked at her. "Don't you want to come home, Jane?" There was a hint of hurt in the tone.

"Oh, Mummy, it's not that I don't want to come home. It's…It's…I don't want to leave this – it's a kind of home too." She gestured round the deck. "It's been… wonderful. It's such a shame it has to end."

"Well, Jane dear, it is over I'm afraid and the future's not looking good. Perhaps

Mr. Chamberlain will get Herr Hitler to calm down, but your father has no confidence that he will."

Jane shrugged, a sad resigned movement. "All right let's go." She went aft to where *Osprey's* skipper-owner was holding court. "Uncle George, Mummy's taking me away now but I'll be back in the morning to help square the boat off and pick up my kit. Is that all right?"

Her captain gave Jane a broad smile. "Yes of course. There is lots to do but it can wait till tomorrow. Enjoy a comfy bed for a change."

"There's nothing wrong with my bunk." And with a wave she went over the side into the dinghy where David was waiting to row them home. Heading up the river, her mother, always prone to saying what was uppermost in her mind, asked "Are you going to settle down now, Jane?"

Jane flinched. "Settle down? In what sense? I'm off to university unless the blasted war gets in the way."

"Yes dear, but that needn't stop you finding a man and starting to look to the future."

"What a horrid thought. That's the last thing I want, Mummy." Jane turned away. Coming home to the Old Grange was an odd mixture of the lifetime familiar and a sense that it wasn't quite the centre of her universe any more. A strong wave of comfort and peace washed over her as she looked around at the well-worn furniture and polished parquet floors.

As the eldest child she had always been boss of her unruly siblings in an off-hand way, but now there was a hint of something else in the way she was treated. Of course, there were hugs all round and the warmest of welcomes, even her undemonstrative father joining in briefly. But there was respect there too.

With a brother, sister Sarah, and noisy ten-year-old twin brothers there was a substantial family at dinner. They were a close-knit family despite only seeing each other in passing in the holidays – or possibly because of it. This was largely through their mother's unremitting efforts to keep everyone in touch. It was expected of all the children that they write home every Sunday, and their mother spent a part of each week drafting a synopsis of everyone's news, which then got sent to them all. So the dinner table, although formal, bubbled with lively chatter and warmth. Inevitably they all wanted to hear about Jane's exploits. Censoring one or two of them, like the night she got leglessly drunk on (highly illegal) absinthe in Cannes, she told them about the backstreets of Tunis, the scents of Corfu and the beauty of dusk off the Iles D'Hyeres, without mentioning the visit to the Isle du Levant. Mostly, she told of how much fun it had been working as a regular deckhand. "I just loved working with the boat, and the boys, but above all being so involved with

CHAPTER 6: On Being a Sailor

the sea and the dolphins and the weather. It was just wonderful and I can't imagine a life that doesn't have boats in it."

Then she told of the abrupt decision to head back to Britain and the charge out of the Mediterranean, pausing briefly at Gibraltar before heading north non-stop to home. For Jane that long sea passage had been the highlight of the trip, and she spoke of the regular rhythm of watchkeeping, of the night sky and the spectacular sunsets and what two continuous weeks at sea felt like. Their one period of bad weather came just South of the Bay of Biscay and gave them twenty-four hours of real discomfort, but even that Jane had reveled in. The whole family, being experienced sailors, understood what she was saying and admitted to feeling more than a little jealous. "Your turn will come," was all she said to that, then "Goodness, I've been talking for two hours."

But they had all listened intently, even her usually semi-detached father. "Aye, quite a trip. It should stand you in good stead, young lady."

Jane smiled at him. "Let's hope so, father. I wonder what will happen next?" She had hoped this might draw him out, but all he did was shrug and shake his head.

Next morning Jane rose early, boat habits overcoming any temptation to laze in bed, and she was just up when her mother came in bearing tea. This caught Jane putting on bra and pants. "Goodness, Jane, you're brown all over. How did you manage that? So Jane showed her the two-piece bathing costume she assured her mother was all the rage in the South of France. "Not like that in my day" sniffed her mother.

"I don't suppose it was, but times change y'know."

"Don't I know it. You've not been misbehaving, have you?"

"No mummy, I'm still a virgin."

"Well thank goodness for that. What else could you be?"

Jane longed to tell her that lots of girls nowadays took a more modern view of their sexuality, but knew it would be wasted on her starchy traditionalist mother. She raised an eyebrow. Her mother humphed and bustled out.

Her exit relieved Jane a bit as she would have had real problems explaining how she came to be brown all over. On her own again, happy memories came flooding back. When it was first suggested on *Osprey* that they visit the nudist beaches of Heliopolis on the Isle du Levant, the boys had looked sideways at Jane. But when it came to the point they were diffident and Jane, after initial misgivings, much less bothered. Their antics amused her hugely, watching them wriggle uncomfortably at the prospect of baring all. Jane at least had the advantage of confidence in her body. At five foot ten, long-legged and lean, strong and athletic, she knew she looked good. Large, high firm breasts enhanced the effect, given how spare she was otherwise. As she matured through adolescence they just grew and grew, rather to her annoyance and embarrassment. Mostly, they were a nuisance; they got in the way, made balance more difficult and had finally put paid to any hopes of being a ballet dancer. She went through fits of hating them, trying to make them less conspicuous. She knew they seemed to excite men but could not see why and hated the way they brought a gleam in men's eyes. It was one aspect of her body that really troubled her 'I do wish they'd go away and leave me alone' she fretted. Her efforts at slumping over to reduce their obviousness achieved little, and anyway her school had drilled all its pupils to stand up straight so slumping was not natural.

At least the boys on *Osprey* had treated her nicely. They often indulged in horseplay, pummeling each other but when Jane had tried to join in they recoiled so sharply that she hastily withdrew. Why they did this, she had no idea but it usually seemed to release tensions that were building up in them so for the sake of peace and quiet she let it go. Having been part of their tight-knit group from early childhood she regarded them fondly as substitute brothers and was much less defensive around them than with other young men. But their pummeling brought on a warm feeling, and it would have been nice to join in.

So the prospect of going nude bothered her less than her nervous English shipmates, despite their well set-up young bodies. In the end they did it, with difficulty, but it never came naturally as it did to Jane. After several weeks at anchor there, swimming ashore naked each day to lap up the sun, she was tawny all over and glowing with health. Then suddenly Uncle George had got twitchy and within a couple of days had announced that they were going home. His young crew were disappointed to begin with, but being made to listen to the news on the World Service brought them round very sharply. Their self-contained idyll was over.

With a sigh Jane came out of her reverie and wandered down to the kitchen, where cook and the maid were already busy. "Good morning Eunice" she greeted the Cornish woman who had been a part of her life from early childhood. Eunice had joined the Beacon ménage just after Jane's father had left the navy and moved his young family to the Old Grange.

"Mornin', Miss Jane, nice to have you home again."

Jane smiled. "How's the teapot?"

"Full as ever" and cook nodded at it sitting on the corner of the range. "Will you be stayin' long? I think the other children are back to school in the next week or two."

"Good question, Eunice. I'm not sure. It sort of depends on whether we start fighting the Jerries or not. If we don't, I'll go to university as planned. If we do, I suppose I ought to do my bit to help the war effort, but I haven't a clue what."

"Well war's looking very likely, though I hope not. I lost my brother Joe in the last one."

"Yes, I remember your telling me about him. Gassed, wasn't he?"

"That's right. Not a nice way to die."

Jane gave her a sympathetic hug, reflecting on the cruelties of a life which had left Eunice to survive as someone else's cook after the farm which had been her home had been taken away when there were no men left to run it. Eunice had been engaged to a marine but he too had been killed, a stray shell at Gallipoli wrecking the boat he was in, but that was rarely spoken about. Occasionally Jane had caught the stocky, strongly-built figure in its big white apron sitting by the kitchen window, looking far out over the river and hills and quietly weeping. She never complained and if offered sympathy simply said there were people a lot worse off than her, thank you, but it was acknowledged in the family that Eunice might otherwise have been a yeoman farmer's wife and more or less their equal. The children had been taught throughout their lives to treat her with affectionate respect. Perhaps it wasn't surprising that she regarded another war with misgivings.

"Your mother was sayin' that she hoped you might be thinking of settlin' down now but this war will mess that up, won't it?"

"Oh God, has she been on about that again? I've told her and told her there's a world out there and lots of other things to do before I have to turn into a housewife, and have babies, and all that stuff. But does she listen? No. At this rate if there's a war it will be a godsend and give me a chance to get away from her pressures."

"Well, you're still a minor Miss Jane so you're not entirely a free agent. There's something to be said for a bit of stability in troubled times, y'know."

"Eunice, please. I'm far too young for that yet. And I'm not going to, so you'll all have to get used to that. Once I can work out what to do I'm off. There's so much more I could do and I promise you that I will, I will make my mark, war or no war."

CHAPTER 7:

On Laying Up

With cook pacified Jane rowed herself down to *Osprey* and was busy about the boat tidying, putting away then gathering up her own gear. Work finished, she looked at her rigger's set: knife, marlin spike and pliers all in a neat leather sheath she had had made in Algeria. 'Oh well, probably not need these again for a while,' she thought sadly, packing them away. By the end of the day Uncle George was satisfied, the food removed, the boat cleaned and tidy with everything where it belonged and bilges sweetened.

With that done, they all retired to the Dolphin Inn in Newton Ferrers to celebrate their homecoming. This turned into a rowdy session of reminiscence and teasing and noisy laughter which would have had them thrown out had Uncle George not been there, his respected position in the village protecting them, as had his quietly taken role as chaperone which allowed Jane to sail with them in the first place. He sat watching his lively protégés with satisfaction. On board *Osprey* they had been a musical bunch with Uncle George's violin, others with guitar and ukulele and penny whistle while Jane played her concertina. She had acquired a passion for the accordion in France, where the Pechot family were keen players. Her own family all played something, and Jane had transferred her early piano playing to the accordion, regarded as a wildly eccentric thing to do but her little squeezebox had proved a great favourite. Leaving the boat they had packed up their instruments but needed little encouragement to get them out again and to keep the pub singing all evening.

Jane could hold her drink as well as any of them, but even so rowed home erratically in the dark feeling no pain. Having missed dinner she was given a fairly frosty reception by her mother. "You know the rules, Jane. You must be in for dinner unless you have said you'll be out."

Jane was going to apologise but something inside her rebelled, her instinctive deference lowered by the martinis she had drunk. Why should she apologise? She didn't feel in the least sorry. "Well that's just too bad Mummy. It was an impromptu party and I don't see why some hidebound rules here should stop me."

"Jane you will not speak to me like that. If I say that's the rule that's an end to it."

"And the other end is that if I want to stay out I will. Good Lord, I was only with the boys from *Osprey*. We were having a farewell session."

"That's not the point. I knew where you were and it wasn't that that bothered me. But you know very well that we try to run this home on regular lines and I won't have you disturbing them. Now go to bed."

"Oh don't be ridiculous. Go to bed indeed. What do you think I am, some five year old?"

"I could wish you were. You're getting altogether too headstrong for my liking. I was afraid this trip might give you ideas beyond your years."

"Oh, come on, Mummy. You're not running a ward now."

"Running a ward and patients was a lot easier than controlling you lot. I dream of those days sometimes."

The two stood glaring at each other, toe to toe. But her mother was cautious; there had been serious incidents before and Jane's temper was notorious in the family. A naturally impulsive creature, when this merged into temper she could be volcanic and there had been times when she had gone totally out of control, smashing things, hitting people and running berserk. This was more than childish tantrums; the veneer of English reserve and politeness drew a skin over a powerfully hot-blooded nature, which had led her into trouble at intervals throughout her life. Self-control had been hard-won. Her revered games mistress at school had used sport to get Jane to channel these forces into a fierce competitiveness and to modify destructive forces into a driving determination. Thanks to that training Jane had a grip of herself but when the red mist rose inside her and she compressed her lips people knew it was time to duck. "You just be careful, young lady" and with that her mother stomped off.

Sharp disagreement was unusual in the family and Jane wobbled for a moment, almost calling after her. But she held on defiantly rather than give in, which meant that she went to bed hungry.

Calm was restored next morning, and over the next couple of weeks she got drawn into the life of the house again. David went back to school first, for his final year, then the twins; Jane enjoyed a couple of days with Sarah, just girls together before she too departed. But the looming threat of war hung over everything. There was a lingering tension in the air, a sense of holding the breath and waiting for the inevitable. Despite Chamberlain's pieces of paper and 'peace in our time' there was little belief in it among people Jane spoke to. Somewhat to her surprise she found a strong streak of willingness to go on appeasing Herr Hitler, almost anything seeming better than going to war again. A few times she met her fellow *Ospreys,* Jane taking along her full size accordion which led to some lively sessions in the Dolphin. The boys were all bursting with plans for what they were going to do – George Junior and Perrie to the Navy, Billy and Horace hoping to fly, Walter defiantly going to look for a job in the diplomatic corps. He was teased by his fellows for being a softie, but quietly replied that he would do as much for peace as any of their more bloodthirsty daydreams. All Jane could do was shake her head and worry. 'I hate being a girl' she thought as she listened to the others out-bragging each other. 'Why can't I be doing something useful as well?' Already she had mentally run through the options open to young women and found them unappealing. Her settled happy life was almost mocking her as she struggled to see any opening.

Caught up in the routine of the Old Grange she briefly put her own prospects to the back of her mind, but in the midst of this small-scale life the tensions burst and on the third of September 1939 war was declared. For a few days they lived with an ear cocked to the radio, the sinking of the passenger liner *Athenia* on the first day alerting them to a new world of danger. Her father, apparently engrossed as ever in his patients, surprised them at the breakfast table as they sat listening to the radio, by saying 'he supposed they had better prepare for a long hard slog. He'd ordered builders to come and make them an air raid shelter at the bottom of the garden, blackout curtains had been ordered to fit every window, and he recommended the women to stock up on food as best they could. It might be scarce before long.' From a man who barely seemed to notice the outside world, this advice startled mother and daughter.

Mid-morning, Jane drifted into the kitchen where the postman was getting his usual cup of tea. As well as gossip from her best friend at school, there was an official-looking cream envelope addressed to her mother. "Jane dear, we're invited to a ball for the young men going off to war. You're invited too. Ten days' time. Do you have anything to wear?"

"Would slacks do? You know my wardrobe as well as me." This only half jokingly.

"Now then, don't be tiresome. We'll have to get something made for you before it all disappears."

"Cotton sailcloth would be nice."

"Jane dear, do take this seriously. It's high time you smartened up a bit. You can be very annoying at times."

"Oh come on, I might be good at dancing but that doesn't mean I want to get tarted up to be ogled by ghastly boys."

"Are you just trying to be difficult? This is a ball, not the sailors' Saturday night hop."

"I'd be more at home there."

"Jane! How dare you say that? Think of your position as a young lady."

"My position, as you so proudly put it, is simply a young female who'd rather be a sailor. Getting polished up for balls isn't my idea of fun."

"Well, it's high time it was so stop being silly."

Jane stamped a foot. "I just don't want."

"Now you really are sounding like a five-year-old. I'll treat you that way if you like. If you want to be treated like the young adult you obviously think you are, try behaving that way. This will be an excellent opportunity for you to meet some suitable young men."

"Suitable for what? A husband? That's the last thing I want just now and you know it. Why do you go on like this?"

But her mother just raised her eyebrows and sniffed, and that was how Jane found herself in her mother's Austin Ruby, that afternoon, heading for their regular dressmaker in Plymouth. Jane went with gritted teeth, determined to hate every minute of the trip. But very much against herself she enjoyed the discussion of fabrics and shape and latest styles. Discussion about colour to match her tanned and slightly freckly complexion, against the deep russet of her hair and grey-green eyes, was actually quite interesting. With elegant drapes pinned in place and instructions about more becoming underwear ringing in her ears they left with both mother and she in better mood. As she drifted off to sleep that night the contrast chafed at her mind, so recently a competent seaman with calloused hands and now a victim of her own femininity. A surge of fright went through her at the thought – being dressed up like that was bound to attract attention and she really did not want that. She sat up with a jerk trying to shake the thoughts away, but it was another half hour before she could relax again.

But next day her other world returned with a visit from her Godfather. "Hello, Uncle George, are you getting used to being ashore again? I'm finding it quite hard."

"Well, I suppose I'm used to those sorts of change but it does feel a bit strange. Tell you what, I came to see if you were free tomorrow. I've been offered a mud berth for *Osprey* up Coflete Creek for the duration and the way things are going I think it's going to be smart to take it. I'm being called back onto the active list so we did the right thing bringing her back to England. I don't think I'll be yachting for some time now."

"I suppose it's sad that we won't be sailing any more but does being recalled mean that you'll be confirmed as admiral? I know how much you wanted it."

"Don't know for sure, dear girl, but probably appointed Acting Commodore to begin with. I have to go and see the boss next week to discuss what I'm going to be doing. Meantime can you come tomorrow?"

"Yes of course, when do you want me?"

"Be aboard three hours before high water. Forecast's good and it's a nice big spring tide."

"Fine, see you then."

Next day was glorious late summer, calm and hot. Surrounded by the beauty of the river's tree-lined steep banks the Yealm was as lovely as any part of the Mediterranean they had so recently left. Jane knew she was looking her spectacular best in a yellow halter top and blue shorts with her rigger's set belted at her waist. This attracted the odd wolf-whistle from the boatyard in passing, and she happily waved back. At a safe distance she rather enjoyed being appreciated; it sent a shiver of excitement through her body, which settled in her groin. Back on board she fell into the ways of the boat straight away. The three of them - honorary Uncle George, George Junior, and Jane - cast off from the mooring; as the boat cleared the pool on the strong-running tide they dropped the anchor so it was just dragging along the bottom. This snubbed the boat's head to the incoming tide and in the time-honoured way of kedging, she gently dropped astern up the river dodging the oyster beds. With judicious use of the rudder, just biting in the tidal stream, they maneuvered backwards the mile and a half to the entrance to Coflete Creek where Uncle George showed his skills by sheering the boat across the tide and into the mouth of the creek. With Jane straining to hold the boat on a quant pole, George Junior heaved the anchor up as fast as he could, and they poled the boat into the narrow confines of the creek. Her berth had already been arranged, so they shoved her into the mud as firmly as they could with the quant poles, got the pram dinghy out and ran mooring lines ashore, tied to a few of the stronger trees lining the creek. Seaman that he was, the skipper had chosen his spot carefully, with a small outcrop close by on the shore where a gangplank could be landed enabling them to walk ashore once *Osprey* was secured. The whole operation had taken just under two hours.

"Never mind blasted balls, this is how I want to be." Jane muttered under her breath but was heard by George Junior who looked at her with ironic amusement. "Sorry, G, I just don't want to be getting all tarted up to go to a ball, but mummy's iron grip is on me and I resent it bitterly." They were both hot and sweaty and mud-stained – and utterly content. 'This', thought Jane, 'this is my reality, not prancing about in a fancy ball gown' and a joyous surge coursed through her.

Now they had to wait for the tide to ebb away so they could be sure the boat was snuggly settled in the mud and would stay upright. With tea made and handed round Jane had time to look about her, and realised that if poor old *Osprey* had to be abandoned in a mud berth, this was an idyllic one. Late flowering chrysanthemums flourished against the dark green mass of trees, and apart from distant gull cries it was silent. The thick blanketing peace of the creek was strangely at odds with the war hullabaloo in the world outside. Uncle George came and stood beside her, quietly taking in the scene. "Isn't it gorgeous? I know it was a shame we had to give up early in the Mediterranean but I can't help feeling we did the right thing.

Abandoning her down there would not have been a good idea."

"Oh well, I got six months out of it and the trip north was a bonus. It was certainly the best six months of my life."

"Do you think so, dear girl? Kind of you to say so. I must say, I enjoyed it myself and I'm feeling very ambivalent about getting back in harness. I could get quite attached to just knocking about in a boat."

She smiled at him and wandered off to tidy up. Coming back on deck, she casually asked "Uncle George, I've been wondering what I should do. I could take up my place at Somerville but I feel I should be doing something useful for the war effort. But really the only practical things I know about are boats and sailing. Could the Navy use me in any way?"

"Well, I hear that they've re-activated the Wrens. Maybe you could join them."

"The Wrens? Don't they just do domestic support and scrubbing things? I'd like to do something active."

"I've a feeling they are going to do more than that. Leave it with me and I'll investigate further."

"That would be kind."

She went and sat on the foredeck, knees under chin and bare feet flat on the deck, quietly absorbed in her surroundings. 'Why does this have to end?' she wondered. 'I could be so happy just being a sailor but it's all slipping away now. I hate it, I hate it.' At least some things didn't let her down. "Well, Old *Osprey*" she murmured "I hope you like your resting place. You're going to be pretty lonely for a while now." And she patted the windlass affectionately.

"I'm glad I'm not the only one that talks to her" The voice from behind made Jane jump. "G, stop that. I nearly had a heart attack."

George junior grinned as he sat down beside her. "Funny how the old girl gets under your skin, isn't it."

Jane spoke softly "Doesn't look good, does it?"

"Oh, I don't know about that. It gives life in the Navy some meaning. I'm told that our term at Dartmouth will be sent out to the fleet pretty soon. The way they're mobilising ships just now, they'll need every one of us. Suits me. The sooner I can get at the Boche the better."

"It's all right for you. How many generations of your family have been in the Navy?"

"Five, I think. We certainly have an ancestor did great things at Trafalgar."

"Me, I'm not nearly so clear. Your father is going to ask about the Wrens but I don't really see myself serving in a wardroom. Not my thing really. Why do girls have to be so constrained? We could do lots more if only we got half a chance."

George snorted. "You, serve in a mess? It's beyond belief. You'd serve the bread on the point of your marlin spike. Don't worry Jane, you'll find something better suited. But don't you want women's things? Y'know, a husband and babies and all that?"

Jane shuddered. "Oh come on G, not yet. One of these days perhaps yes. That's natural for a girl, I suppose, but why is it the only thing I can do? I'm not ready for any of that yet even if there wasn't a war, and all the more so with this nonsense with Hitler going on. At school we used to fantasise about our ideal man, in a giggly sort of way. But first I'd need to fall in love and that hasn't happened yet. You bunch of shipmates were ever so nice to me but it wasn't romantic, was it?"

George grinned ruefully. "We all really fancied you, y'know, but we didn't like to say so. Life on *Osprey* was easy till you joined us and we were all attracted to you. But that wouldn't have been right, would it? We really struggled to control ourselves at the Isle du Levant. That's why we were so shy about it yet you seemed oblivious to just how attractive you were to us."

Jane's return smile was gentle. "I was? Y'know, that never occurred to me. The girls at school used to tease me that I was too practical to indulge in romantic silliness, and I suspect they were right. But it would be nice to be in love, wouldn't it?"

G shrugged. "How would I know? We all have dreams and fantasies but that's not the same as being in love. Or at least, I don't think it is."

"Oh well, I can forget any dreams like that for now which may be sad or may be a blessing in disguise. It's all right for you, at least you can look forward to going off to biff the Boche. Girls don't have that choice." She thought about it for a minute, looking sadly into a murky uncertainty. "Y'know, I was really looking forward to studying French literature and philosophy with all those intellectual people around, and sailing on *Osprey* in the long vac, but that's gone for now."

"Don't you get angry about having that taken away from you?"

"What makes me angry is the way I'm prevented from doing anything useful because I'm a girl. There's so much I could do but it isn't ladylike. Bah, who cares about ladylike? I might get angry if the war went on for a long time and I was a useless old maid before it finished so let's hope it's over soon. How long do you think this silly war is going to last?"

"Well Dad seems to think that it might go on and on. Doesn't know why, just says he feels it in his water. Believe the papers and it will all be over by Christmas."

"That does seem a bit optimistic, but perhaps a year? Then I can go up to college next autumn. That would be nice. Aren't you a bit scared of going off to war?"

G laughed. "No, us fighting Rodmaynes have been doing it for a long time. Remember Dad has a chest-full of medals when he puts a uniform on. It'd never do if I was scared. What about you?"

CHAPTER 7: On Laying Up

"I don't know what to be scared of. I suppose it's expected that a girl should be, but that's just silly. All these great armies and world events going on round you makes you feel awfully small but if we all keep our nerve and do our bit, maybe between us we can come out on top." And she looked thoughtfully across the creek, where seagulls and crows were squabbling over a tattered remnant of fish. In the lengthening shadows she spoke very gently. "It's woman's way just to get on with things, dangerous or not. I expect we'll do the same this time."

CHAPTER 8:
On Being a Girl

Uncle George called "Come on you two, she's settled nicely and it's time to go. We're being picked up in twenty minutes." They packed up and trailed through the woods to where Aunt George was waiting with the Alvis. "Have you heard *Courageous* has been sunk?"

Uncle George started. "No, no. When was this?"

"Well I was chatting to the port admiral's wife and she tells me it's all the buzz round Guzz. The poor old thing was torpedoed apparently, with lots of men lost."

Uncle George buried his face in his hands. "This is going to be a bloody business."

Jane piped up "What was *Courageous*?"

"An elderly aircraft carrier, but a big powerful ship to be lost just like that." And he sat silent and grim for the rest of the journey home.

Next day they were back to empty the boat as soon as the tide made, piled all the lose items into the dinghy and rowed them down to Jane's family boathouse where they were stowed away at the back of the loft. Then, they stripped the sails and running rig, dropped them onto the bunks below decks, sealed the boat as best they could, and made sure a bilge suction pipe ran out to an external pump so she could be pumped out any time. With tiller firmly lashed and a canvas cover stretched overall, *Osprey* was as well prepared as she could be for her abandonment.

All this took the best part of a week. Jane was deeply content, back in the sailor's ways with marlin spike and knife in this quiet backwater, and her calluses returned rapidly. This meant that she was less than prepared for the arrival of her ball gown for final fitting.

"For goodness sake, Jane, would you stop fidgeting. We're trying to get this right and you're not helping."

"Sorry."

But Irritation welled up; this performance seemed so irrelevant to the life she would have liked, and even more to the life it looked like she was going to have. But despite a feeling that trousers on the deck of a boat were much to be preferred, a sneaky pleasure at the ball gown warred with the irritation. In a turquoise and deep green shot silk taffeta, with a tightly fitted strapless bodice and a full, slightly ruched skirt in classic court style, the gown set off her tan and colouring. Dressed in this, she could feel a different person emerging. Perhaps being female was not so bad after all?

Even so the two days before the ball passed heavily. Why did she feel so like a condemned prisoner? On the morning of the ball the dress was delivered looking mockingly splendid. She was eyeing it with undisguised hostility when her mother swept in to her room. "Right Jane, time to get you smartened up a bit."

"What do you mean, smartened up a bit? Isn't it enough that I'm getting dressed up?""

"No, my dear, it is not. We're going to the hairdresser this morning to do something with that haystack of yours."

"Why, what's wrong with it? I run my fingers through it every day."

"Yes dear, and that's what it looks like too. I think we can do a little better."

Her mother, veteran of a thousand such balls, was applying all her wiles to getting the potentially beautiful young woman out from behind the instinctive tomboy. So it was into the Austin Ruby and off to Plymouth again, teeth well gritted. Again, her mother was on about the chance to find a man. "You know, Jane, it really is high time you started to think about your future. You'll have to be ready for when you marry and it's never too early to be considering what that means."

"Mummy, don't be ridiculous. I'm only nineteen for goodness sake with a whole life in front of me. Why are you so desperate to get me married off?"

"Because that's woman's destiny, Jane. If this war hadn't intervened I was trying to get your father to agree to sending you to finishing school – remember you're not twenty-one yet and we can still tell you what to do."

Jane shuddered. "Well, thank goodness for the war is all I can say. Finishing school! What a dreadful idea."

Arrival at the hairdresser stopped this conversation. Under the hands of that lady – a long-established relationship – and her mother's watchful eye, miracles happened. After the hairdresser the beautician took over and despite the occasional splutter – Jane had no idea eyebrow plucking could be so painful – something much more glamorous emerged. Jane had never bothered with more than a touch of lipstick so the application of comprehensive makeup was new to her. The beautician was sensible enough not to cover up her freckles and deep wind-bitten tan, but rather to play them up while subtly toning the whole effect. Her mother was triumphant. "There you are, my dear, you see you can look beautiful if you want to."

Jane didn't know whether to snarl or laugh. It was certainly a dramatic change. As they emerged a low wolf-whistle from nearby demonstrated one result of the improvements. Again that unbidden thrill ran through her, warming her groin.

Back home, the few hours left dragged. But soon the inevitable couldn't be delayed any longer and it was time to change. Even the underwear was a new experience – lacy French knickers identical in colour to the gown, which made a contrast with the serviceable white cotton she was used to, then the slip and finally the dress itself. There had been a brief battle about a corset, with her mother scandalised that Jane firmly rejected the idea. "Look at me mummy. I'm completely flat and firm down the front. Why would I want a corset?"

"Because every lady wears her girdle – I wouldn't even go into the garden without mine and neither should you."

"Mummy that's absolute rubbish and I'm not going to, so there."

Her mother raised her eyes to heaven but said no more. The young could be so untamed at times. But the bodice was so strongly made that it was virtually a corset anyway. It was low-cut at the back and the thought of exposing this bareness to the world was disturbing in a way nudity on the Isle de Levant had never been. Having her hair in clouds round her bare tanned shoulders felt odd to Jane, and she was fiddling with it when her mother came in with a gleam in her eyes. "Well, my dear, I told your father when you were born that you'd be a beauty one day, and I wasn't wrong."

"D'you think so, mummy?" She was looking at this stranger in the mirror, doubting and uncertain, yet with a startling sense that there was a different Jane, attractive and very feminine, looking back at her.

"Yes, my dear, I've no doubt about it – you'll be the belle of the ball. I've been waiting for this day for a long time and I'm delighted to see it come true. Have faith – you'll love it and so will everyone else."

"Oh, come on, that'll be the day."

"No dear, I mean it. And there's something else for you." From behind her back her mother produced a jewelry box. She put its contents round Jane's neck. Jane squealed. "Mummy I can't wear that. It's too….it's too… gorgeous." She looked at the necklace with mixed panic and awe. It was a stunning piece, with a huge emerald in its centre surrounded by amethysts and with a diamond pendant. Smaller diamonds surrounded the centre piece and ran up round her neck. The whole was set in gleaming gold.

"But mummy, but Mummy…." Jane's voice trailed off to a whisper. "Where did this come from? We're not that rich."

"No dear, your father brought it back from Archangel in 1919. He'd saved the life of a Russian prince wounded in the fighting and was given this by way of thanks. It's only produced occasionally but we thought your sort-of coming out was enough. It's not really mine – we regard it as a family possession so I'll have it back tomorrow."

"Does father know about this?"

"It was his idea, dear. Wear it with pride. Now come along, it's time to go." She gave Jane a little hug and smiled, a secret satisfied smile.

CHAPTER 8: On Being a Girl

So Jane, deeply touched but scared at the same time, trooped down the stairs behind her mother to where her father was waiting, smart in white tie and tails with miniature medals on his left breast.

"Good lord Jane, what's happened to you?"

"Thanks, father, that's just what a girl needs."

"No, no, I mean you look wonderful but let's see your hands."

There hadn't been much the beautician could do with the callused hands other than shape and paint the nails, so Jane had decided to flaunt them instead. She held them out palms down but her father wasn't deceived.

"Hmm, going to have to keep those hidden."

"I don't see why I should. I worked hard for them and I'm proud of them. Why should I hide them?"

"Well, not very ladylike, are they?"

"Ladylike, bah." At this point the car arrived to take them, so she gathered up the stole made from the same dress material and an evening bag borrowed from her mother's collection, and set off.

Arriving, Jane felt a chill of nerves running down her bare back – she had watched her parents going to these events for years but actually going herself all dressed up and knowing eyes would be on her, was frightening.

They met Uncle George in the foyer, back in bum freezer and with the single broad stripe on his arm. "Good God, is that you Jane? What happened? I hardly recognised you."

"Oh, mummy seemed to see me as some sort of work of art and has been beavering away."

"To good effect, dear girl. May I have the first dance?"

"Yes of course." So at least she had a senior naval officer's arm on which to sweep into the ballroom. She certainly seemed to make an impression on the gaggle of junior officers hanging about the bar. The ballroom was a brilliant blaze of lights, its ornate Victorian baroque with huge chandeliers complementing the array of ball gowns and glittering uniforms. Jane looked around, and seeing so many other women in their finery, felt less conspicuous.

Something she kept quiet about at home among her boisterous siblings was that she had been the star dancer at her school. Brilliant at ballet until she got too big, but also ballroom, tap and free dance and even the Charleston, she was still not sure if she was sorry that her mother had firmly quashed the invitation to join the Bluebell Girls. Her suggestion that it would improve her French had fallen on stony ground but what a choice - high kicking in Paris or being a bluestocking at Oxford. It meant that taking to the dance floor was effortlessly pleasurable to her;

as they gently fox-trotted their way round, Uncle George, now very much the Commodore, brought her up to date. "Jane, interesting developments. I've been put in charge of vessel movements and port operations here, and I'll need to move around by launch a lot of the time. Meantime I've contacted the Wrens superintendent for Guzz here, and she's happy to enroll you as a Wren as soon as you like. They're expanding rapidly just now. I've also dropped into her ear that I'd like you as part of my launch crew, which she says is highly irregular and never been done before but we might just get away with it. She'll be here tonight and I'll introduce you."

"Well, that would be wonderful. Thanks, Uncle George."

"Incidentally, dear girl, if you do join up I'm afraid you'll have to drop the 'Uncle George' and call me Sir. I know it'll be strange but that's the way it is in the Navy."

"I suspect there will be a lot of things strange about the Navy that I'll have to get used to, er, sir." This last with a mischievous sly grin.

"Yes, and take the sarcastic tone out of your voice when you do it."

Escorted back to her family party, sitting with a group of mainly old Naval friends, Jane found her mother had been filling her card up with enthusiastic young officers, and from then till supper time she was on the floor non-stop. She was feeling a break would be good when supper was called. She had spent several hours discouraging hands from drifting down her back and exploring her bottom. One rather short sub-lieutenant had been very keen on burying his nose in her cleavage; another managed to insinuate his hand down inside the back of her dress and had to be told in short order to remove it. This was just the sort of attention she had been afraid of and could have done without. Why was it that men seemed so keen on getting too close for comfort? Yet she found she only minded up to a point. These young men had a taut brittleness to them, knowing they were about to put themselves in harm's way and this might be the last young female they held close for a long time – or ever, and Jane sensed it. For every one who thought himself a gift to women, there were half a dozen scared and worried and it seemed wrong to be too hard on them. Although she had firmly discouraged the wandering hands she had felt an excitement in her belly when pressed close to her dancing partner.

With the break, Uncle George claimed her. "Jane, I've got the Queen Bee waiting for you. Come with me now."

Yes, ah, Sir. But who's the Queen Bee?"

"Oh, Wren slang for the lady superintendent in charge of a group of Wrens. This one's in charge at Plymouth. You address her as Ma'am."

Jane raised an eyebrow at this but allowed herself to be led to the lady in question. She proved to be a short trim lady with strong features, probably about her mother's age, guessed Jane. She was dressed quietly in long skirt and high-necked blouse, which made Jane feel rather too showy for comfort. Uncle George made the introductions.

"Well, young lady, the Commodore tells me you want to join the Wrens. I gather you have a good deal of sailing experience already?"

"Yes, ah, Ma'am, I've been in boats all my life – we live on the Yealm – and this last six months I've been sailing in the Mediterranean with Uncle George – correction the Commodore."

The lady superintendent smiled at her confusions. "Well, that's a good start and as I know your family and you come highly recommended we'll take you on. Come and see me next Tuesday at ten.

Then it was back to the dancing till the car came for them at midnight. On the way home she explained all this to her parents who had barely been told about her Wren aspirations so she was surprised by how calmly her father took it. "Well, lassie, we rather expected something like this, you certainly should do your bit and we're glad it's the Wrens." Why did he always sound as though he was dictating a letter? Jane had expected another shot from her mother about getting married instead, but strangely there was silence from across the car.

Sitting in front of her mirror back home, getting accustomed to using cold cream to take her make-up off, she felt oddly triumphant. The necklace, carefully laid on the dressing table, glinted and shone even in the dim light, as though congratulating her. Despite the attentions of some of her dancing partners, Jane had surprised herself by enjoying this excursion into being all female, sensing that perhaps there was more to her life than being a seaman after all. But she was still proud of her calluses too. And she was into the Wrens - that was good news although she had little idea what it would mean beyond Uncle George's plan. As she removed the makeup she looked at the face staring back at her with a new appraisal, suddenly conscious of how her looks must seem to others. Her face was a little long perhaps, and certainly her nose was, but high cheekbones and a full, generous mouth improved the effect. She was not classically pretty, for sure, with her features too long and strong, but the overall effect wasn't too bad, as far she could judge. 'And it is all I've got,' she reflected wryly, 'so I might as well get used to it.'

The thought of joining the Wrens was both disturbing and exciting. 'I wonder if I'll be working with the seamen,' she mused. 'Perhaps going around on a launch would mean doing a proper seaman's job?' She certainly hoped so. Suddenly there was lots to look forward to, a war to be fought and a chance to be involved, even if it did mean danger. That would show G. The deep uncertainty, which had been tugging at her for the past few months was rolling away. 'I will do my bit, I will do my bit,' she thought fiercely, punching the pillow. Then she sat up and, as was her wont when trying to put her thoughts in order, she wrote in her notebook.

What lies ahead?
I cannot know.
War must have its excitements
But also its dangers, its fears
And those I cannot see.
But that does not deter me.
We have to, we have to, win.
Let me be there, and be able to say
When we are free
From this terrible shadow
That I did my bit.
What is my bit?
How can I know?
But the need is there
And in answering the need
I will find my own answer.
I will not be defeated.

Even if it took years and no matter how difficult it might prove to be, she would stick to her determination and see it through. 'Hitler, here I come. We've never been beaten before and if I have anything to do with it we won't be now.' And drifting off to sleep a great weight was lifting from her. But she must remember to write to Somerville.

* * * * *

As suddenly as it had come, this vivid living memory rolled away, leaving her in darkness and swirling cloudiness again.

PART THREE:

INITIATION

CHAPTER 9:
Back to the Surface

11 JUNE 1940

It was all very strange. She was heaving and tossing but the light was still. Had she lost her hearing? There weren't any bangs or crashes so where were they? Slowly she opened her eyes and looked up, expecting to see blue sky; instead there was a white ceiling. This was bizarre. Had the cutter got underneath something? The pains in her body were pretty much as she would have expected but the bottom boards seemed very soft. She tried to bring her arms up but found them constrained – by what? And her legs didn't seem to want to move.

She was trying to work this out when a face appeared, surmounted by a white nurse's cap. She looked at it, wondering why a nurse should be hovering above her. Surely this couldn't be heaven? No, that was a silly idea, maybe one of the nurses she'd taken off the beach was still in the boat. Puzzled, she drifted away. Slowly coming back to the surface again she felt around her and realised she was in a bed. But why? A nurse's face re-appeared above her. This time it spoke. "Hello, and welcome back. Just take it very easy, we'll help you sit up in a little while."

Jane tried to ask why she couldn't sit up for herself but no sound came out. This reminded her of being in *Defiance's* sickbay. Realisation dawned. Yes, that was it she was in the sick bay. Were they tending her injuries or something? But there were none of the usual *Defiance* noises – it was all very quiet. The world slowly drifted on with voices faintly echoing in the distance, so perhaps her hearing was still working but who were they? Suddenly there were three of them hovering over her – two nurses and a man in a white shirt. "Right, Beacon, can you hear us?" She nodded - yes she supposed she could hear them.

"In a minute we're going to sit you up a bit in your bed. Just try to stay very relaxed." That seemed a silly comment – of course she was relaxed. Skilled hands pushed under her, gently pulling and lifting. Sudden sharp pain went through her chest and she yelped, instinctively stiffening against it. Well, at least she could still make a noise. Slowly, slowly, they lifted her half upright, the lancing pain easing as she got nearer the vertical. Pillows were plumped behind her and she was able to relax back against them. Now she could see around, and saw a ward with three other beds in it. Her mouth felt thick and furry and she tried to say 'drink'. It just came out as a hissing gargle but they seemed to understand her. A cup was put to her lips and slowly she sipped from it, feeling better for lubricating her mouth.

They left her for a while. Then one of the nurses came back, smiled at her and said "Hello, I'm Sister Donaldson and I'll be looking after you. Can you speak yet?" Jane tried but nothing intelligible came out. "Don't worry, it will all come back soon enough. Now, try to drink some more water."

Jane's hands, now free, seemed curiously unco-ordinated but she managed to clutch the cup in two hands and put it to her mouth. Her mouth hurt a bit – she wondered why. But really it was all too much effort and she lay back against the pillows and dozed off. It was the laughter that woke her up again. She looked across to another bed where three midshipmen were sky-larking with someone in the bed they were clustered round. Why on earth was she with a group of snotties? That didn't make sense at all. Sister Donaldson came back and offered Jane the cup of water again. This time she managed to hold it properly, even if still in two hands, and to drink from it. Again, she tried her voice. "Whe – Whe – Where?" she managed with difficulty.

Sister Donaldson smiled. "Dover hospital. You're in the acute underground bit but we'll be moving you out in a few days. Now just relax, you've been through a very tough time."

This puzzled Jane. Why had she been through a tough time, and what was she doing in Dover hospital? It was a long way from Plymouth. But doubtless it would make sense eventually, so she decided it was all too much effort and drifted off to sleep again.

When next she woke up her memory suddenly came back with sharp clarity – the tumultuous time on the Dunkirk beaches, the trip back, then something about being under arrest. A VAD nurse wafted by, saw Jane awake again and called the sister. This time Jane's voice worked better. "Why am I in Dover Hospital?" She asked.

"Because you were badly injured and generally in a bit of a mess. It's taken us a few days to bring you back to reasonable condition and it will take longer for you to be properly fit again. But we expect you to make a full recovery so don't worry. The doctor will come tomorrow morning to explain it all to you." Sister Donaldson was checking Jane's pulse while talking, and gave a satisfied nod when she finished. "You're definitely on the mend. Do you feel able to take any nourishment yet?"

Jane hadn't thought of that and the idea of food was oddly alien. "Could I try a little soup perhaps?"

Sister smiled agreement and bustled off. The soup wasn't as good as that delicious brew she'd had on waking up in *Defiance's* sickbay, but it warmed her and a gentle contentment spread through her. Again, the world just slipped away.

The night passed in and out of consciousness, sometimes with people quietly going about with dimmed lights, sometimes just gentle darkness and a sense of peace. 0700 was bit of a jolt – the day shift nurses came round with thermometers and cups of tea. Tea! She hadn't had a cup of tea for a very long time and suddenly the idea was very appealing. They eased her up the bed again, sympathetic to her grunts from the pain in her ribs but once upright she enjoyed the tea, the first hot drink she had had since scrounging from the ships she was landing soldiers onto at Dunkirk. Sister Donaldson came on the ward again, checked a couple of other patients lying quietly then came over to Jane. "Good morning, Beacon" she said crisply. "Just looking at you, you're better this morning. How is the pain?"

"My ribs are bloody sore and my face feels odd. It doesn't seem to want to move easily."

"That's not surprising – it's got eighteen stitches in it."

"Eighteen? Good heavens. Was it cut or something?"

"Not so much cut as split open. But don't ask questions just now. The doctor will come and see you after breakfast. You've no idea how pleased we are to see you coming round again. Just briefly we thought we might lose you when you first came in. You'd lost so much blood that it was touch and go but luckily you're a common blood group and we got donors volunteering by the dozen from your Wren colleagues. But you did push it to the edge."

All this puzzled Jane a bit. Her memories of coming into Dover were fuzzy but losing blood wasn't among them. Then a thought occurred to her "Am I still under arrest? They seemed ever so keen on that when I came in."

Sister Donaldson shrugged. "We've not been told that you are not but on the other hand there's usually a sentry on when we have a patient under arrest and there's been nobody near you. But then you couldn't run away if you wanted to so I suppose they didn't feel any need. I'll check it out."

This left Jane less enlightened than she was at the start, but did it matter? She was warm and cosy and being looked after. Anything else was for the future.

A young VAD came clattering in with breakfast. "Porridge?" she enquired brightly.

"Is it a decent burgoo?" Jane growled.

"Our cook is very proud of it. She'll be deeply offended if you don't like it."

"Do I care? But let's try. Plenty of milk and sugar please."

"Cream?" Asked the young nurse.

"Cream? Nobody's offered me cream in a long time. Am I in heaven or something?"

The nurse laughed. "Not quite but we get special rations for our special patients."

"What makes me special?" Asked Jane in genuine bewilderment.

"We don't get many female war heroes in here. You're special." Jane recognised that bright-eyed hero worship which had so discomfited her in the Wren's mess recently.

"All right, lashings of the stuff." And Jane had to admit that it was an excellent burgoo, with the cream an unheard of luxury. Handing her plate back to the nurse she enquired "Any chance of a trip round the buoys?"

The Young VAD looked puzzled. "I'm sorry. I don't think you are to get up for few days yet."

It was Jane's turn to laugh, despite the sharp stab of pain in her ribs. "No, a trip round the buoys is a second helping. Go on, you know you can."

The young nurse looked nonplussed, peering into the pot. "There are only scrapings left."

"Oh, that'll do. More tasty anyway." So Jane got the remains from the bottom of the pot with another generous dose of cream and demolished the lot with enthusiasm. "My compliments to the cook – that was excellent."

Half an hour later, enjoying her third cup of tea, Jane was suddenly confronted by Sister Donaldson in full official mode plus a surgeon commander in uniform. She tried to sit up to attention but the pain in her ribs checked the motion, and actually he didn't have his cap on so she shouldn't anyway. Memories of Uncle George's gentle ticking off surged.

"Well, young lady," he said. At least that was an improvement on 'As for you, young lady' but only just. It struck Jane that he looked desperately tired. 'I know that feeling' she thought.

"You really are going to have to look after yourself better. Two near death experiences in seven months are too much even for a healthy young animal like you. Go on like this and you'll run out of luck."

Jane could only stare at him wide-eyed.

"When we got you in here you were seriously malnourished, dehydrated, suffering severe loss of blood and total exhaustion – to say nothing of badly wounded. A lot of people would have died and we really don't understand how you managed to keep going for as long as you did. The wound in your shoulder was just starting to turn gangrenous and by the time we'd cut the bad stuff out a hole was left, which will heal, but will always be a hollow. The main problem was the shrapnel in your ribs. In a strange way you were very lucky – if that stuff had been an inch or two lower it would have killed you straight away. As it is your rib cage took the blow. We've removed the metal and sorted out your four broken ribs which is why they are so painful just now but they will heal fairly quickly. We've done what we can with your face but that long scar up your left side is there for life, I'm afraid. We've re-set it as best we could but it was days old by the time we got to it and we could only do so much. We'll take the stitches out in about five days. The redness will fade but the scar is permanent, as are the three minor marks on your face. We intend to move you to the *Lynx* Wrens' sick bay in a few days and will monitor you from there. You should be mobile again in a couple of days all going well. That's the medical story. Any questions?" This last growled out.

"Am I still under arrest, sir?"

"You're certainly under restraint but not strict arrest. I don't think the naval authorities are awfully pleased with you, no matter what my staff may think."

Jane nodded in moody acknowledgement. "Could I have a mirror?" She asked tentatively.

He barked a laugh. "Ever the female, eh? Be ready for a bit of a shock. At the moment you're not a pretty sight."

And he was right. The first sight brought a sharp intake of breath, a quietly wailed "oh no" And a sense of despair. The wound ran from just to the left of her mouth, past her eye socket by no more than quarter of an inch, and up into her scalp which had been shaved in a long thin strip to allow for the stitching. Sister Donaldson patted her shoulder. "Don't worry. You'll see a hundred percent improvement in a month or two, I promise. Just believe and you'll see. But you must have a guardian angel – half an inch to the right and you'd have had your mouth mangled and probably lost your left eye. Half an inch to the left would have taken you full in the temple and you would have bled to death."

Jane shook her head, more in sadness than disbelief. What a mess.

CHAPTER 10:
It's not the Body, it's the Mind

Despite the fright on seeing her face, for a day it was pleasant to lie in bed, to be cosseted and cared for by admiring staff and just let the future care for itself. But another day and Jane was starting to feel restless. She snagged Sister Donaldson in passing "Can I get out of bed yet? I'm feeling much better."

"Give me a minute and I'll check you over. How are the ribs?"

"Sore but not agony any more."

"I'll be back." And true to her word she returned ten minutes later, checked pulse and blood pressure and listened to her chest. "Hmm, not quite yet. But tomorrow all going well. There's one other thing I've been meaning to mention and this is as good a time as any. So far as I could tell from the state of your knickers you've had a very early stage miscarriage. Not much more than a fertilised egg but you ought to watch that."

"I what? The rotten shitehawk. He promised to get out at Fratton."

"Well, it looks like he didn't. We would not have noticed it except that I was a Marie Stopes nurse before the war and know rather more about that sort of thing than most medical people. We don't go in for moral lecturing here but it does look as though you've been a bit unwise."

"A bit unwise? You can say so. He wasn't even any good at it. The rotten scumbag." The red mist was rising and colour had suddenly come back into Jane's good cheek. "Would that explain the burst of tummy ache I got after a bomb blast? Briefly, it really hurt but then cleared and never came back."

"Hard to say but it might well have done. How much do you know about contraception? I don't want to sound as though I'm encouraging you to have sex but you really ought to know what you're doing."

"Well, my first one used a sheath – a better type of dreadnought – and this last rat promised to come out at Fratton. It was only a one-night stand. You're right – I really will have to be more careful."

"Best not to do it all but if you must, to take proper precautions. Tell you what, if you want to see me sometime I'll teach you some basics."

"Could you come to the sick bay when I'm transferred there? I'll have time if you do."

"I'll make a point of it, but do be careful."

Jane grimaced and nodded, her brain in turmoil. Pregnant? That was a really

CHAPTER 10: It's not the Body, it's the Mind

bad idea and she realised how close she'd come to huge problems – out of the Wrens by the short route, for sure.

"Have you told anyone about this?" She asked tentatively.

Sister Donaldson smiled gently. "No, Beacon, I have not. With so much of your blood around anyway none of the others would have recognised it and I don't want to be the one to jeopardise your career. But you can't go on presuming on that forever. I'll show you how to avoid trouble but really you must curb any alley cat instincts you have." And with that she was off to the next patient.

Next morning the ward round was impressive – the surgeon commander, a young lieutenant junior doctor, Sister Donaldson, and a couple of younger nurses trailing behind to fetch and carry. They stood round Jane's bed and waited while the commander checked her over. "All right, sit on the edge of the bed."

So she did, in one quick if wincing movement. "Just take it steady now, you're not winning a race. Now stand up."

Jane did and almost fell over. Her legs felt like cotton wool. One of the young nurses nipped in and steadied Jane. "Now just stand, breath as deeply as you can and take it steadily."

"Yes sir" Was all Jane could manage. Supported by the nurse, she walked slowly across the floor, increasing confidence coming with each step. "Now get back into bed and take a breather. We'll come back in half an hour to see how you're doing." She climbed in, legs trembling with the effort.

Half an hour later –on the dot, in naval fashion – the young lieutenant returned. "And how are we now?" He enquired brightly.

"More tired than I'd bargained for, but otherwise fine."

"Not surprising given the state you were in. Try walking again." This time Jane managed it on her own, if still a little shaky about the knees. "Good. You can get up whenever you like now but don't overdo it. Incidentally" – And he hesitated -"Incidentally, what are the scars on your buttocks? We were surprised to see those when we put you on the operating table."

"Oh, I got caned on probationer course for going AWOL." She left it at that.

"Good Lord, that must have been a hammering and a half."

"You could say so."

"I didn't know the Navy still did things like that. It's barbaric."

"The only people who can get it now are junior cadets under training, and Wren ratings and it's extremely rare even then. I know Wren headquarters are trying to get it banned altogether but there's a strange brick wall somewhere in the Admiralty."

He wandered off shaking his head in disbelief. Through the day Jane got up for increasing periods before sudden lassitude overtook her and the sanctuary of her bed seemed very appealing. In the evening the young lieutenant came round again. "We've been giving you strong sleeping pills up to now but it's time to get you off them and we're only giving you a mild one tonight." Jane took the pill and lay back. Sleep came easily but then so did the nightmares. In a watery fog faces swam up to her leering and trying to bite her lips, then detached from their bodies and went whizzing away, circled back and blew bubbles at her.

Screaming, she sat up in the bed. "Go away, go away" She struggled with the night nurse, then with the duty doctor who came over to help. Suddenly she woke up, the faces faded and she went limp, gasping and sobbing. "It was the faces, the faces" she wailed, sweat pouring out and her whole body shaking fiercely.

"All right, all right, just take it easy. Nightmares, eh?"

In floods of tears Jane could just nod and sob.

"I think we'll give you something stronger for now and get the psychiatric people to see you in the morning." Duly sedated, Jane drifted off and woke in the morning feeling heavy, drained of energy and listless. Sister Donaldson had evidently seen the night report and looked at Jane with some concern. "We wondered how long it would be before the memories came back. You'd been taking it altogether too calmly."

Jane shuddered. "It was the faces, the faces" Was all she could say. She refused breakfast and lay there staring at the ceiling. Late morning a brisk middle-aged lady in plain clothes arrived at her bedside. "Hello, I'm Mrs Goodall, the psychiatrist for this hospital. I'm told you started having bad nightmares as soon as they took you off heavy sedation. Can you tell me about them? I've heard a lot about the goings-on at Dunkirk so can probably understand your problems."

Jane shook her head, worry all over her face, pale against the pillows. "It was the faces, the faces," she moaned. Mrs Goodall took her hand gently. "Try to tell me about the faces. Where were they?"

"Underwater, and rolling about the boat."

"I see. How did you come to see faces under water?"

And suddenly the dam burst and Jane told her all about the greatcoat in the propeller and the dead soldier's face coming out of the murk just inches from her own.

"Yes, I can see that would be disturbing. Miss Donaldson, do you think you could arrange some tea for us?" Jane hadn't noticed Sister Donaldson hovering in the background.

"She's ever so nice to me. Please be nice to her too."

Mrs Goodall squeezed Jane's hand a little. "Don't worry dear, Miss Donaldson is well able to look after herself."

"Yes but....She does look after me ever so well." and Jane burst into tears again. "This isn't like me. Why am I crying?"

CHAPTER 10: It's not the Body, it's the Mind

"Because you have a huge store of bad memories in there from the beaches. As you get them out you'll feel better. They are something you will have to learn to live with if you want to be happy again and I am here to help you get there."

"Do you really think you can?" Wailed Jane.

"Yes dear I do think so. Ah, here's the tea."

Sitting up and drinking tea Jane felt calmer. Mrs Goodall gave her a long look and started again. "Now, Miss Beacon, tell me everything. I need to know your story from joining the Wrens right up to your time on the beaches."

"Have you got time? There would be lots to tell you. I only joined nine months ago but it feels like nine lifetimes already."

"Yes, Beacon. I have allowed time for you to pour it all out so start at the beginning."

CHAPTER 11:

Day One

When her mother dropped newly fledged Wren Jane Beacon at the Devonport Dockyard gate at 0730 on 3rd October 1939, neither knew that she was about to be engulfed by a new life far from her family roots. Having presented her crisp new pass and paybook to a cautious gatehouse policeman, Jane entered a place alive with intense activity. Tingling with excitement, Jane made her way past warships being re-equipped, refitted and re-activated for wartime needs. Stepping over cables, past flaring welding torches and covering her ears against the clattering din from riveters, she narrowly avoided being run down by a steam engine shunting truckloads of equipment onto the dockside.

'Report to Flagstaff Steps at 0800 Monday' the instruction letter had said, so here she was, having found her way to the steps under lowering stratus clouds with a whipping wind which was firing light rain into her face and chilling her more by the minute. The stiff South Westerly drove a grey sea into wavelets setting small boats bouncing and rolling and throwing up clouds of spray. Despite her oilskins and sou'wester the wet was finding its way down her neck. The discomfort was acute and no matter how much she tried thinking 'it's for the war effort', the temptation was strong to find shelter and forget about going anywhere near the sea. Boats came and went but none of their crews seemed in the least interested in her and the excitement was draining away by the moment. 'Well, this is a great beginning' she thought. 'What do I do next?'

She really had to show a bit of determination and she supposed that giving up on her orders would be frowned on but what else to do? This internal debate was resolved when an official–looking car drew up and out stepped Uncle George, clutching his cap and bowing his head to the wind. "Hello, er, Sir" she said, trying to smile, "What a dreadful day."

"Yes, not nice is it? Never mind, the boat should be here any minute."

So they stood companionably side-by-side, back to the wind and watching a fast launch surfing its way into the steps. "Right, this is it. Welcome to your new workplace."

"Oh, that's what you meant. Somehow I thought it would be bigger."

The commodore grinned at her "Afraid not, young lady. I hope you can hack it."

Jane eyed it dubiously. Tucked in the lee of the jetty the launch seemed substantial enough but it had been getting thrown around on the open water. 'Oh well, too late to back out now' she thought to herself, picking up her bag and obediently following down the slippery steps. The next surprise was being directed forward to the midships house while her Godfather went aft and disappeared into the officers' cuddy. Stepping in, she was given a cursory glance then ignored by the two sailors crouching by the engines. The two sailors on bow and stern cast off and nipped smartly in beside Jane carrying their boathooks. The launch backed out and within moments was leaping around, bashing into the waves. Jane hung on tightly to a grab rail, balancing against the boat's gyrations and hoping to avoid making a fool of herself.

"Aren't you seasick then, luv?"

"No, why should I be?"

"Most people are when they first come on these boats"

Come to think of it she did feel a little queasy but was determined not to show it. There was a brief respite while they came into the lee side of a cruiser. The Commodore looked into the engine bay briefly, nodded at Jane and said "Good luck," then she was on her own. Suddenly she felt very alone and struggled with a panicky stab of fear. The sailor working the port engine said "See those guys on deck? That's what you're supposed to be doing. Hope you're strong enough." She peered out at them, balancing on the unprotected ends of the boat and hanging on with their boathooks. With the Commodore unloaded they let go and nipped back into the engine bay. The man in charge, who she rapidly discovered was called the Cox'n, gunned the engines astern, they backed out and immediately were heaving and rolling around again. Watching them, Jane thought 'I'm, supposed to be doing that? Crikey.' But already she could see why the Commodore thought she might be useful here.

The matelot on the port engine, who seemed a little more forthcoming than the others, bellowed, "We've got an hour spare now so we'll go back to *Defiance* and have a brew." The rest of the crew ignored her. *HMS Defiance* proved to be three ancient warships permanently moored together off the Cornish coast on the Hamoaze; the launch ran alongside a scruffy old pontoon tucked under the counter of the outboard ship. The two boathook men nipped out, grabbed a line hanging from a boom and allowed the boat to fall back alongside the pontoon, which was filthy and greasy with what looked like food remains – potato peelings, scraps of cabbage, the odd bone. Once tied up, the older man who had been driving the boat left his little control station at the bow and came into the engine bay. As peace descended with the engines' shut down, he looked Jane up and down silently, his round red face closed and wary. There was nothing hostile about it, just a lack of enthusiasm and uncertainty in the face of something entirely new. "I've been in this man's Navy twenty-five years, man and boy, and I ain't never seen this. Boss tells me you're a Wren but I don't see no uniform."

This at least Jane could answer. "They haven't got any for us yet. But I've got an armband - look." And she pulled off her oilskin to show the thing put on her upper right arm, as directed. WRNS it said in large letters.

"An armband?" he muttered. "You can hardly keep an armband tiddley and pusser. And what's the rest of your rig? Almost looks like something official."

"Oh, the rest of it's my yachting clothes. They're not so different, y'know." Her plain white polo neck jersey, blue slacks and white gym shoes had a vaguely uniform air to them.

"Yachting clothes, eh? You've been in boats before?"

"Oh yes, all my life, sailing dinghies and motor yachts and six months in the Mediterranean on a big old sailing pilot cutter just lately. I was with Uncle – dammit no I mean Commodore Rodmayne – and it was his idea that I might be useful in a boat here."

"Well I s'pose that's summat, though I can't say the lads is very keen on a woman on a boat – bad luck, y'know. Right lass, you've got time to go aboard and make your number with the quartermaster, fix you up with a berth 'n all that. We live on this 'ere mighty vessel." And he pointed to the old black hull they lay alongside. Jane looked up doubtfully.

"How on earth do I get from here onto that thing?" All she could see was sheer hull rising above her.

"See that ladder there? We go up that." And he pointed to a set of iron rungs attached to the ship's side rising to the upper deck.

"Oh, right." Bur she felt distinctly dubious.

"That's right luv and you get thirty seconds to do it." She looked doubtfully at the girth of the old cox'n "You mean you can shin up and down that in thirty seconds?" This caused grins and some titters among the rest of the crew. He pulled his generous stomach in and looked at her frostily, colouring more deeply. "Never question your superior officer." he growled. Jane looked a bit startled "Sorry, didn't mean to be offensive."

The old cox'n smiled a little. "That's all right lass, it's your first day in the Andrew isn't it? With no training or induction at all?"

Jane nodded eagerly. "They said I'd be all right here without any induction, as I know what to do on boats. And what's the Andrew?"

Again the cox'n drew himself up and said almost pompously "The Andrew Miller is this man's Navy as seen from the lower deck. You're a rating, see? You can forget whatever fancy ideas you had about Pimms on the quarterdeck – that's for hofficers, not the likes of us." The other ratings, listening intently, nodded.

"Oh all right then, I suppose" said Jane, "I can go up that ladder but how do I get my bag up?"

"Shin up it, get a heaving line from the buffer, and toss it over. We'll bend your bag on for you." This answer seemed to produce more questions than answers but Jane sensed it was time to get on with the job.

She stepped onto the pontoon and immediately an array of heads, all of them male, popped over the upper deck rails, watching. One of the launch ratings, a nondescript little man with thin brown hair and coarse features, called to her "Go and stand on the pontoon for a minute" and directed her to a spot near the after end of it. She stood there irresolute, wondering what to do next, when suddenly a gush of filthy grey foamy water, full of potato peeling and vegetable scraps, shot out of an outlet in the ship's side and all over her almost knocking her off her feet. A great roar went up from the watchers on deck, and the boat's crew who were holding each other up with laughing so much. A red mist came over Jane's vision and, trembling with rage, she squelched back to the launch. "You thought that was funny, did you?" The question was rhetorical as the crew were still howling with laughter. A red fire went through her, her lips compressed as she thought 'I'm not having this'. She stepped up to the matelot who had sent her there and slapped his face. This was no gentle ladylike pat on the cheek, but a snake strike, fierce and too fast to follow. It knocked him over and a second roar went up from the watchers on deck. The old cox'n put a gently steadying hand on her arm. "Hey, lass, take it easy. It w'ar only a joke."

"A joke you say? Well I don't think it's funny." She was still trembling with rage. What a stupid thing to do. "How do I get clean?"

"Up the ladder, lass, like the rest of us."

Rage and determination steeled her. She stepped onto the pontoon and went twenty feet straight up the ladder - hand over hand - without stopping. Stepping onto the upper deck not even breathing heavily, she eyed the laughing party on deck. "All right, you lot, where do I go to get cleaned up?

A sailor in a white jacket said. "Come with me miss and I'll sort you out." He rather minced off in front of her. "They are a dreadful lot, aren't they?"

"Well yes, but if they think that's going to put me off they've got another think coming." He smiled gently, leading her into a little pantry where he helped her wash down, scrape off the stray bits of vegetation and tidy up a bit. It was as well, she reflected, that she had full oilskins on.

De-vegetabled, she went back to the ladder but the boat had gone.

Calming down, she thought 'Oh dear, 'What now?' Then she remembered being told to go and find the quartermaster, so she enquired around and was directed to another well-upholstered old chief petty officer who lounged in a little cubbyhole office tucked under the bridge. "Wren quarters are all on the next ship" he said. "Find the wardroom area, take the starboard alley forr'd from it then the second side alley. You've given us a real problem as the other Wrens living on board are all officers and we can't put you with the men so you've got a little place to yourself at the far end of the Wrens' quarters. But don't bank on that luxury for the rest of your time in the Andrew. You'll mess with the petty officers. By the way, don't disappear. The Commander wants to see you in half an hour." And with that he turned his back on her.

About ten percent of this had made any sense to Jane but she obviously wasn't going to get any more so she wandered off, crossed to the next ship and on a guess headed aft. There she found what had to be the wardroom filling the after end of the ship. It was darkly magnificent with mahogany and bird's eye maple wood paneling, a profusion of gleaming polished brass and two long tables down its length. The seats were well-worn leather, which to Jane had the aromatic smell of Rosewood. The steward who had helped her earlier stepped out of a side pantry.

"Hello, can you help me? I'm supposed to be finding a little cabin near the wardroom on the starboard side. Would you know where that was?"

He smiled gently. "Yes, miss, follow me." Jane seemed to be spending her life obediently trooping after people so one more was no problem. He set off along a long narrow alleyway leading forward then ducked down a side alley so narrow there was only room for one at a time in it. Doors off on each side had names on: '2/0 Jones', one label said. '3/0 Roberts' on another. At the end was a bare door with a blank on it "Put your name on that" said the steward, flinging the door open with a flourish. Well, the quartermaster had said it was small and he wasn't joking. A bunk with drawers under, a tiny desk at one end and hanging space for three or four garments at the other, all ranged down one bulkhead. There was just enough space to stand between the bunk and the bulkhead on the other side. "You've got stores round you here so you shouldn't be disturbed" laughed the steward. 'Disturbed?' thought Jane 'Disturbed by what?'

She spent a little while looking round. Tiny it might be but well fitted out, with tongue and groove bulkheads and solid oak furniture. The only light came from an odd skylight shaped like an orange squeezer and the only ventilation a little brass vent at the far end. 'You wouldn't want to be claustrophobic living in this' she thought to herself. The bunk only had a mattress in it and she made a mental note to find some bedding.

She checked her watch and realised it was time to go and see the commander, whoever he might be. Again she turned to the friendly steward. "I've got to see the commander, do you know where I find him?"

The steward indulged a knowing little smile. "The commander, eh? I'm not surprised. Go back to the ship you first got onto, look for the wardroom area, same as this, and on the port side is an office. The commander works from there." So once again she set off, and after mildly getting lost found the wardroom. On the port side was a small group of officers and, to her surprise, the sailor from the boat whom she had hit so recently, sporting a livid bruise on his left cheek. Those calluses of hers had had a telling effect. A small lectern stood in front of the office door. A senior petty officer stood to the left, looking grim. He looked her up and down without enthusiasm – this seemed to be a naval habit. "Right, young lady step up to here and report yourself."

So she stepped up to the lectern as instructed and said "Jane Beacon, er, Sir." The chief – a master-at-arms - stifled a roar. "That's not how to report yourself. Stand to attention and salute. The correct form is number whatever, Wren Beacon."

"I'm sorry, I don't know how to salute" she said, suddenly feeling much less confident.

"Lord save us, what has the Navy come to?"

She thought the old chief was going to have a heart attack.

Behind the lectern an elderly officer with three stripes on his sleeve cut in. "All right, chief, I'll deal with this." And he looked at Jane appraisingly. "Service number?"

"What's that sir?" It seemed much easier to call this one 'sir'. The officer shook his head in weary disbelief. "You really are completely green, aren't you? The Navy shouldn't be allowed to do this. I must speak to the superintendent."

This worried Jane. "But sir, this is my first day as a Wren and I know I've got a lot to learn but it does seem unfair to get cross with me because I'm new." Simpering was not in Jane's style but she did try a rather uncertain smile at him. "They said I'd be all right because I know so much about boats and I know what I'm doing there."

"Do you now? Interesting. All right, let's start again. Your service number is the number in your pay book – you have got one, haven't you?"

"Yes sir." And she fished under her jersey to pull out the shiny new document. "Here's my number – 1095."

"Right, on all future occasions when you report yourself, you do it in the standard Naval form '1095 Wren Beacon. Once you get the least idea of drill you come to attention and salute whenever you appear at defaulters, then report yourself."

"Defaulters?" queried Jane, eyes widening. "Is this defaulters?"

"It most certainly is, young lady. You are charged with assaulting a seaman and we decided to deal with it right away. The charge is that, at 0912 hours this morning, on

103

the launch '*Amaryllis*' while alongside HMS *Defiance* you did willfully strike another seaman, namely Able Seaman Richard Taylor, before witnesses. Several hundred, in fact. This is an offence under Naval regulations and although Wrens are not subject to Naval discipline, by striking a Naval rating you have made yourself liable to it. "

"But sir," She spluttered, "This idiot deliberately stood me under a gash shoot. Surely I'm not expected to take that without protest?"

"In the Navy we regard that as a prank. Hitting a man so hard he falls over is an offence."

Jane shook her head in bewildered fury. The red mist was rising again. "Well, that's utterly unfair. They can do what they like with me and I can't retaliate?"

The commander grimaced. "Not entirely. Your maidenly modesty will be protected. But if you can't take a joke you shouldn't stay. Getting a disciplinary record within hours of joining is a record even for a Wren, but you now have one. I'm sentencing you to five days CBs and you will be reported to the Wren superintendent. Whether we keep you or not will be up to her. But remember – you must not strike your fellow seamen. Where would we be if anyone could hit a shipmate any time without sanction? It would be total anarchy. Now go and think about that before you get so violent again. Oh, and an apology to able seaman Taylor would be in order."

Jane started and stared hard at the commander. "The rest of it I suppose I have to take but why on earth should I apologise to this idiot? If it wasn't for his stupid prank I wouldn't be here."

"That may be so but who suffered the more? You've given him a serious black eye and we're obviously going to have to watch you. You pack quite a wallop."

Jane, not given to physical violence, looked worried. "Yes sir, I never knew that but it seems so."

One of the other officers – a young man with two stripes on his sleeves – cut in. "Do you think, sir, that this is the time to stop this ridiculous business of letting a woman onto a boat? I mean, who knows where that might lead. And surely they can't be any good at it?"

The commander shrugged. "You have a good point but we have orders from a high level to do it so we'll just have to put up with the nonsense. But we'll be watching closely."

The Commander nodded at the chief petty officer who roared "Wren Beacon, left turn, quick march." So she turned left and walked off as smartly as she could, still seething inside. The injustice of it all was mixed up with anger at the way they had been so casually dismissive of her boating abilities. Why shouldn't she be good in a boat? What had seemed like a bit of an adventure had just got a whole lot tougher. She would show them, she was damned if she would give them the chance to say women were no good. A fierce determination was forming in her mind.

The chief followed her up onto the upper deck. "By the way," she queried, "What's CBs?"

He rolled his eyes "I really don't believe this. CB's is Confined to Barracks - or in your case, this ship, for five days. No shore leave, no nothing except your duties. Just be thankful you weren't given extra duties as well. A matelot certainly would be." By now they had reached the ship's rail; the old Chief watched sourly and turned to Jane, gesturing at the busy scene on the Hamoaze. "Look at it. They call this the phoney war. Not for the Navy it isn't. We've been deep in a sea war since day one and it's already claimed several thousand lives. All around us the dockyards are frantically bringing ships out of reserve. Crews are being enlarged, and I'm horribly afraid my turn will come 'cos wartime compliments can be a third more than peacetime and the extra come from the shore establishments. The Navy will be busy every day of this war, mark my words. It's always been the same."

"Gosh, you do know a lot about it."

"Navy history is my hobby. Ask me anything you like. Now if I were you I'd go and join your friends in the launch – it's alongside the pontoon again."

This scared Jane. She knew she could not back out – pride alone would not allow that - but how would they react to her on the launch now? Feeling distinctly nervous, it was back down the ladder, and approach '*Amaryllis*' with some caution. Coming on board, it was a bit of a surprise to be greeted by friendly smiles and even a pat on the back as she stepped into the midships compartment again. There was no sign of able seaman Richard Taylor but the rest were there, grinning and looking much more forthcoming. There was silence for a couple of moments then the cox'n couldn't stop himself. "Well done lass, that were champion. You keep that up and we'll all be friends. Eeh, we thought you'd be a right toffee nose but you're really one of us." Above all, Jane was confused. Surely this lot ought to be annoyed with her; but evidently not. She smiled uncertainly. "It was entirely instinctive, I promise you. I just don't like being messed about like that."

The seaman on the port engine piped up "Well hello, I'm Nobby. This ere's Taff but he doesn't say much, so don't worry if he just stares at you. He's only seen four females in his life and two of them were sheep. But he's harmless really and you'll get used to him. Isn't that right Taff?" Taff smiled, every bit as uncertainly as Jane had, and nodded. "Pleased to meet you," he muttered and looked down at the bilges, going red as he did so. Jane made a mental note to get to know this shy young man, suspecting it would stand her in good stead. Nobby piped up again "The plonker with the boathook here is Rufus the Red – he's called that because of his ears." Jane looked enquiringly at this but got no enlightenment.

"What about the fellow I hit – Richard Taylor, I think. Won't he be a bit annoyed with me?"

"What you mean Dickhead? Naw, he's too stupid to bear a grudge and he's already enjoying being known as the bloke knocked over by a Wren. He's in the mess now getting sippers on the strength of it."

"Sippers?" Queried Jane.

"Yeah, a sip from other Jack's tots. That's rum if you didn't know."

"Ooh, do I get that?"

"I don't think Wrens are allowed it but there's always some sort of rabbit. Do you like rum?"

"Good question. I like wine and whisky though."

"You'll be right then. We'll arrange sippers for you when we finish for the day."

"That would be kind of you"

"You're welcome, Jenny. Say, what's your name? We can't just call you Red."

She smiled, used to teasing about her mane. "I'm called Jane but I don't mind Red if you prefer."

"Naw, Jane will do. Are you like the Jane in the cartoons in the paper?"

"No, boys, I manage to keep my clothes on. Sorry if I disappoint you." But she could feel the atmosphere warming all the while.

"Just fancy, our very own Jane. You any good at the job?"

"Well, I'm not sure what the job is yet but I've been in boats all my life so I don't think I'll have problems there. I can see the real difficulties coming to terms with the Navy – the Andrew, you call it?"

"Yeah, Jane, that's the lower deck term. Our superiors with brass on their arms call it Pusser. Don't worry, we'll keep you right."

This chat was interrupted by the old cox'n. "C'mon boys, we're liberty boat in five minutes. Taff, go find Dickhead at the double. Nobby, fire her up. Jane you go forr'd with Rufus and see what he does." And without question they all shot off to their jobs. The engines were running, and the boat ready to go when Taff and Dickhead came running down the ladder and on board, panting. "Let go fore and aft, bear off aft." They pulled off the pontoon and then eased astern and round to the starboard gangway. Rufus explained as they went "As well as running the Commodore about, this one's usually the officers' liberty boat – we're too small for the lower deck. Officers come and go on the starboard companion ladder. The port one's the tradesmen's entrance for jolly jack and stores and dockyard mateys and anything else. Don't ever get them mixed up – some snotty will give you grief if you do."

"Snotty?"

"Yeah, midshipmen – kids full of themselves but too young to know sense."

"Oh, my brother's hoping to become one of them next year when he leaves school." She said this without thinking and got a very funny look from Rufus. She was to find it was often the throwaway remarks which would cause her the most trouble.

A busy afternoon followed, running between *Defiance* and the steps, mostly with fairly junior officers. The Commander went ashore mid afternoon, giving Jane an odd little smile as she stood on the bow hanging on grimly with her boathook. He tapped his briefcase significantly. By late afternoon the weather had eased off sufficiently for her to shed her sou'wester, immediately becoming more recognizable, and one group of sub-lieutenants made mocking boxing moves at her in passing. 'Oh dear' she thought, 'This has gone round the ship too quickly for comfort.'

Among them were familiar faces she had danced with. She recognized one short subbie's nose quite distinctly and others had explored her bottom too closely for comfort so recently. "Hello Jane" several called in passing.

"You know these people?" Queried Rufus.

"Oh yes, I was dancing with them at a ball just two weeks ago."

"Really? This is going to be interesting."

Jane gave him an enquiring look but they were letting go at the time and the chat went no further. Mostly she was too engrossed with learning the bowman's job to notice much else, but as they roamed the Hamoaze Jane was able to look around at the multitude of ships lying there.

The Navy's needs were enormous and it showed. She saw not just mighty capital ships and dashing destroyers, but also escort craft, minesweepers and minelayers, submarines, coastal forces - all desperately needed. The first of Britain's extensive fishing fleet were being taken over as minesweepers, boom defence vessels and as the ubiquitous drifters acting as fleet tenders.

For a couple of runs after five o'clock they were taking staff back to the ship from desk-bound jobs in the dockyard, and included in them were a group of Wren officers. The cox'n gravely saluted them and Jane, hanging on with her boathook at the time, was interested to note the same respects being paid to them as any naval officer. Having cast off Jane was heading back towards the engine bay when one of the Wren officers waved to her to come aft to where they were huddled in the officers' cuddy. The group looked her up and down without enthusiasm but with a keener interest than the matelots had and the senior, a three-ringer older than the others smiled at Jane. "Hello, we heard we were getting our very first Wren rating in *Defiance*. What are you doing here?"

"I'm working on this boat – the commodore asked for me to go on it."

"I see, I think. Are you going to go on working on this boat?"

"I suppose that depends on how well I do but I think that's the intention."

"Well, well. The superintendent was saying that it could be a very interesting experiment but I gather from the roars and howls that you've already fallen foul of the Navy."

Jane bridled. "That wasn't my idea – an idiot parked me under a gash shoot and I won't be messed about like that."

"Well, pusser has a capacity for messing us all about. I hope you're not going to go on like that? "

Jane was going to say something fairly strong but a bellow from forward "Bowman to your station" interrupted.

"Sorry, must go" and she shot forward, grabbing her boathook in passing. As the Wren officers trooped up the gangway, the three-ringer said to Jane "We have our own little ante-room just forward of the wardroom. Do join us after supper."

Jane could only nod appreciatively before they were gone.

They pulled off and went round to the port companion ladder. Suddenly a new group came down and onto the boat – a petty officer and four sailors. Nobby smiled "Best thing I've seen all day – oops, sorry Jane - not quite. These 'ere's our reliefs."

"Reliefs?"

"Yeah, the boat keeps running till midnight but we can't work that long so another crew takes her over. And this is they."

The relief crew ignored Jane and her lot wasted no time in disappearing up the companion ladder, so she grabbed her bag and followed them. It was her first time up by this more civilized route and she noted how they came to attention and saluted facing aft as they stepped onto the deck. "Do I do this saluting thing?"

"No Jane, not till you've got a uniform and know how to. You go and stow your bag and we'll meet you by the forr'd companionway for sippers in five minutes – best part of the day, this."

So she scooted over to the next ship, found her little cabin with some minor difficulty having been warned off getting to it through the wardroom, and dumped her bag on the bunk, which she noticed had been made up in the meantime. Coming back on deck she looked round for the companionway without success, but suddenly she saw Taff furtively hanging about near a forward entrance on the next ship and crossed over to him. "Hello Taff, are you waiting for me?

He nodded and tried to speak but seemed to have some difficulty so he just pointed down the ladder and shot down it. Jane followed at a more leisurely pace and found herself in a section of stores and small cupboards. Taff managed to find his tongue. "We're not supposed to be giving you sippers, see, so we've sneaked off to here. Should be left alone." This speech seemed to exhaust him. She smiled and said "Thanks Taff, have you been in the Andrew for long?"

He went bright red. "Two years now. I'll be qualified for leading stoker soon and then go off in something bigger. I'm hoping for a destroyer – not so much bullshit there."

Jane laughed. "It seems that follows us round wherever we go. Is it better on the destroyers?

"A bit. Mostly they're too busy to bother. On the big battlewagons they've nothing else to do." This developing chat was interrupted by the rest of the crew arriving. The old cox'n settled himself on a coil of rope, smiled broadly and said "We've got to keep this quiet – I checked in the mess and Wrens strictly aren't allowed a tot but if we're victualled in for six we'll get six tots and you can have your own and the rum bosun said he'd never notice the difference. Meantime the boys have brought theirs along – want to try it?"

"Thanks, I will. What do I call you? The others have got names but I suppose I should be politer to you."

"You call me 'chief' or 'chief petty officer' if it's very formal and people are watching. When this bunch of herberts aren't around you can call me Stan." And he beamed at her. Dickhead was the first to offer his tot. "No hard feelings, is there Jane?"

"No of course not, I thought it would be the other way round." Now there was a little distance between the event and her, it seemed less infuriating. She took Dickhead's glass and asked "How much is sippers?"

"Oh, a small mouthful or so."

So she took it and rolled it round her mouth before swallowing. It was fairly rough stuff but acceptable. "Now that is rather nice. I could enjoy that." Next up was Taff, still struggling to speak so he offered his glass with a bit of a splutter and a shy downcast of his eyes. Again, she took the mouthful slowly, savouring the taste.

Rufus and Nobby both queued up and she took the offering. The cox'n handed his glass to her. "You be careful now, lass. They've got grog – diluted with water. Mine's neaters and a lot stronger." Filled with curiosity, she took the proffered glass and sipped gently from it. A sweet warm sensation hit her. She coughed gently and said "Wow". They all stood around, drinking their own and watching Jane with curiosity. Suddenly she realized why. She still had vivid if hazy memories of getting leglessly drunk in Cannes on absinthe with *Osprey's* crew who had obligingly carried her back to the boat. She was getting the same feelings now –the rum was a lot stronger than its taste suggested. She struggled to stay upright. "Well you warned me. That's strong stuff. Just as well I've got a good head." They grinned, slightly wolfishly. "We wondered how you'd do. Many a green 'un has collapsed at your stage so you're not doing badly."

"Well, thanks."

The cox'n was sitting quietly, gently gazing at his empty glass. "Will you be all right, lass?"

"I think so but keep an eye on me. It wouldn't be so bad but I've had no food since six o'clock this morning."

"Aye well, it's time for supper so you come along with me and we'll get a bite. Old Fatso tells me you're messing with the POs."

"You mean the quartermaster bloke?"

"That's right but don't call him that to his face if you want to stay alive. He's mighty sensitive about his shape."

She grinned back. "OK, point noted." The cox'n stood up, muttered 'well if that's your tot you've had it' to himself, and motioned to Jane to follow him.

Her legs were still functioning reasonably so far as she could tell so she trailed along behind him, up onto the maindeck, down a midships companionway, and into a big dining hall. It was full of senior rates, mostly mature fully-fashioned gentlemen. Some matelots were running round with plates. Her arrival brought a hush across the whole space. These senior citizens turned and looked her up and down – she was getting used to this direct appraisal and with a good supply of rum inside her she felt no terror. "Good evening gentlemen. Please don't let me stop your supper." This little speech brought an audible gasp from the assembly although it was to be much later before she found out why. Her cox'n led her round to a table at the far end. " 'ere, Billy, budge up a bit and make room for the lass." The Billy grunted and moved up marginally. She slid onto the bench and was surprised to have plonked in front of her a plate of bacon, eggs and cheese with baked beans on the side. "Oh goody" said her cox'n "Cheesy hammy eggy with windy beans. This is a feast." Not having eaten all day Jane was ravenous and demolished the plateful in double-quick time.

The conversation had bubbled up again and the gently rolling rumble of the mess deck flowed over her. Still hungry, she tucked into several slices of bread and butter and a large mug of tea. The men around ignored her, deep in their own conversations which, so far as she could tell, were entirely about the ship and its doings in a way of speaking so complex she couldn't understand more than one word in ten. With food and rum inside her and the effects of a long day in fresh air, complete lassitude took hold. She turned to her cox'n. "Stan, I think I'll go and lie down for a bit. When do you need me next?"

"Turn to is 0630. Be at the boat then."

"All right, see you then." And she wandered off, struggling with a desperate urge to close her eyes. She made it to her little cabin, dumped the bag on the deck without trying to open it, and collapsed on the bunk. Darkness washed over.

She could probably have stayed asleep all night but an hour later a loud knock on her door jerked her back to consciousness. "Beacon, are you there?"

Jane struggled to the surface. "Yes, who is it?"

"Third Officer Roberts – we were expecting you in our anteroom."

"Sorry" said Jane. "I fell asleep." She struggled upright and opened the door to find a Wren officer she'd seen on the boat that afternoon. This young lady – not much older than Jane - looked at her speculatively but simply said. "Well, come along if you're coming"

"Give me ten seconds to comb my hair. By the way where's the washhouse?"

Third Officer Roberts raised her eyebrows in surprise. "Right opposite the end of this alley. Haven't you been told anything?"

"Not a lot, no."

So once again Jane trailed along behind someone. The Wren officers were all smartly dressed in doeskin uniform, skirts, black silk stockings and shiny black leather shoes. Because she had nothing else Jane was still in her yachting gear and felt decidedly scruffy. But the three ringer greeted her warmly enough. "Good evening, Beacon. We're interested to meet you. This is an odd situation with you being the only Wren rating on board. Normally this is an officers-only part of ship but it seemed a bit mean to leave you in isolation and you certainly can't go on the matelots' messdecks so we decided to invite you to join us here of an evening. But that won't happen in other establishments with Wrenneries."

"Well, it's very kind of you to invite me. Do I need to be invited every time or can I just turn up?"

"Just turn up any time after 1930." And Jane nodded acceptance.

A two ringer spoke "Hello, I'm Second Officer Jones. We've been hearing all sorts of tales about your troubles earlier today. What really happened?" So Jane regaled them with the tale as she saw it, including the injustice of being in trouble for someone else's stupidity. They all laughed at the tale but Second Officer Jones warned her "You'd better be careful. Queen Bee was absolutely livid when she heard about it and you'll be getting the biggest bottle going when she gets hold of you. I'm her secretary so I know what's going on. I don't know if you realize it but our superintendent believes very strongly in having Wrens on the boats – says they can do it just as well as the men - and for you to go and get in trouble within hours of joining really disappointed her." The young third officer who had called her then piped up "Yes, and filling yourself up with rum at the first opportunity doesn't help either. Wrens are not allowed it, y'know." Jane started at this, blushed and tried not to look guilty - probably without success.

"How do you know I had some rum? Have they been telling tales on the mess-decks?"

"They may well have been but I knew because you stank of it when I called you. You might think this is all a great adventure but there's a lot riding on it and if you mess up it could set the cause back a long way."

Jane hadn't bargained on yet another wigging and was starting to get fed up with it all. "I'm confident enough about doing the boat job; in many ways it's second nature to me. But coming to terms with the Navy looks like it might be a lot more difficult."

"Weren't you told anything before you joined up?"

"Not a lot. Mrs Welby interviewed me, said that as everything was still in early stages I'd have to work a lot of it out as I went along, gave me an armband 'cos there aren't any uniforms yet, asked if I could swim and sent me off for a medical."

"And you passed it all right?"

"Oh yes, I've been sailing for the last six months so I'm pretty fit anyway and when the doctor found out I was Johnny Beacon's daughter he just wanted to chat about medical gossip."

"You're Doctor Beacon's daughter? He treated my lung problems very effectively."

"Oh yes, that's me."

The three ringer chipped in again. "Well well, I know your parents too. We really are going to have to protect you from yourself. This business of your being a rating is going to cause problems, I can see."

"Yes, I asked Queen Bee about that and apparently it's to mirror how the Andrew does it – apart from middies under training, boats crew are always ratings so Wren officers can't be boats crew. Seems silly to me but I'm learning rapidly that there are lots of silly things in the Navy."

They laughed at that and the conversation drifted off to other bits of scandal, which meant nothing to Jane. She turned to Third Officer Roberts. "I didn't know the Wrens had young officers. Do you mind if I ask how you got to be an officer so young?"

"I simply applied to join the Wrens but I had a good academic background so they said maybe I should be an officer. I came third in the country at maths at Matriculation, you see"

"Oh really? I came fourth in French and English. What school were you at?"

"Guilford Grammar School. And you?"

"Oh, I was at Leadown."

Third Officer Roberts looked slightly startled. "Indeed. That is top drawer. And yet you're a rating. This war is going to give us some very strange mixing of people, I suspect."

"You may well be right. The Navy seems to have it sorted but us Wrens are going to find it very bumpy."

Third Officer Roberts smiled at this and turned to join the others in a debate about some miscreant Wren cook, conversation with Jane over.

Later – much later - as she lay on her lumpy mattress and pillow Jane thought, 'well, what a day'. It was impossible to imagine that at six o'clock that morning she had left home for this wild, strange new world. But the challenge was clear in front of her. 'I can do this job,' she thought 'and they are not going to get away with looking down their noses at me. I will show them.'

CHAPTER 12:
Moving Up

While Jane lay in exhausted sleep, Devonport teemed with activity. Ships came and went, dockyard workers clanged and welders flared so that even out in HMS Defiance, noise and restlessness came across the river. Urgency was all around as the Navy strained to meet the demands of protecting its coasts and shipping from the enemy. Above all, it was clear to even the most hidebound that the battle with the U-boat would be one of the decisive factors in the outcome of the war. Escorts were desperately needed and as in Nelson's time there were never enough.

These concerns, so pressing at a higher level, meant little to Jane as she rolled over groaning to slap down her alarm clock. Right now, her only concern was to get out there and survive in the world she had been dropped into. She just about made it for 0630 in the grey light before dawn. After this struggle it was a let-down to be handed a mop and scrubber and told to go clean the officer's cuddy at the aft end of the boat. "You mean we have to clean the boat too?"

"That's right luv – every day." Jane's instinct was to bridle at this but Rufus was already mopping the upper deck and Dickhead was scrubbing round the midships area in the most humdrum way. So she set to and made a decent job of cleaning the already clean space. Engines checked, brasses polished and the whole boat cleaned, Stan made a quick tour of inspection. Looking into the after cuddy he nodded approval and muttered. "Welcome to the Navy." And with that they were off for the first run of the day. From then on the hectic pace of her first day did not slacken for Wren Jane Beacon in the frenetic atmosphere of mobilisation going on round her. The popular little *Amaryllis* ran virtually non-stop from seven in the morning to midnight, her two crews alternating early and late watches to keep her on the move.

With her five days' punishment finished Jane was summoned ashore to meet her Superintendent and an extremely uncomfortable half hour it proved to be. "Beacon, I really am most disappointed with you. What on earth do you think you're doing getting into trouble within hours of starting?"

"I'm sorry ma'am. But it wasn't my idea to be stood under a gash shoot and I'm afraid I lost it after that. I've calmed down since and I'm getting on fine with them now but I will not be messed about." This last almost a defiant shout.

"Indeed. I'm afraid you will have to get used to being messed about if you want to stay in the Wrens – The Navy does it to us all, all the time. Now listen to me closely. It wasn't just Commodore Rodmayne's whim that you have been put on

CHAPTER 12: Moving Up

the boat. When he came to me with the idea I liked it right away. There are no few senior Wren officers who think we could crew harbour launches very well with Wrens, but we know there are parts of the Navy deeply opposed to the idea. So we felt that you would be an ideal person to quietly sneak into the job, with your combination of boat experience and brains. After a while we'd be able to say that a Wren was already doing it very well, and use that to soften up the opposition. So there's a lot riding on you. We hoped to keep it quiet until you were well established, and you go and blow it by getting in the rattle within hours of joining up so it's all round Devonport. You silly girl, if you mess up you could set this cause back a long way. Now behave yourself, will you?"

Jane gulped. "I'm sorry ma'am, I had no idea anyone was paying any attention to me and I will try to behave. But I actually think I'm getting on better with the lower deck because of this, than if I'd just been a good docile girl."

"Is that right? Interesting. I'd not seen it from that angle and I suppose we all have to stand up for ourselves somewhere but please, make it a bit less obvious, will you? And I hear you are getting a tot. That is not allowed to Wrens and you will stop it now."

Again Jane jumped. "How on earth did you know that?"

"I have my sources and it's my job to know what every Wren in Plymouth is up to. As I explained, you're particularly important so you can be sure I'm keeping a very close eye on you. You will come under a lot of pressure from your male crewmates, and if your response is to behave like them you're not going to last five minutes. Now think about it and try to keep out of trouble. It's also been brought to my notice pretty forcibly that you know nothing about naval drill and ways of doing things. This is our fault but we are starting probationer courses for all Wrens. I've booked you on the second one, in Portsmouth in January, and hopefully you'll get on with the Navy a bit better after that."

"Oh right ma'am, it would certainly help. Will we get a uniform then?"

"If you pass out successfully I think you should. They're still in short supply but some are being put aside for survivors of the probationer courses." And Superintendent Welby nodded to indicate the interview was over.

Second officer Jones – by now a familiar figure - escorted her out and said. "I hope that wasn't too bad."

"Well, it was a bottle and a half but it seems I'm still in so it could have been worse. I'd no idea they were hoping for so much from me – it's a bit scary."

"I did try to warn you but you seemed pretty oblivious."

"Was I? Sorry about that – I'll try to pay more attention next time but there's so much to hoist in."

"Oh, don't worry, you'll manage." And she gave Jane a warm smile and gentle pat on the shoulder. It was the contradictions that Jane found most difficult to cope with

Back on the launch a chastened Jane was rapidly getting the hang of the work on board, acting as bow or stern linesman. She learned what to do with fenders; she learned boathook drill, when to hook on and when to tie up; she learned to throw a line effectively after some early efforts had drawn derision from the audience, and she had grown used to her novelty value drawing crowds of onlookers not shy of making pointed suggestions. She learned to board and leave the boat quickly over the boom and jumping ladder, finding some new shoulder muscles in the process. After the initial bumpiness her own crew came to be curiously proud of their Wren and to treat her with affectionate respect although the teasing comparison with the cartoon Jane did not let up. She blessed this comparison because in an odd way it seemed to make her more approachable to her boatmates. This easy acceptance was no doubt helped by her rapid mastery of the job. Life on a harbour launch required a good deal of nimbleness which her dancing plus life on board *Osprey* made natural and was a real boon in staying safe and inboard when everything was done flat out.

Just eleven days after joining up and as she was starting to feel at home in the job, Jane, taking her turn to fetch the tea for the morning stand-easy, noticed a hush about *Defiance*. Back on board *Amaryllis* she was shocked to find her crew sitting long-faced, Stan almost in tears. Jane looked at them, bemused. "What's up, boys?"

"Haven't you heard? *Royal Oak's* been sunk inside Scapa Flow. It's beyond belief."

"Oh my goodness. Is that bad?"

"Too bloody right it is. Losing a battlewagon inside Scapa isn't bad, it's disastrous. They reckon there's loads of lads been lost."

"But I thought Scapa Flow was safe?"

"It's supposed to be but obviously isn't."

"Did you know anyone on board?"

"Mostly it was young lads under training but my old oppo Jamie Fisher was one of the chiefs. Mind you, knowing him he's probably survived but what a mess."

"How on earth did it happen?"

"It seems some Jerry submarine slipped in and torpedoed the old dear. She was only a stationary training ship nowadays but still a huge thing to lose."

Jane could see her crew were deeply distressed so she poured the tea and left them to their gloom. A bellow "*Amaryllis* away" from the gangway jerked them into motion but they moved on autopilot, all their usual drive drained away. It was the same throughout the Navy, a body-blow which hurt at every level.

As she got to grips with her job on the launch, Jane was also settling into life in *Defiance*. She found her way round the ancient battlewagons, where to go and

CHAPTER 12: Moving Up

where to avoid – she blushed at the memory of blundering into one of the junior rating's messdecks to be greeted by an enormous howl of raw enthusiasm. Eating with the senior rates was helpful because they were mostly very senior: comfortable middle-aged men working as instructors and occupying the less taxing roles which the Navy had in quiet profusion. They were uninterested in her except as a curiosity, but amiably obliging in letting her settle in. She bagged her own bit of bench near the galleys which meant the food was still piping hot when it got to her and she rapidly adjusted to the standard Naval routine of burgoo for breakfast, main meal at midday consisting of soup, a solid main course and pudding, usually on the heavy side, followed by a light cooked supper at six o'clock. In the evening the ritual of nine o'clockers consisting of kye – the naval drink made with shavings of block cocoa with sugar and condensed milk, thick enough to stand a spoon up in – and a light snack also suited her. Working on *Amaryllis* was awkward as the boat was often on the move at meal times and they had to grab a quick bite between trips when they could. But running up the companionways with a plate in her hand and an odd eating iron also became normal. "*Amaryllis*' away" over the tannoy became a dominant theme in her life. It wasn't long before Rufus the Red disappeared on leave and suddenly Jane found herself doing the bowman's job for real but after a day's nervousness she just got on with it.

Jane also discovered why there were so many spotty youths hanging round *Defiance* pretending to be sailors. At first she had simply assumed that, like her, they were there for accommodation, but not so. *Defiance,* she found, was the main school for electrical and torpedo ratings doing their initial training, and this was a far more important role than providing accommodation for odd staff who didn't fit in elsewhere. The trainees were new entrants beginning in their specialist sector and mostly around the same age as Jane. But somehow they seemed incredibly young and callow to her, even when leering at her from a safe distance.

Life on *Amaryllis* was proving tough but manageable, and her early brush with the Navy had instilled some caution in Jane. The life also proved to have its compensations. Just three weeks after her fierce start, she strolled into the Wren officers' anteroom to be greeted in casually friendly fashion. Second Officer Jones, clearly the ringleader of this group, said "There is a Trafalgar Night mess dinner tomorrow night. Mess president has agreed to you coming along as a civilian guest. Would you like to come and do you have a smart frock to wear?"

Jane's eyes gleamed at the prospect. "Yes please I'd love to come and yes I have one smart frock with me but it's a bit crumpled. Where can I find an iron?"

"Leave it with me and I'll get it sorted out. We have our ways of dealing with this".

Sure enough her dress was laid out on her bunk, crisp and fresh, the next day.

Her instructions were to report to the Wrens' anteroom at 1900 so she had to do a quick turnaround after her duty on *Amaryllis*, washing the salt out of her hair, letting it down and hastily running a comb through it before trying to scrub the ingrained grime off her hands. So many of the ropes she handled were greasy and mucky. Then it was a quick dash of lipstick, into her frock and scoot round to the anteroom. The others were there already, elegant in their best uniforms. Second Officer Jones ran an appraising eye over Jane and nodded acceptance. Jane noticed the first officer was missing and enquired after her. "Oh, she's an immobile with a husband who comes home at weekends so she nips off on a Friday afternoon – they live near Marazion so it's a bit of a trek for her."

"I see. This mobile and immobile business – does it make much difference? I put down as a mobile because I quite fancied the idea of moving around a bit but should I have been an immobile?"

"For you, probably not. Except for Third Officer Roberts here we all have domestic commitments somewhere around and use this accommodation as a convenience or for when we're on call. But *Defiance* mess dinners are great fun and we happily give up a night's domestic bliss to come. Let's go, ladies, it's time we made an appearance."

Jane made sure she was at the back of the group when they entered the wardroom, crowded with officers in mess undress, and was relieved to see other women there in civvies. As the Wrens came in there was a distinct pause in the conversation and by the time they got into the middle of the room Jane found a group of young officers gathering round her with no few familiar faces from the ball. Competition was strong to offer her a drink. Despite her superintendent's orders she was still quietly getting her daily tot. Today she had taken the precaution of bottling it and putting it away, suspecting that wardroom drink on top of naval rum might not be a good idea. She had already decided it was time to get acquainted with gin, so turned at random to the young man on her right and said "yes please, a pink gin."

Drink in hand she found herself surrounded. They were all intensely curious about her role, but bearing in mind the superintendent's strictures about keeping quiet she only lightly sketched in her activities and said nothing about future hopes. She did, however, do some gentle sounding out about their attitudes to her being there and found few took it seriously. Basically they all seemed to view her as a bit of window dressing, a nice sight to brighten their days and the Navy having a bit of a frolic at the edges. Underneath the smiling friendliness Jane found this a bit irksome and when she pushed them a bit further she found a smothering sense of protectiveness that fragile femininity should not be exposed to such rough and demanding work, even if she was the exception. 'They'll learn' she thought.

CHAPTER 12: Moving Up

Dinner was called and she found herself between a fairly dour old torpedo specialist on her right, and an obviously foreign officer on her left. Deciding that an evening discussing the inner mysteries of torpedoes might be a bit heavy, she turned to look more closely at the foreign officer and saw his shoulder flash. *"Vous étés Français?"* She enquired. He brightened up.

"Ah Oui, parlez vous Français?"

"Oui Bien sur" she replied and they were off. He was delighted to find a French speaker to talk to and she equally delighted to practise her French, now unused for some months. "Why are you here?" she enquired.

"I am the liaison officer between the French Navy and the English one, working on joint plans for our deployments in *La Manche*. And you?"

"I'm an experiment."

"An experiment? Do you have an extra head?"

"No, no, I'm working on one of the harbour launches to see if Wrens can do the job. So far so good but the Navy's not keen so we have to take it very slowly."

"Well now, are you the girl that flattened a sailor? I heard about that."

She gave a rueful nod. What a thing to be known by. The lower deck had treated her with cautious respect ever since the incident, but she didn't imagine a sophisticated Frenchman would be very impressed. But she was wrong.

"Mon dieu, I didn't expect to meet that lady. May I feel your muscles?"

Jane laughed. "Not here I don't think. Remind me another time."

"I will, I will" he assured her.

Their conversation moved on and she explained about her summers in Paris and on the Isle du Re with the delightful Pechot family, and the trip in the *Osprey* spent largely round the South of France. He asked if she read French literature. "Yes indeed, it was my best subject at school and I was going to go to university to study it if this beastly war hadn't happened. Just now I'm working my way through Victor Hugo and especially his sea stories. I'm reading his 'Toilers of the Sea' at present. Do you know it?"

He frowned. "That's the one about the Channel Islands long ago, where a funny fellow spends six months in a cave with an octopus?"

"That's one way of looking at it, I suppose. I rather admire people who live rough and do things their own way in pursuit of some objective." He laughed and said mockingly "Just like you? Can I be the Octopus and wrap all my arms round you?"

"So long as you don't suck too hard."

Her French officer started violently at this, almost spilling his claret down his front. Jane had to think for a moment before realising what she'd said. Blushing, she apologised for the *double-entendre* and they laughed into each others' eyes. With his fair curly hair and fine weather-beaten features he was quite a good looking man, tallish and probably about mid-thirties guessed Jane.

"*Ma Cherie,* you are the most entrancing young woman I've ever met. How can anyone be so tough yet so appealing?"

"Are you a masochist or something?"

He laughed again. "No, but...." And they moved on to the sweet course. Jane hadn't even noticed the excellent food and wine passing by. With sweet and savoury consumed the port was passed, the toast to the immortal memory proposed, and permission to smoke – and go to the heads – given.

Serving her during the meal had been the same steward who had helped clean her up on her first day. Taking away her sweet dish they had exchanged glances and he gave her a sly smile. "I hope your dress was all right."

"Yes, fine, why? Did you press it?"

"Yes miss, it was my pleasure. I do like looking after young ladies."

She gave him a smile as he moved away but the conversation struck her as odd. She made a mental note to enquire further about the kindly steward.

Mess games followed the meal, which the ladies were largely excused from. But Jane took note of them, thinking that most could be played by women if only they weren't in elegant dresses. With the assembly relaxed and thoughts far from the war, a strength test machine was brought in, doubtless stolen from some fun fair in the past. One had to hit a base plate with a large wooden mallet, sending a pointer up a scale against a spring to register strength. One or two exceptional people got about 80 percent, most were around the fifty percent mark. Then one of the brighter sub lieutenants looked speculatively at Jane "Would you like to have a try? We know how you can knock sailors about"

"That's a bit unfair but yes, I'll have a go." She'd drunk enough not to care, so picked up the mallet, gave it an almighty swing, and stepped back. There was a moment's silence then a roar of approval - she had registered 73 percent.

Her French officer, now Jean-Pierre to her, caught up with her in the general hubbub. "Anyone asking you out will have to careful but I'd like to. How about dinner next Saturday night?"

"I'll need to check my duty watches but I'd love to if I can. What had you in mind?"

"There's a not bad little French restaurant just outside Plymouth that I thought we might try."

Having enjoyed his company through the evening, Jane had casually agreed without giving it much thought. Then it hit – she'd agreed to go out with a mature French officer for her very first real date. Panic and excitement warred inside her. But really it was too late. And anyway, it might be rather nice to spend an evening with him. At the end, trailing out of the wardroom with a couple of the Wren officers, one said. "You must be incredibly strong. I only got twenty percent."

"Oh. I don't know – a lot of it's just giving it everything and not fussing too much about being ladylike." And laughing, they went to their cabins.

* * * * *

The mess dinner may have been a welcome distraction, but in their working lives every sailor was caught up in the relentless pressure of gearing up for war, as the Royal Navy responded to the threat it thought it had to confront. In fact, German naval strength was a good deal less than some feared. In late 1939 the Kriegsmarine was quite modest: The Tirpitz and Bismarck – probably the finest battleships ever built anywhere – were still fitting out, its pocket battleships and cruisers were excellent vessels but relatively there were very few of them - no more than a dozen in total. Its destroyers were overelaborate and not good sea boats which always limited the usefulness of their powerful weaponry and remarkably, it had only twenty-three submarines fit for deep-sea service despite Grand Admiral Raeder asking for three hundred. Like Napoleon, Hitler never truly understood sea power. But even these few u-boats were able to inflict a great deal of damage on British shipping and throughout the war the main threats would come from the air and under the sea with surface action always limited, if spectacular when it did occur.

CHAPTER 13:

Losing It

The mess dinner had been great fun with the wine flowing freely; as a result when she came on duty at 0630 next morning with a thick head Jane wasn't at her most communicative. Stowing the buckets and mops away, it struck her that her boatmates seemed less affable than usual – almost offhand, in fact. But the usual morning rush of staff to take ashore, the captain to collect and the commodore to run over to Mountbatten, the flying boat base on the Cattewater east of Plymouth, gave no let-up until stand easy. It was Nobby's turn to collect the tea, but he pointedly left Jane out. "Don't I get any?" she asked.

"Get your own," growled Dickhead.

"Eh? What's the matter, boys?" She was totally mystified. Stan moved away to his little driving cuddy. She looked round the others. "C'mon, boys, what's up? It can't just have been bad beer last night."

Slowly, unwillingly, Nobby spoke. "Well, we thought you was one of us but you've gone and been officer bait, haven't you? Was it a good dinner?"

Jane was still puzzled. "I'm sorry, I don't understand. Why should my dining in the wardroom last night make any difference to you?"

"Cos we thought you was one of us, not of them lot down aft. " Jane could see Nobby was struggling to explain himself, and the others were sitting there looking deeply unhappy.

Suddenly Taff spoke up. "You've been like one of the boys with us, see, and we wouldn't be invited to a mess dinner in a thousand years. Yet you come along and smile at them and you're in for all of being a rating like us. Just doesn't seem fair somehow." For Taff this was a major speech but light dawned in Jane's mind.

"Boys I'm sorry, it just never occurred to me that it would bother you."

"No, I don't suppose it would" muttered Dickhead with a sharp bitterness.

"All right, can I do anything about it? I can't undo last night and I don't really see why I should. What am I supposed to do? Sit in my cabin all night like a nun? I can't join you guys on your messdecks and there's nowhere else for a Wren rating to go. I do think you're being a bit unfair to me."

At this moment a bellow from the brow quartermaster "*Amaryllis* alongside" put a stop to further discussion. They ran the commander ashore, picked up a couple of civil servants for the run back and delivered them aboard *Defiance* looking distinctly green despite it being a calm day, then ran back to Mountbatten to collect

CHAPTER 13: Losing It

the Commodore. So it was lunchtime before they stopped again and could even speak. Jane had been thinking hard in the meantime but had struggled to come to any conclusions. "Listen, we can't let this spoil everything. I'm damned if I'm going to give up a social life just so you can feel better about it but you can't go on being angry about me spending an evening in the wardroom. What do you want?"

Stan had been standing on the deck by the entrance. "Well, lass, I think the problem's that the boys think you're their Jane and yet you go gallivanting off with the afterguard at the first opportunity. Don't go down well here." The others nodded.

"All right, how about we all go ashore once a week for a beer together? Would that make it better?"

They all perked up at this. "Yeah, that would be great. Let's do it on Saturday."

Jane grimaced. "Sorry, I've got a date on Saturday."

"There you go, that's typical. I suppose it's an officer, is it?"

"Oh come on, I've arranged this already and I'm not going to change it now. Try another night."

"It'll have to be next week – not got another clear evening before then."

"Why not?" Queried Jane.

"I've got a date on Friday, Taff's fixed up to go the cinema on Thursday and we're on late watches the other days."

"Well isn't that just typical – you get cross about me having a date but won't change your own arrangements. I'm quite happy to have a run ashore with you but if you won't bend neither will I. Fix a day next week." By now Jane was starting to get cross with them. Having a possessive man could be difficult, she suspected. Having a whole boat crew like that would be ten times worse and she was damned if she would have it. And yet, and yet – they were her boatmates. She couldn't just turn her nose up at them; life would be impossible. She thought longingly of the young men on the *Osprey* and how easy life had been with them, even as the only female on board. But then she hadn't noticed any competition on the yacht. There didn't seem any obvious way out of this – She had been relaxed and at ease in the wardroom, people like herself. Ah, but they weren't – she was a rating so at best could only partially belong with the officers. So she said to her boatmates "Listen, it looks like I'll always be partly in each camp but that doesn't mean I'm not part of you as well. Let me have some social life and I'll stick with you lot the rest of the time. Will that do?"

And with some bad grace they settled down again accepting the inevitable.

In the Wrens' anteroom a couple of night later she found herself alone with Second Officer Jones and thought to mention her problems with her crew. Second Officer Jones considered it. "I had a feeling your odd status might cause trouble. My father was a chief petty officer and I know how protective the lower deck can be of their own. It looks like you've become that very quickly. In some ways you should be congratulated for getting accepted like that but at a price. Have you managed to settle it yet?"

"I think so – they've accepted my being involved with the officers but I've had to agree to a run ashore with my crew once a week."

"Well be careful – Jack can be a funny beast with a bellyful of beer inside him."

"Oh, I don't think they'd bother me that way – they're ever so nice and protective."

"Is that right? I hope so. I know I shouldn't but I'm wary of them. We've had some dodgy goings-on already with some of our shore-based Wrens and it would be a tragedy to see you fall into the same difficulties. But I think you're too smart for that?"

"I'm glad you think so but really I'm still pretty green. I just think my boys would be better behaved."

"Do you mind if I report this to Queen Bee? We're watching this experiment very closely and this upper deck/lower deck conflict is one we hadn't actually thought about much."

"I don't mind – should I keep you posted on how it's going?"

"That would be good, and do come to me if you are having any problems you can't deal with yourself."

And with that they went their ways, Jane to sit in her cabin in contemplation.

Rufus was back from leave the next day so she reverted to spare hand. This allowed her to get ashore briefly in the afternoon, missing a short trip on the boat, and she made a reverse charge phone call to her mother. It was the first time she'd spoken to her since being dropped at the Dockyard gate that first day. "Jane, what's the matter? Is everything all right?"

"Yes of course mummy I'm fine but frantically busy. Listen, I'm going ashore on Saturday night and I just must have a new dress. Would you mind if I got something at Spooners and put it on the account? I'm only being paid sixteen shillings a fortnight and that doesn't go very far."

"I don't suppose it does. Is that all? Doesn't seem very generous to me."

"Well, we are rather bottom of the heap."

"All right dear but be careful. Do get some nice accessories to go with it. And Jane…"

"Yes, mummy…?"

"Don't do anything silly will you?"

"No of course not. Must dash – bye now."

Jane had wangled Saturday off and her crew had the late turn on Sunday so she had some time in hand. She had arranged with Jean-Pierre to meet ashore at half past six so when she went ashore mid morning it was with the fixed intention of not coming back till pipe down. First, it was off to Spooners where she ended up with two dresses, a handbag, shoes to match and a nautical brooch that pleased her. A silly little hat topped off the purchases. Blessing the family account she then went to the hairdressers where she startled them by saying she wanted her great mane cut short. With her curls a pageboy bob was impossible but under the hairdresser's expert fingers the Wren regulation that hair had to be off the collar became a lot easier to comply with. Then it was into the beautician's lair where she got a demonstration of how she could handle make-up herself, watching closely as the layers and eye linings were applied. The beautician just looked in despair at Jane's hands. A collection of potions and paints were added to her shopping. She arranged to leave her purchases there and to come back and change just before they closed at six. The rest of the day she spent visiting old haunts and ducking out of the way when she saw one of the Wren officers in the distance.

This was the first time she'd been ashore since joining up and going to *Defiance,* and it struck her there was a difference in the air. It was hard to put a finger on till she looked at the sand bags piled up round shops, gas mask bags being carried by everyone, and a lack of food in the shops. Posters exhorting the populace to dig to win, to save for victory, and not to indulge in careless talk, were everywhere. Already there was much less motor traffic on the roads. She found a jaunty defiance in people she spoke to convinced it would all be over quickly and that peace with Germany was just round the corner. This struck Jane as odd, given that the Navy was clearly gearing up for a major and prolonged conflict.

Jean-Pierre did a double take when he picked her up, dressed as she was by then in elegant black chiffon. Knee length, with a low-cut fitted bodice and little cowl sleeves over a flared and floaty, flirty skirt, the ensemble was set off by the new brooch and patent court shoes. "*Mon dieu,* Jane you are absolutely beautiful. What happened?"

"Why do men ask that whenever I smarten up? Am I such a scruff the rest of the time?"

"From what I've seen you don't make an effort when you're working."

"Well, what do you expect? I'm up at 0630, scrubbing and polishing, then splashing about in the oggin and handling dirty ropes all day. Doesn't encourage one to try terribly hard."

He laughed "Never mind. The effort is worth it when you do make it. Why aren't you on the stage?"

"I could have been, got invited to join the Bluebell Girls. But my mother wouldn't have it at all. I must say I'm really enjoying being out from under her thumb now."

Jean-Pierre shook his head and roared with laughter. "Let's play adults for tonight then." And he hailed a passing taxi.

The 'little French restaurant' proved to be a slightly ambitious description, but it was welcoming enough. It was a converted old cottage, long and low, whitewashed, set in a nook in the hillside. Inside was a low-ceilinged room, bare floor boards and cream-washed rough walls with French posters on them. It only had eight tables, each set with crisp linen tablecloths, shiny cutlery and glasses in profusion, and candles stuck in wine bottles. And if the staff proved to speak no more than menu French, at least the chef-proprietor was genuine Gallic and Jean-Pierre disappeared into the kitchen to bellow at him in happy native terms. Jane got bored on her own and strolled in as well, joining in the lively debate. This got them an exceptional meal, far removed from the menu's offerings, along with the best claret the place could produce. By coffee and liqueurs they were very relaxed with each other and Jane was thinking 'If this is going on a date I could take a lot of it'. Then the conversation turned

"Jane, have you ever made love?"

"Jean-Pierre, how could you? No, of course not. Nice girls don't, y'know, and to ask really is a bit offensive."

"Even in wartime?"

"Especially in wartime. How could I look a potential husband in the eye and promise him everything when I'd already given it away?"

"Ah, such an old-fashioned English attitude. There's another world out there, Jane, where people give themselves freely inside or outside marriage. Surely you've seen that."

Jane considered this for a moment. "No, I don't think I have. I suppose I've led a pretty sheltered life at a girl's boarding school and in a loving but strict family."

"A very sheltered life. In France we think nothing of a little extra fun in our lives. And making love can be so marvellous – the finest thing in the world."

"*Vraiment*? I'm afraid I've never thought much about it – my life just hasn't included that sort of thing. Mummy seems to regard it as a necessary evil, although I suppose she must have done it enough to have had five children."

Very gently Jean Pierre took her hand, looking her in the eye across the candle. "Jane, you're a young woman now. Your time has come and with a war on there's no point in holding back. We could all be dead next week."

"Oh really Jean-Pierre. I've never been near sex and frankly the thought scares me."

"If I was to promise that you would find it a wonderful experience, would that make it any better?"

"Isn't that what all men say?"

"Maybe, but I mean it."

"Come off it, Jean-Pierre. The answer's no – I'm just not ready for that sort of thing yet."

"Not ready, Jane? You ooze sex from every pore if only you knew it."

She gave him an enquiring look then lapsed into silence while he looked at her with a wry encouraging smile.

"Come on, it's time to be catching the liberty boat." And after pleasantries with *monsieur le patron* they stepped into the waiting taxi. Somehow it seemed natural to lean back against her date, stretching out and relaxing in the arm round her shoulder. From there it was a short voyage to his gently fondling a breast. Jane tried feebly to push his hand away but with a little persistence he infiltrated her bra. To her surprise, Jane found it very agreeable. He murmured in her ear "at least let me come to your cabin and kiss you. That can't be so terrible."

Encouraged by the warm pleasure spreading from her breast, Jane nodded while saying "We shouldn't really. Isn't it against the rules?"

"Who's to know? I'll go on board by a different route and see you there."

Back on board Jane strolled down to her cabin by her usual route, noting that the wardroom was empty. She left the door on the hook and sat on the bunk waiting, her brain slightly numb. All the while she was trying to sort out conflicting thoughts in her mind, which didn't seem to be working properly. At a conscious level everything told her she should be shutting her cabin door firmly and refusing to let Jean-Pierre anywhere near her. Then she thought that an odd kiss would do no harm while another bit was murmuring something like 'come off it, you know what he wants. If you don't say no you know what to expect.' And a bit of her didn't mind at all. What was it she was defending? He was a nice bloke who looked like he might know what he was doing, so why not let it go? She had to do it sometime and yes, there was a war on and they might all be dead soon. Somehow her mind and her body seemed uncoupled from each other. Then fright took over 'This is stupid' she thought 'why am I thinking of letting him near me? I don't want, I don't want' and a spasm of fear ran through her. But it had a strange edge to it, that fear, a tingling something else from deep in her body, which held her and stopped her shutting and locking the door.

She was struggling with this confused jumble of thoughts when he silently slipped into her tiny cabin, closing the door quietly. He embraced and kissed her in a way wholly new. She'd heard the term, French Kiss. Now she knew what it meant. "I mustn't, I mustn't" she murmured trying to push him away but clear thought seemed at odds with the hot feelings running through her body.

"Please, no, Jean-Pierre, this is wrong. Please stop."

But his only response was to kiss her again and gently but firmly run his hands over her back, unzipping her dress. She wasn't entirely sure how it happened but in no time she was naked on her bunk, the fire in her body pushing aside her conscious scruples. She turned her back on him but that just allowed him to reach her breasts again and the tingle from there left her feeling weak. Those gentle but insistent hands moved down below and she instinctively turned away, pushing at his hands, but that did nothing to stop him either. Warmth turned to fire and suddenly her body was seized by fierce gripping shocks as all conscious thought evaporated.

"Now, *ma cherie,* you are ready for me." And he rolled on top. A brief stabbing pain was followed by a fiery sensation inside her then she gave up all resistance, wrapping her arms and legs round him.

Ten minutes later it was all over and her conscious brain returned. "Jean-Pierre, what have we done?" she sniffled, tears flowing. "I'll get pregnant"

"No you won't, my lovely. I have a protective sheath." He guided her hand down to the sticky rubber. She gave him a weak smile. "What happened to me? My body was on fire."

"That was a climax you had. Girls can have them just like men."

Jane looked at him through her tears. "I had no idea that happened. Can I do it again?"

"Any time you like – girls can do it again and again."

"Wow, that would be something but even so we shouldn't have done it, it's all wrong and now I can never get it back."

"Ah, Jane my dear, you'll come to see that it isn't such a loss. Your body was ready for it."

"Maybe but this should be a part of love and commitment not just me losing control. Do you love me, Jean-Pierre?"

"I just have, my dear."

Somehow that didn't quite seem the point but she let it go.

Some cuddling later he tried roaming hands again but she stopped him. "I'm all sore there now, please leave me alone."

He smiled. "All right*, ma cherie.* Don't worry, I won't abandon you but I can't stay here till morning – we'd get found out." And he kissed her again, very gently, then dressed and went.

Sated, sleep came instantly.

CHAPTER 14:
On Relative Morality

Wren Jane Beacon stretched and rolled over in her bunk, warm and languorous and feeling good. Then, as her brain came to the surface, last night's events hit her. She threw the covers off and looked down at her naked body but saw no sign of anything different. Quite what she'd expected to see, she didn't know. So she snuggled down again and tried to understand what had happened. As the enormity of what she'd done rose up, terror, shame and confusion roiled around in her mind. She'd never be the same again, that was obvious. One couldn't be partly a virgin and now that was gone. She quailed at the prospect of the frightening new world she was in whether she liked it or not.

'My God', she thought, 'I'm a fallen woman. How on earth did I let it happen? What got into me? A lifetime's strict moral code has been drummed into me and the first time I'm tempted I just blow it all away. Was that seduction? Yes, that's it – I was seduced so it's not really my fault.'

But a nagging voice at the back of her head said 'Come off it, you wanted to give in or you would have just locked him out. You can't pass the blame like that. So now you have to live with the consequences.'

And yet... nothing she'd been taught had even hinted at how nice sex could be. Oblique references at school about saving oneself for marriage, and her mother's awkward explanations based on pleasing one's husband and making babies, grumbling about 'having to do her duty', had given no hint of how enjoyable it could be. Had her mother ever had a climax? Somehow Jane suspected not. Nothing Jane had heard, or read or been told had even hinted at the overwhelming physical pleasure of sex. 'I could enjoy more of that' she thought then tried to suppress it as her ingrained moral strictures warred with the thought.

And what, Jane worried, would happen if she was found out? Quite apart from the naval consequences she shrank from the thought of the trouble if her mother ever found out what she'd just done. Now she had to live with a knowledge she couldn't share, that she was a fallen woman.

How on earth could she go out and look people in the eye after last night? Then the practical voice at the back of her head replied 'Oh, don't be stupid. Married women are at it all the time and have no difficulty behaving normally with everyone. Why should you be different because you're not married?' But it was difficult to get away from guilty conscience, and a sense of trepidation.

Suddenly she was seized of a tremendous energy, and leapt out of her bunk, grabbed her dressing gown and went for a bath. Returning feeling cleansed she looked at the chaos in her cabin: clothes strewn about, with stains on her nice new bit of black chiffon. And the sheet was bloody and distinctly messy. She pulled on her yachting gear and ambled towards the wardroom where she met the nice friendly steward. "Excuse me, do you know where I can get a clean sheet?"

"Oh, leave it to me miss, I'll fix it."

"I'd rather do it myself – I've had a – a – feminine accident" and she blushed furiously, never having discussed her personal hygiene with a man before. "Wait one" he said, and a minute later was back with crisp white cotton. "Just put the soiled one in the bag in the pantry" he said, pointing to a cupboard in the far corner.

Jane smiled thanks at him – he was so discreetly helpful at times.

Back in her cabin Jane re-made her bunk, remembering the naval superstition to put on the counterpane anchor flukes down so the ship wouldn't sink. All the while last night's shattering events gnawed at her mind. With two medical parents Jane, like her siblings, had had her basic biology explained at puberty and knew – in physical terms – what had happened. But her mother's awkward, strictly anatomical explanations were entirely based on warning Jane what would happen on her wedding night - sex just didn't happen any other way. Her mother had made society's rules quite clear: Nice girls were still virgins on marriage – "This is the way it is, Jane. The only sure way of staying safe and pure is not to do it until your wedding night. Anything else is dangerous depravity."

Too late for that now.; she had a suspicion that she had crossed a Rubicon and joined a different set of females. Jane had seen women whose behaviour showed their enjoyment of men without a ring on their finger. And from her study of French literature knew that this had always been the case down through history. Such women understood men, understood their own bodies and knew how to keep out of trouble. Married or not, made little difference to them. Then she thought of the girl at school who got caught out and came in deep distress to Jane as head girl. "I didn't mean to and it was only one night" she wailed. The boy involved had promptly disappeared. A little gentle questioning showed that this wretched girl had even less understanding of what had happened than did Jane, who was at a loss except to suggest the girl ask the school nurse. Suddenly the girl was no longer there and from somewhere a rumour went round Jane's group that she had been disowned by her family and had had the baby taken away from her at birth for forcible adoption as a result. The next thing was the school magazine recording her death 'suddenly, tragically' without saying what had happened. The word was that she had committed suicide. The sad events had had a deep effect on the senior girls, and it tugged at Jane's conscience that she might have done more to help – even save – the girl. But what? It had been the first time Jane had felt helpless in the face of social adversity. With hindsight she saw where she might have been more sympathetic but the girl was pregnant and Jane's instinct was that there nothing she could do to combat the ranks of disapproval. Now, Jane could see a wider picture and knew equally instinctively that like or not, to survive she had to join that other, more knowing, group of women. She knew enough to see that the unfortunate girl's story was typical of what happened to the ignorant and naive, and it would pay her to make sure she didn't go the same way. And what of Jean-Pierre? Worrying thoughts ran through her mind: 'Supposing he just abandons me now like that boy? Uses me like a tart, treats me with contempt for being an easy lay then discards me? At least I shouldn't get pregnant which is some relief, but the rest is terrifying.'

By the time she'd sorted her cabin out it was dinnertime and Jane set off for the mess deck, firmly convinced that when she came in it would be as though there was a big arrow pointing at her saying 'scarlet woman'. But the old chiefs were used to her and no-one paid any attention when she eased gingerly into her usual space. Her subconscious brain was saying to her that somehow her appearance should be different, but it seemed not so.

    Throughout her years at boarding school it had been required that the girls sat down after supper on Sunday night and wrote home. Old habits dying hard Jane had continued to do so each Sunday while in *Defiance*. As she wrote this time she smiled gently to herself, thinking that for about the first time ever she wouldn't be telling her family everything that had happened in the past week.

Jane loved the late watches on *Amaryllis*, driving around in the dark of the blackout with shaded ships' lights their only guide. Shapes, which seemed humdrum in the daylight took on a looming blackness and the silvery gleam of moonlight on the water stirred a deep romantic pleasure in her. She thought that perhaps her boatmates gave her an odd look as she joined them at the brow that evening ready to take over, but if so it was fleeting and probably just her guilty conscience at work. Returning to her cabin at midnight tired but at peace she was startled to find a figure in her bunk already. "Jean-Pierre" she exclaimed in a soft undertone, "I didn't expect you here."

    "*Pourquoi non, ma chérie?*" And suddenly the full enormity of what she had done hit her. He was evidently expecting this to be a regular thing, and somehow Jane hadn't thought it through to that extent. It moved the involvement from a romantic dream sequence to a raw reality. She panicked, thinking to tell him to get out, "Jean-Pierre" she whispered, "this is all wrong. I can't go on doing it"

"Why ever not, *ma cherie?*"

"Because....because I shouldn't do this. It's just wrong. I'm sorry, Jean-Pierre, I'm all mixed up and frightened and just can't go on with this."

"How very English of you, my dear, come here" He reached out to her, gently but firmly pulling on her arm. "I can't, Jean-Pierre. And anyway, I'm all sore between the legs. You'll have to wait."

He smiled in the semi-darkness. "All right, *ma petite.* I can wait. But come and cuddle at least." Climbing in beside him, she became aware of his body – trim, a bit hairy, strongly muscled. In his arms but safe from heavier demands she relaxed and found being pressed up against him rather pleasant. He whispered. "I told you I wouldn't desert you and here I am. Was I really your first?"

She burst into tears again "Yes, Jean-Pierre, you were. I've always been scared and hated it when men got too close but this is different somehow. Do you love me?"

"What is love? I find you adorable and beautiful and that's a good start. Let's get to know each other better."

When Jean-Pierre left an hour later Jane lay awake in the dark, groping for context to it all. Her last thought as she drifted off to sleep was that having a reasonably mature Frenchman for her first lover just might have been a good move, however much of a chance thing that was. 'Jean-Pierre, I could love you.'

Five days later she was feeling much better below and, with some trepidation but re-assured by his continuing presence and gentle affection, allowed her lover to get intimate again. As before, his hands produced the explosive result before he entered her. This time there was a feeling of warmly welcoming him in, rather than the sense of invasion of the first time. With it all over he explained "That is a climax you are having. You have a thing called a clitoris which is especially made to give you them when I rub it and it gets you ready for me to come into you. Now you are ready for loving and enjoying it regularly."

In the semi-darkness she smiled. "If it's always as nice as this then maybe it being wrong doesn't matter so much. But you can promise never to get me pregnant, can't you? "

"Yes of course. That's one thing we don't want."

She giggled, starting to relax and feel less worried about this business which had so scared her. "Let's do it again now."

He looked startled. "But it takes me a little while to get going again. Here, let me pleasure you for now." Which he did with spectacular effect.

CHAPTER 14: On Relative Morality

Days then weeks whizzed by in this strange new world she found herself in, as busy as ever on *Amaryllis* where Dickhead had gone on leave so she was working crewman again, followed by nights of enjoyment in which she felt increasingly relaxed. Her feelings for her French lover were growing by the day, his combination of skill, gentle firmness and kindness overwhelming any resistance she might have felt. A loving contentment ran through her stifling the moral scruples, which still gnawed at her regularly.

On her third Wednesday-night crew run ashore, she'd told Jean-Pierre he would have to do without for that night. He's grumbled briefly, even enquiring if she had anything going with any of the crew, but had been placated by her "Have mercy, you're quite enough." She debated what to wear: They would all be in their tiddley uniforms, but it seemed a bit demeaning to wear her by now rather scruffy yachting clothes. Thinking 'Oh for a uniform', she settled on a tweed skirt she'd brought along just in case and brogues to go with it. It was a raw, windy night so a coat was necessary.

Meeting them at the brow she enquired. "Where are we going?"

"We thought we'd take you to one of our favourite pubs this time, not far from the dockyard gates." Stepping into the warm smoky atmosphere she found the place full of matelots and women in various states of dressiness, and a small group of Wrens in uniform huddled together in one corner. 'Lucky so-and-sos' thought Jane 'I wish I had one.' Jane had never drunk beer before these runs with her crew and its bitter edge took a little getting used to. At first she wasn't impressed, but in the name of friendly relations she had persevered. They found a vacant table, sat Jane down on the banquette, and started gossiping about various people on the ship. Three pints later Jane decided she'd had quite enough; she was feeling bloated and a little drunk.

Mostly she had just sat quietly while her crew chatted round her, not that they were ignoring her but she was just included in the same offhand way as she was on board *Amaryllis*. For some reason a casually sarcastic remark about Froggy Frenchies rang an alarm bell for her. "Why do you say that?"

Rufus gave her a distinctly odd look. "You should know" he shot back.

"Eh? Why?"

"Well, you know Frenchies better than anyone else on board" And they all cackled, a sly knowing laugh that sent Jane's heart into her boots. "Come on boys, level with me, what's this about?" She had a sudden desperate need to know what they knew.

"Hey Jane, you made a chief tiffy from the torpedo school a lot of money."

"How on earth did I do that?"

133

"There were two sweepstakes running on the messdecks for weeks and he got the date right. But no-one guessed the Froggy as the guy to do it." Jane had had enough beer to loosen her tongue. "Are you seriously telling me that you know what I've been doing, and with whom?"

They laughed uproariously. "Yes of course – you're the most watched person in *Defiance*. Your sheet was ceremonially paraded round all the messdecks the next day."

"Oh no, no, no, that's too horrible. My God, what a disaster" and she blushed deeply, beating her temples feebly with clenched fists, struck to the core with desperate embarrassment.

"Disaster, why?"

"Because I'm not a loose woman and I thought it was a secret and… and… and…. Oh, this is too ghastly. I'll never be able to look you in the eyes again and I'll probably be chucked out of the mob for it."

"Naw, don't you believe a word of it, Jane. We're all shaggers given half a chance and you've just made yourself even more one of us. Hey, it was obvious when you arrived you were goin' to get trapped by someone – we just didn't know when and who the lucky chap would be. But why the Froggy?"

"He's an intelligent sophisticated bloke and because I speak French we got on well from the start."

"Is he any good in bed?"

"That's my business but let's say I'm not complaining."

"Do you love him?"

"It's going that way, I think, but I still don't know him all that well."

"You don't know him? Come off it Jane you know him inside out"

Again Jane blushed deeply, struggling to make sense of this skewed conversation.

It struck Jane that her loosened tongue was getting her deeper into difficulties. But what was she to do? It couldn't be denied and they were remarkably relaxed about it. Their almost approving attitude seemed a long way away from the morality she'd had drummed into her so far in life.

"But if it's known about, surely I'll be chucked out?"

Her crew looked at each other for a moment, smiling among themselves. "Probably not, Jane. It's only known about on the mess decks and you'd be surprised how good the lower deck can be at keeping things quiet. We don't want to see you go over the wall."

"Well great but how can you lot work with me again? Surely you'll not want to know me now?"

"Naw, we're enjoying having a celebrity in our crew. We've had lots of sippers because of you. We're all a bit envious of your Frenchie but hey, you're obvious officer bait so we just enjoy the show from a distance."

"Yes but even so...... I've been a nice girl really and now what am I?"

"One of us, Jane – a matelot even if you are going with a Wardroom Willy. You were bound to get trapped sometime so don't fret."

She shook her head in bemused worry. Why was she bound to get trapped? That made no sense to her. What had seemed rather nice had turned into a nightmare. There was no going back so she really didn't have any choice but to put a brave face on it.

Stan had said little during the evening pulling on his pint and watching the drama go by. Now, as they walked back to the steps, on impulse Jane turned to him. "Stan, what am I to do? This is a disaster."

"Aye well, lass, you might've done better not to get started 'cos it's an offence to do it aboard ship. But it's too late now. Remember there's no such thing as a secret on board a ship. Let me tell you summat. I've been in this man's Navy for a long time and the dividing line is very fine between being seen as a living Jane like the cartoon so the boys like you, and bein' seen as a tart. You're a nice girl, no doubt about it. So long as you stick to just this one bloke I reckon you'll be all right an' everyone will cheer you on. But if you were to start putting it about – an' I'm not saying you will, but if you did – you'd be fair game for every canteen cowboy in the outfit and your life'd not be worth living. The boys know the difference y'know, so if you stick to the right side of it I reckon you'll be all right."

"Do you really think so, Stan? I'd no idea this would lead to such a mess."

"It's not really a mess, lass, you just carry on calmly doing your job an' glare at anyone who tries coming smutty with you and you'll be all right."

But on the liberty boat back to *Defiance* Jane felt that every ribald remark – and there were plenty of them – was aimed at her. Knowing that they all knew what she'd been up to was a kind of torture from which she wanted to curl up and shut out the world. But what could she do? Far from condemning her, they had an air of amused tolerance of her situation. There only seemed two alternatives: pack it in and run away, or brazen it out and hope naval authority didn't get to hear about it. She loved the job so much she really didn't want to run away. Should she dump Jean-Pierre? Somehow that seemed a bit feeble too, giving in to her moral doubts and the worrying sense that she was in a goldfish bowl. She loved him, didn't she? Well yes, so she'd damn well brazen it out, keep Jean-Pierre going and go on with the job too.

A sudden surge of angry defiance rose up, red tinged.

As the only Wren rating living in *Defiance* Jane had no other females she could talk to on a level with her. The Wren officers were kind enough but always a little distant and certainly not people she could have a confidential chat with, girl-to-girl.

So for ordinary human contact she had to turn to the men around her and had little realisation of just how considerate they were, given her vulnerable position. But it did mean she was falling into their male ways of thinking and doing, and was slowly becoming a matelot herself. Ladylike propriety seemed a distant concept, living among men to whom any opportunity for sex would be gleefully pounced on then related to an amused audience back on the mess deck. Her own activities might be a source of gossip but in a strange way also a strengthening bond between herself and the ratings around her. At the same time having a lover was actually a kind of protection – it meant that the mass of men among whom she lived and worked saw Jane as spoken for and hence not a serious target for their own opportunism. Isolated as she was, Jane had no idea how untrammelled a life she was leading compared with other female ratings in the services so her own scruples were fading by the day.

* * * * *

As I listened to Jane telling her story it became clear she had little regard for history or the wider world beyond the Navy and the war. When quizzed she admitted that the world she lived in was so all engrossing that she rarely thought about matters beyond it. Given that she was an intelligent and observant woman this narrowness of view showed how utterly dominated by the war and her place in it, her life had been. To do my journalist job I had had to study these matters much more broadly, which gave me scope to talk about them in ways she hadn't really considered before. Although Jane hadn't known it at the time she had been in at the start of a revolution, which changed forever how female sexual morality was viewed.

One word lay at its root: mobility. From the constraints of a static traditional world where they lived under controlled family conditions until married – and then only exchanged one control for another – mobility gave women freedom. The intensity of 'live for the moment' in wartime has always exaggerated such effects and from the powerful loosening of morals of the First World War, the Second War packed into a few years what might otherwise have taken decades. From the start of this disorienting period women – and very largely young, lively and hormonal women – had been uprooted from their sheltered, controlling, home backgrounds and redistributed round the country in vast numbers. The results of this blew like a gale through the female population. In uniform, doing demanding real jobs, often living close to danger, riding round in lorries singing group bawdy songs; all this was powerfully liberating to women whose lives had been constrained until then.

CHAPTER 14: On Relative Morality

This more liberated approach to life, more open and more freewheeling was gleefully grasped by most women so affected. Every one of them felt they were doing their bit for the war effort in a wide new world and the bracing effect of knowing they were needed was profound. This gave their authorities challenges throughout the war as such attitudes tended also to lead to a more masculine view of morality. These women were desperately needed, so losing them to mass pregnancy was not a good idea but inevitably their work and play was close to men with all the temptations that went with that. Deep ignorance about how babies were made, the contraception to prevent that, and about venereal disease with primitive unreliable treatments, made the problem doubly complex. Apart from strict practical controls, Authority did what it could to lift the fog of ignorance by lectures on anatomy and what was called moral hygiene. The only sure way of avoiding pregnancy and diseases was not to indulge in the first place, but powerful emotional pulls could play havoc with rational thought in the most determined and intelligent of women and with the extra pressures of war this effect was hugely magnified. Perhaps the surprise during the intensity and uprooting from their moorings of the Second World War wasn't that female morals become looser but that so many women did manage to stay 'respectable' under the severest of pressures.

But by no means all, as Jane ruefully admitted. "Not that I'm complaining" she emphasised, "My personal life has had wonderful ups as well as dreadful downs and has been nothing if not complex. You know, it's something I've always tried to treat as very private but I suppose when I think about it in the context you're talking about, how I've lived does fit in to that wider pattern."

CHAPTER 15:
The Water Takes and Gives

For some days after the revelations in the pub Jane was on edge, watching for the rejection she feared. But although there were sly comments and 'Wot abaat it?' invitations, it quickly become clear that they were amiable and that, like her thumping of Dickhead, her fellow ratings did not think badly of her for it. The sense of her becoming almost a man and being absorbed ever more into their fundamentally different set of standards grew stronger. The female in her wanted to hide, to be an invisible member of the herd, to deny to the mass of matelots around her the exposed sexual overtones of her activities. But her highly visible position made that impossible and only by behaving in the same way as the men was she able to achieve a degree of fading in to the crowd.

She reflected on Stan's advice and decided it was just about the most helpful thing anyone had ever said to her, with its deep understanding of lower deck psyche. She warned Jean-Pierre that they had been rumbled, but he just laughed once it was certain there wouldn't be any problems for him from being found out. If anything, it seemed to increase his enthusiasm and the nightly visits became more adventurous. He introduced her to the bits of her own body she hadn't known before and to their effects, encouraging her to explore for herself - another climactic revelation. He seemed to take great delight in playing with her breasts while she pleasured herself below and the whole-body sensations could be mind-blowing.

She was beginning to relax again and feel that she was getting the best of both worlds when this idyll was brutally disrupted. She was quietly enjoying her tot in her cabin after a busy day watch when there was a knock on the door, followed by it being opened without invitation. One of the jossmen came in – a big solid bloke probably in his mid-thirties who was a brow quartermaster she knew only by sight. He came in, closed the door and parked himself on her bunk. Startled she looked at him and said. "Yes?"

He responded with a grim smile and said, "Yes, you're not so bad looking, are you?"

Fear gripped her - this did not look like good news. "It's like this, Jane. I know all about your nocturnal activities but pusser doesn't. If he did you'd be out on your ear tomorrow. So I reckon it's worth something from you for me to keep quiet about it, and I'd like you to be nice to me."

CHAPTER 15: The Water Takes and Gives

Panic rose in her throat 'Dear God,' she thought, 'this just gets worse.' "What had you in mind?" she asked cautiously.

"See this," he said, taking out his penis "I want you to take it in your mouth and pleasure me."

"You filthy old beast" she growled, as much puzzled as horrified "why on earth would I do that?"

"Because if you don't I'll make sure pusser gets to hear about it and you'll be in the rattle and over the wall directly."

"But that's blackmail" she wailed.

"You catch on quickly, young lady. Now how about it?" He grabbed her arm and pulled her down towards him. Revulsion, panic and worry all boiled in her but above all fear of being found out. Terrified, she pulled against the downward force, fighting to keep a grip of her horror. She struggled violently and as he came off the bunk she tried to knee him in the crutch. But like all Jossmen he was trained in unarmed combat and parried her knee with ease. "Got some spirit have we?" he growled with a grim smile. She pulled her right hand free and slapped him across the face, the same ferocious snake-strike that had floored Dickhead. But this one just shook his head and growled "You bitch, you'll pay for that. Stop struggling or I really will get tough with you. You've no choice unless you want to be slung out in disgrace. Now calm down and get on with it." She looked at him, pleading, but saw only a fierce determination. She eyed with loathing the half erect object now only inches from her face, with a sense of losing something precious, of going somewhere beyond revulsion where she really did not want to go. But he rammed her head down and said "you know your choices. Now get on with it." So she did as she was told and with instructions in how to do it - "No teeth, no teeth" - finished the task in five minutes. The shooting, with its frantic jerks, just about knocked her head off – and the result tasted vile. But his hands, laced into her hair, made sure she did not pull away.

"Swallow, swallow" he roared. Calming down, satisfied, he sat back on her bunk with a contented smile. "You could get to be quite good at that" he said, clearly intending it as some sort of commendation. "Now, I'll come around whenever it suits and we'll have some more. Get me?"

Jane had collapsed in a heap on the deck, gagging and retching. Struggling to control her waves of nausea, she nodded slowly. Her brain was still just about functioning despite the desperate fog clouding it. She managed to speak. "This is horrible. Please don't tell anyone else what I've just done." She retched again at the taste in her mouth.

"I could give you a tot to make it better."

"Make it two of neaters – one before and one to take the taste away afterwards."
He reflected for a moment. "Yes, I could do that."

He got up "See you tomorrow." And with that he was gone. Giving it a minute till the coast was clear, Jane shambled to the heads, shaking uncontrollably, and was violently sick. 'At least that got rid of him' she thought. Struggling out again she encountered second officer Jones who looked at her, worry all over her face and asked "Are you all right?"

"I think I will be. Probably something's disagreed with me."

"Yes, you have to watch those eggs sometimes"

Which, in a manner of speaking, was about right, reflected Jane. She tottered back to her little cabin, somehow transformed from cosy nest to entrapping cell, and fell down on her bunk shaking and sobbing uncontrollably. What had been fun and a great adventure had just become soiled and tawdry. How many more were there like him, she wondered, and what will I do if any more come? The thought terrified her. But mercifully no-one else came. Eventually she cried herself to sleep and when Jean-Pierre arrived he got very short shrift. "Go away, go away, I hate you all."

"*Ma Cherie,* what has happened?" He was totally perplexed. But Jane couldn't bring herself to explain, just shook her head, burst into floods of tears again, and lay on her bunk sobbing helplessly. He shook his head, muttered something about the feebleness of women, and left. For about the first time in her life Jane felt defeated, crumpled and defiled and quite unable to see a way forward. But there had to be some way out of this, and she'd find it. That thought stiffened her a little and she drifted off to sleep trying to think of ways out and of revenge.

But the rest of her life had to go on, so she turned out in the morning puffy-faced and woebegone but driven to keep going. She kept getting fits of the shakes, trembling all over, but by getting posted aft on the boat she mostly managed to avoid prying eyes and to keep her deeply disturbed state hidden. This was helped by the weather. From early December 1939 it turned wintry. Going out in the launch ceased to be a pleasure, each day a battle against icy conditions and biting winds which chilled to the bone. Stan quietly arranged for her to acquire a duffle coat, heavy-duty oilskins and sea boots, and thick white socks but nothing really kept the cold and wet out. More than once she found herself wondering if it was really worth it. The various pressures on her never relented and it had all become a grim struggle. On the other hand, Stan was starting to let her drive the boat from time to time and she found again her natural flair for boatwork, which was some compensation.

CHAPTER 15: The Water Takes and Gives

Amaryllis was alongside *Defiant's* port gangway on yet another rough grey day with the early dusk closing in. Stan had come out onto her little foredeck to bellow at the brow quartermaster as a large tug charged past at full speed. Its wake caught *Amaryllis'* crew unawares, heaving the boat over violently. Stan was flung against the companion ladder, bashing his head before disappearing over the side, drifting away face down on the three hours' ebb tide, which was running. Jane and Rufus looked at each other in horror. "Do something, Rufus."

"I can't swim. Let's get help."

"That'll be too late." Jane ripped off her oilskins and seaboots and dived in after Stan. A powerful swimmer with a Lifesaving Award of Merit, she caught up with him, turned him onto his back and held him by the head in the approved fashion for unconscious people. She looked round but already they were drifting clear of the ship's lee and clearly there was no way she was going to swim back to it – the tide was running at a brisk three knots. Out of the lee, short steep waves, wind over tide, caused breaking crests which flung sharp spray into her face and made breathing difficult. She figured her only hope was to turn her back to the weather, drift with the tide, and hope to be picked up. But she must not let go of Stan.

The cold was intense and bit in, leaving her gasping for breath. After a little while the cold started to fade, and a gentle nothingness spread through her as the world drifted away. It didn't hurt any more, and somehow it was ceasing to matter whether she survived or not. Grimly she hung on to Stan but senses faded. Then there was blackness when suddenly she was subject to a violent jerk. Looking up, a boat towered over her, its port sidelight shining redly on the water. People on board were lowering a net, which they got round the two in the water and hastily hauled them up onto the deck. There the crew had to prise Jane's hands from Stan's head. For some reason her legs didn't seem to be working so she was carried into the boat's cabin where they gave her resuscitation and pushed a fair amount of water out of her lungs. It all seemed very vague and far away but she was dimly aware of the boat roaring at speed back to *Defiance*. She was rolled onto a stretcher and hurried up the companion ladder. Bright lights and anxious faces drifted in and out of view before the comfort of the sick bay was followed by a jab in her arm, then blessed nothingness.

Her first thought on coming round again was to wonder why Jean-Pierre wasn't in bed beside her. Then, with returning consciousness she realised that the sense of warm comfort came from the cot in which she was tucked up, in the sick bay. An SBA - Sick Berth Attendant - was sitting next to someone in another bed across the cabin and she tried to call to him, but for some reason she could only manage a croak. He looked up, saw her awake, and came over. "Well, are we pleased to see you coming round again. Hang on to the slack a minute while I get the doctor." This puzzled her. Why was she here? Why were they pleased that she was awake? It didn't make sense. She was startled to see her father come in and look at her carefully.

"Well, lassie, I'm glad to see you awake again. Just let me check a few things." And he expertly checked temperature and pulse and breathing before nodding happily and said "I think you'll live. But don't push it so close next time, huh?" She nodded in turn, bursting to ask questions but not able to get her voice to work. "Just relax now. Explanations can come later. Can you sit up?" And with some assistance she pulled up the bed a bit. The soup must have been from the wardroom – she'd tasted nothing as good on the mess deck. Then she was lowered down again and, watched by her wary father, drifted off to sleep.

Over the next day she was able to piece the story together. Memory of getting Stan came back, a steady stream of visitors called by and she gathered that hypothermia had nearly killed her. Her father had been summoned by the ship's doctor and had attended to her during the twenty-four hours she'd been unconscious as they slowly brought her core temperature up again. She found her voice again and her first question, hesitantly, was "Stan?" The SBA nodded at the person in the other bed. "That's him there. If you nearly died he came within an inch of it but we expect him to pull through now. You're both very lucky people."

"I don't know that I'd call it, luck." ventured Jane.

"No, but another five minutes in the water and you'd both have been dead. The boat only just got to you in time and that was by an inspired bit of guesswork. Now just relax and take it steady."

Among the visitors was the ship's captain, a tall imperious gentleman of the old school, recalled from retirement. He clearly didn't have a clue how to talk to a Wren rating who had just done something special.

"Ah-hem" He cleared his throat. "I have to congratulate you, Wren Beacon. We are conscious that you did something very brave in saving the life of Chief Petty Officer Roberts and have decided to recommend you for a 'Mention in Despatches'. I have forwarded your name to Superintendent Welby and you should receive your ribbon in about a month's time."

"It was entirely instinctive, sir."

A slight hint of humanity showed in his eyes as he smiled and said "We could do with more of that kind of instinct, then. Well done" And he marched off.

CHAPTER 15: The Water Takes and Gives

The young surgeon lieutenant left in charge came in that evening looking very cheerful. "Have you heard? They've hounded the *Graf Spee* into Montevideo."

Jane looked puzzled. *"Graf Spee?"* she queried.

"Yes, Y'know, the pocket battleship that's been commerce raiding in the South Atlantic."

"Well, I didn't know, but I suppose it must be good news for the Navy?"

"Too right – best morale booster we've had since this wretched war began."

A day later the young doctor came in for morning rounds looking exultant. "She's gone. Scuttled herself yesterday."

"Who's gone?"

"The *Graf Spee,* of course."

"Oh, right, I suppose that is good news."

'I really must learn more about the Navy and the world situation,' She thought.

* * * * *

The action that became known as the Battle of the River Plate was the Royal Navy's first real success in World War Two. Whilst no more than a skirmish set against the tapestry of the whole war, it was a bravely fought action, which sent a strong message through the fleet that the Navy was still up to the job. Having found the pocket battleship, the three light cruisers: 'Exeter', 'Ajax' and the New Zealand Navy's 'Achilles' of Force G under Commodore Harwood fought tenaciously despite being heavily outgunned. Like wounded terriers they kept at the more powerful beast and hounded it into Montevideo, damaged but still potent. The battered ships of force G kept watch, waiting for the battleship's next move. After that it was down to bluff: the Germans were led to believe that a heavy force was outside ready to pounce on the Graf Spee as soon as she left neutral Montevideo. When the permitted seventy-two hours expired her crew scuttled the Graff Spee just outside the harbour. Her captain shot himself. This would not be the last time the British successfully deceived their enemies during World War Two.

* * * * *

Jane's world remained the smaller one of the sick bay for another day, although she was recovering rapidly. Second Officer Jones called by and brought her up to date with Wren doings, confirming the Mentioned in Despatches and explained a bit what it meant. "The Navy weren't entirely keen on giving you this as simply saving someone's life didn't merit it. But we pointed out a few cases where sailors have had it for less than you did, and they've relented. Secretly, I think a lot of them are really rather proud of their first Wren Mention."

She carried on. "As Chief Roberts won't be fit for service again for some time and his crew are temporarily disbanded we've agreed with boats officer to put you on the Admiral's launch *Vosper* for a couple of weeks for a bit of variety. You're getting leave from 23rd December until 29th so you can have Christmas with your family, then back to *Amaryllis* until mid-January. Then you'll go on draft to the probationer course at Pompey - I think it's on Whale Island - before coming back here. Superintendent wants to talk to you about where we go after that. Incidentally, she's delighted with the recommendation for a Mention in Despatches – it's a first for a Wren and she's so pleased that you are working out well."

Jean-Pierre called by and sat by her bed chatting for a while. As it was all done in French they could more or less say what they liked and Jane was left with a warm glow of love and affection. They made a date to go back to the French Restaurant on Saturday night provided Jane's duty rosters allowed. After a sound night's sleep, interrupted only by nightmares of water slapping into her face, which brought her upright in the middle of the night snorting and blowing to the alarm of the duty SBA, Jane was ready to go again. Out of bed she dressed in her old but freshly laundered yachting clothes then went over to the other bed. Stan was lying there, his head bandaged from the injury when it hit the companion ladder, and was very still but his eyes were open.

"Hello Stan" she said quietly, perching on the edge of his bed, "I'm told you will be all right."

"Yes, so they tell me but I'm still feeling pretty ropey. Listen, Jane, I…..I…..I" and to Jane's alarm he burst into tears. Gently, she took his hand. "It's all right Stan, you'll be fine and I only did what I had to. You don't have to get upset about it."

"But you saved my life, lass. How can I ever thank you?"

"By getting better and back to work. There's a war on, remember?"

He smiled weakly. "Yes, you're probably right."

CHAPTER 16:
The Highs and Lows

Back in her own cabin everything seemed neat and tidy. The Black Chiffon was laid out on the bunk, clean and pressed. Who was doing this, she wondered? Her wristwatch, which had been ruined in the water, had disappeared. Next day she took the first boat ashore in the morning – ironically *Amaryllis* with a different crew and found *Vosper* at Flagstaff steps. *Vosper* proved to be a different proposition, a bigger and beautifully built version of *Amaryllis* used by the port Admiral and various senior officers so kept in immaculate condition. Stan, working with his regular crew, ran *Amaryllis* strictly enough but with little need for overt discipline. By comparison *Vosper* was very tightly run. Her crew were all seasoned two- and three-badge men– long service ABs with the 'badges' that is chevron stripes denoting seven and thirteen years' good conduct and long service. Working on *Vosper* was a quiet sinecure away from the more fierce elements of Naval life, and her crew knew very well that the way to keep things that way was to run their boat with extreme efficiency. So they were wary when Jane came aboard but by now she was something of a celebrity throughout Devonport and after a couple of days' cautious observation they accepted her with nothing more than the odd growl. She learned in those two weeks just how efficiently a harbour launch could be run, and what to do with an admiral on board. The admiral had been dubious about this Wren boat crew experiment, but watching Jane go about her business with quiet efficiency he saw that perhaps there might be something in it. The word that got back to the superintendent was distinctly encouraging. Meantime Stan had gone on sick leave as soon as he was fit to travel. Jane saw him off at the brow, to avoid any more heavy emotional scenes. The rest of *Amaryllis'* crew were dispersed temporarily, some to other boats, a couple to long leave.

Reuniting with Jean-Pierre had been pure pleasure, and on the Saturday night they made a real event of it, *M. Le patron* excelling himself with as fine French cuisine as his limited supplies would allow. It was also *adieu*, with Jean-Pierre due to go home on Christmas leave so the later night should have been special as well. But over dinner he had made a casual reference to 'my son' which Jane puzzled over and once they had enjoyed themselves fairly spectacularly in bed she lent up on an elbow, looked at him and asked, "What was that reference to your son?"

"Oh, I have three children, two girls and my lovely little son."

"Does that mean you're married?"

"Yes of course my love. Didn't you realise that?"

Horror filled her. "No I bloody well did not. How could you deceive me like that?" And she burst into tears, collapsing with a wail.

"My dear, my dear, what's wrong? There's nothing unusual about a married man having a mistress as well."

"Maybe not in France but here girls don't give their virginity to passing men who fancy a bit on the side. Oh Jean-Pierre, how could you? I thought I loved you and you cared for me and all the time it was a sham. I hate you, you rotten deceiver."

"Now, now, Jane, calm down. I really do care very much for you, y'know, and I never thought my being married would bother you."

"Not much. I know it felt good but do you really think I gave myself to you like that just for a bit of fun? If so, you don't know much about women. I did it because I believed I loved you, you rotten scumbag and now I feel so betrayed. Get out. Go on, get out." She gave him a huge push so that he tumbled out of the bunk. Gathering up his dignity he pulled his clothes on watched by glistening eyes, blew her an ironic kiss and was gone. In the dark of her little cabin Jane cried silently and steadily for what seemed like hours. How could she have been so blinkered and stupid, not to have asked him long ago if he was married?

As if that wasn't enough her gruesome Jossman was soon back to be dealt with. After the horror of his first few visits Jane had tried to see a way to survive the revulsion that swept over her each time he came as she didn't see how she could avoid his visits. She racked her brains for some way out, perhaps calling his bluff and taking her chances, but the danger in that was obvious. Might she get her boat crew to warn him off, even beat him up? Again, she rejected the thought as too risky; that blackmailing threat of exposure seemed to hang over any ways out. She dreaded his coming but struggling to be rational about it – given the depths of her instinctive revulsion this was difficult – she saw that she wasn't suffering any physical harm from his visits, just a degrading sense of being invaded and abused. At least the two extra tots were welcome and the whole thing was mercifully brief. She was startled to be complimented by him on how good she was getting at it, and snarled "What I'd really like to do is bite it off." But he just laughed. She found herself getting spurts of rage at the whole male sex, and carrying round a sense of being soiled like a used rag. There had to be a way to get rid of him, but how? This sense of degrading helplessness was new to her, and she hated it.

But life wasn't all bad. Jane was pleasantly surprised to be invited – still as a nominal civilian – to the pre-Christmas mess dinner in the wardroom where her other new dress passed muster. It was a spectacular affair in iridescent petrol blue velvet, which shimmered, and changed hue in the light. It was a tight, sleeveless full-length sheath with high Mandarin collar and a long kick-slit up the back, relying on figure-hugging like a second skin for its effectiveness. Looking at herself in the mirror Jane saw her knicker line showing clearly over her rump which wouldn't do at all, so after trying to smooth it over she thought 'what the hell' and went knickerless. Did modesty matter now? The only drawback to its spectacular display was the crowd of admiring young officers who clustered round her after dinner, competing for perhaps more than a smile. But a smile was all they got. Her aching heart was still deeply in revolt against men in general, a mixture of crying after lost love and hatred of their demands.

With her two weeks on *Vosper* completed, she had an odd day's make and mend before going on leave. After supper she was surprised to find Taff knocking at her cabin door with a request to come down to the mess deck. Mystified, she trailed along behind him onto the mess deck which she was startled to find full of matelots. A cheer went up as she came in. They were all there: spotty nozzers from the torpedo school, various boats' crews, a bunch of regulating types and a phalanx of the well-upholstered senior rates she messed with.

From the throng Nobby stepped forward; he'd always been the mouthiest of *Amaryllis*' crew. "Jane, it's been great having you with us but specially we wanted to say 'thank you' for rescuing Cox'n Roberts the way you did. That was the bravest thing any of us has ever seen. So we decided to club together and get you something to show our appreciation, and here it is." He thrust a small box into Jane's hands.

She opened it tentatively; there was a watch inside. Not strictly a lady's watch, a bit bigger and chunkier but obviously very high quality. "We saw your old one had been ruined when you went in after the cox'n so we thought we'd get you a new one. It's waterproof and shockproof and self-winding so it won't matter if you have to jump into the oggin after any of the rest of us. Go on, put it on." Smiling, Jane took it out of its box then saw inscribed on its metal strap '*To Jane with thanks. From the boys of HMS Defiance 12.1939*'. She put it on and held her arm up so everyone could see it. "Speech, speech" roared round the messdeck.

She stood on a bench and said "Boys, this is so kind of you. I really don't think I deserve this. You probably know I've been put forward for a 'Mention in Despatches' but really this means more to me. Thank you, thank you." Suddenly it all got too much for her. She sat down with a thump and burst into floods of tears, the surge of emotion overwhelming her. A roar of "Jane, Jane" went round the messdeck whilst

– of all unlikely people –her gruesome Jossman stepped up and gently hugged her shoulder. A strong urge to throw the hypocrite's arm off and slap his face spoilt the joy of the moment but somehow that didn't seem the right thing to do so she just wriggled out. Again, the contrasts and contradictions of life in the Navy were just too much. But back in her cabin later a certain glow of pride went through her as she looked at the watch on a hook by her bunkside.

Going on leave next day, Jane was under instructions to report to the Superintendent as she came ashore. She smiled sweetly at Second Officer Jones as she came into the office, although the curt nod in reply seemed less forthcoming than usual. Going into the Superintendent's office she was not invited to sit down, but was scowled at. "Beacon, what on earth am I to do with you? No sooner do I send off the papers recommending you for a 'Mentioned in Despatches', than I discover you've been entertaining a man in your cabin more or less since you started. What are you, some sort of alley cat?"

Jane, who had been expecting a pat on the back and good wishes for Christmas, was taken flat aback. She blushed violently. "But, but…"

"No but but with me, young lady. I take it you don't deny the charge?"

All Jane could do was shake her head, too embarrassed for speech. She found herself wishing the floor would open up and swallow her.

"Why did you do it?"

Jane wanted to shout that she'd done it because it felt so nice, the most wonderful physical feeling she had ever known, but somehow that didn't seem like the right answer in the austere surroundings of the Superintendent's office so she just shook her head mutely.

"Right, quite apart from the morals of the situation, are you aware that it is totally against regulations to indulge like this aboard one of His Majesty's ships? You have blithely been committing a serious crime and by all rights you should be getting thrown out of the service right now. What is really frustrating is that you've received glowing reports for your work and your recent bravery has been noted in high places. Is this some sort of self-destructive impulse you have?"

At last Jane found her voice. "No ma'am, it's not like that. I didn't know I was committing any crime and we did take precautions."

"Hah! The only true precaution is not to do it in the first place. Are you in love with this man?"

"Not now, ma'am. He has admitted that he's married anyway, back in France and that destroyed it all. I am so sorry Ma'am, I just got carried away and had no idea I was committing a crime. No, I don't love him, not now, although I thought I did. He was so charming, and sophisticated, and we did enjoy chatting away in French."

"Which is all very well but hardly justifies what you've been doing. Do you intend to go on like this? Because if you do, there's no place for you in the Wrens. We are trying very hard to make this the good women's service and won't have it undermined. And I find that what you've been up to is known right round Devonport, which just makes it worse. It's such a disappointment to me because we had huge hopes of you."

"Well I'm sorry ma'am but the job has gone really well and I had no idea that what I thought was a quiet thing in private could have exploded like this. Bit naïve of me, I suppose."

"You can say that again young lady. I gather you feel some affinity to the cartoon Jane. If so, you would do well to note that she doesn't actually get up to anything – just flirts with it."

"The affinity to the other Jane came from my crew, not me."

"Your crew? You're supposed to be the junior there, not the senior. How can you say that?"

"Well, that's the way they think of it – and so does everyone else on the mess decks. There does seem to be a wide gap here between the official view, and what I've come across on the lower deck. They've known about it all along and were really very relaxed about it."

"If you're adopting Jack's morals there's no hope. We worried about this business of your being a rating when you had the capacities to be an officer but hadn't bargained on your taking sides with them so much."

"But ma'am, I had to and they've been so good to me. They've not tried to take advantage of me much or been hard on me and they all seem to have taken me to their hearts. I've been put in a situation where I've got to live and work with them and I would have got nowhere by being toffee-nosed about it. They have been so helpful and if this idea is going to work we've got to find ways of reconciling the contradictions."

"This may be true but doesn't excuse why you went to bed with an officer in the first place. I know your mother well and have some responsibility to her for your wellbeing. How on earth could either of us explain this to her? Your family would be devastated to know that you're being seen as a trollop round the fleet here."

"But it was only one man and I certainly wasn't going to go any further. Nor was I going to try explaining it to my mother. She has very firm views on this sort of thing and just wouldn't understand. I don't know, ma'am, I was sort of seduced and just drifted into it. Let's face it I was an ignorant virgin when I arrived and I certainly didn't intend to do anything like this but it just happened. And no, I don't intend to make a habit of it. I suppose there's a lesson in it somewhere about being a bit more discreet. I think I've learned more in the last three months than the rest of my life. Somehow being able to parse Virgil doesn't seem so important now. I am so sorry to have let you down. Can you forgive me?"

The superintendent shook her head in slow sorrow, looking at something lost and far away and briefly appearing old and worried and a bit vulnerable. But she wasn't the Queen Bee of Guzz for nothing and taking a deep breath she fired up again.

"Right, Beacon, let us think forward a bit. Because you're so good at the job we're not going to throw you out just yet. We can try to protect you from yourself but one more performance like this and there will be no saving you. Your service record was marked as suitable for officer promotion but for now that's being withdrawn. If you want to identify with the lower deck you must live with the consequences. Your disciplinary record will have this gross infraction recorded, two disciplinary notes in three months is not good. You will go on draft to the probationer course, then to try to get some sort of control over you we're bringing you back here afterwards. We have to think a bit about the complications of your position and so do you, young lady. Have you anything else to say?"

"I don't think so. I feel terrible about it all now but he was ever so skilled and good at it and I couldn't have asked for a kinder first lover."

The shock at this on the superintendent's face was obvious. Briefly she went pale and big-eyed. It was rare for the superintendent to lose her temper and shout, but this explosion was fierce. "That is utterly irrelevant and if you don't want me to change my mind about keeping you, you will shut up now! Get out!"

Jane scuttled out of the room. Second Officer Jones gave her a wry sideways look and said. "I'm afraid you asked for that."

"So it would seem." Jane was white-faced and trembling, struggling to hold back tears. "I will not be defeated." she muttered.

"In some quarters they call that self-destruction. Have a nice Christmas."

* * * * *

Looking back on it, Jane admitted to me that the wild roller-coaster she had been on since joining just three months earlier had been with very little thought beyond her immediate world. She was blithely unaware of the Navy's long history of coming to terms with sexual urges. I explained that in Nelson's time the men were cooped up in their ships for years at a time, because of the very real fear that they would desert if allowed ashore. To compensate, whores by the hundred were allowed on board when the ships anchored near a port. In the UK these whores tended to be thin undernourished (and often very young) country girls, frequently diseased, left with no other means of survival. Their life expectancy was short. "Poor things" said Jane "So we've made some progress." On the gun decks each sailor had eighteen inches of space, in which to sling his hammock and they lived jammed up against each other. Coupling was done in their hammocks in full public view and totally shamelessly – 'like dogs' as one senior admiral put it. Jane wrinkled her nose at this. "So I've been seen like those wretched country girls? Oh dear."

I grinned at her and carried on. "At the end of the Napoleonic wars the Royal Navy went from being the largest fleet in the world to a peacetime rump of a service. Britain has ever been thus with its Navy. The multitude of pressed men were discharged and slowly the ratings who stayed became more professionalised. Ashore the swing in public morality trended towards a high-minded prudery. The armed forces have always been a reflection of the civil society they spring from, and from 'coupling like dogs' naval ratings saw women completely banned from their ships by mid-Victorian times. In theory they always had been but reality was another matter."

"Good Lord" interjected Jane "No wonder my antics caused so much concern."

I continued "This deeply felt and strongly enforced ban was to survive for a hundred years and more and was as potent as ever at the start of World War Two. Women were welcome on board commissioned warships as visiting guests, but for any further involvement both they and their sailor partners were expected to go ashore."

"What a shame nobody told me that" she said ruefully. "I might have been a bit more careful if I'd known just how totally I was contravening their shibboleths."

I could only give that an ironic laugh.

PART FOUR:

PROBATIONER BEACON

CHAPTER 17:
Back Among the Girls

Christmas at home was much like any other, give or take a few shortages and the intensely cold weather. But Jane felt herself distanced from the cheerful rowdiness of her family, and was gripped of a sense that she no longer fully belonged – her real life was now some miles away on the Hamoaze. When she got home she had launched into an excited description of her life on *Amaryllis* only to be brought up short by her mother "You know, dear, you've been talking at me for ten minutes and I've not understood a word you've said." A few strongly salty oaths also raised eyebrows; it was only when she got away from *Defiance* that she saw how much of their way of speaking she had picked up. Her dinner table story this time was all about rescuing Stan. She showed off the watch to everyone's admiration, although only her father and brother David had much idea what being 'Mentioned in Despatches' meant, but they were thrilled. Despite some fishing by her mother she managed to avoid Jean-Pierre as a topic and her edgy worry that her changed state might show in some way, proved groundless. Her mother remarked that she seemed to have a new warmth about her but Jane managed to pass that off as enthusiasm for the job.

Pleasant and relaxing though it had been to be with her family, there was some sense of relief when her leave was up. Returning, her interview with the superintendent had been brief – simply told to go back to work on 'Amaryllis' and to keep out of trouble – and by the way, her precious Frenchman wouldn't be coming back, thank you. They had arranged for the French Navy to send someone else and had had no hesitation in saying why. As she came out of the superintendent's office Second Officer Jones stopped her with a rather cold hard stare. "I'm afraid you will not be able to come to our ante-room any more. We can't be seen to condone your sort of behaviour." This crisp and slightly brutal reminder of the price she was paying for being found out disturbed Jane; she found the contrast between that and her warm welcome back on board *Defiance* was marked. Her little cabin was just as she had left it, except that it was shiny clean and the bunk was freshly made up. Even the crusty old petty officers gave her a friendly welcome on the messdeck.

Amaryllis' crew had re-formed as she returned at the same time as Stan, he glad to get away from the caring but cloying attentions of his two sisters. Next day they all defied the biting cold to give the boat a thorough clean. Somehow the temporary crew just hadn't looked after it so well. As they got going a still profoundly thankful Stan allowed Jane to do more of the driving. Deeply knowledgeable, he proved to be a good teacher, showing her how to read the tide to put a boat alongside always bows-on, how to allow for wind and tide in narrow waters, how to use the two screws to manoeuvre and turn in tight spaces. Jane loved this – when driving the boat nothing else existed for her.

It had occurred to her that with her nocturnal activities known anyway, the gruesome Jossman no longer had any hold over her. So when he turned up looking for servicing she took a good deal of pleasure in saying no. "It's quite simple" she explained "I've been found out and survived so now the boot's on the other foot. If I were to go to the authorities and tell them how you've been harassing me, guess who'd be over the wall? So you can clear off and leave me alone – as far as I'm concerned you can stick your horrid cock in a motorised mincing machine and fry the result for breakfast. And if you breathe a word of this to anyone I will go to the authorities, so I suggest you keep it very quiet." He slunk off shaking his head in slow disbelief, leaving Jane surprised by the roughness of her own tongue. Her transformation into a lower deck sailor was getting ever stronger.

* * * * *

This theme of the contrast between the male Navy she learned to live with, and the gentler mores of the women's naval service, became a central thread of Jane's life through the war. Having adapted to male ways, she never lost that unfeminine edge and openly told me of her life much as the men would that I was accustomed to interviewing. Once into her stride, I found Jane spoke fluently and easily. Her reminiscing was a mixture of pleasure and pain, but a certain raw honesty kept her going. Clearly, those early months on the boats were formative and as the later story unfolded so much of its roots lay in that pioneering period, both personally and professionally. One of the break points was the return to a female world on the probationer course and I asked her if she had any idea what to expect when she went off to it. "None at all" she admitted. In this she was not alone. My conversations with Superintendent French had given me some view of the Wrens' beginnings and I saw that Jane had been part of the first tidal wave of women into the forces.

To get the WRNS going, Lady Superintendents like Mrs Welby had been appointed at the major naval seaports and told to get on with recruiting Wrens locally. Varying standards from port to port rapidly made it clear that some form of standard initial induction was needed to produce uniform newly-minted Wrens but this understanding came too late for early entrants like Jane Beacon. They had started without such training and some corrective was needed. The first probationer courses were largely made up of Wrens who had already joined without much knowledge of the Navy or its ways.

Miss French had explained: "The re-formed WRNS was based on the ethos of our distinguished predecessor service which had flourished from 1917 to 1919, when it showed so clearly that women could do enormously more than had been asked of them. There was a fierce outcry when the Navy insisted on that original being disbanded. We would have loved to have gone on but the atmosphere in 1919 was not helpful as many of the women had been doing jobs in war time which could be done by men in peace time and there was an inevitability back then that 'jobs for returning heroes' meant women giving theirs up for these 'heroes'. It was sad but that was life at the time. That reaction after the first war set back women's rights a long way just when it looked like they might be getting somewhere. You should have seen what happened when the re-formation of the WRNS was announced in early 1939: it was inundated with applications, many from women who had been Wrens in the first war. These women, more mature now, formed a large part of the early backbone of the Service in World War Two."

That much history I understood but I was less clear about how they had evolved into the powerful force they were later on. Jane laughed "Perhaps it's my turn to give you a history lesson. You see, we came of age in the Second World War. From a standing start in 1938 we had 74,600 members by mid-1944 – smaller than the other women's military services but stronger, more tightly bonded and more highly thought of. Although the Navy was the most hidebound and reactionary of the three services, it took the Wrens to its heart from the start. Somehow there was an atmosphere in the Wrens that we would remain feminine no matter how demanding or technical the job was. The black stockings helped a lot. Quickly, the system settled down that Wrens were answerable directly to (male) naval officers for performance of their duties but all other aspects of their lives and careers remained in the hands of the WRNS all-female structure. Unlike the other two services we are not auxiliaries; despite the 'never at sea' bit, we are fully integrated and very rapidly the Wrens became the Navy in a skirt. I'd like to think that given the opportunity, we Wrens seized the openings with both hands, doing brilliantly well in the many tasks we were set. A die-hard rump of Naval traditionalists did not like it at all, but demand to "Free a Man to go to Sea" overwhelmed all objections as gaping holes in manning ashore arose from the desperate need to send sailors to the ships at sea.

Back in 1938 the Navy's concept for the WRNS had been for 1,500 part-time assistants in domestic and secretarial roles. Ha! Little did they know – we were into all manner of areas very quickly and by late 1940 a statistical freak briefly showed a service strength of exactly 10,000."

Jane continued: "There's one other point which is relevant at this stage. From its earliest days the reborn WRNS adopted a highly beneficial policy of ensuring that its senior officers with real power over the mass of Wrens, were mature ladies with some experience of working with younger women. This avoided the difficulty encountered in the other services of very young women officers, possibly better educated but otherwise much on a level with their charges, having great difficulty exercising any authority. Senior Wren officers were respected from the start and, being less susceptible to the temptations of a giddy social life, formed the iron backbone of the moral respectability, which – apart from me – was such a feature of the Wrens. The 'prigs and prudes' jibe from World War One might still echo down the years but in difficult circumstances this sometimes starchy morality has served us well. We have lots of young Wren officers but they're specialists, trained –sometimes highly trained – for the many demanding technical roles placed on them. While expected to do duty officer turns and possibly to exercise authority over a limited group of Wrens they are working with, young officers are never asked to assume wider disciplinary authority. It all sounds a bit girl guides but believe me it works and has been a major factor in the Wrens being so successful."

I had to admit I'd never thought of it that way, but reflecting on what I'd seen it was obvious, and all the more successful for being so much the everyday way the service ran. "You found that on the probationer course?" I asked.

"Well, yes and no, but let me come to that."

* * * * *

For Jane, there was a sadness in leaving *Defiance,* but a comfort in getting away from the worst winter in a hundred years. Knowing that she would be coming back afterwards, Jane had decided to slide away with minimum fuss, leaving at sparrowfart by a different boat on the first run of the day. Inevitably the trains were packed, but as they were also unheated only the mass of humanity jammed together stopped people freezing. Changing trains at Salisbury was not enjoyable, an icy blast blowing along the platforms on people waiting for trains, which came hours late. Eventually she made it to Portsmouth, only to find she had a two-mile

CHAPTER 17: Back Among the Girls

walk to *H M S Excellent* on Whale Island. Whoever decided to hold a probationer Wren course there in January had a warped sense of humour: the Navy's primary gunnery and drill school was a tough place at any time. In sub-zero temperatures it was miserable. Jane hiked across the causeway, close-hauled on port tack against the biting wind, and reported to the guardhouse. "You another of these Wrens with no uniform? Shouldn't be allowed, either you're in the Andrew or not."

"Well, I've got an armband" she said defensively. She was in her full oilskins, sou'wester and seaboots, so there were a few layers to divest before she could show her armband, and dig out her identity card and draft chit. She looked at the grey sleet-swept scene "Bloody hell, d 'you get hard liers just for being here?"

The crusher laughed. "You'll not get away with swinging the lamp here, Jenny." Jane grinned back at him.

Then, with ill grace he let her through "You're in Block Three, far side of the wardroom. Report to reception there." He disappeared back into the warmth at the double, leaving Jane to cover up again and carry on hiking. Under other circumstances she would have been interested to look around this new place, but following the vague waft of the crusher's arm she beat to windward across the front of the wardroom head down.

Pushing through the front entrance Jane found a straggling queue of young females waiting to register; some well covered up, but others inadequately dressed, soaked through and shivering violently. 'Poor things' she thought, 'They must be frozen.' A couple of harassed writers were entering each girl's details, watched by a quarters officer. When her turn came Jane took her sou'wester off but was still in her full pusser's oilskins and seaboots. This drew the ire of the officer, "Don't you think you could at least take those dripping oilskins off? I don't want you splashing all over our desk. Where did you get a full set of Pusser's foul weather gear anyway?"

Jane shook her hair out and looked at this bossy lady. "They were issued to me for the work I do. Sorry if I'm making a mess - I kept them on for warmth – er – ma'am."

She handed over her paybook and draft chit, automatically saying "1095 Wren Beacon." The writer looked at her in a more amiable way. "Done this before, have we?"

Jane nodded. "Yes, been in three months now – it feels like three years already."

This got a sympathetic smile. "Right, we're trying to spread the experienced ones out so you'll go into cabin three with mostly newcomers. Try and guide them a bit, will you? Our C.O. wants everyone in the messroom at the far end of the block at 2000. Meantime there's supper next door if you can bear to go outside again."

"You bet I will. I'm famished." Cabin three proved to have a dozen double-deck pipecot bunks in it; Jane selected the lower one furthest from the door, dumped her bag on it, pulled on her sou'wester again and fought her way to the canteen.

159

"Oh goody, cheese oosh and windy beans on a raft" got a wry look from the cook. "We decided to make a special effort for the first night. Don't bank on it lasting."

She didn't, and by smiling nicely at the cook managed to wangle a trip round the buoys when no-one was looking.

After another brief battle with the elements she went dripping into cabin three again. Jane's bag was upside down on the deck and an attractive blonde girl was emptying hers out on the bunk Jane had selected. "Excuse me, I chose that bunk. Who are you?"

"Merle Baker, pleased to meet you." She held her hand out. Jane ignored it. "I said I chose that bunk. Why are you in it?"

"Well, I decided I wanted it so - too bad."

This defiance irritated Jane. "There's no too bad about it, gobshite. Now shift your hook pronto."

Merle looked startled by this "I really don't see why I should. You can find another one." Her voice rising to a squeak at the end.

During this exchange Jane had been steadily taking off her oilskins and thick outer layers, as the cabin was cozily warm. "Out, I said". But Merle sat there staring defiantly; Jane lowered her head so they were eye to eye. Struggling to control her temper, Jane hissed, "Get out now or I will remove you. Do not mess about with me." Merle shrank back but stayed put. Suddenly Jane's carefully developed control went; she grabbed the girl by her shirt front and pulled her forward "This is your last chance. Get out." Merle shook her head, more in fear than defiance but that did it. Jane yanked her out of the bunk and tossed her onto the floor with an audible bang. Her bag was hurled at her, followed by the loose clothing item by item. Finished, there was an appalled – a terrified - silence in the cabin broken only by wailing from Merle. Jane turned and looked at the rest of them, staring in wide-eyed terror. Taking a deep breath she said. "Don't worry, I'm not usually like this and you're all quite safe. But I will not be messed about, d 'you hear me?" As abruptly as her temper had risen, it evaporated and something akin to horror rose up in her mind. What had she done? This was no way to start with a group of girls who would live by a different set of rules to those she had adapted to on the matelots' messdecks. But too late now.

Jane turned back to Merle, still lying on the deck sobbing. She struggled to contain the fierce irritation rising up again, but three months as a matelot took over. "Oh for fuck's sake get up, you snivelling wimp. There's a bunk for you by the door." She grabbed Merle's hand, jerked her to her feet and dusted her down a bit, picked up her bag and carried it to the remaining bunk, an upper one next to the door.

CHAPTER 17: Back Among the Girls

"There you are, you can sleep comfy there. Don't mess with me again, shitehawk."

Most of the girls had stared in speechless amazement during this altercation, but Jane had noticed one that didn't seem bothered. A big girl with a broad square face weathered like Jane's. She had given Jane an initial appraising look then calmly carried on unpacking, untroubled by the drama. Ambling down the cabin again, Jane stopped by this big girl. "Hello, I'm Jane Beacon. Please don't think I'm always like that – it's just that I can't stand being messed about with."

When she stood up the girl's size showed. Jane was no miniature but this one topped her by several inches, and was strongly built with it. Her handshake was crunching. "Hello, me name's Violet Johnson but everyone calls me Punch." She spoke with a distinctive country accent that Jane couldn't place.

"Why Punch?"

"Oi'm from Lowestoft – that's in Suffolk and the big carthorses there are Suffolk Punches. So I'm called after them. Oi s'pose I am a bit of a carthorse."

"Well, that seems a bit unkind but if you're happy about it I'll call you Punch too. Have you been in for long?"

"A month now but they can't decide what to do with me. Me dad owns a spreetie an' I've been in boats all me life but they don't seem to have any use for girl seamen. Seems a shame somehow."

"A spreetie? What's a spreetie?"

"A barge - y'know the kind that run from the Thames to East Anglia?"

Jane was puzzled. "But there aren't any canals from the Thames to East Anglia?"

"No, no – a spreetie's a sailing barge with a big diagonal boom to set the mainsail."

Light dawned. "Oh, you mean a spritsail barge."

"That's right, a spreetie."

"And you've sailed with your Dad?"

"Oh yes, ever since I can remember. Me mam often sails with him and when she went I went too."

"But can't the Navy make good use of your abilities?"

"It seems not – they said Wrens don't go to sea."

In view of her experimental status Jane decided to say no more than "I'm in boats too. And you never know – things might change about Wrens going in boats."

"D'you think so? That'd be nice."

They smiled at each other and drifted on. The other girls had started chatting again in the meantime and the atmosphere was relaxing. Merle had climbed into the upper bunk by the door and was gently trying to stifle her sobs. One or two were having difficulty unpacking and stowing their clothes away in the two drawers each was allotted so Jane helped here and there, chatting to them as she did so and trying to get beyond the terror she saw in their eyes when she arrived towering over them.

Abruptly there was a rasp on the Tannoy. "D'you here there. Clear lower deck. All hands muster in the messroom."

Some of the girls looked puzzled by this so Jane said. "Come on girls. That's all of us in the messroom now. Let's find it." Coming to the door Jane saw Merle still inert on her bunk. "Come on, Merle, that's you too." She reached up to give Merle a hand, but Merle effortlessly vaulted to the floor, glared at Jane and stalked out, head held high. As they filed into the messroom two ample hard-faced women in petty officers' uniforms were counting and checking the chattering crowd. Jane recognised one for a chief petty officer by the buttons on her sleeve and thought 'that's quick promotion'. As Merle passed by, her face puffy with crying, this chief pulled her over. "Are you all right?" To her credit Merle only nodded and said "Yes, just feeling a bit homesick, I suppose." Jane, close by, noted this and smiled appreciation. Merle glared at her and hissed. "I am not a snitch," which rather took the wind out of Jane's sails.

A tall grey-haired example of the mature senior officers policy stood up in front of the assembled probationers. "Good evening, and welcome to *HMS Excellent*. I am First Officer Brown and I am in charge of you for this second probationer course. The intention is to introduce you to the Navy, how it works, who is who and what is what. We will also be teaching you drill although how we will manage with the weather as bad as it is, remains to be seen. There will be tours of several of the establishments around Pompey of the sort you may end up in, and talks on the various specialisations open to you. While here you will be subject to strict discipline and control – probably stricter than you have known so far. Apart from the block duty group there will be limited shore leave from after supper each evening, but there will be a general requirement for all of you to be back on board, in these quarters, by nine o'clock. Each of you will be allowed one late pass to ten thirty and when you use it you must take it with you to show to the guardhouse - no excuses will be accepted. If you go ashore you have to sign out and back in the register kept at reception here. We hope none of you have to be disciplined but believe me, we will deal very firmly with anyone who does not obey the rules. 'Pipe down' – that's lights out – is at ten thirty every night regardless. For tonight you will just stay in your quarters and get settled in. There will be kye available from the canteen at nine o'clock. You will have to get used to working by the twenty-four hour clock, so nine o'clock in the evening is 2100. The daily routine will be 'call the hands' at 0600, then clean and scrub the entire block until 0730 when first sitting

CHAPTER 17: Back Among the Girls

for breakfast will be called. Second sitting is 0800. Classes will normally start at 0845 until midday, when you will have your main meal. After dinner comes drill, as mentioned. Tomorrow will be a bit different as you will be issued with your working uniforms called 'bluettes' at 0845 and you will be given time to change into them. You will each get two bluettes and you will wear one at all times you are on duty. You will be examined on your classroom work and tested for drill at the end of this course and will have to pass if you want to stay in the Wrens.

Now, there are girls from all sorts of different backgrounds here. Let me make it quite clear: there will be no class distinction on this course. You are all ordinary Wrens on probation and no one of you is better or worse than any other. Try to see each other as fellow ratings with a mutual goal, to help each other work together for the common good. I hope you understand this for we will enforce it rigorously.

One more thing: headquarters has instructed that the girl who gets the best overall results for classroom work and drill and shows some leadership qualities, will be promoted leading Wren. So there's an ambition for you to aim at. Questions?"

"Please ma'am, my husband's here in Portsmouth. Will I be able to get a night off any time to visit him?" A titter went round the assembly.

"I am afraid not. It has been decided that all Wrens must sleep in during the course, so your husband will just have to do without you for three weeks. You can, of course see him from secure until 2100 unless you are on block duty."

There were no other questions so they dispersed back to their cabins, chattering like a flock of their namesake birds. Jane unpacked herself then it was time to fight through the cold and snow to get at the kye, although many girls didn't bother. Back in the cabin she encountered the occupant of her upper bunk for the first time. "Hello, I'm Alicia D'Aincourt."

"Jane Beacon, how d 'you do."

They looked at each other with hovering recognition. "Are you The Honourable Alicia D'Aincourt, by any chance?"

She pulled a face "Well yes, but keep it quiet please – I'm trying just to fit in here."

"That's where we've met." said Jane with a burst of recognition. "You're Roedean aren't you? I played hockey against you back in '38. I'm Leadown."

"Oh really? Yes, I do remember now" and she smiled in recognition. "But you didn't learn to behave the way you did earlier at Leadown, surely?"

"Well no, but I've been three months in the Andrew now. I was in *Defiance* and was the only Wren rating on board so I picked up what are probably lots of bad habits from the matelots."

"The only girl in lots of men? Oh wow, that must have been fabulous."

"Not entirely – it was like living in a goldfish bowl. Everything – and I do mean everything –I did was observed. But they were a nice bunch. Have you been in for long?"

"Six weeks now as a driver. I'm hoping to become a despatch rider but it's full up just now."

This chat was interrupted by one of the chief petty officers putting her head round the door saying "fifteen minutes to pipe down. Time to turn in."

Jane grabbed her toothbrush and scooted along to the washhouse. Preparing for bed, she and Alicia changed in the automatic way that years of boarding school had taught them. It was casually effortless and they nodded at each other in mutual recognition of well-adjusted habits. But looking round there was chaos. Clearly a lot of the girls had never undressed in company in their lives. Some struggled to get their stays off without revealing anything, a couple just piled into their bunks in their slips and underwear, others kept vests on with pyjamas on top.

But, beyond the chaos Jane noted that Merle changed as she had done, and was equally at ease with a quick change in a crowded dorm. Punch simply stripped off defiantly and pulled on a bell tent of a nightgown. Settling down on her hard lumpy mattress Jane thought over the events of the day – leaving *Defiance* that morning seemed a long way away.

Perhaps she had been a bit hasty with Merle, and as she drifted off she turned over in her mind what she could do to sort it out without backing down. What on earth had possessed her to behave that way? Despite her temper she'd never been given to violence beyond giving little twin brothers a clip round the ear, so why this now? It didn't really make sense but had seemed so natural at the time. She'd never been a bully and to behave that way now was – she hoped – out of character. Perhaps that was the worrying bit about it. She really would have to try harder to be friends with this lot – would it be so different from trying to stay on good terms with the matelots in *Defiance* – but was that perhaps the root cause? They were quite capable of being fairly rough with each other and she'd seen it happening. Was she really turning into a matelot? Had her behaviour been so changed by three months in sailor company that she had ceased to be feminine? Superintendent Welby certainly seemed to think so but she really would have to try harder to control herself. She knew from school days that the awkward and the bullies never really got accepted, and this was bound to be similar. Back to being a girl among girls, but could she, would she, adapt?

CHAPTER 18:

Mixing in

It felt like only five minutes before the tannoy rasped again with the piercing notes of the bosun's call. "Call the hands, call the hands. Wakey wakey rise and shine, you've had your time, now it's mine. Lash up and stow." Jane rolled over and groaned. She was accustomed to the call but could never pretend she welcomed it, not helped by the cabin having gone cold overnight. She rolled out of her bunk, pulled on underwear under her pyjamas and dived into her warm yachting gear. She grinned at Alicia lying snuggled down with just the top of her head showing. "Lovely day for sunbathing. We'd better jump to it."

"God, I hate mornings. Pass me that bag of clothes, be a dear."

So Jane did and Alicia managed to get half dressed by wrestling under the covers before emerging tousled but triumphant. Elsewhere in the cabin there was chaos as girls struggled out and tried to dress without exposing themselves. Jane, accustomed to this sort of thing, made an early sprint to the washhouse and secured a basin with some hot water before it ran out. Round her girls were splashing, some applying complex makeup, others just dragging a comb through their tangles. Turning to leave she found two waiting politely in line behind her for the sink. Clearly, there were going to be benefits from getting up sharp in the morning.

Back in the cabin she found one of the petty officers waiting, with buckets, mops and brushes. "I want four for the messroom, four for the heads, two for the reception area and the rest in here. Get 'em organised." With that she stomped out. 'Well thanks' thought Jane. 'Why me?' But orders were orders and as girls came back she detailed them off to the different places. Punch she put in charge of the group doing the messroom, Alicia to the reception area and she resisted the temptation to send Merle to the heads. Several of the other girls seemed more self-confident, including a stocky Scots girl with a guttural accent that rang a bell with Jane. "Hello, I'm Jane Beacon and the Chief has asked me to organise the cleaning parties."

"Aye, nice to meet ye. I'm Fiona McPherson frae Buckie. You ever heard o' Buckie?"

"Well, yes I have actually." Jane was hastily tuning her ear to speech patterns familiar from her childhood. "My father's family were farmers from Buchan – near Huntly. We used to holiday there so I got to know the area a bit. Granny still lives there but the others have moved on, like my father. But I think there are still cousins farming round there."

"Oh aye, ye'll ken fit I'm spiering then?"

Jane smiled. "Give me a minute to get used to it again and I should manage."

"That'll mak a braw change. Naebody roond here can mak' me oot at a'."

"Well, it is a bit different."

"Ye didna learn to spier like yon in Buchan?"

"No, I'm born and bred in Devon, went to an English boarding school so quite different really. But my father can still sound quite Scots when he gets upset. Why did you join the Wrens?"

"Och, I aye wanted to get awa' frae that life tae something mair couth. I workit at the fishin' – following the herring fleet an' gutting the fish. See these?" And she held up her hands, red, rough and covered in scars. "That can be a rough way o' living. By the bye, I saw fit ye did last nicht – dinnae try that wi' me lassie or ye micht get a muckle big surprise."

Jane laughed. "Don't worry, I've no intention of trying it with anyone unless they mess me about. Shake on it" and she held her hand out. Jane thought she had calluses, but this girl's hands were like sandpaper. They smiled at each other in respecting acknowledgement. But Jane was still curious. "So you saw the Wrens as an improvement?"

"Och, the fish guttin's a hard trade and I aye wanted to get awa' frae it. I was top quinie at school an' the auld dominie aye spiered me wi' my brain I cud do better. So I thocht maybe the Wrens was a wiy oot."

"Y'know, I hadn't thought of the Wrens as a way to better yourself. But I suppose it could be once you get past this bit."

"Pah, this is naething."

A clatter of buckets brought Jane's mind back to the job in hand.

"Would you mind taking charge of a group to clean the heads? Not much of a job I know but it's got to be done."

"Oh aye, I can dae yon. Far's the gear?"

This time the dialect defeated Jane. "Pardon? I'm not with you."

Fiona took a deep breath. "The mops an' thingies?"

"Oh, I see. Good question – I imagine there're there already. Let me know if they're not." Fiona nodded and sauntered off. 'Now there's a tough one' thought Jane, 'who gives best to no-one'. Faint echoes of her father's way of speaking rang in her mind – his much trimmed by thirty years living in England but the same broad vowels showed. Perhaps that would help Jane understand this interesting girl.

She got the rest of the girls going with scrubbers and mops, put Merle onto dusting round the bunk frames, chests of drawers and window ledge, and kept the buckets filled. She showed several of them how to wield a pusser's scrubber, and knowing the standards that would be expected, chivvied a few of them to try a bit harder. Most of them were still wary of her, but working with her the fear was easing. She noted with interest that Merle did a good thorough job, and gave the windowpanes a polish without being told. After a quick check on the other areas being cleaned, Jane felt reasonably confident when the chief came back to inspect, but wasn't surprised when fault was found in various corners; such is the way of the Navy. Grumblers dealt with and the recleaning completed, she found out where the cleaning gear was stowed and saw it all tidied away. The Chief Wren in charge was being distinctly hostile. "You'll have to be a lot quicker than that to keep us happy."

"Oh come on, this is their first morning and a lot of them didn't have a clue what to do. We'll get better."

"Don't give me lip, girlie. I'll bust you if you get uppity."

"You what? That's not lip, just a statement of fact. Give me a chance."

"The only chance you'll get from me is out the door." The Chief stomped off.

Overnight the snow had stopped so at least they could cross to the messdeck canteen without needing to pull on waterproofs. The burgoo wasn't up to *Defiance's* standards but filled a hole, with bread and – luxury of luxuries – marmalade on the table. Having gone to first sitting there was half an hour spare and as ever a fair number of the girls sloped off for their first cigarette of the day. Jane had never been a smoker and really couldn't understand why anyone would want to be. There was a slightly aimless sense of waiting about until 0845 when a different chief petty officer collected the course and led them off to the clothing store to draw their uniforms. The issuing petty officers sized them up by eye and handed a pile to each Wren, topped off with a pudding basin hat. Punch gave them a problem but eventually they found something big enough, buried at the back of the store. Jane had noticed with interest that Punch didn't have any fat on her – she was trim and solid with a suggestion of fitness about her, just very large. Back in quarters the Wrens realised just how horrible these bluettes were, shapeless navy blue serge coat dresses almost down to their ankles, up to the neck and long-sleeved. Mostly they were faded and obviously well used. Alicia said in disgust. "Are they trying to put us off? It's enough to make you want to leave now." The hats were even worse – shapeless and battered, brims highly variable, and with a musty air to them.

The tannoy suddenly blared. "All hands muster at the entrance. All hands." It struck Jane that, all dressed alike and even if they hated the things, a levelling process was going on. From the socially glossy to the fishwife, they now looked the same and as they congregated in the reception area the chatter was more animated, laughing at each others' sad appearance. A buzz was going round that these Bluettes were leftovers from the First World War, put away in store and now being dragged out again. They certainly smelt as though they could be. Fiona gave Jane a sideways grin, "Och, I thocht oor fishguttin' gear was rough but Good Goad amichty, this is worse." Still grumbling, they were led round the back of the wardroom and into a classroom, which didn't have enough desks so some had to share.

The morning flew by with lectures on badges and ranks, basic ship recognition, and the beginnings of the paperwork they would have to master. By midday they weren't sorry for a break and trooped back to the canteen. Although still bitterly cold with packed snow on the ground, the day had brightened up and a weak sun shone. On the way the petty officer pointed out the NAAFI, the hallowed ground of the quarterdeck –"Never go on that unless you're on a specific duty there" – and the regulating office. The petty officer smartly saluted a couple of officers they passed, and ignored a group of matelots who cheered and whistled as the Wrens went by. Dinner at midday, the main meal of the day for the lower deck, is a solid three-course meal, finishing with a golden pudding. Jane was accustomed to this but some of the girls had difficulty coping with such a large meal then. Around her, adjustments were being made – to habits, to hopes, to humour. A giant hand was taking a grip of them, carrying them along into a new world with its own ways, its own rhythms and language.

During the morning they had each been issued with a small card. It laid down the attributes and attitudes expected from Wrens. Jane sat down to read it with dinner. It said, in part:

"Every person in the Women's Royal Naval Service is to conduct herself with the utmost respect to her superior officer and with strict obedience to his or her orders; she is at all times to discharge every part of her duty with zeal and alacrity and to strive to promote the interest of the Naval Service. Every member will on all occasions endeavour to uphold the honour of the WRNS and by the good order and regularity of her conduct prove herself worthy of the service to which she belongs."

There was more ,but Jane was riveted by this section. She turned to Alicia sat next to her. "Crikey, have you read this stuff? No wonder they've got a bit excited about my behaviour so far. Zeal and alacrity, eh? I suppose it depends on how you interpret it."

Alicia grinned at her. "Hey, I bet you have anyway but just never thought of it that way."

"Well maybe but that's because I just love what I'm doing. The Andrew has been a very mixed blessing so far and look at us now. How can you be zealous in a dress like this?"

"Rise above it, dear heart."

"Yes sure." But they laughed with each other from a sense of mutual determination and set off to find the parade ground..

When they arrived there for the first time pro course 2 found the ground under six inches of hard-packed snow. This made a treacherous surface on which to walk; the cold was intense and once more there was a hint of snow in the air.

A shivering gaggle of girls assembled in the drill shed. The Chief G I allocated to them (Gunnery Instructor, the Navy's drill specialists), with his black leather gaiters and shiny silver whistle chain, looked at this untidy group in some despair. "Do any of you know anything about drill?"

"No, chief, not really."

He raised his eyes to heaven. "Right, we'll split you into two squads. Form into three lines with the tallest on the ends and the shortest in the middle." And with that they were off. They learned to get their dressing right (that is, forming straight lines with each person an arm's length apart), the duties of the right marker were explained and they were initiated into how to salute. They were right and left turned; here the first major snag arose as some of the girls didn't have a clue, which was right or left and bumps and collisions were frequent. Jane found herself right marker for one of the squads. Inevitably Punch took the other squad and surprised people by showing a lightness of foot and a certain elephantine grace in her movement. By 1630 they were tired out, warm and starting to lose concentration. Instead of simply being dismissed they were ordered to march in their squads up the hill and back to their quarters which caused a good deal of hilarity as people slipped, crashed into each other and turned the wrong way at crucial moments. Several times they were overtaken by squads of male ratings going at the double, one of Whale Island's defining characteristics being that all trainees moved about at the double at all times. As the third squad of matelots overtook the girls their chief GI said. "You'll be doing that before you're finished" which produced a loud groan from the ranks.

Sub-zero temperatures, driving snow and exhaustion meant that few took the chance to go ashore in the evening. But a hot bath and a decent supper of HITS – tinned Herrings In Tomato Sauce – saw some general revival and the chat reverberated in the messroom in the evening. Already groups were forming, but Jane made a point of trying to talk to different lots. There was a London gang, a bunch of Janners to whom Jane would naturally belong, and some who had already been together in Pompey. Jane was sitting with Fiona scratching for recall of the impenetrable Doric when Alicia came over and said "Jane, you must come and meet Camilla. She was at Benenden and I think you played hockey against her in '38 as well."

Jane turned to Fiona "Do excuse me, it looks like I'm being dragged off."

Fiona gave the pair a very ironic look "Oh aye, on ye gang."

Walking across, Jane said. "I like that girl. She's got something unbeatable about her."

"Is that right? I must try to get to know her."

"You'll have problems. Her dialect is so thick I struggle and I thought I knew it. But there's a lot of spirit there."

Cabin Two was a mirror image of Cabin Three; the girl was sitting close to the stove. "Camilla, this is Jane I told you about. Jane meet Camilla."

They smiled, shook hands and looked at each other. Again there was that sense of half recognition. "Were you full back when we played? I've a funny feeling it was you flattened me at one stage."

"You were the one I got! Sorry."

"Took me a week to recover."

They looked at each other cautiously. "How long have you been in?"

"A fortnight now. I'm to be a teleprinter operator apparently. And you?"

"Three months now. I'm being tried out on the harbour boats down at Guzz to see if Wrens can work on them. Going well so far but it's early days."

"Three months makes you a positive veteran. Alicia was telling me you got quite violent with one of the girls last night." Camilla was small and dainty and clearly didn't fancy anything physical.

"Oh yes well, the stupid girl tried to mess me around and I won't have it. I'm not normally like that but I'm finding the hard way that I can occasionally lose it. Don't worry, I won't jump on you."

"Well that's a relief I suppose. Was your father in the services?"

"Yes and no, he's a doctor, but he started out in the Navy. We're based down near Plymouth but he's fairly widely known for his chest work. And yours?"

"Oh, that's interesting. Mine's a surgeon at Guys – specialises in heart work."

Suddenly there was a thawing between them, a recognition of mutual standings.

Coming back into cabin three Jane found it deserted except for one girl huddled by the stove. "Where is everyone?" asked Jane. The girl jumped and whirled round looking at Jane in sheer terror. All she could say was "Kye, kye." The girl was thin and scrawny, with lank brown hair and a pinched narrow face. Her only striking feature was a pair of light hazel eyes, which had a wary intensity. Whatever age she actually was, she looked like a child. She shrank as Jane tried to approach her. She had changed out of her bluette and her clothes were thin too, inadequate for the harsh weather outside and her shoes little more than sandals. 'No wonder she looks frozen,' thought Jane. "What's your name?"

With an effort the girl spoke "Dora".

"Don't worry, Dora" said Jane "I'm not going to bite you."

The girl just shook her head, blank fear obliterating all else.

"Don't you have any other clothes?"

She found her tongue. "Naw- they said we'd get something when we got here, but I didn't know it would only be a couple of crummy dresses and a stupid hat."

"So why aren't you wearing one now?"

"Got to save 'em for best, 'aven't I?"

This perplexed Jane. "What? These things are made for rough treatment. Surely you'd be better in one?"

"Naw, they're too good to use unless I have to."

The girl's East End twang was strong but somehow it wasn't Cockney.

"Where are you from?"

"Gravesend." Suddenly the dam burst. "I didn't know I was going to be with a bunch of toffs like you lot. I thought this might get me away from me pa and his tricks, but I'm all wrong here, aren't I?"

"What tricks did your father get up to?"

"Oh, y'know, he'd want to do things to me when he came home drunk. Horrible it was."

Jane didn't know but suspected there was something deep and dark here, in a different world.

"So you joined the Wrens to get away from that?"

Dora nodded vigorously, the first sign of real life she'd shown.

"How did you get in?"

"I told 'em me dad was a waterman, which is kind of half true. Watery connections anyhow. The vicar organised two references for me and me mam forged the third one. And I can read and write, y'know." This last had a defiant edge to it.

"But when you got here it wasn't what you expected?"

Again Dora nodded vigorously. "I've made a right mistake being here, I don't belong and I'm going to pack it in, in the morning. I can't keep up with you lot with your fancy clothes and lah-de-dah ways."

"Dora you mustn't do that. The Wrens can take you in, they can give you sanctuary."

"What's one of them?"

"A sanctuary is where you're inside and safe and you're part of the others around you. You can be too."

Bitterness suddenly broke through. "Ow the 'ell can I do that? I've only got the clothes I stand up in, I ain't got your polish or, or,........" suddenly she gave a brilliant bit of mimicry. "*You must come and meet Camilla, she played hockey against you in '38.* I can't compete with that. And what's Benenden? A reformatory?"

Jane winced. 'It might as well have been,' she thought. That jibe was very close to the bone. Something strong but still only half-formed was stirring inside Jane. "Dora, you mustn't give up. You just mustn't. I think it's much more important that you should stay in than any of us gals who can fall back on our families any time."

"Aw sure, but how?"

Jane could see pride warring with unhappiness and desperation. "Would you accept help from the rest of us?"

There was immediate wariness. "Wot kind of help? I can't do much favours in return."

"Oh, we've got spare clothes and toiletries we could give you and perhaps a warm pair of shoes. I can arrange that if you like." Jane had no idea how, but it never occurred to her that she couldn't. She'd already heard of a good hairdresser in cabin one.

"Yeah, but you're goin' to want somefink back, ain't you?" In her distress Dora's accent had become much stronger.

Jane pondered this for a moment. "I don't see why. I think you might find the girls a lot kinder than that."

Pride suddenly flared. "I don't need no charity. I can go back on the game if I have to."

"But Dora you don't have to. What I'm talking about is nothing to us and if it helps you to stay in and keep off the game, it'd be stuff well used. Listen, I don't have to tell the others what you've just told me but I'm sure I could get something organised for you. Please, let me try before you give up."

Dora wavered, pride and a cautious, almost timorous hope struggling inside her. "Ow would you do that?"

"We can get you a good haircut, some good warm clothes, - would you like underwear? And we'd try to keep you in with us. We're not that snooty y'know. Remember what First Officer Brown said – we're all just pro Wrens."

"Yeah but we're not really, are we? I've seen you palling up already with others of your own kind."

CHAPTER 18: Mixing in

"Oh Dora...." Jane shook her head in frustration. It was all so true but there was another side to the coin. "Listen, please let's us both try. Don't do anything until I see if I can help. I promise you I don't want anything in return. Just to know you'd managed to pull through would be enough."

"Oh, all right, I s'pose I've nothing to lose."

Jane smiled and on impulse pulled the girl to her feet and hugged her. Dora expected that to be a sexual contact – she knew no other - and was ready to respond as she'd been taught so didn't quite know what to do when Jane just let go again. "I promise you, no hidden agendas, no wanting something in return, no hoity-toity charity. Just a wish to help. Maybe that's hoity-toity in itself but it's all I can do."

Quietly, over the next couple of days, a haircut was arranged which left Dora with a smart, just-off-the-collar style with curled ends. A pile of warm clothing anonymously appeared on her bunk and a pretty bag of toiletries, soap, shampoo, bath salts, lipstick, talcum powder, a facecloth, a hairbrush and hair curlers, even a toothbrush and toothpaste. Jane had had a word with the chief Wren who had taken them to get their bluettes; a small pile of naval underwear and a new pair of black leather lace-up shoes materialised – serviceable rather than smart but practical in a sub-zero January. Equally quietly Jane had dropped a word in the ear of her own lot who started to make a point of including Dora. A week later the thin scared face had some fullness to it, she was seen to experiment with a little lipstick, she had a tentative little smile as she looked at herself in the mirror and the instinctive wariness was easing. From hiding in a corner Dora was starting to join in.

* * * * *

Looking back at those early days from 1944 Jane smiled, a gentle reminiscent smile, which told me a new tale was emerging. "Y'know, on that pro course we turned out onto the parade ground in sub-zero temperatures and worked so hard we ended up hot. Of all the places to learn drill in, Whale Island had to be about the toughest. Its parade ground is one of the most hallowed places in Naval mythology. Generations of sailors have learnt their drill there, and in the open-fronted drill shed beside it. I found that the Naval approach to drill was at an angle, and not what I expected. It is seen as an adjunct to forming individuals into cohesive groups, and developing a sense of smartness and pride in the uniform. Unlike the Army, marching and drilling for its own sake has only ever been a minor part of the naval life. There is limited call for it on board a ship. From the start there were serious doubts about whether drill had any part to play in the training and utilisation of Wrens: did it make a cook or a writer/secretary a better

173

one? Apparently there was a brisk debate about whether our pro course should do it or not. But our director, Vera Laughton Mathews, was a strong advocate for it and she got her way. Being an articulate lady she expressed her views very clearly in response to the fundamental question:

"A march is different. One loses the sense of individuality.
There are no longer single human beings but one unit,
one soul, one aim. And marching oneself one forgets
one's own small life and becomes merged in something
bigger, a great comradeship, 'shoulder to shoulder
and friend to friend.'"

"And so we learnt to march and salute and lots of other strange things you wouldn't otherwise do." She shook her head in sad recall. "The silly thing is I really did very little ever again – usually managed to get out of it by being on the water. And did it do us any good? Strangely enough, our director was right: at the time it achieved its purpose in giving us a common goal that we had to do jointly to get anywhere. No, I've no regrets at having mastered it but I'm in no rush to go through it all again. And getting the hang of it did help us all to merge into the Navy throughout our time in the Wrens."

All of this fitted a pattern, a pattern of women fitting in to a powerfully male world and adapting to its mores. Since first meeting Jane I had become intrigued by the background to this and had researched it. One of the more startling things I found was that the Wrens in World War Two were in an anomalous position. The Naval Discipline Act was never applied to them and legally, throughout the war, they were civilians. They were subject to various disciplinary sanctions from loss of pay and confined to quarters to the ultimate, which was discharge from the service. Anything criminal was referred to the civilian courts. On very rare occasions more fierce treatment was meted out. Although it was fading fast from the armed services, corporal punishment for juveniles was still a quite normal part of everyday life in the civilian population.

Apparently Senior Naval Officers blanched at the Naval Discipline Act being applied to fragrant females, and when the other women's services came under military discipline acts in 1942, the Admiralty refused to countenance that for the Wrens despite active lobbying in favour by the WRNS Director. This was eased by the Wrens themselves: competition to get into the Service was fierce and although there were the inevitable failures they were few by comparison with the other women's services. Desertions were rare, helped by a humane policy towards Wrens who had a genuine reason to want out. Very largely, the WRNS was a disciplined and well-regulated service because its members chose to be.

CHAPTER 19:
Solidarity in the Abyss

In Jane's probationer group an unspoken determination had quickly grown up to surmount all the demands and challenges thrown at them. It didn't stop them grumbling about chilblains and sore feet, as they had to drill in their own shoes. Uniform footwear had not been issued and quite a few girls didn't have really suitable shoes for the hard useage they were now getting. Jane was fortunate in having her sturdy brogues, even if they were brown which caused their Chief GI some initial pain. Ironically, the best-shod girl on the course was now Dora, with her stout naval lace-ups designed for the job. Wren probationer course 2 took some pride in mastering drill, determined to be as good at this military attribute as any mere male. Being shouted at troubled the girls not at all.

The miserable weather persisted and there was little encouragement to going ashore. On her third evening there Jane got out her concertina and began playing quietly to entertain herself. A slow Tango, so natural for the instrument, gently rolled round the cabin and in no time a group had formed round Jane. She livened the tunes up a bit. Then Fiona pushed forward and asked to have a go. "You play too?"
 "Oh aye, I play accordion in a dance band back hame."
 So Fiona took over and played lively Scottish dance numbers for a while before handing back to Jane. Another little bond had formed between them. Then Jane played some songs, and by the fifteen minute warning for pipe down a rip-roaring sing-song was going on with girls from other cabins joining in. The sense of camaraderie among this uniformly bluette-clad but mixed group was growing stronger.

Each day, events followed the same pattern, with the squads dodging between the snow showers and trying to keep warm. For all but a few, drill became easier; Jane found a similarity to dance in its choreographed and rhythmic movements, which helped. On day five when they came back from more marching and saluting, there was a letter for Jane pinned on the notice board, hand delivered to the guardhouse. Puzzled, Jane opened it and found a note from Jean-Pierre inside.

Ma Cherie,
I am here in Portsmouth to see you. I must see you
before I go again on Sunday. Can you get away for

a while? Leave a note at the guardhouse and I will
pick it up.
Love
Jean-Pierre

This put Jane in a quandary. Already, in her mind Jean-Pierre was the past, a bit of a mixed memory with its warmer elements, but no longer relevant. Why must he see her? Presumably there had to be some problem, which she'd better find out about. She went to the quarters officer, who had thawed a lot since their first brush, and explained the matter, asking if she could have her one ten-thirty pass in the next day or two. "Is he your boyfriend?" queried the quarters officer.

"He used to be, but I thought he'd been posted back to France permanently and I'm surprised to find him here now. I'd better find out what his problem is."

"All right, you can have your pass for tomorrow night but don't be late back, whatever you do." Jane nipped down to the guardhouse to leave a note saying she'd be there at six thirty.

Day six passed routinely enough. It was a sharp clear day without snow so they practised their drill on the parade ground, although there were skids and falls enough whenever they tried to change direction. Back in quarters Jane had a quick bath then debated what to wear. The temperature had been falling all day from an already low level and the cold was intense. She settled for the tweed skirt and her thickest polo neck jumper, the serviceable brogues which were starting to show signs of wear, and just in case, her oilskins and sou'wester on top. She told Alicia what she was up to then headed down to the guardhouse, presented her identity card and late pass, then strode briskly across the causeway trying hard to warm up a bit. Jean-Pierre was waiting as she reached the shore. They embraced and kissed. "Jean-Pierre, *qu'est que fait?* Is something wrong?"

"No, my lovely, nothing is wrong but I just had to see you one more time. I've been dreaming about you all the time since I went home."

Relief mixed with irritation flooded through Jane. "Really, is that all? When I got your note I thought something terrible must have happened. I've got my only late pass for tonight but I must be back by ten-thirty. What are we going to do?"

"I'm booked into a little hotel in the middle of the town and fixed it with the people there for us to use my room. We can have dinner there as well."

"You what? You've got a nerve. We're finished Jean-Pierre. I thought about it a bit and decided I don't want to get involved with married men, starting with you. So forget about the bedroom."

He smiled, shook his head and shrugged. "Well, let's go for dinner anyway." The walk was long enough in trying conditions so Jane wasn't sorry to get there. The hotel proved to be a dingy little place with a sad-faced receptionist who looked at Jane without enthusiasm. Surprisingly, the food was passable and they managed a half decent bottle of burgundy, Jane relaxing as the meal went on. Echoes of previous similar occasions crowded into her mind as they laughed and reminisced about the problems of making love in *Defiance*. She was being reminded again what fun and good company Jean-Pierre was and by the end of the meal was thinking 'Oh, so what. Enjoy one more session with him' her fondness for him resurfacing and overriding her doubts. He was obviously wound up and needing it.

With dinner over and time to spare they went upstairs and thoroughly enjoyed an hour in bed. He had lost none of his skill at pleasuring her. At the end of that they agreed this had to be the end, Jean-Pierre to forget about her and return to France, his Navy and his family, Jane just to get on with her life in the Wrens. Her deadline for being back in quarters always at the back of her mind, Jane kept checking her watch to Jean-Pierre's annoyance. "But Jean-Pierre, I can't be late. You're an officer. You must know how important it is not to miss end of shore leave."

"Yes, I suppose so. Let's get you a taxi back."

They went down to the entrance to find things had changed while they were tucked away. The world was coated in ice. Heavy rain was falling but as it landed it instantly froze, covering everything. The streets were deserted – no traffic, no people, just silence. 'This doesn't look good' thought Jane 'Getting back isn't going to be easy'. She said her farewells and stepped out into the deep darkness of the blackout, but struggling even to see her feet she hadn't gone more than a few yards when she slipped, went her length and found herself rapidly getting coated in ice as well. Worried, she retreated to the hotel to try to ring the guardhouse to pass a message that she wouldn't be able to get back. But the phone lines were dead. "Jean-Pierre, what am I going to do? I just can't stay out."

"It looks like you will have to, my lovely. You can stay here."

"Well thanks, but I'm in deep trouble. I dread to think what will happen if I don't turn up." She made another attempt at walking back but again didn't get very far, so gave up and came back. Shrugging off the worries about what awaited her when she did get back, she snuggled up with Jean-Pierre and they enjoyed themselves all over again. The buzzing glow through her body by the time they'd finished went some way to stilling the apprehension in her heart.

She was up early in the morning, managed to coax some tea and toast from the management, said good-bye all over again and stepped out as soon as there was daylight to see. The freezing rain had lightened, making walking possible if perilous. Everything was thickly coated in ice and she had to step carefully. There was virtually no-one about but as luck would have it she made it back to the guardhouse just as First Officer Brown arrived. She gave Jane a startled look. "Are you just coming back now, Beacon?"

"Yes, ma'am, I tried last night but it was impossible. No taxis, no buses, walking dangerous in the blackout and the rain freezing on me when I stepped out."

"I see. Let Wren Beacon through, please." This to the guardhouse crushers regarding the little tableau with amusement. "Where did you stay, not being able to get back?"

Jane paused for a moment. "With a friend, ma'am. I was offered a bed for the night."

"So not only are you hopelessly adrift over leave, but you're admitting to spending the night with a 'friend'. I am not impressed to say the least."

"Yes ma'am but I did try to get back. It simply wasn't possible."

"Hmm, we'll see about that. Get changed into your bluette then report to my office in half an hour."

She was subject to nervous giggles and sideways looks by her cabin mates when she arrived back, a tension in the air. Saying nothing she changed quickly and presented herself to First Officer Brown's office as instructed. There she found the quarters officer and an unknown naval Commander, looking grim-faced. "Beacon, you must be aware that staying out all night is a serious breach of the disciplinary code, no matter what excuses you might think the weather gives. I have investigated this with the quarters officer and it turns out you were going to see a man – a former boyfriend, I believe. You were told very clearly you could not do things like that on the probationer course yet you did it. We cannot allow a breach of discipline like this to go unpunished and we feel we have no choice but to give exemplary punishment for it. I have checked with Commander Parker here and we are within our rights to do so. Unless you have anything more to say we will proceed." First Officer Brown gave Jane an enquiring look.

Jane shook her head, feeling that she was in some sort of nightmare. 'Not again,' she was thinking 'that bloody Frenchman has brought me more than enough trouble.' The whole thing seemed detached and far away, as though watching a film about someone else.

"But I couldn't get back, ma'am."

"That is no excuse. You should not have gone in the first place if you weren't going to get back. Go to the mess room and we will meet you there."

As she came in to the mess she was surprised to find her entire course assembled, sitting on the benches and keeping very quiet. Both the Wren petty officers were waiting at the far end and beckoned to Jane to come to the front. There she was startled to be seized, flung face down on a table, her arms and legs tied to the table legs despite struggling against this treatment. First Officer Brown came in. "As you are aware, Wren Beacon here elected to stay out all night with her boyfriend. Quite apart from the morals of it, we made it plain when you started that you would be subject to strict discipline and curfew while on this course and a deliberate flouting of the rules on this scale cannot be condoned. Therefore Beacon is to be subject to exemplary punishment. Proceed, chief petty officer."

To her dismay Jane saw that Chief Jenkins, with whom she had had sharp words half a dozen times was waiting with a cane in her hand. Jane's skirt was flung up over her back and her knickers pulled down by an unseen hand. Chief Jenkins stepped forward, swishing the cane. Jane, who had never been chastised in her life, looked at this with horror. "You can't do this. It's assault" She screamed.

"Oh yes we can, young lady." And the first stroke fell. Jane gritted her teeth and tried not to shriek, but with the third one she gave a yelp, which lengthened into a wail then a continuous screaming howl with each succeeding stroke. A mixture of rage, humiliation and agony coursed through her, tempered slightly by relief when the blows ended after the tenth one. Try as she might she couldn't stop herself bawling, a keening howl of despair and misery driven by the pain. She could feel trickles of blood running down the back of her thighs. Her knickers were pulled up, the skirt dropped and she was untied but unable to move – it hurt too much. In the distance she could here Wrens crying and retching as they left the room.

A voice said "Better take her to the sick bay. Those cuts may need treating."

'What have they done to me?' wondered Jane. She was picked up and dumped – face down – onto a stretcher. The sick bay VAD nurse specially imported for the Wrens' course had had virtually nothing to do and was looking forward to a patient to deal with, but took one look at Jane's cuts and called the doctor. He went pale when he saw the mess on her buttocks.

"Good God, what have they done to you?" Jane was still struggling with gasping sobs and couldn't give a coherent explanation but managed "Punishment – caning – assault – bastards."

"I think we might just give you some pain relief here" And a minute later an injection brought blessed relief before she drifted off into oblivion.

CHAPTER 19: Solidarity in the Abyss

When she came round again she was tucked up in bed, face down, and for a moment hazy wonderings passed by. Then she tried to move and the stab of pain brought her fully conscious with a squeal and a jerk. It all came back too vividly. A VAD nurse heard her and came over. "How is it?"

"Sore. Bloody sore. What's the time?"

"Around nine o'clock in the evening. Can you move at all?"

"I can try." She eased off the bed and stood up. "God that hurts." As she tried to move her face screwed up in agony and she muttered "fuck fuck fuck" under her breath.

"That's not surprising. We've treated your cuts and covered a couple with gauze but I'm afraid you'll just have to live with the bruising until it fades. I wouldn't sit down for a while if I were you."

"I don't think I was going to try. Any chance of anything to eat? I'm starving."

She tucked into a plateful of spam sandwiches and a cup of tea – standing up - and felt slightly better.

"Is there a mirror here? I'd like to look at this lot."

Yes, but maybe that's not such a good idea – it looks pretty horrible."

"I can take it, don't worry." But even so she was appalled at the deep weals, raw flesh showing through in places where the skin had been flayed off, the cuts surrounded by a black bruised mass that had been her buttocks." Can I stay here overnight? I don't think I want to go back to my cabin."

"Well yes you can but there will only be an SBA on overnight. Do you mind?"

"A mere male? Naw, doesn't bother me." For some reason Jane couldn't fathom this sent the VAD nurse into fits of giggles.

Jane lay down and turmoil took over. Her mind roamed over the day's events and rage, humiliation and sheer fright boiled inside her. She started to tremble uncontrollably. Suddenly it all became too much and she started to scream and howl. The VAD hurried over and held her hand then wrapped her arms round the shrieking shaking mess who tried to speak but it was incoherent gabbling in which 'Bastards ' was occasionally decipherable. Terrified, Jane stared blankly into the middle distance, all rational thought boiled away in the seething but helpless rage inside her, until the howls settled into a steady keening as some part of her young self left her never to return. This went on for perhaps fifteen minutes before she subsided into sniffling sobs, still crying her heart out and muttering "It's not fair" in a petulant childish whimper but suddenly she went limp and flaked out on the bed.

The nurse, with her apron tear-soaked down the front, looked at Jane sadly. "I'll get the doctor" she said and went to the phone. Ten minutes later the night duty medic arrived, had the situation explained to him and came over to Jane with a couple of pills. This set her off again. "I don't want your bloody pills. I want my bum fixed."

The young newly qualified doctor looked helpless. "What else can I do? You need to calm down, young lady, and these will help."

In the red confusion in her brain a sudden shaft of clarity shone on some corner and her determination came surging back. She shouted at the doctor "I will not be defeated. Do not mess around with me, d 'you hear me?"

Now the doctor looked startled and puzzled. "Well, all right, suit yourself but these will help y'know."

"Give me one then leave me alone, please."

He shrugged his shoulders, handed one pill over and left. The VAD returned and helped Jane to take the pill, then was asked to help her to the heads. As well as the necessary, done with difficulty standing up, Jane stripped and basin washed as best she could then shambled back to the cot in the sick bay. Feeling mentally cleansed as much as bodily, with difficulty Jane lay down on her tummy again. The VAD nurse pulled up the blankets and wished her good night. From there, all emotion spent and the pill taking effect, deep nothingness came quickly.

She woke early, struggled to her feet and stiffly moved over to the sick bay desk where the night SBA was dozing gently with his feet up. "Excuse me." This woke him with a start. "Yes Jenny, what is it?"

"Can you give me some of the ointment they put on my cuts? I think I'm all right for going back to my quarters now." He rummaged around and gave her a pot-full. Arriving back in her cabin shortly after morning 'call the hands' she found her cabin mates in various states of half dress, lots of buzzing activity and chatter going on which silenced as she entered the cabin. They all looked her as though she were from another planet. "Please carry on," she said. "I'm only here to pick up some clothes." She put on her other bluette and moved out stiffly, going over to the canteen for a cup of tea. Sitting being impossible she stood by the window looking out over the frozen ice which blanketed everything. In a way it was rather beautiful, but clearly there wasn't going to be much outdoor activity that day. The freezing rain continued to fall.

After breakfast she was summoned to the First Officer's office again. Grimly she marched in, glaring at First Officer Brown. "Right Beacon, you must realise that we had to do that. If you had been allowed to get away with simply turning up in the morning we would have had anarchy on our hands in no time at all so we decided to make an example of you."

"Yes, but I told you it was impossible to get back until morning. This is grossly unfair as well as a sadistic assault which I'm going to take up."

"Well, that's up to you but be assured we were within our rights. We did check first and junior Wrens under training can be subject to corporal punishment."

"But that wasn't just corporal punishment – it was a vicious attack. It looks like I'll be permanently scarred."

"As far as we're concerned you asked for it. At the end of the day it's better for us to lose one Wren, no matter how talented, than to lose lots more because they think they can get away with it too. You may be quite sure that the rest of the course will now be very careful not to be late."

"Lose one Wren? Why? Am I being put over the wall as well?"

"Well, we didn't imagine you would want to stay after that punishment. You're here voluntarily so you don't have to take any more."

The red mist was rising. "I will not be defeated. I will not be driven out!" she shouted, glaring hard. She banged a fist on Brown's desk. "You will have to throw me out to get rid of me, because I'm not going voluntarily."

First Officer Brown was thoroughly taken aback. "Oh dear, I hadn't expected you to be like that. If you're going to be stubborn about it that does rather change things. I suppose we could let you finish the course then we'll make a decision. In fact I think I'll refer this to higher authority for a ruling. Are you sure you can manage the marching?"

Jane pulled her mouth down grimly. "Let me make it quite clear. I will do everything that's required of me for as long as I'm allowed to stay on the course. If I have to do handstands I will, pain or no pain."

"Very well, in that case you should join the rest in the classroom. But you will be confined to barracks for the rest of the course and this will go on your disciplinary record."

"Hah! My disciplinary record is already peppered with injustices so one more doesn't make much difference."

"Yes, you do seem to have spent most of your time so far in trouble. I'm not sure we want girls like you."

"Oh this is ridiculous. Isn't it enough that I am doing well on the course?"

"Not for the Wrens it isn't. And you do not speak to me like that."

"Do you really think I care? After what you've done to me already any other punishment is meaningless. You've lost it with me I'm afraid." And Jane lowered her head to be level with Brown's and glared deep into her eyes. She hissed quietly "let me make it quite clear. I want to stay in the Wrens because of what I do. So I will behave myself and not give you trouble but you needn't fool yourself for one moment that I'm doing it from fear or respect for you."

First Officer Brown had gone white and her hands trembled as she tried to return the fierce stare coming to her. Taking a tremulous breath she said. "You can go now."

Jane stalked out still seething with rage. Negotiating the icy conditions was not easy but she got there, quietly easing into the back of the class. Come lunchtime the group marched over to the canteen with Jane struggling along at the back. Everyone was avoiding her eye while giving her quiet surreptitious glances. Alicia broke the tension. "When are you going, Jane? We'll help you pack."

"Get this straight. I am not going. I've told them they'll have to throw me out to get rid of me and it seems they don't want to do that, so I'm staying here. It may not be easy but I'm damned if they will push me out like that. It's all being referred to a higher level now anyway."

"But Jane, do you want to stay after the way they've treated you? That was appalling."

"Yes I do. My job is wonderful and it's only this bunch of sadists that spoil it. Besides, there's a war on and they'll need us all."

"Why did you stay out all night anyway? We knew it wasn't allowed."

"Because I couldn't get back with the ice falling. No transport, impossible to walk in the blackout, phone lines dead, I was stuck so just stayed with the ex all night."

Abruptly Merle chipped in. "The ex, hm? You were out sleeping with a boyfriend all night and expected the weather to excuse you in the morning? No wonder they took a dim view of it."

"Oh come on Merle, I could wish it was only an excuse."

"Jane, we've been lectured in the classroom already about how they expect us to behave. You sat there and listened to them then went off and did exactly the opposite. Has this boyfriend being going for some time?"

"About three months now, but it's finished and he's gone back to France."

"French, eh? How romantic. I bet he wasn't your first."

"Yes he was dammit. How dare you!"

This argument had drawn in a large part of the course, listening avidly. To her surprise Dora spoke up. " 'Aven't you ever stayed out? That's nothing compared with a thrashing like they gave Jane. Give 'er a break."

In Jane's absence Camilla had rather taken over leadership of the group and she piped up "Sorry to break this up but its time to get over to the gym. We're doing our stuff there instead of skating over the ice." As they got up to go Camilla wandered over to Jane and said. "I do think you're awfully brave to keep going. I don't think I could. Are you sure you can manage? We'll all help as much as we can but it's not going to be easy."

"I don't suppose it is but I'm not going to let them defeat me."

The afternoon was as difficult as she had feared, the pain intense at times but she battled on, driven along by anger and determination.

Back in quarters after supper she quietly slipped off to the heads and examined her backside as best she could with a makeup mirror. The weals didn't seem to have broken open although the bruising was as deep as before, so she re-applied ointment and eased her way back, collapsing face down on her bunk. In no time a group of girls had gathered round, all offering support. On the one hand they seemed to see Jane as something apart now, on the other there was a strong sense of group solidarity and sympathy for her state. Jane tried to make light of it. "Instead of kissing the gunner's daughter, I suppose I am the gunner's daughter now."

"Apparently the doctor who dealt with your cuts has written a letter of protest to the Captain here, with a copy to our Director. He's let it be known that he considers it barbaric, what was done to you. Did you know that he'd taken a couple of colour photos of your battered backside?"

"What? That's horrible, unless he's going to use them in evidence. Come to think of it, if there are any repercussions it might be quite useful to have them."

Alicia picked up on this. "Do you think we should write and complain as well? I'm not sure I want to stay in a service that can do things like that to you, war or no war."

Jane looked doubtful. "Thanks Alicia but there's no point in you getting into trouble too just for me. It would have to be all of you and does everyone feel that strongly about it?"

"I think you'll find they do. The general feeling was that it was utterly disgusting and right out of proportion. While you were in sick bay Brown spoke to us at lunchtime and warned us that we were all in line for similar treatment if we didn't behave. Nobody mentioned that to me when I joined up."

Punch had said very little so far but now joined in. "I'll sign it for sure." She said "And take it round an' make sure everyone else does too. Oi've seen some dodgy things on the docks but nothing as bad as that."

Camilla suddenly took charge. "All right, what shall we say? Presumably it has to go to our Director. 'Dear Mrs Director, we are utterly disgusted and frightened' "

Here Alicia cut in "Don't be too melodramatic about it. Just state things plainly. Remember what we were taught in English class."

So Alicia and Camilla put their heads together to draft the letter, helped by a load of suggestions from the group. They were progressing well when Merle, who had sat on the fringe of the group, suddenly said "It might be better if we acknowledged a bit of guilt, but that the offence didn't merit the level of punishment." Jane looked up, startled by this. "Oh, are you going to sign it too, Merle?"

"I most certainly am. I still think you asked for it a bit but dear me, I don't want to see that going on regularly. I wonder if the Director knows this can happen? There's nothing in the draft disciplinary code about it."

They all swung round to look at Merle. "You've seen a disciplinary code? That's more than I have" said Camilla, and the others nodded agreement.

"Oh yes, when I visited my mother at HQ I was invited to have a look at it and comment and it all seemed very fair and sensible. No mention of this savagery. So yes, I'll sign because of the principle involved. I'm damned if I would allow myself to be caned like that."

There was short silence, then Camilla asked "Your mother works at Headquarters? I don't think we knew that. What does she do?"

"She's a first officer on the intake staff. They're desperately rushed with all the applications just now."

"Might that be a way of getting our letter into the Director's hands?"

"You don't need to. Our Director has a principle that she has to see every letter that's addressed to her personally. I'll tell you how to address it correctly for that."

"How useful. Thanks Merle."

"There's just one thing – officially any complaint should be handed to First Officer Brown here – there's a system for taking up complaints which goes through your own officers. For a group to get together and go straight over her head is effectively mutiny, I think you'll find, which is punishable by hanging."

The group laughed uneasily. "Do we really care?" Asked Alicia. "I can't imagine they'd want to hang forty-odd Wrens – think of the publicity. And besides, I'd rather be thrown out than stay in an outfit which treats people like this. To hell with it, let's take the chance." And the others nodded agreement. "Merle, are you still in?"

"Oh yes, I'll take my chances but I thought you should know the risk you're taking."

"You certainly seem to know about these things, Merle. What did you do before joining?

"I was training to be a solicitor and I've always had an interest in naval law."

"Well well." And they all nodded in agreement.

After another half hour's debate and pencil chewing the draft was agreed. Punch proved to have beautiful copperplate handwriting – this huge girl was full of surprises – so she wrote out a fair copy.

Letter written, the girls sat around wondering what else they could do, if anything. A fair-haired and deeply sunburnt girl who had said very little except to introduce herself as Evadne, suddenly started talking in a low sing-song almost trance-like way. Her clipped accent was strong. "Back in Rhodesia I've watched the elephants a lot. Did you know that herds of elephants are all female? They kick the males out once they mature. There's a tremendously strong group solidarity, all sisters together and if one takes sick the others all gather round to protect her from predators. Same for their babies - maybe we should be like that too - gather round to protect our sick sister."

There was a low murmour of approval at the thought and Merle laughed. "Real light-weight elephants we'd be, but I like the idea. Come on girls, are we like elephants too?" The mood lightened as they all laughed at the idea

"Too right and we are. All for one and one for all."

With mock solemnity Camilla intoned "We elephants promise to protect each other." The confusion the staff had with elephant jokes and secret trunk communications for the rest of the course was enormous – as big as an elephant, really.

After the elephant debate it went quiet and reflective in the group. Fiona got up, picked up Jane's concertina and started playing, gentle lullabies and highland laments. A restorative peace settled over them. This ruminative atmosphere was abruptly interrupted by the chief Wren putting her head round the door "Fifteen minutes to pipe down. Shake your arses."

Jerked back into a harsher world they moved.

Jane eased off her bunk with difficulty, Fiona lending her a hand to get upright. "Come on, sick elephant. We're gathering round."

"Take me to the watering hole." But even cleaning her teeth was difficult and, having stiffened up, she just managed to shuffle back as pipe down was broadcast. Heading to her cabin she met Chief Wren Jenkins who had caned her. The red mist suddenly came over her again. She looked the woman straight in the eye and hissed "I'll get you for this one of these days. Just you remember that."

The chief looked at her contemptuously "Save your breath, little girl. You'll never get near me."

"Don't you bank on it? I shan't forget you." And they passed on.

CHAPTER 20:
Not Defeated

As Cabin Three's inmates settled for the night, the buzz of gentle determination that had been so alive, calmed down with them. But Jane lay awake in the dark for some time, her anger after the encounter in the alleyway oozing away. Then doubts came creeping in. Perhaps she should get out? She thought of all the fun that working on *Amaryllis* had been; that alone made staying in worth it. But this was far worse than her gruesome Jossman or even the Superintendent in a temper. As she lay there the doubts got bigger in the darkness and she had a poor night's sleep, not helped by stabs of pain whenever she rolled over enough to put pressure on her damaged bits.

Dragging herself out in the morning, Jane was about ready to quit. By 'Call the hands' she was feeling very small and frightened and the thought of a safe and loving home seemed tempting. As they dressed the chatter in the cabin was all about the letter and several of the girls told Jane, how brave she was to keep going. Despite feeling anything but inside, she pulled on her bluette and joined the queue for the washhouse. The burgoo seemed particularly horrible that morning and a rumble of complaint went round the canteen, but Jane felt better for it.

The ice storm had ceased and there was a breathless stillness in the air. It remained bitterly cold but the sun shone on a brilliant white world and it seemed a better place. They went on a day out, mercifully by bus, to visit a major communications centre being developed at a stately home near Petersfield. Jane felt conspicuous standing at the back but the driver didn't seem bothered – his attention was much too taken up with keeping the slithering bus on the road. By the time they got back to their quarters late in the afternoon Punch had collected all but five signatures. The five were simply too scared to do anything that might draw attention to themselves and even Punch standing over them looking significant couldn't penetrate that fear. Taking no chances Alicia and Camilla went ashore in the evening and posted the letter at the main post office. Next day, coming back to the cabin Jane found her other bluette and knickers neatly pressed and laid out on her bunk, freshly cleaned with the bloodstains gone.

"Oh, what happened here?" she asked. Alicia gave her a grin and said "We decided to wash them for you. Regard it as a small token of solidarity. I'm sure those elephants would have."

CHAPTER 20: Not Defeated

This really took Jane aback. "Well, thank you, that is kind." Somehow this little gesture lessened the pain a bit. In her emotional state she couldn't help having a little weep once no-one was looking. Slowly over the next days the discomfort eased, although sitting down was still impossible.

At the same time the worst of the ice coating started to melt a bit; it was still bitterly cold but the icy grip eased sufficiently for the main roads to be cleared – and also the Whale Island parade ground. A large group of naval defaulters were set to clearing away the ice with pick and shovel, to the dismay of the rest of the trainees. Conditions eased enough for some of the girls to try a run ashore in the evening, but when Jane was invited to join she had to say sorry – she was CB'd and couldn't risk another transgression. This caused some fresh indignation but it was agreed that looking for more trouble wasn't terribly smart. They were all back, signed in again, by 2100.

Finding herself stuck in quarters, Jane made the best of a bad job and spent her evenings studying. She had resolved that no matter what disciplinary fate awaited her, she was going to do well on the course and not give them any excuse for chucking her out on those grounds. And the learning, basically memorising lots of detail, was simple enough. Drill was more difficult to begin with but it actually did some good by making her get mobile and move around each day. The weals were healing well and the bruising had gone from black to a vivid rainbow of colours. It still wouldn't take any pressure but a week on from the caning she was moving freely if cautiously. Towards the end of the course she had become very knowledgeable about the Navy, its systems and structures, its badges, stripes and ceremonial and could identify most ships and naval aircraft. She had reclaimed her place as right marker to her squad and they were all coming on well with their marching and drill. Her salute drew praise even from their chief GI. Her seething resentment still bubbled but, recalling the formative guidance of her school games mistress, she channelled that into really going hard at the work in front of her.

With two weeks of the course gone, the evenings saw girls in many odd corners of their quarters, all with their noses in their books. It wasn't at all clear what standard would be expected from them when examined, so most on the course were taking no chances. Even Dora was doing her best, and waved offers of help away with that defensive, "I can read an' write, y'know". She came to Jane and asked "would you test me on this stuff?" Testing completed well, Dora said. "I'm still wondering if I should stay in. This is all fine an' dandy but what'll it be like doing a job?"

"Better than this I'll bet – for a start not so strict. I've been watching you, Dora. You're quite a smart cookie aren't you? There's a brain there and if you can get used to using it you could go far, y'know."

"Aw, come off it. I'm just a scrubber from the backstreets an' my sort don't go nowhere."

Quietly listening in to this had been Fiona, a gentle half smile on her face. On impulse Jane turned to her. "Fiona, you've seen a bit of the rough side of life, I'll bet. Can you tell this silly girl there's a life for her here?"

"Aye, well, the life'll be fit ye mak it but it could be good. We're a' just Wrens the same, ye ken, and wi' a war on if you're ony good the road will be open for ye."

Dora looked at them, a hungry longing in her eyes. "I'd love to but......" and she looked deep into some dark pit. "Can you two keep a secret?" They were already in a quiet corner of the cabin and Dora motioned to them to come close. She was almost whispering. "I told you I was forced to go on the game, didn't I? That means I'm not like all you nice respectable virgins. Can I ever get past how my body's been used? I'd be terrified that my past would catch up with me an' that would be that. Easier to get out now."

Jane and Fiona looked at each other, an ironic curl on each lip. Jane spoke first. "Listen Dora, why was I caned? For spending a night with my boyfriend. That means I'm no virgin, doesn't it? And frankly I don't give a damn that it's known about. How about you, Fiona?"

"Och, dinnae tell onyone 'cos in my home community girls are supposed to be unsullied when they marry but maistly we're onything but." Fiona smiled quietly, reminiscently. "There's been ain or twa good-lookin' lads frae the fishin, an' so what. We're a' awa' frae wor ain homes noo an' naebody to look at us. Hey, Dora, you've done mair o' it but nane o' us is pure. Have ye nae noticed that the untouched ones dinnae ken fit it's aboot onywiy? They woudna ken fit you're on aboot. Dinnae let yer past fash ye. I'll bet no-one ever asks."

Dora looked from one to the other. "It'd be nice to get away like that. You really think I could in the Wrens?"

Jane nodded. "I was given some really good advice –by a man, believe it or not – when I was rumbled. He said to keep quiet and not spread myself around at all, and I'd probably be all right. You can maybe do a little for pleasure but discreetly."

"Pleasure? What's pleasure got to do with it? Girls are just there to let men have their way, aren't they? I'll be happy if I never have to do it again."

Jane shook her head in slow sorrow. "How sad for you. It can be wonderful for women too, y'know, if the bloke you are with knows what he's doing. But it has to come naturally so don't go looking for it. Come on Dora, stick in, do well and you could go places."

Fiona chipped in "Jane's richt, Dora. We'd better keep this conversation tae worselves but if you stick at it there's nae limit for ye except fit you put on yersel'." They went back to their studies without further comment but there was no more talk of leaving from Dora.

A couple of days from the end of their course formal divisions were held and the Wrens doubled from their quarters to arrive rather puffed. They proudly marched on to the parade ground swinging their arms to the strains of 'All the nice girls love a sailor' from the marine band. Divisions are when all the crew or staff of ship or shore establishments make formal squads and attend the ceremony of colours, probably with a short divine service included. There was more marching and evolutions at Whale Island with a march-past a saluting base with *HMS Excellent's* captain taking the salute. Whale Island divisions are not like the rest of the navy – they are marked like a competition and message matelots run out in front of each squad holding up a board showing how well they had done. The Wrens were pleased to see a 'very good' given them and when they marched off at the end they were given three cheers. Their Chief GI was a very relieved man. That night Jane was invited to join a handful of Wrens to take part in the ceremonial lowering of the flag at sunset. They had been through the colours and sunset routine in training but actually taking part had a much deeper significance for them and Jane found herself quite moved despite trying to maintain a cynical view of it. Dora and Alicia, next to each other, were sufficiently moved for the odd tear.

With sunset over a group of the Wrens rather conspiratorially went ashore. This group, led by the unlikely but effective combination of Camilla and Fiona, had invited their GI out for a drink with them. Still feeling deeply relieved, he had not needed two invitations. The group all got their late passes for that night, and by ten o'clock they had him blubbering gently into his beer. They had heard that his wife was a serious battleaxe so they took him home in a taxi, propped him against his front door, rang the bell and ran. Next day he was sporting a vivid black eye but grinned at his Wren charges in waving away their concern.

Exam day had them all in a bit of a flap, but the questions were straightforward and Jane found she could answer them all. After the challenges of matriculation and Oxford entry they were undemanding. Right after breakfast on their last day they were all assembled in the messroom and told the results –everyone had passed, one person had got 98% and a couple of others 90%, so First Officer Brown was really quite pleased with them. They were also warned that an important person was coming to give them their certificates and talk to them about their futures. The buzz was that this would be the Captain of *HMS Excellent.* Dora, sat next to Jane, was in ecstasy."I've passed, I've passed" she squeaked. Jane gave her an ironic lift of an eyebrow. Dora whispered, "I've never sat an exam, never mind passing one."

Jane gave her hand an encouraging squeeze and smiled. This felt like more of a victory than her own results.

Then the girls got even better news – their uniforms were waiting. "Stand fast Wren Beacon" said First Officer Brown. "You can all go to the clothing store and be fitted up." So there was a good deal of chatter as they marched over to collect their new garments. Back in quarters there was lot of excited trying on, spoilt only by the way most of them didn't quite fit. But quick work with scissors needle and thread dealt with the more glaring misfits. They had even produced an extra large set of uniforms for Punch which delighted her as she'd been afraid of trying to squeeze into a normal sized outfit. The only serious drawback was the black-outs – long droopy woollen bloomers, navy blue, down almost to the elasticated knee, which the quarters officer made quite plain they were expected to wear. A mixture of disgust and affronted horror greeted this, but those who did put them on were surprised by how comfortable they were. But hardly feminine. Jane was left in a corner expecting the worst. 'Oh well,' she thought 'at least I tried. Now what do I do?'

After a special dinner they assembled in the messroom in their smart new uniforms, black lisle stockings and shiny black lace-ups to the fore. Jane sat quietly at the back in her bluette. First Officer Brown came in, followed by the Captain, then – to everyone's surprise – the WRNS Director.

First Officer Brown spoke first. "You have all done very well and I am delighted to see you all passing the course despite the difficulties the weather has thrown at us. The Captain will be giving you your certificates in a minute but first I have to say a few words about the results. You may recall that at the start of the course I said that the Wren who did best overall would be promoted to leading Wren provided she showed some leadership qualities. This has given us a problem, as the girl who has done best is Wren Beacon. She would have got the promotion without question had it not been for her disciplinary record which means that she can't be considered. Indeed, her whole future in the Wrens is being reviewed although no decisions have been made yet. Therefore we are awarding the leading rate's hook to the next best results, and it goes to Wren Merle Baker. I will now call each one of you forward to get your certificates from Captain Ellis-Green. Congratulations."

CHAPTER 20: Not Defeated

At the back Jane felt she wanted to curl up and die. To have got so far – and done so well – and still be chucked out felt deeply humiliating. And to see Merle get the hook hurt. Thinking about hurt, Jane was just about managing to sit down now but it was still a painful effort, and she stood up to ease the discomfort. All this did was give her a better view of Merle getting her certificate and the single anchor badge. Awards over, the director stepped forward and gave the assembly a five minute pep talk about their future in the Wrens and what a difference they were making to the war effort. Somehow the war had seemed very far away these last few weeks. Dismissed, the girls filed out, quite a few giving Jane a brief commiserating hug in passing. First Officer Brown called Jane forward. "Beacon, we want you in my office in ten minute's time." In her misery all Jane could do was nod, although she noticed the Director giving her a sharp look. In the Navy 'ten minutes' time' means be there in five minutes and wait, so Jane made her way to Mrs Brown's office in good time and on the stroke of ten minutes knocked on the door. She was surprised to find only the Director inside.

* * * * *

Vera Laughton Mathews – ultimately Dame Vera – had a long history with the Wrens. She had gone from being a suffragette to a dynamic young Wren officer in the First World War, already noticed by high authority. Between the wars she married and had three children, practised her journalist trade, and was internationally active in social and women's affairs. She was also deeply involved with the Sea Rangers, a nautical offshoot of the Girl Guides, which did much to bring girls into the marine orbit and produced many of the early Wrens. A devout Catholic, she held strong traditional views on morals, sex and marriage, but managed to combine that with a warm humanity and generous consciousness of the frailty of human nature. And long before the term acquired common currency, she was a fierce feminist – the word was in use even then. Her other defining characteristic was a bulldog-like energy and determination – not for nothing was she known affectionately as 'Tugboat Annie' (although never to her face). In World War One the Wrens were often referred to as the 'Prigs and Prudes', reflecting the strong views of their Director, Dame Katherine Furse. She had trained Laughton Mathews and a lingering echo of that attitude attached to her and hence the Wrens in World War Two in drastically different circumstances. Laughton Mathews was director right through the war and if any of the services were a reflection of the views and values of its leader, it was the WRNS.

* * * * *

When Jane found herself looking at the Director's appraising eyes, she could feel the sense of being in a powerful presence. On the desk were a killick's hook badge and also two small strips of cloth with an oak leaf on them, and a similar metal clasp. To one side was a letter, which Jane recognized as the one the girls had sent protesting about her treatment. At one end of the desk was a pile of Wren uniform.

Jane stepped forward, came to attention and saluted. "1095 Wren Jane Beacon, Ma'am." The Director returned the salute then took her hat off, laying it on the desk. "At ease, Beacon, and sit down." By now Jane knew enough of Naval ways to keep quiet and wait. "Beacon, I rarely get involved in the affairs of individual Wren ratings but you seem to be a bit special and have given me more heartache and concern than any other I've come across. Your story has raised a series of matters I must get a full understanding of. You have the most lurid disciplinary record I've ever seen; three serious infractions in four months are remarkable and if you go on that way there's no saving you."

Jane drew breath to try to protest but a peremptory hand was held up behind the desk. "Let me continue. You must be aware of our determination to maintain a standard of behaviour and morality, which you seem to have gone out of your way to flout. Yet at the same time you have received glowing reports on your work, which I'll discuss later, your bravery in rescuing your cox'n was exceptional and I was delighted when the recommendation for 'Mentioned in Despatches' came through. All of which puts us in a quandary. On the surface of it you should simply be dismissed the service – we don't want anyone with loose morals contaminating the rest of the Service nor do we want our reputation in the Navy to be sullied like that. Yet when I look into these disciplinary infractions there seems to be mitigating circumstances in all of them. Now, the Navy has a rigid approach to discipline and as a fighting force it has to have. So there is very little room for mitigating circumstances. But we know that sometimes good people can come unstuck and we have to exercise a little discretion to avoid losing them. You just might come into that category. How old are you?"

At last Jane got a chance to get a word in. "Nineteen, ma'am." Jane was going to go on talking but again the raised hand stopped her.

"Young enough. And did you have any experience of the wider world before joining the Wrens?"

"Well some, ma'am. I was head girl at Leadown and was going to go to Somerville until the war came along. Before joining up I spent six months on a yacht in the Mediterranean with Uncle George – I mean Commodore Rodmayne - and sailed back to England in her. Then I joined the Wrens and because I was put straight onto a harbour boat I was quartered aboard *HMS Defiance* same as the rest of the boats' crews, which was interesting because I was the only Wren rating on board. I learnt a lot about the lower deck in those three months."

"Yes I can imagine you would. This is something I wanted to discuss with you. It seems clear to us that putting odd Wrens into the sort of position you were in, is not a good idea. You'd have been a lot better off in a Wrennery living with other girls and we will avoid making that mistake again if we can. It appears that you've adopted all too many of the attitudes from the messdecks, presumably as a protective cover?"

"Not consciously or deliberately, Ma'am. I was very alone in some ways, and I'd never have survived if I hadn't worked in with them. They were very good to me – far nicer than officialdom although the few Wren officers on board were kind enough. Look, when I rescued my cox'n the men clubbed together and got me a super watch to replace the one I'd lost." Jane took off her watch and passed it over. The director examined it closely. "Hm, very impressive. And you say they were good to you?" There was a hint of something else in the question.

Jane picked up on it. "Yes they were. There were lots of dodgy invitations but none of them really meant anything – most of them would have run a mile if I'd said yes." This got a slightly wintry smile from the Director.

"Mostly they were just helpful and kind and friendly. Beyond that the Navy is so set in its ways that you've got to go with it. The biggest problem by far was one I wasn't aware of to begin with, and that is that I was being watched the whole time. I was sort of spied on and everything I did was noted. My cabin might as well have had glass bulkheads. This had a lot to do with my problems in taking a boyfriend."

The director cut in. "Yes, that's something else we have to consider. I was appalled to hear about your behaviour, and the way it was all so public."

"Put that down to naivety, ma'am. Thinking about it now I am so ashamed of what I did. I was sort of seduced, not that I minded at the time. But you learn. I've only been with the one man yet people are going on about it as though I was touting for business in the red light area. What was silly of me was not to realise that it was all being noted so that something I thought was quiet and private was in fact public. Given half a chance to stay in the Wrens I'll be a lot more careful about it."

"Which implies that you might do it again?"

"Ma'am, I wasn't looking for it last time and I certainly don't intend to go looking for it again. But who knows what may happen? I've got a life to live."

"Hm, that's only half an answer to my mind, but I suppose it's an honest one. I must say you are remarkably offhand about your behaviour. A bit of modesty and contrition would not go amiss."

"Well ma'am, when I found out that the whole lower deck knew what I was up to, I was horrified and in despair. I suppose I could have retreated into my shell and tried to hide from it, but somehow I was damned if I was going to be so weak-kneed. Which meant that I had to brazen it out and look them in the eye when they got smutty with me. Maybe that has rubbed off onto my approach in general."

"Yes, talking to you is almost like talking to a sailor – the same brass-necked openness. I fear we may have done some irreparable damage leaving you to survive among the seamen but do try to remember that you are female, won't you?" Jane couldn't help laughing ruefully at that. "I get reminded pretty often, ma'am but it's a two-edged sword, you know. Yes I suppose I am a bit brass-necked about it now but it does mean I am well able to deal with Jolly Jack in his more frisky moments. Some of the other girls I've come across are terrified of them."

""Well, Beacon we take note of that but my concern remains. Now, let's look at your work so far. You came out top of this probationer course by some margin, which in itself tells us something. You're obviously intelligent and a quick learner and that counts for a lot. You've had glowing reports on your service on the launch, which apparently you've taken to like the proverbial duck. Do you think other Wrens could do it?"

"Yes of course ma'am. It's a bit challenging physically sometimes but nothing we couldn't manage. I've been doing quite a lot of driving the boat, which is just wonderful and I'm sure if I can do it lots of other girls can too. Do you think we might be allowed to crew the harbour boats?"

"Not yet I'm afraid. There is some serious opposition to the idea at higher levels in the Navy so we're hoping to continue with the experiment with you. Not that your behaviour has helped."

For the first time Jane perhaps detected a glimmer of hope. "But it might come in the future?"

"We intend to keep trying but it won't be quick."

"How would it work if we got one Wren crew together quietly and let them run a boat somewhere?" Here Jane was thinking of Punch especially, but others of the girls on her course had really fancied the idea as well.

"Nice idea Beacon but not yet. You keep your nose clean and go on getting such glowing reports, and things might change eventually. Now, the other matter I have to look at is this beating you were given here. It is undoubtedly unfortunate you got caught by the ice storm but even so you merited some sort of punishment. However, this letter here" and the Director picked up the girls' protest letter. "Makes it very plain that beatings of this sort are counterproductive. We can't have whole courses threatening to resign. I was more than a little surprised myself when I read it and the doctor's note of protest. He sent me copies of the pictures and I must say they

CHAPTER 20: Not Defeated

are not a pretty sight. But it does seem that your course officers were legally within their rights to have you beaten. I've looked into it and there's a loophole in the set-up for the Wrens. When we were first discussed in 1938 - before my time - someone in the Admiralty decided that ordinary Wrens would be the equivalent of boy cadets. Now, the only people still subject to corporal punishment in the Navy are boy cadets and by formally equating Wrens to boy cadets the lawyers tell me that Wrens can also be caned although there's nothing in the Wrens' disciplinary code about it. But I must say I think it is a very bad idea and I am giving explicit instructions that this is not to be used except as an extreme last resort when no other punishment is available for serious crimes. I have emphasised that it is never to draw blood. Better to dismiss people from the Service or let the civil law deal with them than have this sort of barbarity. I'm trying to get the cadet equivalence removed altogether and hence the legal possibility of girls being given a hiding in the first place.

Your refusal to be pushed out has taken everyone by surprise although I think it shows just how strong a person you are, or could be. Losing you would be a real loss to the Service but let me make it quite clear that one more serious disciplinary offence with moral overtones and you – will – be – out." The Director rapped the table with each word. "Do I make myself quite clear?"

Jane nodded vehemently, the sudden surge of realisation that she wasn't being chucked out briefly robbing her of speech. Then abruptly she found it again.

"Ma'am, what really hurt was the loss of control. Not being in charge of myself is something new for me and I hate it, I hate it. Believe me, they'd never have got away with the caning if they hadn't caught me by surprise."

The director interjected "Being in uniform inevitably means a degree of losing personal control."

"Yes ma'am I know that and the likes of our drill GI didn't bother me at all. But this was different. The only reason I didn't walk out there and then was the thought of what we're trying to do with me on the boats. There is such a wonderful opportunity for us women, us Wrens, to show what we can do here and I know, I just know, that I can do it." Quite unconsciously Jane had stood up and was walking up and down the room, waving her arms about. "I could so easily jack it in here and find a job on a fishing boat or something, but that utterly misses the point. The active Proper Navy is surprisingly willing to be shown what we can do, y'know, and so far as I can tell the opposition comes from deskbound wallahs with no real understanding of what we're about. So I will bloody well show them all. But it's bad enough having to cope with the blokes without our own side turning against you as well. You must, you must, support this."

The Director had listened to this tirade with a half smile on her face, but now held up her hand for silence. "Beacon, you have no idea how much sympathy I have with this. Please sit down again. Now, you do not order me about, however well meaning your intentions. Your passion is noted and will not be counted against you. But I must remind you that your beating was for a major breach of basic discipline and for moral reasons which had nothing to do with your enthusiasm for the boats. The one can never condone the other and you will do well to remember it."

As abruptly as it had risen, the fiery tide inside Jane ebbed away. She slumped and nodded sadly. "All right ma'am. I understand that and will try to behave accordingly."

For a minute the silence lengthened between them. Then the Director drew breath, looked Jane in the eye and said "Right, Beacon. Here's your uniform. These are the ribbons for your 'Mentioned in Despatches'. They sew onto your left breast at the end of the other medal ribbons I suspect you may accumulate. The metal one is to pin onto any other dress outfits where medals are worn. And finally"- here she pushed the killick's hook across the desk – "We've decided to take a big gamble and promote you leading hand. I gather you were pretty much the dominant personality on the course and showed real leadership qualities. But just remember it can all be taken away again. Here's your course certificate and draft chit back to Plymouth where Mrs Welby is waiting for you."

"Oh thank you ma'am, thank you." And to her chagrin Jane couldn't stop herself bursting into tears.

"Can I put them on now?"

"Yes of course. And put up the badge and ribbon."

"Oh wow, the sun has just come out again."

The director smiled gently, got up from behind the desk and surprised Jane by coming round and giving her shoulder a hug. "*Courage, ma brave*" she murmured. "Women's natural approach will always be a little at odds with the Navy's rigidness but that can never be an excuse. Just go and do your job well now and keep out of trouble." And with that the Director popped her hat on and marched out of the room leaving Jane open-mouthed. It was the contradictions that were most difficult to cope with.

This prolonged interview had lasted well into the afternoon and when Jane got back to her cabin she found it empty except for her own gear and a note on her chest of drawers. The note was from Alicia:

Dear Jane,
We're all packed and the bus has come to take us to the station so we can't say goodbye to you but we really do wish you all the best in whatever your fate is. Please keep in

CHAPTER 20: Not Defeated

touch, we're longing to know what happens to you. It's been great getting to know you. Let's hope this horrible war doesn't last too much longer.
Love,
Alicia (and all the other elephants).

Attached was a list of ten addresses including, interestingly enough, Merle's.

Jane spread her new uniforms out to look at them. Throughout the war, the appeal of an attractive and becoming uniform was a major draw for the Wrens. It was an adaption which was kind to almost any female shape of the male officer's fore-and-aft jacket. Along with navy blue skirt and black stockings and, for the officers, a smart tricorne hat, the uniform for Wren officers and ratings was fundamentally the same – different material, buttons, badges and stripes were the main differences and details such as kick pleats in the officers' skirts. It was a naturally neat and tidy outfit which, combined with white shirt and black tie, made any girl look smart. Wrens felt good in it, which contributed much to their sense of self-respect. But how they hated the stiff detached collars with their awkward studs. The collars rubbed and the studs – one at the back to secure the collar and a folding one at the front to tie in the two ends were fiddly and took some getting used to. The black stockings were a major feature – much the greater part of the male Royal Navy was obsessed with them. The only real disaster was the rating's first hat: carrying on from its First War predecessor which had been adapted from a yachtswoman's hat of the Edwardian era, it was a pudding basin shape with broad floppy brim, supposedly waterproof but never so in practise. It was replaced in 1942 with a smart beret variant of the matelot's round hat, which was such an outstanding success that versions of it became a fashion item in the general population and even worn by the Queen.

Jane's course had been lucky to get their uniforms. Supply of Wren ratings' uniforms was to remain a problem for some time, as the factory making them and holding substantial stocks was twice bombed into oblivion. It also affected the supply of Matelots' uniforms and this led to one of the most infamous signals ever put out by the Admiralty: *"Wrens' uniforms will be held up until the needs of the Fleet have been satisfied."* Whether this was by some deliberate joker or not was never established.

So Jane was pleased at many levels with what she now had. Jackets and skirts did not quite fit and she was sitting sewing, her huzzif spread out on the bunk, when the quarters officer came in. "Right Beacon, it's too late for you to travel today so you can stay here till the morning. Here's your travel warrant and transport is arranged for you at 0830 tomorrow morning. Quite what you've done to deserve a car of your own I don't know but the Director ordered it so it's organised. Leave your bluettes and stuff at the reception area." The quarters officer had come close to Jane and looked over her shoulder at the handiwork. "Is that a 'Mentioned in Despatches' oak leaf? How on earth did you get that?"

"Yes ma'am, it is and I got it for rescuing my launch's cox'n after he'd gone over the side. I had to dive in and keep him afloat for some time."

"Indeed. You really are a bundle of contradictions, aren't you." She wandered off shaking her head in mild disbelief.

With bust let out and minor tailoring done, on went the oakleaf ribbon and the single blue anchor, a sneaky sense of pride going through her at the finished articles. There was no supper so she had to scrounge sandwiches and tea for herself but that seemed a small price to pay, and the evening was spent writing short notes to all the names on the list.

Next morning she put on the uniform for the first time and was waiting at the door of the quarters when an Austin Seven drew up. It was the smallest possible car but to Jane it was a limousine, the respect its fairly mature Wren driver gave her suggesting something had changed. Having cleared the guardhouse the little car chugged across the causeway; Jane turned and looked back. A sudden surge of anger and bitterness washed over her, tears welling up as she looked at the place which had brought so much pain and grief to mix with the happiness and success. For a brief moment it all just seemed too much and a bit of her wanted to run away and hide. Then suddenly she banged the dashboard and shouted. "Dammit, I will not be defeated." This so spooked the driver that the little car swerved violently and the unfortunate lady almost lost control. Looking startled and not a little scared she quavered, "Please don't do that again. I could lose my job if I have a crash."

As abruptly as it had come the surge of emotion drained away and Jane sat back, patting the driver on the shoulder. "Sorry about that – I promise to behave now."

"Well thank goodness. I'd heard you were a bit different but nobody warned me about your temper."

"Oh, not really temper, just a determination not to be defeated by this lot which spills over sometimes."

The driver gave her a nervous side glance and concentrated on getting to the station. As the train pulled out Jane looked over the town to the masts in the distance, her mind a confused jumble. Pulling out a writing pad, she tried to set her thoughts in order in the way she knew best.

CHAPTER 20: Not Defeated

Goodbye Whale Island
You rough old hump.
Now I know what they mean,
Those who rail against
The military mind.
Toughness and cruelty
Are so close that
They can fuse in the mind, it seems.
'Discipline must be maintained' they say.
When you are driven into the face
Of the guns you have to be
Beyond your own feelings.
But does that justify wanton cruelty
A savageness sprung from dark heart,
Not military need?
That I cannot answer but
What I do know is that
It defeats itself.
Such treatment puts me
Beyond fear of retribution.
Now there is no thing, no-one,
That can scare me.
That can make me
bob my knee before your exalted
So-called authority
From anything more than politeness.
I will not be defeated.
Do you understand that?
I thought not.

PART FIVE:

VOYAGER

CHAPTER 21:
Back Home

THE winter of 1939/40 was the most severe for a century. Although the ice storm, which had caught out Jane Beacon was its most extreme happening, for months the whole of Europe was in the grips of sub-zero temperatures and mountains of snow. The Thames and the sea froze, trees, power lines and telegraph poles snapped off and fell over and birds died, encased in ice, sitting on tree branches which were themselves thick with ice. The ice storm, which engulfed the South of England was caused by supercooled raindrops, already below zero as they fell but still liquid, freezing instantaneously on contact with a sub-zero surface.

In Continental Europe it was even worse and the war effectively came to a halt for several months as serious movement was impossible. Not only was it freezing but the weather wild and the U-boats found conditions in the Atlantic so bad that they had to call off the campaign until spring 1940. In the pocket war in Finland battles were fought in minus 35 degrees Celsius. This hiatus in Germany's warlike moves brought some benefit to Britain, which used the precious time to continue mobilising and to build up its defences. The Royal Navy struggled on through the harshest of weather but there were times when smaller warships could not get to sea.

* * * * *

Catching the train home from her probationer course, Leading Wren Jane Beacon found her killick's hook had some uses, which included ordinary matelots being willing to move up and make space for her on the seat. Again, it was a boon that the train was stuffed with humanity as the mass of bodies provided some warmth in an otherwise unheated carriage. Getting off at Plymouth, Jane had found no buses. She phoned home and was directed to contact her father who was working in the hospital; he would pick her up when he finished. After several hours nursing a mug of tea in the station buffet she was collected but her father seemed unimpressed by her new status. "Aye, I suppose you look like a Wren now" was his only comment. But then he'd always been an amiably remote figure in her life. Her mother, rather more caring personally, simply didn't understand the import of the oak leaf or the anchor on the uniform's left sleeve.

CHAPTER 21: Back Home

Back at the Grange, for a few days Jane found it pleasant to lie in bed for half the morning, be looked after and do very little. The bitter cold persisted and Jane found childhood memories coming back with ice on the inside of her bedroom window in the mornings, which did nothing to encourage her to get up. Enjoyable languor or no, it was not long before she started to feel restless to go back to her other life. Her siblings were all away at school, which meant that life at the Grange was peaceful but a bit dull. Her *Osprey* companions had all joined the services so although she took her accordion to the Dolphin a couple of times it was much less fun on her own. She debated consulting her father about her battered posterior but decided against it. He had strong views on physical violence and she was afraid he might start making trouble in high places if he saw what had been done to her. But the bruising was dying away rapidly, the weals had healed to rough striped ridges and she could move around and sit down more or less normally.

"Jane darling, have you thought any more about settling down? At the moment you seem to be getting more and more embroiled in Naval stuff which can't offer you a future."

"Mummy if that means 'are you thinking of finding a man', the answer is no, and I mean no. I can do without them thank you very much." The vehemence of her reply even startled Jane herself.

"Oh dear, have you had a bad experience?"

"Not really bad but getting involved with them is too bloody dangerous for my liking and as for getting hitched to one, you can keep it. I like being myself."

Her mother shook her head in sad bewilderment. Her daughter was changing in front of her and although she longed to do more, she felt helpless to do anything except snipe from the sidelines.

With her leave end looming Jane caught her father enjoying a port after dinner and generally in a mellow mood. "Father, do you think you could sub me a bit? I'm finding a Wren's basic sixteen shillings doesn't go very far." She had in mind to ask for a couple of pounds a quarter to tide her over.

He smiled at her. "I suppose I should do my bit for the war effort too. Would five pounds a month keep you right?"

Jane gulped. One part of her brain was thinking 'that's ridiculous. I don't need that much' while another part said 'Go for it. If he's offering that much he must be able to afford it.'

"Well that would be more generous than I really need. Are you sure you can afford it?"

Her father leaned back and smiled. "My dear girl, if I couldn't afford it I wouldn't

205

offer it. Would you like me to open a bank account for you? I can then arrange to pay the money straight in. I'll instruct them to send you details and a cheque book."

"That would be wonderfully kind. I'm not sure I can use that much but I can save the rest."

"Y'know, Jane, we've been worried about you working on the boats but it seems you can cope. Is it very tough?"

"Yes and no. It's huge fun, for sure, and I can see some weaker females struggling but most matelots are ever so kind and helpful and I think we Wrens could do a lot more. But I'm told there is enormous opposition to the idea so I just have to try to do my bit well. Being a pioneer is interesting if a bit frightening at times."

He laughed gently "We're actually quite proud of our pioneer Wren. It seems like a good use of money to support a venture like this so enjoy it and look after yourself."

"I will father and thank you, thank you." To her surprise her undemonstrative father came round behind and hugged her, kissing her left ear gently. Abruptly he coloured, straightened up and left, his port unfinished.

Food and petrol rationing were introduced at the beginning of 1940. Her father was given an allowance to enable him to go about on his duties but there was little left over for her mother's Austin Ruby, forcing her to plan any trips much more carefully - to her dismay. On the last day of her leave Jane had arranged to go into town with her father, who dropped her at the dockyard gate while grumbling that it might make him late. Her records were out on the superintendent's desk as Jane came into the office, having paused to say hello to a slightly friendlier Second Officer Jones. The superintendent was quietly looking through the papers and for a full minute did not look up. Jane waited silently.

"Well, Beacon, another one. Are you trying to set some sort of record? And how is your bottom now?"

"Getting better ma'am and I think I should get full mobility back."

"I've been looking through this and see the Director's annotations. I suppose I should congratulate you on coming top and making Leading Wren but I do have misgivings. If only we could sort out the exceptional Wren from the wayward girl. How do you see it going now?"

"Well, ma'am, no more Frenchman – he's gone for good. After the troubles with him I'll be very careful about any other entanglements with men. Having survived in the Wrens by the skin of my bottom I'm going to try very hard to make sure I stay in. I presume I'm going back to *Amaryllis*?"

"Yes Beacon, and briefly you'll be back where you were living on board *Defiance*. But when I'm finished, Commodore Rodmayne wants to see you to discuss some fairly major changes, which I'll leave for him to explain. I've not got any more to say just now but please keep out of trouble. You really are on your last chance now."

Jane waited silently. That was it so she just said "Yes ma'am" and left at the nod of dismissal.

She had to ask Second Officer Jones where to find the Commodore's office. A phone call through confirmed that he was waiting for her on the other side of the building. Stepping smartly into his office she came to attention, saluted and reported "1095 Leading Wren Beacon, sir."

"Yes congratulations on the hook, rapid progress indeed. Incidentally, you don't salute an officer who is sitting at his desk without his cap on. You only salute when the officer can return it."

Jane was mildly crestfallen at this – she had been looking forward to showing off her newfound drill expertise and had been found wanting at the first attempt.

"But not to worry. Now, I've been following your exploits from a distance throughout. I annoyed your superintendent by laughing about the affair with the Frenchman until I heard you'd been doing it in a warship. That really is seriously naughty and you just mustn't ever do it again. But I was right about your value on a harbour launch, wasn't I?"

Jane's eyes gleamed with enthusiasm. "Yes indeed, sir. I've been having a lovely time and I'm just hoping I can go on. It seems such a shame we can't do more of this crewing them with Wrens. There's ever so many good ones would just love to do it."

"Patience, dear girl, patience. If you only knew the massed ranks of crusty old opposition to this idea, you'd not be tugging at the bit so much. Now, the main point of asking you to see me isn't the pleasure of your company, but to discuss your future. This has all been cleared through the Wren hierarchy, incidentally. I am being appointed to Dover in a few weeks. I've been tasked with doing a similar job there, control of movements but also local control of convoys passing through, anti-submarine patrols and minesweeping in the Straits and that sort of thing – very much a co-ordinating role. They're short of harbour launches there so I'm taking *Amaryllis* with me. After some debate it's been decided to sail the boat up there with its own crew. This leaves a choice for you: either you can stay here and carry on doing boat's crew with some of the other boats, or you can go with *Amaryllis* and be drafted to Dover. Do you have any idea which you'd prefer?"

"Does that mean I'd do the passage up Channel in her?"

"I suppose so, although we hadn't thought of it that way."

"Well you know from the *Osprey* trip that I can navigate and keep a watch, so why not? I can sleep in the officer's cuddy aft and leave the fore part of the boat for the men."

"Yes, that might actually work. We were going to have to draft an extra watch keeper in but there's no reason why you shouldn't do it. Weather permitting it should only take five days, day running."

"I'd love that – going to sea again would be great fun. Is the rest of the crew going with her?"

"There have been a couple of changes but otherwise, yes. Your cox'n will be in charge. Congratulations on your MiD, incidentally. You've been cramming the incidents in."

"It just seems to happen that way."

He smiled at her. "There's one other thing to mention. I'm being made up to rear-admiral on taking up my appointment at Dover."

"Oh that's wonderful. You've finally made it – congratulations sir. Makes my leading Wren seem a bit tame."

"Well, it's only taken me thirty years to get there. You've done it in a few months."

"Yes but the Wrens are so short of people that they don't have any seniority listing. What happens now?"

"You go back to *Amaryllis* while I square things for you to go up the coast in her. She's coming out of the water next week for her crew to clean and paint her underneath, so that'll be something new for you to do. Then she'll be off as soon as the weather looks reasonable."

Coming on board *Defiance* had a real feel of coming home again. There was one difference: as she came over the brow in her smart new uniform she faced aft, came to attention, and saluted the quarter deck. By chance her gruesome Jossman was duty quartermaster, watching Jane arrive with undisguised amusement. "Been learning something then?"

"I certainly have. We can do this drill thing now so the Navy doesn't scare us any more. It's all go in the big ships y'know."

He snorted with amusement, watching her trim black-stockinged figure disappear aft and commented "Wrens, don't you just love 'em," to no-one in particular.

Jane found her cabin shining clean and the bunk freshly made up. Too late for dinner, she scrounged a bowl of figgy duff from the galley then unpacked and settled into her cabin again. Later, coming into the chief's mess for supper she spotted Stan in his usual corner. "Hello there, had a good course?" He took in the new uniform and the anchor on her sleeve. "Ee lass, that's quick promotion – took me ten years to get me hook up."

"Yes well, the Wrens are a bit short of killicks just now so they promised the top person on the course their hook. So here I am, although I'm not sure what I'm supposed to do with it."

CHAPTER 21: Back Home

"You can boss Dickhead about for a start. He needs it. I hear you're coming back to us – that's champion."

"Has anyone told you I'm doing the passage up to Dover with you as well? I'll be coming as watch keeper."

"Do you know your navigation lass?" Stan looked a bit worried.

"Oh yes, I can navigate and recite my Rule of the Road and generally run a watch."

"In that case it'll be great to have you. Are you staying with us once we get to Dover? It'll be a lot livelier there, y'know."

"So far as I know I am. The Commodore offered me the choice of coming with you or staying here so it was no contest really."

"You know we're being hauled out next week to clean and re-coat her bottom?"

"Yes, so I gather. Which leads to my other problem. This Wren's outfit is all very well for a tiddley uniform but I can't see me doing deckhand on a launch in a skirt and stockings. Nor scraping and painting the boat for that matter. I wondered if I could come by something a bit more workable?"

"Let me have a word with our chief storekeeper. He's an old oppo of mine. Might be able to do something. I'd have thought bell bottoms would be best for you."

Jane smiled her thanks and when she turned-to at 0630 the next morning in her well-worn yachting gear to scrub out *Amaryllis* Stan told her to go see the storeman right after breakfast to discuss getting kitted out. A fruitful hour ensued with the amiable but sharp-eyed old storeman who went bright pink when she gave him a hug on completion. A short conversation with Second Officer Jones that night got another four Wren killick's blue badges ordered and she wrote away for two more MiD oak leaf ribbons.

She signed for two pairs of bell bottoms, two of the white square-necked shirts known as cottons or white fronts, three of the blue uniform shirts the petty officers wore for workwear under their uniform jackets, and not least two voluminous boiler suit overalls. She was also issued with a seaman's clasp knife and the white lanyard to secure it. A balaclava helmet, thick polo neck jersey, six pairs of socks, a new pair of pusser's daps, two pairs of white heavy seaboot socks and a new pair of heavy naval wellington boots completed the issue. None of the clothes fitted properly so she set to with her huzzif to trim and sew and adapt them to her shape. The bell bottom waistbands needed taking in five inches. Suitably attired in her new bell bottoms, blue uniform shirt with black tie and uniform jacket topped off by her dreadful pudding basin hat, she sallied forth to join *Amaryllis*. She was startled to get stares, wolf whistles and salacious suggestions all along the upper deck, which came to a halt to look at this new apparition. It amazed Jane - surely they knew her better by now? Puzzled, she asked Stan what their problem was. "Well lass, I don't think they've ever seen a woman in bell bottoms before. You do something to them. I must say matelot's clothes look different on you. You know how it is when cartoon Jane comes out with some nice adaption of uniform and all the men fancy it? I'd guess you were having the same effect here." It didn't make much sense to Jane but then there were still moments when she didn't understand the men at all. But the outfit proved practical and for a week she was happy running round the Hamoaze again.

The only other change came when Dickhead looked at her hat and was appalled at the way she'd tied the ribbon. "Get me a pair of scissors and a sixpence and I'll do it Proper Navy for you." Despite his lack of intellect Dickhead was a two-stripe AB and knew the ways of the lower deck. So he set to with scissors and sixpence, pulling and tucking until the ribbon sported a beautifully neat bow with two ends sticking up like cat's ears just over her left temple. The hat was always going to be an abomination but she found that by soaking it she was able to pull the brim down at the front, up at the back, and wear it tilted well back on her head to give it a more rakish air. She also nipped ashore to the family dressmaker. There she commissioned a tailor-made tiddley uniform, in doeskin (which strictly was not allowed for ratings), made exactly to fit her and to look good. She transferred one of her oak leaf ribbons to it, along with one of the new killick's badges, and was delighted with the result. Now she could look all those smart officers in the eye and not feel a scruff.

CHAPTER 22:
Up The River

Chatting with her crew at stand easy, Nobby asked if she'd got settled in again all right. Yes, everything was fine, her little cabin all ready for her and shining clean. "Just one thing I've never understood, how does it get kept so well? Someone must be doing it but I never see anyone."

Her crew roared with laughter. "Oh Jane, you can still be so innocent at times. Eustace does it."

"Eustace? Who's Eustace?"

They gave each other sly knowing looks before Stan answered "Eustace, lass, is the right kind steward who looks after you."

"Well, that's very nice of him, but why? I'm not entitled to it."

Again her crew looked at each other, enjoying some secret shared joke.

"Come on boys, level with me. What's so funny about this?"

"Have you never noticed his effeminate manner?" Asked Nobby.

"No, can't say I have. Why?"

"Because Eustace is a shirt lifter – y'know, a brown hatter."

"Eh?"

"An arse bandit, Jane. He loves everything to do with being feminine and gets a real kick out of his involvement with a young female."

A light was coming on in Jane's mind. "I suppose you mean a homosexual? I thought you only get them among academics?"

"Naw, there's another lot get involved in things like stewarding. The Andrew's got plenty, I can tell you."

Jane's mind was running ahead a bit. "So was it Eustace that spied on me all the time? I've wondered how you all knew so much about me."

"Yes of course. He's not needed to drink his own tot since you came aboard. He's always trading some juicy titbit for gulpers somewhere. That's how your sheet got taken round the mess decks. We rather thought you knew that."

"No I didn't. The rotten shitehawk - I'll have his guts for garters."

As was often the way, Stan had said little during this eye-opening chat. But now he chipped in. "Eeh, lass, I wouldn't. Right now you've got a big ally there. But Eustace can be real mean when he's crossed an' given that we're leaving soon anyway I'd just stay on the right side of him if I were you."

Jane suspected she was getting good advice again.

"I did wonder why he seemed so keen to clean and press my dresses and things – now it makes sense. But he seemed so kind – was it really just to satisfy his perversions?"

"No, lass he is genuinely kind to those he likes – and you're number one. You'll be smart to keep it that way."

Jane nodded. "At a price."

In a vague way she knew about homosexuals from scandals in the newspapers and gossip at school, but had no real comprehension of what it meant. Obviously, a man who liked to be a bit feminine himself. She puzzled over it for the rest of the day.

Jane found cleaning *Amaryllis*'s underside therapeutic after the recent traumas. Day by day they scraped off the barnacles and weedy growth, blow-torched the rough patches then rubbed them smooth, applied primer then just before the boat went back in the water there was a frantic rush to get a full coat of anti-fouling on. Again Jane was struck by how adaptable the seamen were, cheerfully and skilfully going about the work. She watched with interest as a chief petty officer shipwright shook the rudder, examined the propellers in minute detail before giving their edges a meticulously careful rub with a fine rasp then felt his way round the boat's bottom, poking and prodding as he went.

Scraping away under the boat with shell and paint scraps landing on her new boiler suit, Jane pondered why getting cold and damp was so satisfying. 'I suppose it's all wrapped up with enjoying the rest so much,' she thought. 'So much physical challenge but plenty of mental demands as well. I've never enjoyed anything as much as driving the boat. I've only been in six months but I'm completely changed in so many ways. Maybe Wrens can drive harbour boats and I can do my bit to make it acceptable. And in a way it's showing affection for the boat by looking after it. Here, under this boat, I am fulfilled. Despite the best efforts of school to make me an academic this is where I belong. And the bad bits? 'Oh well, not much I can do about them now although I still think my three disciplinary offences are unfair. My bum will never be the same again, will it?' And a surge of fierce resentment went through her at the memory of her caning. Angrily she stabbed at the boat, digging a gouge which brought her up short. 'Oops, better be careful with that sort of thing. But I'm damned if I'll let them defeat me, I will not, I will not be defeated.' And she rasped her scraper over the boat fiercely in time with her thoughts, almost shouting out loud. Her mind drifted to her reputation for loose morals, which again she didn't really feel she deserved. 'All right, I'm not a blushing virgin anymore but it was only one man. And it was so nice and such fun– what's wrong with that? Have I lost anything?' An inward grin at that – 'Too right and I've lost something but I'm

CHAPTER 22: Up The River

not that sorry. Am I a woman now, is that what marks the difference between girl and woman? And what of the future? Let's just hope there are some understanding men come out of this horrible war.' Then it was back to concentrating on digging the paint out of an awkward corner.

When the boat was put back in the water Jane was sent to the boats officer's lair to get a weather forecast and to see if he had any orders for *Amaryllis*. This officer had been wounded at Jutland and was unfit for sea duty but his huge knowledge of boats kept him in uniform doing a meaningful job. He had always been in the background in her efforts to become a good boat crew rating, and although she didn't know it had been quietly encouraging throughout. He was a Proper Navy taskmaster well known for being a stickler for correct procedure so she was cautious as she came in, saluted and reported. He had already helped her by authorising her to go to the depot and collect charts and pilot books for the trip up channel; some general advice about planning the passages was useful as well, as Stan had already charged her with doing the planning for the trip.

This day, however, attention was on the immediate. He looked at her mildly, "Right, Beacon, the forecast is dreadful – southerly gales and heavy rain turning to snow for the next forty-eight hours. So I've got a special job for the boat. We need to send a couple of surveyors up the Tamar to the old lock for Gunnislake to look at some barges there that we can't get to by land. You can pick them up from Flagstaff steps tomorrow morning at 0800 then bring 'em back when they have finished. It will probably take two days so it will give you all some practise at living aboard the boat. Then report back to me."

Jane saluted again. "Aye aye, sir," and took the news back.

There followed two of the most enjoyable days she had had on *Amaryllis*, pottering up the river on two hours' flood tide away from the filthy weather that was making life on the Hamoaze unpleasant for small boats. The two surveyors settled in the officers' cuddy at the aft end, and Jane pushed Nobby out of the way so she could work on the little chart-table he had fixed up for her at the fore end of the midships house.

Running up the river they passed under Brunel's magnificent tubular bridge and, with the wide lower reaches of the river before them, Jane settled down to work out her passage plan for the trip to Dover. She read the Admiralty pilot book then her father's yachtsmen's pilot, which she had borrowed, and it was clear that careful planning was needed.

213

'*The English Channel requires great care in navigation,*' she read. *It is wide open to the Atlantic and can get very large seas and swells sweeping up it. Both coasts are rock-girt and dangerous although there are many places for the small boat navigator to find shelter.*'

'Well, there's a start,' she thought looking out as the river narrowed approaching Cargreen. The Spaniard Inn, set close to the riverbank, had some fond memories for Jane and her crew. But back to the pilot book: '*Strong tidal streams are felt throughout the Channel, but these are particularly marked around the main headlands; sail and small low-powered craft are advised to time their passage to have the tide in their favour as they pass these headlands.*'

'Well, we're small but not low-powered,' she thought. Looking up, the river seemed to disappear in front of her, with nothing but low cliffs ahead. Suddenly the river opened to the West and *Amaryllis* swept round, doubling back on herself into a narrower channel. Then, dramatically, the river turned back on itself again in a huge meander and they were heading north once more. She turned back to the pilot book. '*Tidal streams can set unpredictably towards the land, especially at the main headlands, and reflection swells can come from any direction as the Channel narrows towards its Eastern end. Great care should be taken with navigation at all times but especially approaching the major headlands.*'

Again, Jane had a feeling of 'Yes of course' but the warning stayed with her as she looked at the charts. Her instructions were to plan a series of five one-day trips and Stan had emphasised that stops had to be in naval ports. This made sense: facilities, repairs and supplies would be more readily available and wherever they stopped Stan would be sure to have some old oppo ready to help them out.

As she looked at the demands of making a safe voyage it became clear that in a small craft it would also pay to know where the nearest down-weather refuge lay at all times and how one could get into it. Places like Salcombe, she learned, may look tempting on the chart but the bar at its entrance means that it is only accessible for a few hours around high tide and trying to get in at other times, especially if it is a lee shore, could spell disaster.

While mulling over these requirements, Jane looked out ahead. Cotehele Quay passed by, looking neglected but with ammunition barges tied up alongside. Ahead the river seemed to be heading straight at a large hotel, and disappear. Much narrower now, the river's half-tide mud banks seemed to press in on the boat with no way out. Abruptly, the river opened to the East and as they swept round the sharp bend a tall viaduct loomed into view, its spectacular arches spanning the river in confident strides. A train passed over it high above them. Intrigued, she went forward to where Dickhead was on the wheel with Stan keeping a wary eye on him.

CHAPTER 22: Up The River

"Where is this?" she asked, "Isn't it stunning."

"This 'ere is Calstock, lass. Striking isn't it."

Jane watched as they passed under and was going to head back to her chartwork when Stan said. "Ere, it's time you learned to steer in a narrow channel. Take the wheel from Dickhead."

Jane gulped but did as she was told. "Just follow the river, and remember that the deep water is on the outside of bends." Jane found the boat more skittish in its behaviour with the tide behind it and more inclined to sudden sharp changes of direction that had to be corrected on the instant. But after the first couple of bends she started to get the hang of it and found she could anticipate the boat's sudden lunges. Morwelham Quay passed by, another memory of the river's past as a major industrial artery, now looking run down but it had clearly been a major shipping point. An abandoned sailing barge lay half submerged at one end of the quay, quietly rotting away. The wooded banks were getting higher and the river ran in a deep, steep-sided valley. A couple more sharp bends and the eastern bank rose to be high imposing cliffs clad in greenery. All around were woods and fields and a deep air of peace. On the Western bank some old barges appeared, quiet and forlorn. "Lay alongside those lass" said Stan, "And don't go beyond them because there's a weir just below the surface and I'll have to fill in lots of forms if we go aground on it."

Jane nodded, concentrating hard on coming alongside the barges neatly. She spun the boat to stem the tide then eased it backwards and across the tidal stream, checking its sternward drift with gentle bursts on an engine. Contact was so gentle an egg would not have been broken between boat and barge. Stan nodded his approval; Jane puffed out a heavy breath of relief and satisfaction at a job well done. The surveyors went ashore and surprised *Amaryllis*' crew by pitching a tent on the riverbank. Nobby and Dickhead knocked up a corned beef hash on the little primus stove and after a preliminary look around the barges in the gathering dusk, everyone gathered round a camp fire the surveyors had started. There was Naval chat then a bit of a sing-song as the old Naval favourites came out. Some of them were distinctly bawdy and Jane was given surreptitious sideways glances but she was much too fascinated to feel embarrassed or to protest. A general air of peace settled over the group and they turned in to country sounds of owl and sheep around them.

There was a gentle rustling in the trees, sheltering the boat from the gale raging not far away, and lying in the after cuddy, open to the elements, Jane felt a tranquillity of soul which she hadn't known for some time. The past few months had been so hectic that she had rarely stopped to reflect on her life and where she was going. In this quiet secure spot, somehow the sea and the Naval aspects fell in to place and she saw a path forward. 'I will show them. I will not allow Naval prejudice and rigidity to stop me doing this and doing it well. You will not defeat me, d 'you hear? I can take whatever you throw at me and I bloody well will.' She rolled over and looked at the darkened world beyond the boat. 'If I can do the job well on the run up to Dover and show a different Command that I am up to it then perhaps we will be able to get an all-girl crew together. This blasted war is also an opportunity for us, which I'm sure lots of girls will be able to take. And won't I just enjoy showing those crusty old opponents how good we can be.' She smiled gently to herself, and more at peace than she had been for some time, Jane drifted off to sleep.

Next morning people were up early for bacon butties, then with Dickhead holding the other end of the tape measure the surveyors passed the day in closely examining the barges. Built of ferroconcrete, they were relics of World War One, which had survived remarkably well despite their scruffy appearance; the verdict was that they could reasonably be pressed into service. While this was going on, Jane continued planning the trip to Dover. She had been told that when day running each passage has to be calculated to ensure arrival at the destination – preferably in daylight – is reasonably achievable. The boat itself had to be capable of staying out if access to shelter was not available and have sufficient fuel and supplies to keep the sea for a significant period. She found many factors to take into account in laying the plans.

She looked out at midday and again was struck by how the calm beauty of the upper reaches of the Tamar, with its steep wooded banks and smell of the land made such a sharp contrast to the rumbling drum beats of war in salty Devonport.

Surveys completed, Stan was told to lash *Amaryllis* alongside one of the barges and tow it down to Devonport. This was much more of a boathandling challenge than the potter up had been. Boat and barge filled the narrow upper reaches of the river. Jane watched closely as Stan struggled to keep control of the ensemble, which was slow and erratic. Several times they went aground. They passed under Calstock viaduct in gathering early evening gloom and once the river opened out handling boat and barge became easier. They tied the barge up alongside in Devonport at 2200 and with a sigh of relief withdrew to *Defiance.*

Coming back to the reality of Devonport was a bit of a jolt. But with their excursion completed they got their sailing orders: the forecast was much better for some days ahead and there was a reasonable prospect of being able to make the run up Channel. The gentle trip up-river seemed to have refreshed the whole crew who were keen to get on. So they victualled for five days, topped up the primus stove and brought their kitbags and hammocks on board. Jane had had her inflatable camping mattress and sleeping bag sent from home; they just about fitted in the small after cabin. She – and the boat – were ready for sea.

CHAPTER 23:
Weathering the Storm

They sailed after a final breakfast on board *Defiance*; as they cast off Stan muttered, "Good bye, old dear." Jane felt the same tug but excitement at the trip to come welled up to overcome any sentiment. As they reached open sea a great surge of pleasure coursed through her. In the forward steering cuddy with Stan she said "See the Great Mewstone over there? My home is just behind it. It's lovely to be out on the sea again."

Stan grinned, trying not to look too cynical.

They worked their way down the coast to Prawle Point, the southernmost point on their entire journey, arriving just after low water at 1400. "Nice to have a decent quiet day for it" remarked Jane as they brought the point abeam. Start Point came in quick succession. Then they squared away for Dartmouth where they arrived at three in the afternoon, to Jane's quiet relief. Stan went foraging ashore and came back with a couple of old friends, one a chief petty officer steward who despatched a large cooked meal – leftovers from dinner – to the boat.

Jane volunteered to stay on board in the evening as duty watch which let the others find the pleasures of Dartmouth, rolling back to the boat in amiable mood. She enjoyed the deeply satisfying sense of having the boat to herself in the evening, of closeness to boat and water. This brief possession of the boat, hers to care for and to be at one with in its watery home appealed to her inner core and growing sense of professionalism. She loved the responsibility, knowing that her crew were close by but keeping a respectful distance. This was a bit like having the anchor watch – a relaxed but careful eye on the boat, yours to look after on your own while all around you trust you to keep the watch.

They were up again at first light, Stan looking more than a little bleary-eyed. He checked the fuel situation with Nobby, as this was a crucial consideration for the next passage. They had shipped two forty-gallon drums of reserve fuel, lashed next to the engines. At her economic speed of twelve knots *Amaryllis* could run for twenty-four hours, but if she was pushed up to full speed she could empty her tanks in six hours. So balancing speed against consumption and distance-to-go was quite tricky. While Stan and Nobby debated fuel, Jane was despatched to the boats office to get the latest forecast, which was promising: light sou'westerlies freshening to moderate gale later in the day.

Dartmouth is a good jumping-off point for the passage across Lyme Bay to Portland, with Start Point already doubled and open water ahead. In early 1940 Portland was a major naval base, and therefore a logical next port of call. Jane had consulted the pilot books about the crossing. She read. '*The small boat navigator has two choices in crossing Lyme Bay. Either to go straight across, which is a distance of fifty miles but takes the navigator twenty miles to seaward of a coast with few easy refuges if the weather turns foul from southeast through to southwest. Or to follow the coast, always close to a refuge but taking a track almost twice as long as the direct route. Close attention to the weather forecast is advised before deciding on either route.*' Jane had also investigated The Shambles, the notorious area of breaking waves three miles to seaward of Portland Bill, which can be a serious threat to small boats. The pilot book reported that *'Portland Race, known as The Shambles, is caused by tidal streams meeting and running over an uneven seabed and deflecting up to form standing waves on the sea surface; if the wind is against the tide these waves can become standing overfalls, easily capable of sinking a small boat.'*

Jane had briefed Stan on the choices – not that he wasn't well aware of them anyway. He looked at the forecast's predicted light south-westerlies and estimated that they would be tucked up in Portland before it freshened. He took a deep breath, looked at his crew and said "Right lads, I reckon it's the direct route for us. Let's get breakfast quickly and get under way." By 0800 they had cast off. Jane, delegated to do the navigation, set a course of East-Nor'-East, calculating that it would be better to make landfall somewhere around Chessil Beach and coast round the Isle of Portland than to end up to seaward and have to dodge the Shambles.

But whoever made up the weather forecast got it dreadfully wrong. Within an hour of leaving a great bank of black cloud had loomed up to the west; by late morning it was raining hard and the wind freshening from South-West all the time. Stan increased speed to fifteen knots hoping to outrun the weather but in the rain visibility had decreased to a mile or so and they were straining through the murk to spot the land. The sea got up quickly, short steep breakers that pushed *Amaryllis*'s stern around and made steering difficult. Although reasonably seaworthy, this harbour launch design with its flat transom stern, single rudder and twin screws, is designed for efficient handling in confined spaces and sheltered waters, not for running before breaking seas.

Jane was aft securing her gear when the inevitable happened. A rogue wave, much larger than the others, reared up its glistening breaking crest, towering over them. It gripped the boat's stern, spun it round and put her into a broach. Looking over the stern Jane saw the breaking crest coming and for the first time in her life afloat, felt pure terror. For a heart-stopping few moments *Amaryllis* rolled wildly downhill, the wave crest broke on board flooding her from end to end and stopping the starboard engine. Jane, trapped in the after cuddy was flung against the boat's side and rolled around under the breaking sea, which filled the cuddy. Everything was roiling water. Coming to the surface as the boat stabilised in the following trough she spat out sea water looked around and realised that she was still above the surface. Up forward on the wheel, a cursing and spluttering Stan pulled her round until the boat was lying head to the seas and slowed the port engine.

They had survived, but only just. The launch, heavy with water, was now rising to the seas in a slow laboured way. Jane, battling her way forward, was struck by how quickly the matelots responded without specific orders. Dickhead put the new deckhand on the little hand pump, grabbed a bucket and frantically started to bail the water sloshing about up to their knees. Nobby immediately started to strip the starboard engine's fuel system to look for the failure, his new oppo acting as fitter's mate. Bruised and thoroughly shaken up, Jane struggled forward to find Stan grimly hanging onto the wheel. "How far from Portland bill, lass?" he bellowed.

"I reckoned about eight miles to go" she shouted back.

"No point in trying to make a run for it then, we're too far out."

"So we'll just have to wait till things get better?

"Looks like it. We certainly can't turn again till the starboard engine's fixed. Here, take the wheel while I go aft and see how they're getting on. Just keep her head to sea." Jane nodded acknowledgement and took over. She imagined that her light touch on the wheel seemed to calm the boat a bit. Stan was back ten minutes later. "Nobby hasn't found anything yet but he reckons he'll have checked everything out in half an hour. We'll just have to wait till he's finished. You happy to keep the wheel?" Jane nodded, concentrating on holding the boat ,which with only one propeller turning was proving erratic in its steering. Stan eased the engine back a little more until they were just holding their own – dodging, the fishermen would call it, and set to with the bucket he had brought to bail out their forward steering position. An hour later the boat was pumped out and Nobby had run through the various parts, which might have caused a failure, bled the systems and was ready to go.

But the starter motor was dead - water in the electrics somewhere had shorted it out. Again Nobby went to work to try to fix it but in the end had to admit defeat, and they were down to one engine. Disappointed, Stan came back to where Jane was battling with the boat. It was now blowing a full gale with ragged spume blowing off the tops of the steep-faced waves, grey-green with menace. The semi-sheltered steering position was a cold wet place to be, not helped by the wild plunges and gyrations of the boat. "It looks like we'll have to stay here till the weather eases. We can't take a chance on trying to turn or run before this lot. And where are we now anyway?"

"Good question. I think if anything we're setting further to the north and we should be clear of the strongest of the tide's run, but who knows? I presume the chart's a sodden mess now?"

"Afraid so, it's mark one eyeball from now on."

"Which would be all right if we could see anything. Don't think we've got more than half a mile of visibility now."

So they settled down, dodging into the weather and seas through the afternoon with Jane and Stan taking half hour about on the wheel. They were startled when Dickhead appeared with a can of bully beef and a loaf of bread. Conditions were too harsh to eat properly but they tore off chunks of bread and meat and stuffed them down their throats as best they could, dripping with salt water. Later he came back with a bottle of fresh water, which they sipped carefully. At dusk Jane battled her way aft to see how the others were doing. Mostly they were fine if cold and worried, but the new deckhand – Rufus's replacement was curled up in a corner whimpering. "We're all going to die" over and over. Jane tried to pull his head up and talk to him but he threw her off and curled up even more tightly.

Nobby intervened. "Best leave him alone Jane. We'll keep an eye on him. Fancy some soup?" Miraculously Nobby had warmed up a can of pea and ham soup, and its pungence spread through her comfortably. She filled a bottle with some more for Stan and struggled forward again, nearly going over the side in one of *Amaryllis's* wilder lurches. After dark conditions always feel worse. By curling up in the corner the off-duty helmsman could keep out of the wind and driving wet but it was still a cold and soaking place and there was no rest to be had.

Jane took over again at midnight, blessing the luminous hands on that waterproof watch which allowed them to keep track of the time. She was just getting into the rhythm of the boat again when a black mass reared up in front of them. "Watch out, watch out" she screamed as she pulled the boat round to starboard, shipping another wave top. A warship, probably a destroyer, charged past them at speed, darkened ship, and missed them by no more than twenty feet. If Jane had not swung the boat round they would have been run down. She knew what to expect next and pulled the wheel hard to port as the destroyer's churning screws threw heavy spray over them. Hampered by it being the port engine that was running, *Amaryllis* was slow to turn to port, and the wall of the destroyer's wake reared up over them. But the launch had turned just enough to put its shoulder into the raging mass and although it bucked and reared wildly, coming down with a crash, the boat stayed upright. "My God that was close" roared Stan. Jane was trembling all over, hardly able to hold the wheel. "Take her for a minute, please Stan" and she was violently sick over the lee side. The pea and ham soup made it an aromatic moment.

Calming down if still shaken, she took the wheel again, remarking to Stan "At least that tells us we're not too close to the land. If he is heading for Portland it looks as though we've set South rather than North, which would be good. Let's hope so." Stan grunted.

Just after four in the morning the rain got even heavier, driving down in solid sheets while the wind rose to a howling crescendo. In a matter of minutes it veered a couple of points and ten minutes later the rain abruptly stopped. The front had passed through. Half an hour later they were left with a sloppy swell and calm conditions. To the west the horizon was clear; to the east the retreating weather system still obliterated everything. An hour later a darker mass could be seen out to the east – the Isle of Portland emerging from the rain, and by dawn it was clear that they were lying no more than a couple of miles from land and more or less west of Portland Point. Stan eased the stiffness out of his legs muttering. "I'm getting too old for this sort of thing" and went aft to check on the state of the engine. The port engine seemed to be all right so he took a look at the swell, now no more than lumpy rollers and remarked. "I think we'll give it a go. You ready for a roll or two, lass?" She nodded, glumly eyeing the swells which although easy enough were still higher than the boat. But *Amaryllis* came round steadily with just one heavy lurch down the face of a swell before settling with her bow to Portland Bill. Half an hour's careful steering had the point abeam close to port as they passed inside the Shambles, and soon after they were in the lee of the Island. The sudden easing of the boat's motion was a blessed relief.

They were sitting stupefied on a pontoon in the boat pool looking at the salt-encrusted *Amaryllis* with a gentle sun easing warmth into their faces, when a petty officer came down the ladders. "Where are you lot from?" He queried.

"Doing a transfer from Guzz to Dover" Grunted Stan. Like the rest he hadn't even removed his sou'wester and looked grey with exhaustion.

"You mean you were out in that lot last night? You're lucky to be afloat."

"Don't we know it. You from the boats' office?" Getting a nod Stan went on, "Right, we've got an engine out. Can you get a tiffy to look at it for us? We need to get up to quarters for a bath and a clean and could do with a square meal. Is old Davey Giffard still in the boats office?"

This made the petty officer pay attention. "Yeah, he is indeed."

"Then tell him Stan Roberts is in town an' would like to say hello."

"You know Davey?"

"He was my oppo in *Hermes* on the China station back in '32 –'34."

"Oh, right I'll let him know."

With the petty officer gone Stan looked at his crew and smiled. "That'll get things moving. Old Davey will have a finger in every pie in Portland or he's not half the fixer he used to be." This rumination was interrupted by the boat's recently acquired replacement for Rufus the Red suddenly appearing from the midships cuddy, kitbag on shoulder. "Right, I'm off. You mad bastards can carry on with this crazy trip but I'm finished. I don't care if I do get in the rattle, that'll be safer than taking this tub to sea again." With that he swung up the ladder and disappeared.

Stan looked at his crew. "Probably best to let him go. I'll have to report him and Lord knows where he's going now but there's no point in trying to hang on to him. The rest of you thinking like that?" But they all shook their heads slowly. As ever, Nobby spoke up. "Could do with a rest and getting the engine fixed before we go, though." At that point the petty officer came back and called down to Stan from the quayside. "Chief Giffard says would you come up to the office? He'll sort you out."

Proper Navy through and through, Stan Removed his sou'wester and oilskins, clapped his cap on and puffed his way up the ladder. "You lot stand fast till I get back. You could make a start on squaring her off below while you're loafing about with nothing to do."

There was a collective groan at this, but slowly they got moving, extracting soaking kit and mashed up food and tattered bits of chart from around the midships cabin.

Half an hour later things suddenly started to happen. Two tiffies arrived and set about the starboard engine. A Tilly (utility vehicle, the Navy's term for all lighter commercial vehicles) pulled up on the quayside and the driver called down to them. "Collect your gear and come with me." Jane was dropped at the Wrens' quarters, where a friendly killick met her. "We were told to look out for you. Bath's waiting for you. Does your gear need drying out? Leave it with me."

Sinking into a deep hot bath was bliss and a great feeling of lassitude took over; Jane was sleeping peacefully when a loud knock on the door woke her up. "Are you all right? You've been half an hour in there."

"Sorry, I was dozing. Have you any of my kit available?"

"There's a pile by the door – the rest is so full of salt that we've sent it to be washed."

Clean and dressed again Jane felt much better and a solid naval dinner left her at peace with the world. She tried to explain to the quarters officer what she was doing there but struggled to stay awake so was despatched to a spare senior rate's cabin with a warning to say nothing about it to those senior rates, who would not be pleased at a junior's incursion into their little redoubt. She sank into oblivion until tea time. Turning out for tea in her usual rig of adapted bell bottoms, blue shirt and uniform jacket she stepped into the mess hall and noticed a Wrens' table at the far end. Walking through the mess she had the same effect as the first day she went onto *Defiance's* upper deck – the whole place went silent and stared in disbelief. They had never seen a Wren in bell bottoms before. With Jane's long legs the effect was spectacular. Joining the Wrens' table they all looked at her in puzzled amazement, and she found herself explaining all over again what she was doing and why she was dressed as she was. They were a friendly group of writers and teleprinter operators and catering staff, and she noticed that it was largely Wrens who served the tables. Tea over, she flaked out again and didn't budge till 'call the hands' the next morning.

Ambling down to *Amaryllis* she was surprised to find the rest of the crew busy washing her down with fresh water. "Morning Jane, the engine's fixed and I've got fuel, food and charts coming today so I think we should be good for going tomorrow morning if the weather holds. Get your boots on and start scrubbing." And the rest of the day was spent shining the launch up to something like its usual standard. At stand-easy Stan said to her "Come and look at this" and led her to the end of the jetty. Round the corner was a destroyer with its upper works bent and broken. "Apparently they got their navigation wrong in that gale and ploughed into the Race. Can't help wondering if it's the same one that nearly ran us down. That'll teach them to pay more attention." He indulged in a sardonic chuckle. This surprised Jane as Stan was usually most unjudgemental and had shown little emotion at the time. Clearly he had been more affected than he showed. However, maverick destroyers were not the only danger that lay ahead.

CHAPTER 24:
Planes and Prejudice

Another good night's sleep and Jane was ready to go; they slipped at 0830 and headed out for the Solent and Portsmouth on a mild spring morning with the gentlest of northerlies and a good forecast. After what they'd been through this trip seemed like a holiday excursion. By late morning Anvil Point was abeam and they altered up for the Needles. Their route had been briefly debated as they could easily have gone south of the Isle of Wight but the true small boat route is through the Solent, and with *Amaryllis'* power the strong tides were not an issue. With fifty-seven miles to go they would make Portsmouth in easy time.

Overhead, the RAF were practising and a couple of Hurricanes made dummy attacks on *Amaryllis*, with much waving and thumbs up. So when a third Hurricane came zooming down on them they thought nothing of it until it opened fire on them. "Bloody Hell" screeched Stan and put the wheel hard-a-starboard. But too late – a line of bullets ripped through the boat, there was a scream from somewhere aft, and the ensign was neatly shot away. By chance the boat was still watertight below the waterline, although the row of holes in her topsides would be a problem if the weather got up. Stan stopped the boat and went aft to see Dickhead who had a flesh wound in his thigh. Expertly he and Nobby stripped the wound, cleaned and bandaged it, and lashed a splint to it. Puffing and looking grim Stan came forward again to where Jane was idly holding the wheel and keeping lookout.

"He'll be all right but it needs proper attention. We've plenty of fuel so I think I'll rev her up a bit and go straight through to Haslar. He'll be better off in our own hospital. Then I'm going to do some serious complaining about that mad crabfat. We even had our ensign showing clearly – what was he thinking about?" Jane could only shrug and shake her head in sympathetic agreement. It had been her first experience of being under fire and it had all happened so quickly that she hadn't had time to be scared – but thinking about it sent a shiver through her, the line of bullet holes down the boat's side going no more than a foot from where she'd been standing. She had already heard the old military saying that sometimes your own side are more dangerous than the enemy, and now she saw why.

Stan turned East, towards the Needles which were in plain sight, and pushed the launch up to sixteen knots. He then turned the wheel over to Jane while he wrote up the log book, with several heavy bits of underlining. Charging up the West Solent was fun on a clear sunny day, and by mid afternoon they were easing down to pass Fort Blockhouse and turn up Haslar Creek. Jane looked around with intense interest as they came in, as this was new territory to her – somehow Whale Island, further up the harbour, seemed like a different world. Again, Stan clapped his cap on as soon as they arrived and disappeared ashore, logbook under his arm. Ten minutes later an ambulance was on the jetty above them, looking for Dickhead. Its solitary driver was not inclined to come down to the boat but passed his stretcher so they were able to carry Dickhead up the ramps onto the jetty and see him off. Half an hour later Stan returned with news that preliminary examination suggested that the wound was bad enough to keep Dickhead in, and he wouldn't be going any further with them. So they packed his gear and landed it, Nobby taking it into the hospital. Stan had also arranged shoreside accommodation for them, Jane in the Nurse's Home as they hadn't yet got a Wrennery. Dockyard mateys would be down in the morning to repair the damage.

For the rest of the afternoon they tidied up on board and did some cleaning. Jane was peacefully polishing the sidelights when a full four-ringed captain appeared on the pontoon. A tall angular man with the requisite bushy eyebrows, piercing gaze and his cap at the Beatty angle, he looked every inch a naval captain. A hasty grabbing of caps and they came to attention as he arrived at the boat, Stan giving him the honours of his rank. "At ease, chief petty officer. I'm told you have a woman on board. Is that right?" Jane was a bit startled by the question as mostly she found it was perfectly obvious that she was female despite – or more probably because of – her retailored bell bottoms. But the question was directed at Stan and by now Jane knew enough of naval ways not to butt in. "Yes sir, Leading Wren Beacon here." And Stan motioned to Jane. The Captain continued to look at Stan. "And what are you doing here?"

"We're on a delivery run from Devonport to Dover sir. We're the launch of Rear Admiral Rodmayne who's being transferred from Devonport to Dover and he's taking us with him. We got shot up by a Hurricane this morning and put in here to land an injured sailor. You can see the line of bullets down the side." Stan pointed to the neat line of bullet holes.

"Hmm. I find this most irregular. You pop up here full of holes, with an injured seaman and this…. Thing," And here he gestured vaguely in Jane's direction "And expect me to believe you're on a routine port transfer? I don't believe it and you're being detained while I look into it. There's something fishy here and I aim to get to the bottom of it. Report to my office in half an hour's time – and bring the thing with you." Jane bristled fiercely but held her tongue.

Suitably smartened up they reported the necessary five minutes early, and were summoned on the elapsed dot of the half hour. They were startled to find a three ring commander, a sub-lieutenant writer, and two regulating chief petty officers also in the room. Stan obviously knew one of the Jossmen as they exchanged the briefest of recognition looks. "Right, chief petty officer, tell me the story from the start." Stan explained it all again, going back to when Jane first joined the boat around the time they were nominated to act as Commodore Rodmayne's launch and how, when he was appointed rear-admiral at Dover, it had been agreed that *Amaryllis* would go with him due to a boat shortage at Dover.

"And you are a lifetime rating?"

"Yes sir – joined up in 1915"

"Were you at Jutland?"

"Yes sir. Boy in X turret in *HMS Inflexible.*"

"Hmm. And survived - that is a respectable record.. Yet you have deliberately undermined Naval tradition by allowing this thing on board your boat?"

"I was given orders from a very high level sir. And I have to say that she is very good at the job, sir."

"That is utterly irrelevant. There is a serious matter of principle here"

The captain then turned his attention to Jane, looking her up and down in that cool naval way. "Report yourself, young lady" Jane took a step forward, came to attention, gave him her very best naval salute and said "1095 Leading Wren Jane Beacon, sir."

"This oak leaf you have on your jacket. Do you know what it is?" The question startled Jane a bit as she thought someone like a captain would know. "Yes sir, it's a 'Mentioned in Despatches."

"And why are you adorning yourself with it? That could be a serious offence, y'know."

"Because I was awarded it, sir. It's in the Gazette in early January if you want to check."

"Don't get lippy with me young lady."

This puzzled Jane. "I only answered your question sir."

"Indeed. So I'm expected to believe that a female can get an award? Has the Navy no pride left? How long have you been in the Wrens now?

"Almost six months sir."

"A real old salt, aren't you." He sneered. "The whole thing is preposterous. Women's place is barefoot in the kitchen. I'm damned if I'm going to have them pretending to be seamen, in the Wrens or not. Scratch, check with Devonport about this Admiral Rodmayne. And see if there is some ghastly female office that thinks

CHAPTER 24: Planes and Prejudice

it's to do with the Navy. We can't be having this. Chief regulators, make sure that none of this dreadful crew leave *Dolphin*. And Commander Jones, please make sure the boat doesn't move." He turned to Stan and Jane. "Chief Petty Officer Roberts, I'm putting you on a charge. I don't know what it is yet. But I'm damned if I'm going to have the Navy undermined by its own people. And as for you young lady, I'm going to have you slung out directly, be damned if I'll have women interfering in my world."

Jane just couldn't stop herself "But what about 'Free a man to go to sea, and all that?" She queried quietly.

"That's for stewards and other poofters; not proper seamen. Now clear off and don't argue with me." So they came to attention, saluted and backed out.

Outside they looked at each other in puzzled dismay. "What on earth was all that about? Who is this guy anyway, and what's it all to do with him?" The regulating chief who had exchanged glances with Stan caught up with them. "Hello Daisy" said Stan. "Can you explain all this?"

"Hello Stan. Funny way to meet up again. That's Captain Gribben you've just tangled with; the most detested man in Pompey. He's a notorious bag of prejudices and none more than women. His wife's a terrifying battleaxe and he can't stand the sight of them. So having one turn up on his doorstep in bell bottoms is like throwing petrol on a fire. Keep a low profile and we'll see what tomorrow brings. You're to report again at 1000 tomorrow. Meantime I'll make sure you're comfy. Fancy a jar tonight, Stan?"

"That'd be nice, Daisy." And the two parted amicably.

Jane packed her kitbag and found the nurse's home, where they gave her a cubbyhole of a cabin. The nurses at tea were a distantly affable group, very strict in their behaviour and obviously viewing Jane as something a bit strange, a bit exotic from a different planet. But she was able to get a good hot bath and the hard mattress didn't stop her having a sound night's sleep. She pulled out the rest of her Wren's uniforms first thing in the morning, scrounged an iron, pressed the worst of the crumples out of them, and dressed properly – white shirt, skirt and black stockings – for a change. In the captain's office once more he ignored them, and turned to his secretary. "All right, scratch, what have you found out?"

"There is a Commodore Rodmayne, sir, recently recalled to the active list and was gazetted a week ago as rear-admiral. The boats officer at Devonport confirms that the launch *Amaryllis* left there by sea six days ago to go to Dover but he hasn't heard from them since so turning up here would not be unreasonable. He knows about Wren Beacon, who is well known in Plymouth and is seen as an experiment in whether women can crew harbour craft." Here the captain cut in across him.

"Is that so? Well, I'm going to put a stop to that right now. I'm damned if I'll have these horrible women coming into men's work. Detain the boat, and have this impudent girl put on a train tonight. This has got to stop now." He crashed a fist down on his desk, face puce with rage.

Back outside, Jane looked at Stan and asked. "What can we do about it, Stan?" He shrugged. "Sorry, lass, there's nothing much I can do. Once it's a four-ringer my connections don't count for much. You're pals with your admiral. Can you speak to him?" This was a thought that hadn't occurred to Jane, somehow focused on the immediate and worrying problems. But yes, she could try. "Can you get me a quiet telephone? Maybe I could speak to him." She nipped back to her tiny bedroom, collected her address book and found Stan in the regulating office, talking to the large and impressive Jaunty Stan seemed happy to call Daisy. Jane certainly wouldn't. She was led into a side office and left with a telephone. She knew her Godfather would still be on leave prior to transfer so got the operator to try his home number first. Mercifully, he was there. There was a gentle, only half articulated, understanding that off duty and in domestic surroundings he would remain Uncle George. So she decided to push that angle. "Hello, Uncle George? Jane Beacon here. Listen, we've got to Pompey and have hit a big problem." She went on to explain about Captain Gribben, his prejudices and that *Amaryllis* was being detained. It was Captain Gribben's detaining the boat that seemed to bother the new rear-admiral most. "None of his damn business and I need her" was his comment but when he'd listened to Jane he said with quiet grimness "I know Gribben, he's a menace. You just keep quiet and leave it with me. If he's still giving you trouble for being female you could do worse than speak to Wren headquarters and see if they can sort him out."

"Thank you, sir"

"And Jane"

"Yes sir?"

"Keep very quiet when the shells start exploding above you. Things could briefly be quite bloody."

"Yes sir. And thank you."

Uncle George growled farewell.

Jane debated for a minute then thought. 'Why not, let's do it now,' and asked the operator to connect her to Admiralty House in London. Through a series of connections and extensions she got the WRNS general office and asked to speak to the Director. "Good morning, ma'am, it's Leading Wren Beacon here. Do you

CHAPTER 24: Planes and Prejudice

remember me? Your one and only boating Wren?"

"Oh yes, Beacon, I remember you. I hope your backside's all right now. What is it this time?"

Jane went through the story again, this time with more emphasis on his views on women. The director was clearly not impressed. "Yes well, we have to be a bit careful about treading on the Navy's corns but we do have ways of dealing with it when prejudice gets threatening. Leave it with me and keep a low profile in the meantime."

"Thank you, ma'am, and I'll take your advice."

The director laughed and rang off.

After that there was little to do. Jane packed up completely in case she did have to get on a train that night. The dockyard mateys made quick work of plugging the bullet holes in the launch's topsides, and by mid-afternoon she was fit for sea again if still a little rough looking. Jane followed them along and put a quick coat of paint over each of the raw repairs as it was completed. The boat was otherwise immaculate so, sailor-like, they settled down to do nothing but wait. Around 1600 Daisy was seen trundling his large frame down the gangway and arrived alongside *Amaryllis* with a quiet smile on his face. "Which one of you is related to an admiral?" He queried. "Gribben has just had the worst two hours of his life. It started with two rear-admirals giving him earache, one of them bellowing at him and ordering the immediate release of his boat. Then some virago of a female, apparently in charge of all you Wrens? Gave him grief about allowing prejudice to cloud his judgement and he'd better move into the twentieth century sharpish, and what's more Wren appointments were not his to unpick, and to cap it all some bloody Sea Lord calls him up and tells him to wind his neck in pronto unless he wants to see out the rest of his career in command of a coal barge in West Africa. You have some interesting friends. He's so consumed by rage he can't speak at the moment but managed to splutter 'Get them out of here, if they're still here at 1800 I'll blow my career by sinking the bloody thing.' So I think you'd be smart to go while you can. How on earth did you do it Stan?"

Stan smiled, slowly and expansively. "Well, y'know Daisy, we all have our level of contact. But this is a bit of an eye-opener."

Daisy looked round. "You ready for sea?"

"We could do with some bread and bacon but otherwise yes. Repairs finished; bunkered; fully refreshed; yes, I reckon we can go. Do we need to report to boats officer?"

"No, I don't think so Stan, I'll let 'em know. What's your plan?"

"Well, I didn't mean to go to sea at night but it looks like we'll have to. I'll head up to Newhaven now, should be there by breakfast tomorrow easy, and lay over there while the nausea settles. Then it's last lap to Dover."

"Fine, I'll let 'em know. Good sailing."

"Thanks Daisy. See you at Aggie's sometime."

"Yeh, right. You owe me one."

Stan just laughed and waved as Daisy marched off the pontoon.

CHAPTER 25:
Sailing to the Future

Ten minutes later a breathless young matelot arrived with half a dozen loaves of bread and a pile of bacon – 'half a pig there' muttered Nobby. By now they were down to four on board so there was no question of Jane not pulling her weight. They slipped at 1730 with Jane on the bow, and quite deliberately she slowly went through full boathook drill as they went, still in her skirt and black stockings. Although they didn't know it Gribben watched this and it reduced him to such hysteria that he had to be tranquilised for his own good. They pushed out into gathering dusk, rounded the Nab Tower, ran down to the Owers light vessel and set course to the East. Portsmouth to Newhaven is forty-eight miles so, with ten hours before dawn, there was no rush. Stan shut down the port engine and they ambled along easily at five knots. By Jane's reckoning the tides would just about cancel each other out in that time and the forecast was calm.

"Right, lass, are you as good at watchkeeping at night?"
"I think so, Stan, I've done it often enough before."
"That's fine then. Watch out for darkened ships and call me at midnight."
"Sleep tight."

And as Amaryllis headed East into the deepening night sky, Jane had an enormous sense of relief flood over her, driven by a suspicion that the curious incident in Portsmouth had been a close-run thing. Briefly, she turned over the thought that had she not been able to phone for help as she did, she could have been in serious difficulties. But then she'd never have been there in the first place had it not been for those powerful interests keeping a distant watch on where they had put her. Encountering someone like Gribben had really shaken her. Such naked prejudice was new and to meet someone prepared to damage other peoples' lives by their own blinkered actions was scary. It would take her a long time to forgive being referred to as a 'thing'. That really rankled. How much of that was there in the Navy, she wondered? Uncle George had hinted at it but meeting it face-to-face like that was a frightening experience. She was discovering that she had a capacity to remain calm and *insouciant* when events were getting tough, but when the reality struck home afterwards she could feel really scared.

Stan and Nobby were asleep aft, so the new stoker, replacing Taff who'd got his destroyer, came forward to chat to Jane. He'd been a silent withdrawn character since joining and they'd been on the go so continuously that Jane had never really got to know him. He turned out to be a young Geordie, out of a shipyard and basic naval training. "It's George, isn't it?" she enquired.

"Nick Barmelow really, but Ah've got used to George now. We always get Barleymow anyway so whatever you like."

She settled down to get to know him, chatting about home and his wide-spread family. The men were mostly merchant seamen or fishermen, the women had jobs in the yards and shops and the fish quay around his home turf of North Shields. It appeared to be a spreading clan that Jane had difficulty keeping a handle on. She remarked that he'd done well to stick with it through their troubles and difficulties, but he seemed to feel that he'd seen worse out fishing, including a boat that sank under him. "A bad feeling that," he said. "And Ah tell ye Jane, Ah've several sisters'd love to be doin' what you are. They'd be canny hands."

"Tell 'em to join the wrens and when the call comes we'll see about getting them in. It's going to come but we just don't know when. What are you hoping to do?"

"I'm quite happy here for now, thanks. I hadn't thought much further."

At ten he made them a mug of Kye on the little burner, and at midnight called the watch after a peaceful evening. It was 0500 before Stan called Jane again and by then he was worried – they were in dense fog. The sea had an oily calm to it with slow undulating swells just moving the boat, but they were completely shut in, visibility no more than fifty yards at most. "Jane, can you figure out where we are?"

"Well, I can do a dead reckoning run for you and see but it'll be a bit of a guess. When did you last see the land?"

"Half an hour ago. I could make out the black mass of it against the horizon but there was nowt to take a bearing of. Looked like it was still a good way off."

So Jane took the log book and plotted as best she could. That put *Amaryllis* about five miles from Newhaven, or at least the land round about. Stan eased the engine down to tickover and they crept ahead, eyes and ears straining for any sign. Sound acquires a curiously dead effect in dense fog, actually carrying over long distances but giving the impression of being close by. Everything was dripping damp, and in the dark any sense of size or distance disappears. They all jumped at a snort and splash alongside the boat. "Bloody seals" growled Stan.

Daylight brought little respite. Instead of black wooliness they now had white, but remained just as walled in by the stuff. By seven they had more than run their distance by dead reckoning to have reached land of some sort, but nothing showed.

Shortly after eight Jane whispered. "I think I hear something different ahead and to port. Might be sea on the shore." Nobby, standing with them, nodded agreement. Stan listened intently, heard nothing to begin with then picked up the gentlest of rattling sighs. "You're right, I think. Nobby, minimum revs please." It is one of the curiosities of navigating in fog that the first thing seen is often low down and in the foreground, below the natural middle distance focus of lookouts, and so it was this time. Right in front of them, alarmingly close to, was a fuzzy line of boulders, seas gently washing them as they broke. "Full astern" cried Stan and as it was the starboard engine that was running, the boat swung sharply to that side. They came to, parallel with the still indistinct rocks, and peered at them. Studying them with the binoculars, Stan said. "I reckon those are white, which means we must be off Beachy Head somewhere. They're darker further west. See what you think, lass." Looking closely she saw they were indeed white, not that she could tell any more. Stan stared morosely at them for a minute or two. "It looks like we've arrived East of Newhaven. I think we'll turn to port and slowly follow the beach along just on the edge of visibility. It's a pretty clean shoreline here, isn't it?" Jane checked the chart and agreed. "There are one or two offlying rocks but we'd be unlucky to hit them. If we're on the West Side of Beachy Head we're a maximum of seven miles from Newhaven – be careful you don't run up the back of the breakwater."

"Right now that's the least of our worries lass." Stan spun *Amaryllis* round, set minimum revs and ghosted along, the faint shoreline keeping them company.

Twenty minutes elapsed uneventfully, eyes straining forward and to the side. Suddenly there was a rattle and a brief check to the boat's movement. Stan winced – that was a propeller briefly touching something. He just hoped it wasn't too hard. At the same time the shoreline dropped away sharply to starboard and he swung the wheel to follow it, not wanting to lose sight of the land. Jane, acting as his eyes and ears, suddenly said "Stan, there's land to port too."

"What? Bloody hell, where are we?" For on both sides low shingle banks were showing. They were also stemming a noticeable current, which meant Stan did not follow his first instinct to stop the engine but kept it ticking over at minimum revs.

He went to the boat's side, scooped up a handful of water and tasted it. "Almost fresh. We must have got into a river somehow, but how?" They were gently moving ahead, just overcoming the current, when a fence strung across the river loomed up in front of them. Muttering curses Stan backed the launch down. "I think we're just going to stop here until this harry thickers clears away. We're probably safe enough. Jane, go and drop the anchor. Give it short stay – there's not much room to swing here."

With anchor down and holding, they stopped the engine and prodded about with the boathook. "About four feet under us, I wonder if that'll keep us afloat?"

Jane responded. "It's an hour and a half before low water Newhaven and wherever this is can't be much different. With any luck we'll just about stay afloat but we'll need to watch her sharply when she swings to the flood." Stan nodded gloomy agreement. With the engine shut down the silence was total. As they grew used to it they could hear cattle in the distance and the odd seagull calling. Then a heavy machine started up, quite close by. "Well, at least there are other humans somewhere about." Muttered Stan. "Nobby, how about a brew and some bacon butties? I'm famished." Nobby grinned agreement and soon enough the wonderful evocative smell of frying bacon filled the boat.

Swinging to the flood gave no problems, so they settled down to wait – one person on watch, checking for dragging the anchor. Stan, having been up since midnight was tired and slung his hammock, soon snoring peacefully. Through this strange closed-in day they took watch turns and waited patiently for the weather to change. Around four o'clock the next morning the fog abruptly rolled away, and when daylight came they saw they were in a narrow river, low green fields on each side and the mass of Beachy Head close to the East. A man in a coastguard uniform came to the river's edge and hailed them. Mouth still full of bacon Stan replied and explained how they'd ghosted in during the fog. "Where are we?

"You're in Cuckmere Haven." The coastguard replied. Jane dived for the chart. "Good heavens, how did we squeeze in there? Oh, I suppose it makes sense." And she pointed out to Stan the little river tucked in on the western edge of Beachy Head.

"Are we all right for getting out of here?"

"Well if you got in all right you can get out. Tides are making. I'd leave it till at least half tide flood to be sure of getting over the bar, not that it's much of a thing. Where are you bound?"

"We were heading for Newhaven from Portsmouth."

"You'll not have any problems then. It's only five miles to the west. You'll get going this afternoon? "

"Too right. We're way behind schedule now."

"Good luck and good sailing."

But things didn't work out that way. By late morning the wind was rising strongly from the South, and by 1500 when Stan had hoped to move out the mouth of the river was a mass of broken water. The wind was starting to howl around them and the cows had taken shelter. "Someone up there doesn't want us to get to Dover." Growled Stan in dismay. Not only was the mouth of the river a line of dangerous breakers, but the sea beyond it looked distinctly rough. Shaking his head sadly Stan called off any attempt at getting out that day. "I think we'll be safe enough tucked up here" was his prediction and for twenty-four hours that held true. It blew a screaming gale outside but apart from a short swell that set her nodding for an hour round high water, *Amaryllis* lay snug as a dog in its basket. Anchor watch was kept up and Jane on the middle watch found it odd, lying so close to foul weather in this tiny little nook yet safe against the storm which she could hear booming outside. Odd it might be but there was a sense of something almost like cosiness, of unlikely protective hands being held round the boat and gently caring for it.

Next morning the gale had blown itself out, the barometer was rising and so were hopes. By early afternoon they had swung to the first of the flood tide, the river mouth looked quiet enough although there was still a swell running on it, and by 1600 Stan was impatient to be off. Both engines running, Jane heaved the anchor up, a physical challenge right on the edge of her strength but she was damned if she'd ask for help - and they eased gently down the half mile of river, waved to the coastguard as they cleared the entrance without touching the bottom despite a couple of scares in troughs, and were once more on the open sea. It was now calm outside, so Stan opened both engines to near full throttle and twenty minutes later they were easing down again, entering Newhaven. As well as the regular cross-channel ferries there were some strange new naval vessels around – landing craft and coastal forces motor boats. There also seemed to be a good deal of construction work going on ashore. There was no sign of any officialdom or a boats office so Stan found a hut with some shipwrights in it and managed to wheedle unwilling use of their phone. He reported to Dover boat's officer who grumbled about how long it had all taken, and then they cleaned the boat and decided on a run ashore that night. Jane dug out her skirt and stockings again and all of them, best tiddley uniforms on, made a round of the pubs where they met quite a few of the new Volunteer Reserve Navy. This was a strange experience for Stan used to regular Proper Navy for so long, but they were a cheery sociable crowd and a brisk evening was had. They all – officer and rating - treated Stan with the deepest reverence; for many he was their first contact with the old Proper Navy outside their training officers.

This new Navy were a mixed bunch, keen enough on all things maritime but without having sold their souls to the Navy. They had been through basic training so knew who to salute and how the Navy worked, but carried its social distinctions very lightly. During the evening Jane met a handful of Canadians as well as former country solicitors, bank clerks, milk rounds men, an insurance salesman, shop managers, and not least general labourers. Like Jane they had joined for the duration to 'do their bit' so did not have the heavy vested interest in seniority or promotion lists that regular naval officers lived by. Everything was light-hearted and fun, especially when let loose ashore and Jane, by now accustomed to moving up and down the Navy's social scale fairly effortlessly, enjoyed meeting them. Most were young like her and viewed their world with cheery optimism.

Whether it was the release of tension or just the enthusiastic company, Jane rather disgraced herself that night, getting thoroughly tipsy and having to be helped back to *Amaryllis* by her grinning shipmates while gently warbling the hair-raisingly obscene song they'd been teaching her. The crusher on the gate was inclined to record this in his log but Stan put him right "Do us a favour, she's been through a lot has this one. Needed the break."

"Who was Eskimo Nell?" she innocently enquired of the crusher who to his credit just laughed and let them pass. Although she had barely noticed it, Jane had made a deep impression on the rather green young men she chatted with. A tough sea-going wren, and a leading wren with a 'Mentioned in Despatches' at that, was something new to them and with her increasing looseness of tongue through the evening she regaled them with embellished wild salty yarns all in complex Jackspeak. Her lean weather-beaten and freckly face made a stark contrast with the soft pale white of the other girls around.

Turn-to the next morning was a painful affair, her throbbing head and shaky innards reminding her all too painfully of what she'd been up to. Stan was impatient to be off so she had to pull herself together rapidly and by 0930 they slipped, Jane on the boathook drill on the bow. She couldn't understand why the various boats they passed all came to a halt and their crews waved and whistled furiously. Nobby gave her a sly grin "You were in cracking form last night Jane. The whole damn lot are in love with you now."

"Spare me, no tell me, what did I do?"

"Well, you certainly talk a good story and taught them some interesting new swear words. Then when you got on a table and danced a Charleston in the 'Smuggler's Rest,' it brought the house down."

Jane shuddered. Outside with good conditions and plenty of fuel in the tanks Stan pushed the speed up and the forty-five miles to Dover passed in quick time.

Once the White Cliffs were in sight, they stirred a deep passion in Jane. These were the ramparts of the moat, the iconic face of defiance over which no invader had come for a thousand years. Away to the South East gun fire and columns of smoke spoke of active war on the doorstep and were a sharp reminder that they were now entering a new and dangerous area. Jane had passed through Dover often enough on her summer trips to join the Pechot family but the cliffs seemed quite different this time.

Looking at them she thought 'I am here to do my bit, help defeat the threat across the Channel, and I will do it, I will do it. I hope I can be strong enough to withstand whatever this posting throws at me so we can look forward to a better tomorrow. These cliffs are a wonderful wall; but on their own they are nothing. It needs the people around them to turn them into a barrier and I am about to become one tiny bit of that. I must not fail.' She looked ahead to where the pier ends of her new posting were approaching rapidly 'My future, my worth to this effort will be decided in the challenges I find here and soon.' Please let me be up to them.'

Amaryllis berthed in Dover boat pool at 1415. Plymouth seemed a long way away.

BIBLIOGRAPHY

TITLE	AUTHOR	PUBLISHER
WOMEN'S ROYAL NAVAL SERVICE (WRNS)		
Blue Tapestry	Vera Laughton Mathews	Hollis & Carter
Britannia's Daughters	Ursula Stuart Mason	Pen & Sword
The Wrens 1917 – 77	Ursula Stuart Mason	Educational Explorers Ltd
The WRNS	M H Fletcher	B T Batsford Ltd
The Story of the W R N S	Eileen Bigland	Nicholson & Watson
Never at Sea	Vonla McBride	Educational Explorers Ltd
Blue for a Girl	John D Drummond	W H Allen
ALL SERVICES		
Women in Uniform	D Collett Wadge	Sampson Low, Marston
World War 2 British Women's Uniforms	Martin Brayley & Richard Ingram	The Crowood Press Ltd
Service Slang	J L Hunt & A G Pringle	Faber & Faber
The Girls who went to War	Duncan Barrett & Nuala Calvi	Harper Collins
Queen and Country	Emma Vickers	Manchester University Press
BOAT CREW WRENS		
I only joined for the Hat	Christian Lamb	Bern Factum Publishing
Entertaining Eric	Maureen Wells	Imperial War Museum
Maid Matelot	Rozelle Raynes	Nautical Publishing Co.
Ten Degrees below Seaweed	Paddy Gregson	Merlin Books Ltd
An intriguing Life	Cynthia Helms	Bowman & Littlefield Inc.
Sea Change	Yvonne Downer	Dreamstar Books
Land Girl to Leading Wren	Lucia Hobson	Hobson Books
WRENS		
Services Wrendered	Sonia Snodgrass AKA Jack Broome	Sampson Low, Marston
Changing Course	Roxane Houston	Grub Street
Wrens in Camera	Lee Miller	Hollis & Carter
WRNS in Camera	Lesley Thomas & Chris Howard Bailey	RN Museum
Love and War in the WRNS	Vicky Unwin	The History Press
Thank You – Nelson	Nancy Spain	Arrow –Hutchinson Authors
Dancing on the Waves	Angela Mack	Benchmark Press
The War Years	'One small Wren' –Lillian Pickering	Athena Press
From Little Ships to Comets	Audrey Iliffe	Self-published

BIBLIOGRAPHY

TITLE	AUTHOR	PUBLISHER
WRENS continued		
Bellbottoms and Blackouts	Louisa M Jenkins	iUniverse Inc
Hostilities Only	Brian Lavery	National Maritime Museum
Wren's Eye View	Stephanie Batstone	Parapress Ltd
Secret duties of a Signals Interceptor	Jenny Nater	Pen & Sword
ROYAL NAVY		
Steam Picket Boats	N B J Stapleton	Terence Dalton Ltd
A Seaman's Pocket Book	Lords Commissioners of the Admiralty	
Jackspeak	Rick Jolly	Palamanando Publishing
Not Enough Room to Swing a Cat	Martin Robson	Conway Maritime
The Royal Navy Day by Day	A B Sainsbury	Ian Allen Publishing
Coasters go to War	John de S Winser	Ships in Focus Publications
The Battle of the Narrow Seas	Peter Scott	Seaforth Publishing
True Glory	Warren Tute	Harper & Row Publishing
German Kriegsmarine in WW II	Chris McNab	Amber Books Ltd
The War at Sea 1939 – 1945	Stuart Robertson & Stephen Dent	Conway Maritime
Naval Life & Customs part 1 & 2	John Irvine	Web site
Hold the Narrow Seas	Peter C Smith	Moorland Publishing Co.
Nelson the Commander	Geoffrey Bennett	Pen & Sword
Men Dressed as Seamen	S Gorley Putt	Christophers
On going to the Wars	Godfrey Winn	Collins
The Hour before Dawn	Godfrey Winn	Collins
Home from Sea	Godfrey Winn	Hutchinson & Co.
One Eye on the Clock	Geoffrey Willans	MacMillan & Co
The British Sailor	Kenneth Poolman	Arms & Armour Press
The Lower Deck of the Royal Navy	Brian Lavery	Conway
Dunkirk Revisited	John Richards	Website off-print
The Evacuation from Dunkirk	W J R Gardner	Routledge/Taylor & Francis
Sunk by Stukas Survived at Salerno	Tony McCrum	Pen & Sword
WOMEN IN WARTIME		
Sisters in Arms	Helena Page Schrader	Pen & Sword
Debs at War	Anne de Courcy	Weidenfeld & Nicolson
Jane: A pinup at War	Andy Saunders	Pen & Sword
As Green as Grass	Emma Smith	Bloomsbury

TITLE	AUTHOR	PUBLISHER
WOMEN IN WARTIME continued		
Corsets to Camouflage	Kate Adie	Hodder & Stoughton
Women in Wartime	Jane Waller & Michael Vaughan-Rees	MacDonald & Co
Our Wonderful Women	Cecil Hunt	Raphael Tuck & Sons Ltd
Sisters in Arms	Nicola Tyrer	Weidenfeld & Nicolson
Love Lessons and Love is Blue	Joan Wyndham	Mandarin
The Secret Ministry of Ag. & Fish	Noreen Riols	MacMillan
Britain's Secret War	Chris McNab	Pitkin Guides
What did you do in the War, Mummy?	Mavis Nicholson	Pimlico – Random House
Women in War	Celia Lee & Paul Edward Strong	Pen & Sword
Priscilla	Nicholas Shakespeare	Harvill Secker
Forties Fashion	Jonathan Walford	Thames & Hudson
The WAAF at War	John Frayn Turner	Pen & Sword
A Writer at War	Iris Murdoch	Short Books
The Girl from Station X	Elisa Segrave	Union Books/Aurum Press
Wartime Women	Dorothy Sheridan	William Heinemann Ltd
WAR		
A Muse of Fire	A D Harvey	The Hambledon Press
Love, Sex & War	John Costello	Collins
What Britain Has Done	Ministry of Information	Atlantic Books
The Battle of Britain	Richard Overy	W W Norton & Co
Battle of Britain	Len Deighton	Book Club Associates
The Great Crusade	H P Willmott	Potomac Books Inc
Moral Combat	Michael Burleigh	Harper Press
Lightning War	The Editors of Time-Life Books	
The Second World War in Photographs	Richard Holmes	Carlton Books
All Hell let Loose	Max Hastings	Harper Collins
Blitz Spirit	Jacqueline Mitchell	Osprey Publishing
Home Front	Juliet Gardiner	Andre Deutsch
Britain at War	Maureen Hill	Atlantic World
The Spirit of Wartime	None	Index/Orbis Publishing
The Blitz	Gavin Mortimer	Osprey Publishing
Greasepaint & Cordite	Andy Merrimam	Aurum Press Ltd.
Wartime Britain 1939 – 1945	Juliet Gardiner	Headline Book Publishing

BIBLIOGRAPHY

TITLE	AUTHOR	PUBLISHER
WAR continued		
We shall never Surrender	P Middleboe, D Fry, C Grace	Pan Books
Cheer up, Mate !	Alan Weeks	The History Press
Millions Like Us?	Nick Hayes & Jeff Hill	Liverpool University Press
Never Surrender	Robert Kershaw	Hodder & Stoughton
Careless Talk	Stuart Hylton	The History Press
Listening to Britain	Paul Addison & Jeremy A Crang	The Bodley Head
Human Smoke	Nicholson Baker	Simon & Schuster
Home from Dunkirk	J B Priestley	British Red Cross
Forgotten Voices of Dunkirk	Joshua Levine	Ebury Press/Random House
Secret Forces of World War II	Philip Warner	Pen & Sword
Churchill and The King	Kenneth Weisbrode	Viking
PLACES		
Dover at War 1939 – 1945	Roy Humphreys	Alan Sutton
Hellfire Corner	J G Coad	English Heritage
Life in 1940's London	Mike Hutton	Amberley
FICTION		
The Cruel Sea	Nicholas Monsarrat	Cassell
The Seafarers	Nevil Shute	The Paper Tiger Inc
A Wren called Smith	Alexander Fullerton	Peter Davies
H M S Marlborough Will enter Harbour	Nicholas Monsarrat	Cassell
Not so quiet….Stepdaughters of War	Helen Zenna Smith	The Feminist Press
MISCELLANEOUS		
Etiquette for Women	Irene Davison	Chancellor Press
Etiquette in Everyday Life	F R Ings	W Foulsham & Co., Ltd
Table & Domestic Etiquette	Mary Woodman	W Foulsham & Co Lrd
West End Front	Matthew Sweet	Faber & Faber
Gypsy Afloat	Ella K Maillart	William Heinemann Ltd
Since Records Began	Paul Simons	Harper Collins
Careless Talk Costs Lives	Fougasse/James Taylor	Conway
Private Battles	Simon Garfield	Ebury Press/Random House
The War Within World War II	Thomas Fleming	Perseus Press
Breverton's Nautical Curiosities	Terry Breverton	Quercus

About the Author

Douglas J Lindsay was born to the sea. His parents both came from sailor families and when his father went to sea for the duration of the Second World War, his mother followed the ship to its new base at Scrabster on the Pentland Firth, Scotland where the author was born in 1941. His father sailed on the small coaster *Drumlough*, which the family owned. It ran as a supply ship for the fleet at Scapa Flow, operating up and down the east coast of the UK, although from 1939 to 1945 it was never touched by enemy action. The family lived in a wooden shack on the Scrabster harbour wall, and the author's playground was the harbour and ships berthed there until 1945.

Douglas J Lindsay left his public school in Edinburgh soon after his fifteenth birthday and attended the T/S Dolphin at Leith Nautical College before going deep sea in 1957 as a cadet with the Clan Line – a major cargo liner company - operated to Africa, India and Australia. He settled into a merchant shipping career of which the highpoint was being appointed Captain at the young age of 28, on the large ro-ro freight ships of the Tor Line. Later, he worked in the family shipping office before setting up his own ship management business. In 1985, this business went bankrupt and the author and his wife lost everything. They moved to Berkshire where his wife found work as a housekeeper to a retired colonel, a position which provided a roof over their heads.

About the Author

Very new Captain

The author then took up shipping consultancy and with an interest in square riggers started sailing them intermittently between consultancy jobs as well as continuing with his lifelong passion for writing. His first published piece, in 1965, was titled rather grandly *Improvement of Navigation Lights and Signals* published in the Journal of the Institute of Navigation. In the 1980s he attended creative writing classes run by John Fairfax and Sue Stewart, who founded the Arvon Foundation. He has written essays, short stories and poetry and many technical reports.

It is with his depth of naval knowledge that the idea was born for *Wren Jane Beacon Goes to War* as the first book in a series of well-researched books about the Wrens during the war years. The author has had vignettes from his own life published in *The Marine Quarterly* as his life in the maritime world has had its adventurous moments.

As well as his years in commercial shipping, the author was for many years a reserve officer in the Royal Navy, sailing as watch officer and/or navigator and gaining a thorough understanding of the Navy's ways and mores.

Tailpiece by D J Lindsay

WHOSE SONG IS IT ANYWAY?

Whose song is it anyway?
Deep-voiced in the masts
Always there from times long past
Then off to the far horizon.

Whose song is it anyway?
In cadences of blow.
A tropic murmur, soft and low
Or a raking Arctic blast.

Whose song is it anyway?
We always try to catch.
What wasted work; not one snatch
Will stay within our souls.

Uncaught, it sings it song, and goes………

Coming next:

Wren Jane Beacon at War – Volume Two – Survival
Wren Jane Beacon in War – Volume Three – Running The Tideway

Printed in Great Britain
by Amazon